Project Genesis

by

Brian Phillipson

 **New Generation Publishing**

Other books by Brian Phillipson

Thor's Hammer
Pharoah's Treasure
Ares Rising

About the author:
Brian was born and raised in Hull, East Yorkshire. He married Renate in 1984 and eventually moved to the village of Woodmansey where they live with two terrapins, dozens of fish and where the wildlife in the garden threatens to eat them out of house and home. Brian has worked as a civil engineer at both Hull City Council and Beverley Borough Council and currently works as a Senior Project Manager (Civil Engineering) for East Riding of Yorkshire Council. For several years Brian was a director of a garden design firm in his spare time, but had to choose between the security (and regular pay) of engineering and the pleasure of working with plants.

He wrote his first book after Renate asked what he thought of the book he was reading at the time, "It's not bad, but I could have written a better opening," he said. Renate suggested he should give it a go and the idea blossomed. 18months later he had completed Thor's Hammer.

For Zena

Good luck to:

MWF
RSL
APC
PGS
&
Me
Because we're worth it!

And to Renate
Here's to many more holidays together.

Chapter 1

2000 Years Ago
Calvary

The soldier turned towards the midday sun and let the gentle heat kiss his face. The climate here was as warm as his beloved Rome, but far drier. In Rome, the olive groves would be casting their enticing aroma across the countryside, the gentle breeze blowing in from the coast refreshing the air in the streets. But here in Calvary the heat was dry and sapped his strength. The memory of Rome brought back even sweeter memories of his time as a Legionnaire serving Emperor Tiberius. But that was no more. He was getting old, beyond his fortieth year, and his eyesight was failing. He could make out light and dark, vague shapes, but details and colour were things of the past. Without his eyes his days as a Legionnaire were over. He was lucky that the regional commander was a benevolent man and had kept him on as a demoted foot soldier. At least he had food, shelter and companionship, if not his eyes.

They were carrying out the sentence on three criminals today. Prefect Pilot had made it clear that these three were to be executed together, even dictating the order of the crucifixion. Two of the men were petty thieves. Already caught on two separate occasions, there would not be a third. But it was the third man that Longinus felt sorry for. As the law required, the soldiers had stripped him of all his goods, sharing them out between themselves. They had then flailed and beaten him before he had carried his own cross to the hill outside of the city walls. But it was the man's crimes that made Longinus question the Prefect's decision. He had proclaimed himself the King of the Jews, hence the crown of thorns the soldiers had placed on his head. Proclaiming yourself royalty and usurping the power of Rome was punishable by death. But this man was not interested in power, not in the normal sense. He claimed to be the spiritual leader of the Jews, seeking no taxes or favour, simply offering them salvation and spiritual guidance. For some time his following had been growing and the sheer numbers were a threat. He was becoming too popular and questions had been asked, threats made, but it was silver that had finally drawn out one of his own followers who had betrayed him in the gardens.

Longinus could not help thinking that the punishment was far from just, but it seemed as if Prefect Pilot was acting under orders to make an example of the man.

And so they were here, on the low hills of Calvary, just outside of the city walls as befitted a place of execution. A place the locals called Golgotha, which apparently meant the place of the skull. The crowd was smaller than expected. Since his arrest, many of the man's followers had gone into hiding, fearing persecution. The Prefect had ordered extra guards out today to ward off trouble before it started. But even Longinus with his poor eyesight could tell that the crowds were thinner than usual.

Looking up, he saw the vague outline of the three crosses. The prisoners' arms spread along the crossbars, nails driven at an angle through their wrists and into the timber. Their feet held in place by more nails through their ankles. Longinus has seen some men hold on for days before succumbing to the loss of blood, dehydration or asphyxiation. The two thieves flanked the third man, a sign of further humiliation as if the crucifixion was not enough.

"Longinus, new orders. This is taking too long, the Prefect wants this over and done with. Break the legs of the third prisoner." The centurion spoke quietly so his words did not carry to the crowd.

Longinus hesitated, looking from one figure to the other. The centre figure was the one the authorities feared, Jesus the Nazarene, son of Joseph. Breaking his legs would cause excruciating pain, additional internal blood loss and put all of his weight on his damaged arms and wrists. Painful asphyxiation would follow.

"Sir, the man is already dead. There is no need to waste any more time on him," Longinus said.

"Are you sure? Show me."

Longinus had hoped it would not come to this. Why had the Legionnaire not simply taken his word? He shuffled along, careful where he placed his feet, not wanting to step on a loose rock and lose his footing. As he approached the middle figure, he placed the sun behind the man's body. The man and the cross cast a shadow over the soldier. He could see the man's outline and could make out the shape of his body. He raised his lance and aimed for the man's right side just below the ribcage.

There was surprisingly little resistance, the head of the spear easily piercing the skin. Longinus expected to hear a cry, perhaps of pain, perhaps of fear. Instead all he heard was a gentle sigh, a sigh of almost contentment.

The Legionnaire was several feet away and obviously had not heard the sigh. "Very well," he said. "I'll report that the prisoner is dead." He turned and walked away.

As he withdrew the spear, Longinus felt the warm stickiness of blood flowing down the shaft and onto his hands. He looked down and saw the rich red blood as was characteristic of a wound to the liver. The sight brought back memories of his training as a Centurion. A blow to an opponent that elicited that amount of dark red blood was unquestioningly fatal within a few short minutes. The man's pain would soon be over. But there was something else. As he looked at the red stain spreading along the shaft, he also saw what appeared to be a clear liquid. It looked and felt like cool spring water.

With shock, Longinus realised that the memory of his training had come at the sight of the blood on his hands, a level of sight that had been beyond his ability for several years. Looking up, he peered over to the horizon. He could see the scrubby trees in the distance, see the individual branches. The colour of the yellow sand on the next hill streaked with darker rocks, the brown stains from previous executions standing out in sharp contrast. The individual grains of sand seeming to stand out in relief against their neighbours. The sun was bright and almost overhead, but he did not have to squint against its light. It was as if the sun were softened, bright but not harsh.

Longinus was still in the man's shadow. He stepped to one side, the sun beating down on his upturned face. The sun was intensely white, yet it had the softness of a candle flame with a multi-coloured halo.

Looking at the man's face, he was surprised to see a gentle smile, a smile of peace and acceptance, a smile of love. As he watched, the man's lips parted and he spoke. No sound came from those lips, but Longinus knew what he was saying as clearly as if the man had spoken directly into his mind.

"Thank you, be at peace, go in love."

Chapter 2

Temple of Solomon, Jerusalem
1122

The sunset was a dusky red. The dust from the desert hung in the air dulling the light as the sun dipped slowly for the horizon. It had been a long day. Richard de Skuner had risen early to meet with the pilgrims along the trail. They had met as planned and relieved the other guards who had a leisurely breakfast before heading back along the trail. An hour later, Richard and his charges had rendezvoused with Hugues de Payens and his relative Godfrey de Saint-Omer, the founders of the order. They had travelled in good spirits until the early afternoon when they had stopped for a short lunch of bread, cheese and biscuits.

The order had formed following the last crusade when several French knights had asked King Baldwin to allow them to protect pilgrims as they travelled along the trail to the Holy Land. The king had not only granted their request, but had also given permission for them to use the various temples and ruins along the trail as places of safety. Most significantly, they were granted permission to use the sacred ruins of Solomon's Temple as a base. Hence the order's generally recognised name of Knights Templar.

The order grew steadily, each of the knights swearing a vow of poverty. They would forsake all worldly goods that they did not need to fulfil their tasks. Their seal showed two knights travelling on one horse and their white mantle with the bold red cross was viewed with reverence by the pilgrims and feared by those who opposed them. Trained in many forms of

9

combat and battle hardened by the crusades, the knights were a force to respect.

But that did not guarantee a peaceful passage. Bandits and robbers still plagued the pilgrims and the knights who protected them. During the afternoon a small group of bandits had approached the group of travellers demanding a 'toll' for the road. The knights had respectfully declined, ready to back up their words with action if necessary, when another ten bandits had appeared, several with bows.

"It appears that this is going to be an unfair fight," said one of the bandits who seemed to be the spokesperson for the group.

Richard looked around at the fifteen men, weighing up their appearance and weapons. The men looked mean and physically hard, but had clearly not been trained. They were thugs, used to people standing down at the first sign of conflict.

"You're right. Fifteen to three would be unfair. But we are not in a hurry, we can wait until you call for reinforcements," said Richard.

The fight had been short. Although outnumbered five to one, the knights had driven the bandits off, but not without casualties. Three of the pilgrims had been injured, although not badly and Richard had taken an arrow to the side of the chest. At first he bore the wound without complaint until they had handed the pilgrims over to other knights for the final leg of their journey. But gradually it had become clear that the wound was worse than they had at first thought. By the time they returned to Solomon's Temple, Richard was coughing up blood and could barely stand. That was two hours ago, and he was slipping away.

Since establishing the Temple, the knights had been renovating the structure in His glory. They had rebuilt sections to act as a place of worship, quarters for the knights and somewhere to cook and eat. Hugues and Godfrey had carried Richard to his quarters and made him comfortable. Godfrey helped to remove Richard's armour while Hugues had fetched water to bathe and cool him.

As they laid Richard down to rest, the two knights applied oil and holy water before speaking prayers to pass his soul to God's keeping. As they finished the prayers Hugues stood and bent to retrieve the metal bowl containing the water they had used to bathe Richard. The oils made his hands slippery and the bowl fell from his grasp, spilling on the dusty floor and washing away layers of dirt.

The rays of the dying sun cast long shadows and shafts of light across the floor and reflected from something previously buried under the dirt.

The floor had originally been part of the lower level, adjacent to the crypt and as such would not have been generally accessible to the worshippers. The two knights bent and found the solid stone floor contained a trapdoor with a large, heavy ring-pull. The ring and trapdoor lifted with little effort revealing a steep stone staircase. Looking at each other wordlessly, the two knights descended the steps.

The area appeared to be a natural cavelike structure, a Mithraeum, used in early worship to hold the worshippers and reflect the 'universe on Earth'. Newer churches were often built over such places, sometimes with the heathen Mithraeum being sealed up.

The cave was quiet and peaceful. The quiet was not simply a lack of sound, instead it was as if a comforting hand had been placed over the knights as they entered, a protective fatherly embrace that promised peace and security. The natural cavern was not large, maybe thirty-five feet by twenty. Two rows of benches ran along each long side, a crude stone altar stood at one end raised by six inches on a small dais. At the opposite end were the bottom two steps of a staircase leading upwards. A solid looking stone wall had been built across the staircase blocking any possible exit. A thick layer of dust covered all the surfaces.

As the knights cautiously stepped across the cave, they saw several chests and crates of various sizes sitting on the last row of pews.

"Where is the light coming from?" asked Godfrey in a whisper.

The main entrance was sealed, the trapdoor the only opening and the light from the burning torches in Richard's room was barely noticeable. Yet the two knights could see by a diffused dim light that seemed to have no source.

Godfrey looked down and saw their footprints in the dust and looked back at the crates. "Why is there no dust on the boxes?"

The two men approached the nearest box, a solid looking crate with no sign of hinges. Godfrey removed a twelve inch dagger from his belt and uttered a prayer of apology for bearing a weapon in a house of worship. With caution he inserted the blade in the lip of the crate and prised it upwards with a protesting squeal from the nails.

The box held books, ancient bound tomes, some with metal straps others in delicate soft leather. Some appeared to be official and expensive, others cheap as if they had belonged to peasants.

Hugues examined a second box, this one long and thin, twelve inches wide and deep and around six feet long. Three metal catches were evenly spaced along one side. At his touch, the first one snapped open with only a slight protest of old, dry metal against metal. The middle and bottom catches were more corroded and snapped rather than opened. Hugues lifted the lid cautiously and the concealed hinges opened with little resistance and no sound.

Inside was a rich green and gold cloth lining. Hugues lifted the cloth and folded it back, draping it over the edge of the open box. Underneath the cloth was an old looking spear, perhaps five feet six inches long with a crude iron head. The shaft was of a solid looking wood jointed in the middle with a balancing metal sleeve that would double as a throwing point. The shaft had a brown staining running its length. As a knight, Hugues was used to handling weapons; they held no fascination or fear for him. He reached into the crate and carefully removed the spear. The weapon was crude, its counter-balancing handle and the iron head caused it to balance just above half way along the shaft. As he weighed the weapon in his hands, Hugues saw a small sheet of vellum in the crate. Removing the vellum, probably calfskin, he saw the writing was an old form of Latin. As all Templar Knights, Hugues was well educated. He had learned Latin many years ago, but some of these words were strange to him, older than he had ever seen.

After a few seconds he looked up and handed the paper to Godfrey. "Read this," he said.

Godfrey took the paper and studied the writing for a few seconds before looking up with reverence and awe on his face.

"We should show this to Richard. It will ease his passing, knowing that his life has not been in vain."

The two knights climbed back to Richard's room, Hugues carefully carrying the spear. Godfrey described to Richard what they had found in the Mithraeum and read the inscription from the vellum. Richard smiled. He had given his life to the protection of others, fighting for the Lord's followers and His glory. It was fitting that he should see this before going to His side.

13

Richard parted his lips to speak, but all that came out was a rough gasp. He tried to raise his hand, but his strength failed him. No matter, Hugues knew what he wanted.

"Here my friend. Hold this." Hugues placed the spear along Richard's side, the shaft going through his right hand, the cold iron head resting against his cheek.

Richard gave a contented sigh and took a deep breath. The peace was a warm blanket covering him with love, the softness reminiscent of the finest furs. He closed his eyes and slept.

Hugues and Godfrey looked down and said a pray for their fallen comrade. He was at peace. His breathing was deep and regular, the clammy sweat that had been on his brow was dry and he had colour back in his face. Godfrey bent down and peeled back the dressing covering Richard's wound. The bleeding had stopped, the wound was dry and pink, no sign of infection.

Richard stirred and his eyes opened. "Thank you my friends. I can feel my strength returning. Praise the Lord."

Richard caressed the spear and held it up to Hugues who took it reverently.

"We have a new task. We must gather the holy relics and protect them from those who would use them for their own ends rather than for His glory."

Chapter 3

Distant Shores
Autumn 1314

The ten ships swayed gently at anchor, the calm inlet giving a lie to the vicious storm that had been raging for the last week. The sailors aboard the ships went about clearing the decks, splicing new sheets and canvas and making the ships seaworthy again. Many of their passengers were not so calm. The men were all battle hardened soldiers, but most of them had spent the majority of their lives on dry land. The seven week journey across rough seas had been a new and unwelcome experience, one they were not in a hurry to repeat.

There had originally been twelve ships in the fleet, but bad weather had claimed two of their number. Many of the sailors were amazed that the loss had been limited to two ships and spoke quietly of salvation being granted by God. A sure sign that this voyage into the unknown was indeed His will.

It was already late afternoon when the last of the ships cast its anchor, but many of the passengers were not willing to spend another night aboard ship. The longboats and rafts were cast afloat and the men and their supplies, including 100 horses, were transferred to the sandy shore.

"So this is Le Merca," the man stated.

"Yes, the land promised in the ancient scripts. Here we shall set up home before we return to fight for His glory." The two men stood watching the sun as it dipped across the vast expanse of rolling countryside. The trees that covered the surrounding hills were afire with hues of bright reds, oranges and yellows. A heady pine scent hung in the air.

Already the temperature was dropping. If this was to be their new home it would not be a Paradise without hardship. Still, these men were no strangers to hardship. They had sworn their lives and skills to the service of the Lord. And in thanks, the church had persecuted, hunted and killed many of their number. They had been accused of everything from homosexuality to necromancy, abortion to use of the Dark Arts. King Philip of France had been the driving force behind the purge, simply to further his own ends. But Pope Clement V had been a willing participant and had issued a Papal decree outlawing their order.

But the knights knew the truth. Better than the church. Better than the Pope himself. They had been willing to follow the church's teachings, willing to keep their own counsel and not speak out. But the truth and their power had proven too frightening to the church and those in authority. So the church and European royalty had gone on the attack.

William Forester, son of Gawain, looked at the scroll. It showed a sailing ship following a star, much like the star the wise men had followed so long ago. The star was labelled 'Le Merca' and gave its name to this new land. William looked up at the sound of movement on the beach. The first of the boats bringing the cargo ashore was being pulled up the sand. Most of the cargo would stay on the ships until the morning, but not this cargo. This was the reason the knights had left their homes and the land they knew. These chests and crates held the truth they all held dear, the truth that the church so feared. There was not a man on the beach or the ships that would not lay his life down for the knowledge or contents of the crates.

"We need to stand guard until we can build a

fortification. We don't know what form of native may dwell in this land," said William.

"If there are men here, they are bound to be heathens, unaware of the word of God," replied Hugo de Bonn.

"Heathens are simply men who have not heard His word. They can be taught."

"Not like the Holy Church of Rome. They don't want to know the truth," Hugo almost spat the words.

"I fear it is worse than that. They know the truth and deny it. It is blasphemy in itself."

The Templar sailors and soldiers reverently carried the various crates and chests ashore. Several needed two men to lift them. Further along the beach another boat ran up onto the sandy shore and a knight wearing the white robe with the red cross stepped slightly unsteadily from the small boat. He straightened and stretched before looking around and heading towards William and Hugo.

Although the knights wore no rank or insignia, this Holy Knight was the most venerable of the order. Unofficially the knights and soldiers looked up to him as their true leader, the elder they all respected.

"Richard, welcome to the new land," said William with a smile and slight bow.

"Thank you William," Richard's face was lined but his speech and bearing were still strong even with his advanced age.

"But how new is this land? The scroll you hold led us here. Whoever drew that left it as an instruction to follow their lead. To follow where others had already been."

William and Hugo nodded at Richard's words.

"This land holds promise. We will be safe here, at least for the time being."

Spring 1315

The winter had been hard. The knights had quickly set up camp half a mile inland from their landing place. The trees in the surrounding woods were tall and straight and offered good building blocks for the timber cabins they had built to house their number. They were fortunate, only five souls of the 280 that had landed had been consigned to God's keeping. The natural shelter of the inlet had protected the ships and they were all in good condition and ready to sail when required.

The trees were coming back into rich deep green leaf, and the meadows were sporting wild flowers of white, yellow and a most vivid blue. The smell of the flowers was fresh and reminiscent of an English country estate.

"It is a good day," said Richard as he strode up the hill to stand next to Hugo.

"Indeed, Richard." Hugo noticed that Richard was breathing slightly harder than he used to after the climb. Was his age finally catching up with him?

"It will soon be time to start the next leg of our journey. Some of us will return home to fight for the Lord, spread his word and uphold his teachings. Some will remain here and spread out. Taking our treasures to safer places, exploring this land and seeing what it holds. Bringing the Word to the natives, teaching them the true way."

"Do you know who will stay and who will return?" asked Hugo. Richard looked off across the rolling hillsides, his gaze miles and possibly years away. At length he nodded.

"Yes. I finalised the list last night. I'll call a meeting at midday and explain to everyone."

Richard continued to stare off into the distance. He knew that Hugo was too polite, almost reverential, to ask the question that was eating away at him. After a few seconds Richard smiled and put him out of his misery.

"I'm going to ask you and William to stay here and head up the garrison. I would like William to set up a more permanent base and for you to take the majority of the men and explore this land. In a few years we will return with others so that you can return to your home. While we are away you are to spread far and wide, find the resources we need to survive and prosper. Integrate yourselves with the natives of this great land and teach them. Remember, they do not have our history as a foundation. You will need to explain things in terms they can comprehend. Do not be too literal. We are here to spread the wisdom and teachings of our Lord. We do not need to teach the exact words to get across the message. But most of all, above all else, you need to keep the holy relics safe. They represent the core of our beliefs, the truth that we live by. In the wrong hands they could be a force for evil. Men will want them at the head of their armies, the belief in the relics and teachings could destroy the world."

"Thank you, Richard. I will not let you down." Was Hugo relieved at staying or disappointed?

"And are you staying or returning Richard?"

The old knight looked off to the horizon for several minutes before answering, his breathing now calm and measured. "I will return. My place is back home, trying to bring understanding and acceptance to the church. I doubt I will see this land again, or you." Richard turned to look at Hugo and held up his hand to ward off the younger knight's protests.

"It is God's will. I have served him for many years. I do not have many more left. But your time here will set the foundation for the future. You must learn to adapt, turn the other cheek. Wars are not won by fighting every battle. Some battles are best lost for the good of the cause. You must learn a new way of fighting. Not just with strong arm and sharp sword, but with words and persuasion. There will be others who arrive in this land in years to come. They will be looking for leadership. You must prepare yourself to provide that leadership. It is by working from within that we will be most effective."

Richard looked around at the land that had been his home for the last seven months.

"Come, let us return to camp and prepare for the meeting. There is much to do before we finally say goodbye."

Chapter 4

23:35hrs, 6th January 1945
Schloss Wewelsburg, Alme Valley,
Germany

The snow was thick and crisp with the sky holding the promise of more to come by midnight. For months the German forces had pulled back to the Motherland to draw in the enemy and give the appearance of impending defeat. In truth this was simply a delaying tactic until the German H-bomb was complete and ready to use, and that would be any day. Werner Heisenberg had developed the technology almost three years ago, and it was only the limited supply of heavy water from Norway that had delayed the production this long.

Already the laboratory testing was complete and the prototype Junkers Ju 287 with its six jet engines was being readied for the first mission, a mission that would bring the war to a sudden end. The scientists wanted more time to carry out field tests, dropping live weapons from the aircraft, but that would not be possible. The first attack had to be successful and a complete surprise. A small version of the H-bomb had been detonated on a remote island just off the Antarctic, taken there by U-boat two months earlier. The test had proven the science and technology. The next detonation would be decisive. They would destroy the advancing allied forces.

The Führer had already selected additional targets, including the city of London. Along with Hermann Göring, the head of the air force, they had devised a plan they felt would lead to a decisive victory. Shortly after a British raid, the bomber would take off with British markings and limp back after the returning British bombers. Once across the channel the aircraft would peel off and head for London. It would be over the English capital before the fighters or anti-aircraft gunners knew anything was wrong. If all went well, New York would be wiped off the map four days later.

The three German officers, all wrapped in heavy blue-grey uniform coats, leant into the wind with their heads down as they approached the door leading from the large courtyard to the interior of Wewelsburg Castle. The lead officer knocked on the heavy door as large snowflakes swirled in the turbulent wind.

The Schloss Wewelsburg was the SS occult teaching centre and home to many of its most treasured possessions. From being a teenager, Adolf Hitler had been fascinated by the occult. He had studied under many of the masters of the age. Von Liebenfels and Dietrich Eckardt had set the foundations with their beliefs in the superior Aryan race. A race, they insisted, that was both ancient and pure, with psychic abilities. These abilities had only been lost when its members started to interbreed with the lower races.

However, it was the people around Hitler after he came to power that were perhaps the most devout in their beliefs. Heinrich Himmler – The Black Magician – was a grand master of several secret societies and guided the Führer's thinking and many of his acts. He formed the SS and set up the Ahnenerbe, the archaeological research arm of the SS. It was the Ahnenerbe that scoured the world looking for relics. And it was the SS and Ahnenerbe that Himmler ruled as Grand Master of the thirteen ruling priests in the 'Knights' Great Council'. So fanatical was Himmler that he firmly believed he was the reincarnation of the

10th Century Saxon King Heinrich I. Under his guidance the Nazis had spent years and vast sums of money in procuring ancient relics from all religions and from all corners of the Earth. And it was here at the Castle Wewelsburg that the Knights' Great Council worshipped Lucifer, Satan and Set.

The three soldiers, two colonels and a major, knocked on the courtyard door and waited for the eye level hatch to open.

"Ja?" the hatch opened and a pair of vivid blue eyes looked out. The eyebrows were an almost white blond as befitted an example of the master race.

"We are here to meet with Hauptsturmführer Muller." The men had done their homework, they knew the man was in residence.

"It is late, Hauptsturmführer Muller cannot be disturbed until the morning."

The men had been expecting the rejection. Their senior rank counted for little to the occultists of the SS.

"I suggest you reconsider. We are here on the orders of Aegis."

The eyes behind the hatch changed as the man recognised the self-imposed title of Heinrich Himmler. With a series of metal against metal scrapes the man pulled the bolts back and opened the door.

"Bitte." The man stood back and indicated for the three senior soldiers to enter.

The first two men entered and glanced around the large open room, one hundred feet on each side with a double stairway leading to a balcony running along the back wall. Coats of arms and ancient armour were hung on the 17th Century stone walls, but the most prominent symbol was the red, black and white SS flag hung floor to ceiling. The two men looked around and nodded back to the third.

As he came in, he turned back to see the guard close

and lock the old oak door. Stepping up behind the guard, the major quickly and quietly put his right hand over his mouth and pulled his head back exposing the neck. His left hand quickly drew the razor sharp knife across the exposed throat cutting through to the spine before lowering the guard's limp body to the floor.

The three men quickly found the door they were looking for and headed down a wide stone stairway. The stone steps were worn in the middle from years of footfalls making for a precarious footing. As they descended, the electric lights of the ground floor were left behind to be replaced with flickering torches hung at intervals in sconces.

They reached the bottom of the stairs and looked along the wide corridor. Like the stairs, it was lit with flickering light from torches interspersed with pools of black shadow. Two guards stood to attention at the far end of the corridor guarding the double embossed doors. Seeing the three men approach, the guards unslung their weapons and pointed them forward. Waiting until they were within twenty feet, the guards commanded the men to, "Halt."

Stopping as commanded, the two men wearing colonel's insignia stood to the centre of the corridor, with the major just behind. One of the guards stepped forward to examine the men's IDs. The three German officers had very well forged papers that had got them past the outer guards and into the courtyard, but no papers, real or fake, would get them through these doors.

The two colonels casually parted to hand over their cards. As they did so, the major raised a silenced pistol and put two bullets in the rear guard's head before adjusting his aim and placing another two bullets into the front guard before he could raise his own weapon.

The three men quickly moved to the double doors

and swung them open.

The scene was straight out of an occult directory. The room was a large circle with thirteen semi-circular alcoves each lit by burning torches in twisted iron sconces with a fourteenth ornate burner at the head of the room. This was the eternal flame. There was a large pentagram painted on the floor in a dull brown colour and various occult runes painted on the walls. An ornate gold swastika sat on a pedestal behind the eternal flame reflecting the flickering light, with an SS flag hung on the wall behind. A black marble stand stood to each side. On the left the stand held a horned ram's skull, to the right a large golden bowl and a wickedly curved dagger. The air was permeated by a strong smell of sulphur. But it was the black marble altar in front of the eternal flame that drew the men's attention.

The altar had only one adornment, a stand with an upright pointed spear. The old smooth shaft was topped by a dull metal head. The centre of the shaft had a metal cover, clearly designed as a hand hold and counterbalance.

The three men stood in front of the altar and crossed themselves. One of the colonels stepped forward and carefully removed the spear. The second colonel placed a leather briefcase on the floor and bent down to unfold the bag into a six feet long leather wrap.

"It's time to go," said the major.

The first colonel placed the spear from the altar into the padded pouch.

"Ready?" asked the major. The other two men looked at each other and nodded.

Exiting the room, the three men stepped over the bodies of the two guards and quickly climbed the steps back to the lobby.

Their staff car was where they had left it. Heavy

snow had started to fall covering the car and courtyard with a half inch of large flakes in the twenty minutes the men had been in the castle.

The car came to life on the first turn of the starter and the major put it into gear and headed across the courtyard towards the exit. As they approached the closed barrier, the car slowed and came to a halt. The second colonel stepped from the car and walked deliberately over to the guard post.

The guard came to attention at the sight of the colonel's insignia and saluted, "Heil Hitler."

As the guard reached out for their papers, the colonel fired two rounds into the man's chest from his now unsilenced weapon. The major accelerated hard away from the guard post, leaving the second colonel standing in plain sight, the case with the spear falling to the floor as he looked around for a new target.

The major and first colonel heard more shots from behind as guards rushed from the old castle into the courtyard. Stopping after sixty yards, the major quickly stepped from the car and removed the sniper rifle from the side of the front passenger seat. He put the rifle butt to his shoulder and took careful aim.

The second colonel fired at the first two guards that came rushing from the castle. Both fell to the snow-covered courtyard, red stains quickly spreading and melting the pure white snow. He paused as he heard the car come to a halt, fired another four shots and turned to face the car. He took a deep breath and crossed himself, his lips moving in a silent prayer.

The major squeezed the trigger and the rifle kicked against his shoulder. Through the telescopic sight he saw a shower of blood and grey matter erupt from his comrade's head. He watched as the figure slumped to the floor and again took careful aim. The second hollow point bullet destroyed what remained of his friend's head. He threw the rifle back into the car and quickly stepped in pulling the door shut and heading away from the castle.

The two men drove on in silence for several minutes along the narrow winding road, the snow making the turns treacherous, but the major was unwilling to slow down.

"I still do not see why Francis had to die," the first colonel's voice from the back seat held an accusing note.

"He gave his life for the cause. His name will be honoured," replied the major with little inflection and even less emotion.

"But why did he need to sacrifice himself?"

"We have been through this, you know why."

"Tell me again," snapped the colonel. "We could all have gotten away."

The major took a deep breath and concentrated on taking a corner with a two hundred foot drop to the right, the rear wheels slipping as he straightened the car and accelerated along a short straight.

"If we had got away they would have quickly known that we had taken the spear. They would have closed the borders tighter than ever. We would never have left the country and they could have got the spear back. The only way was to sacrifice Francis, make it look as if the guards had killed him and recaptured the spear. They will still look for us, but with less vigour. We will go into hiding for a while and then hide the spear in plain sight. Somewhere where everyone will see it yet pay no attention. We will wait for the tide to turn against the Nazis, as it quickly will, and join the allied forces. Francis understood all this, it was his idea."

"But the guards did not kill him, you did. That will also be suspicious."

"The guards will probably take credit for the killing to cover up their mistake in letting us get past them in the first place. Even if they tell the truth the fact that we killed our own comrade to prevent him falling into their hands and revealing our secrets will simply add weight to the deception."

The major glanced in the mirror. The man wearing the colonel's insignia was sat back, obviously not happy but appearing to be resigned, the real spear in the leather cover resting on the seat next to him.

They drove twenty miles before pulling over and changing cars and clothes. The uniforms they placed in the staff car and drove it to the edge of the steep drop. Both men pushed the car and as gravity took over, the major pulled the pin to an incendiary grenade and threw it in through the open window. The car careened thirty feet down the cliff side before erupting in flames and starting to roll and tumble the remaining eighty feet to the rocky valley below.

The two men drove all night, covering two hundred miles, before stopping at a small village. The location was prearranged, their accommodation ready for them. As the sun came up, they entered the Tyrolean cottage and headed for their rooms.

The major removed his outer clothes and lifted the pendant hanging from the silver chain around his neck and kissed the white shield with its red, even legged cross. He then knelt and prayed for the soul of his fallen comrade, Francis, and forgiveness that he had killed his only brother.

Chapter 5

20:15hrs, 9th November 1989
Berlin

The atmosphere was electric. The night was cold and crisp, but no one cared about the temperature. The crowds had been gathering all day, nothing had been planned, no adverts had been taken out, no TV or radio broadcasts had called for the gathering. The people had simply appeared, drawn to this place at this time as if by a siren's call. They were mostly German, but almost every race was represented somewhere in the city. This night would go down in history and these people were going to be part of it.

After the Second World War ended, the city of Berlin was split between the Russians, French, Americans and British to administer as a condition of the reparations owed by the German nation. The French, Americans and British promoted the residents to regain their independence and rebuild their lives as the authorities rebuilt the city. But the Russians felt that the citizens should not simply be administered but should be repressed and suffer the same hardships as their own people.

In 1961 the Russians decided that simple political segregation was not sufficient. Over the space of one month the infamous Berlin Wall was erected forming a physical barrier that would last for twenty-eight years. But tonight that segregation would end.

The crowd were already standing on ground that until recently would have earned them a bullet fired from one of the guard towers. The surge of bodies was starting to force the people at the front against the wall.

There was only one place for them to go, up, to the top of the wall.

The atmosphere was not simply electric, it was joyous. The crowds were spread along the wall, concentrations gathering at areas of easy access, but there was no length of wall that was unpopulated.

In several locations the wall actually split in two, the two halves of the wall surrounding significant areas that did not belong in either half of the city. One such area was the Brandenburger Tor, one of the old city gates. The gate was one of the original eighteen inner gates of the old city. Constructed almost 200 years ago, the gate consisted of twelve Doric columns, six on each side. These columns formed five passageways, with citizens originally only allowed to use the outermost two. The inner passages were used by various ranks of the nobility, with the centre passage being reserved for the exclusive use of royalty. On top of the gate is the Quadriga, a chariot drawn by four horses driven by the Roman goddess Victoria, the goddess of victory. Designed by Carl Gotthard von Langhans, the design is based upon the Propylaea, the gateway to the Acropolis in Athens, Greece.

Walking steadily among the throng of people, cheering and smiling with the crowd, but not actually joining the celebration, the man passed by unnoticed, just one of the thousands of faces on the street. But rather than simply enjoying the atmosphere and meandering aimlessly, he had a destination in mind.

He crossed the road heading south through the old French section towards the area originally occupied by the British. The border between the Russian and English quarters was the shortest, but held some of the best known sections of the wall.

By now the crowd was turning into a party. The spectators were either drunk on the euphoria or, in some cases, something a little more liquid.

Up ahead the man saw his target, the floodlights illuminating areas that had been off limits for years.

"Val, I thought I'd missed you in the crowd."

The man turned at the sound of the familiar voice.

"Francois, I knew the crowd was going to be big, but I wasn't expecting this." He spoke with a middle England accent, well educated but not upper class. His physique was lean and he looked younger than his fifty-one years, with the keen awareness of a hunting big cat.

"These people have been separated for too long, it's time the world gave them back their city," Francois spoke with a distinct French accent. Like the first man he was lean and fit, but seemed to be paying little attention to his surroundings. "Is everything ready?" he asked.

Val nodded. "I've already seen several people on top of the wall. That slow drip will soon become a torrent. We can scale the wall with the rest of them. Blend into the crowd."

Francois looked around at the swelling, heaving crowd. Joy was etched on many of the faces, light reflecting off sparkling eyes. Faces were turned to the light rain that was starting to fall, but the precipitation was not dampening any spirits.

The two men started to pass among the crowd, generally heading south. Without warning Francois stopped, Val only just avoiding walking into his friend.

Francois' look had gone from mild amusement at the crowd to a look of intense inspection.

"What is it?" asked Val, looking around.

"Ahnenerbe."

The name made a chill run down Val's spine. Based at Castle Wewelsburg, they were officially disbanded at the fall of Germany in 1945, but it was suspected that the organisation and many of its members had simply gone underground, working covertly and biding their time until they could again emerge in force.

Val looked around, what had Francois seen? There, a face in the crowd, seen three quarters from behind, but familiar none the less. The man was laughing and smiling, but like Val and Francois, he was not really joining in.

Francois headed off at an angle, putting himself and Val behind the man and out of his sight. Was he here for them? Was he here for the same thing they were, the treasure that had been hidden for so long? Or was it simply coincidence?

Francois led the way, constantly checking the crowd for familiar faces, someone who was not part of the crowd, movement that went against the flow. Val glanced behind as they moved, checking for the same thing. But he had to be more careful, turning to examine the crowd, seeing if they were being followed could draw attention to the men if someone was indeed looking for them.

After two minutes they were completely out of sight of the familiar face. Francois headed slightly away from the crowd and sheltered in a shop doorway. In the shadows of the recess they were out of sight from the sides, but could still see the crowd. There was nothing out of the ordinary, the crowd was moving like the ocean, ebbing and flowing, no one was causing ripples, maybe it had been a coincidence. The majority of the Ahnenerbe were German, so one of them being here was to be expected. But neither man liked coincidences.

"What should we do?" asked Francois. Although both men were in the order, Val was the senior of the two and had the final say on how tonight would play out. But Francois was several years younger and had only recently left the French Foreign Legion, and his instincts had not been dulled by inactivity for several years.

"Split up. Meet at the east end of Ludwig Strasse in ten minutes."

Francois nodded, glanced around the crowd and headed out. Val watched him move away and examined the crowd. Was anyone watching Francois? Was anyone following?

Within a few seconds, Francois was out of sight. Val slowly counted to one hundred, all the time watching the crowd. With one last glance around, Val stepped out and headed after Francois. He stayed at the edge of the crowd, close enough to appear as part of the celebration, but far enough away to be slightly separate from direct attack.

Val stopped at a store front and watched the crowd through the reflection, checking behind him without having to turn around. Turning back towards the street, he was stunned to come face to face with the man they had seen earlier. The surprise that he had got so close dulled his instincts and that hesitation was to prove fatal. The man stepped closer, his left hand going to Val's shoulder in a friendly gesture, his right flashing forward into Val's midriff.

The blow to his stomach brought Val back from the lethargy of surprise. His right arm came up and over the man's left arm that was still around his shoulder and forced it down. There was an audible snap as the man's tendons stretched beyond breaking point. To his credit, the man twisted free and took one quick step away before turning back with his right arm arcing towards Val's throat. Val reacted quickly and pulled his upper body back, allowing the man's arm to pass inches from his face. He then snapped forward and snagged the returning arm in a severe hold, forcing the arm down and around, his right foot snapping up to connect with

33

the man's face. As the man started to go limp, Val stepped in and raised his right hand to bring it down on the man's exposed neck.

Before Val's arm could connect, the man twisted and brought his knee up into Val's groin, his now free right arm slashing upwards into Val's stomach while his left arm hung loosely at his side. The man's face had turned from benevolent friendship to feral hatred.

Both men gasped and staggered back from each other. Val could only watch and struggle to get air into his burning lungs as the man hobbled away and into the crowd. It was only then that Val felt the warm trickle of blood as it flowed freely down his stomach and legs. With shock, he realised that the man must have been holding a small knife and his blows to Val's stomach had been knife blows and not simply punches. He needed to get to Francois to warn him.

Val straightened and pulled his coat around him, holding the wounds as best he could, and trying not to draw attention to himself as he walked unsteadily along the street. He was surprised at the lack of pain, almost numbness spreading outwards from the wounds.

As he approached the end of the street he looked around for Francois. He should have easily been here by now, had they found him as well?

"Any problems, Val?" asked Francois; again he had managed to approach without Val noticing.

Val turned and almost collapsed into the other man's arms. Francois caught him before he fell and helped him over to a nearby bench, sitting him down gently.

Val took a few unsteady breaths and briefly explained what had happened, warning that his attacker was still out there.

"It's nearly time. You need to go. Retrieve the relic. I'll be okay here until you get back. Go."

"But recovering it by myself, that was never the plan. I was only supposed to be your backup. You're the leader."

"As my backup you were more than a simple lookout. You were my substitute. You know what you need to do. Go, before it's too late."

With obvious reluctance, Francois moved away, heading towards the crowd, glancing back at his fallen comrade sitting on the bench.

The temperature was still dropping and the light rain, little more than moisture in the air, was eating into Val. His mind was not focused as it should be due to a combination of the cold and blood loss. The partying crowd, the singing, cheering and laughter was sounding hollow.

Val's chin touched his chest and he woke with a start. How long had he been asleep? Seconds? Minutes? He looked around, everything seemed the same, and he recognised several of the crowd. He had probably only been out for a few seconds.

Suddenly his clarity came rushing back. There, at the edge of the crowd was the man that had attacked him. His left arm still held close to his body, but he was walking with determination, heading the same way as Francois. Val needed to help Francois, he was now Francois' backup.

He stood and pressed his hand to his side, staunching the blood as best as he could. He broke his own rule and headed directly for the floodlit area, hoping to cut off the two men.

Pushing his way through the crowd, excusing himself at every other step, he found himself at the foot of the hoarding set up to hold the crowd back from the ancient monument. He lent against the stout timber as he tried to regain his breath. Had he missed them?

An attractive young woman wearing a short skirt

and skimpy top jostled Val. He looked around as she went on her way, laughing with her friends. There, Francois was heading towards him. Val looked past him at the crowd behind. Just before he reached him, Val saw the attacker closing fast. Val pushed off from the hoarding, staggering slightly at the pain now burning in his side, his legs turning to jelly. He grabbed for Francois' shoulders and pulled his friend around just as the attacker swung his arm in an upward arc. The knife bit into Val's back, the pain spreading out to cover his full torso. Francois recovered his balance but was encumbered by Val as he tried to lower his friend to the floor. The crowd was unaware of what was happening. They made room for the fallen man, probably assuming he had been drinking and could no longer stand.

Francois turned to the attacker just in time to feel the keen blade slice through his shoulder. It was only his unconscious reaction that made Francois pull his head and neck back from the blow, the knife blade leaving a thin red line across his neck and cheek. Francois jumped back and collided with the hoarding, breaking one panel and half falling, half stumbling through. Francois fell to the floor, falling over the knee high scaffolding supporting the boards. The attacker followed, he was off balance, but recovered quickly. He swung his leg and kicked Francois viciously in the head. Francois saw the blow coming and pulled his head as far to one side as he could, the man's foot connecting with the side of his scalp and making his head swim. He rolled away from his attacker and sprang to his feet, the warm sticky blood running down his arm and dripping from his fingertips. The attacker pushed the broken board to one side and advanced in a slight crouch. He was obviously experienced in knife fighting and had already proven his ability. Francois took a second to weigh the man up. He was around six feet and lean, probably around mid-thirties, blond hair and blue eyes, an ideal candidate for Hitler's Aryan race. He was well balanced, but he was protecting his left arm, holding it close to his body.

The two men circled one another, each looking for an opening. Francois feinted to the right, aiming a blow for the man's head but pulling it at the last second and springing to the side, his foot lashing out at the man's knee. His foot connected, but it was a glancing blow. The other man was fast.

The Ahnenerbe stepped to the side and in towards Francois, his hand flashing upwards. Francois blocked the blow, but before he could counter-attack, the man jumped backwards and in one fluid motion snap kicked Francois to the head. Francois was taken unawares and the kick snapped his head back, stars swimming in his vision. He staggered back, putting distance between himself and his attacker. The man advanced quickly in a low crouch. As he approached he feigned another kick, seeming to jump up but instead twisting around and driving his elbow into Francois' face. This time Francois saw the blow coming and reacted on instinct. He pulled his head out of the way and, as the man's arm passed his face, he took a half step to one side and drove his fist twice into the man's left shoulder. The man gave a strangled cry of pain at the blow to the already damaged tendons and muscles. Francois pulled his arm back to deliver the same blow again, but the man jumped back and brought his right arm slashing forward across Francois' face, the blade digging deeply into his cheek and grazing his eye.

Francois cried out in pain, falling backwards and losing his balance, collapsing to the floor, his hand raised to his face. He knew his attacker would attack immediately. Forcing himself to lower his hands, he looked around for his attacker, blood obscuring his right eye. The man was almost on him. Francois kicked out at the man's legs. But from the floor he had little purchase and the man easily sidestepped the kick, bringing his foot down onto the side of Francois' knee. The dislocated joint sent white hot pain through Francois' body and he automatically curled up into the foetal position to protect himself.

The man looked down at Francois. "Tell me where the relic is and I'll let you live." As expected, the man spoke German-accented English. He bent and pulled Francois onto his back, his shirt tearing and opening to reveal a small tattoo on his chest, a white flag bearing a red cross.

The man knelt on Francois' chest and put the tip of the blade to his left eye.

"Tell me, or you'll lose the other eye."

Francois drew a ragged breath, "Go to hell."

The Ahnenerbe grinned at the reply. "It is not us that will go to hell. Certainly not before you." With that he drew his arm back, the lighting from outside catching the edge of the blade as he held it poised to deliver the final blow.

Val half fell, half dove onto the man, his hands scrabbling for the knife as his weight drove the man to the ground and off Francois. The Ahnenerbe was taken by surprise and lost his grip on the knife. Val was already numb, the pain little more than a dull ache. He knew he had at best a few seconds before he lost consciousness. He only had a loose grip on the knife. He lashed out blindly as hard and quickly as he could. Several of the blows hit flesh, but he could not be sure where the blows were landing of how much damage they were doing. After a few seconds Val simply lost his grip on the knife. His body giving out, he could do no more. But he realised the man under him was struggling with less energy. After a few seconds Val felt himself being rolled off the man as he struggled free.

The man crawled a few feet before staggering unsteadily to his feet. His breath was ragged and he was holding his side and chest. He looked around at the two men lying on the floor before staggering back through the hoarding.

Val was too weak to move, it was all he could do to turn his head to look at Francois. Francois looked back at his mentor.

"I'm sorry I failed you," said Francois.

"You did not fail. You protected the relic at the risk of your life. That is not failure." It took all of Val's strength to say the words.

"Our cause is not won or lost in one night. The Templars have been protecting God's secret for hundreds of years. This was but one battle in a long war. You did well." Val smiled at his friend before closing his eyes and resting for the last time.

Chapter 6

15:00hrs, 24th October 2009
Eyjafjallajökul, Iceland

In October, at a height of 4,000 feet, the temperature was minus ten centigrade with snow on the ground and ice on the rocks. The expedition had been on site for two weeks, setting instruments, monitoring readings and assembling data. The four man team were living in the town, but spending twelve to fourteen hours a day on site.

Iceland was one of the most active volcanic regions on Earth. The Eyjafjallajökul volcano was a reliable, if unpredictable, performer. The last eruption had been a series of explosions and venting starting in December 1921 and culminating in an explosive finale in early 1923.

There were signs that pressure was building in the 100 square kilometre magma chamber where superheated molten rock was gradually filling the reservoir.

"Here, I think we may have found the vent we need." The man stood from his position bending over the instrument and looked around at the others in the small group. He was blond and had not shaved in the last fourteen days giving him a Nordic appearance that matched many of the locals.

"A direct connection with the chamber?" asked a second man. Like the first, he was also blond, but clean shaven with piercing blue eyes.

"I think so, Adam. The readings are showing a direct link. The speed of the return signals are the fastest we've seen. The intensity and sensitivity are beyond the predictions. And the readings have been consistent for over a week. I'm sure this is the vent we need."

Adam nodded and called the other two group members over via the radio.

"This could be the breakthrough we've been looking for. The instruments are giving clear readings that show volcanic predictions are possible."

The other two men checked the readings themselves and after several minutes confirmed the conclusion. The software they had been using had predicted the readings within less than one percent variation.

"Okay, set up the disruptor. We'll leave it to calibrate overnight and check it in the morning," said Adam, clearly the man in charge. His voice had the clear tone of command without arrogance, he spoke English with the slightest of accents that was not easy to pin down.

One of the men walked the half mile back to the large wheeled, 4x4 Toyota. Driving it back to the small group, he stopped a few feet away from the men. Between them, they lifted several large aluminium cases from the rear and started to set up the machine. One of the cases held a large laptop and peripheral computer equipment. The other three cases contained non-descript metal and plastic boxes and what looked like audio speakers.

The three men set about connecting the equipment, turning dials, connecting leads and calibrating readings. One of the boxes unfolded to reveal a small dish antenna which they set up with small adjustments until they got the best signal. They then tidied up and placed all of the now empty cases back on the pick-up before heading across the frozen glacier to town and some hot food and cold beer. By now, even from this raised platform, the sun was sinking below the horizon, casting long blue shadows across the landscape and turning the sky a deep fiery red.

"What is it the English say? 'Red sky at night, sailors' delight' meaning that tomorrow will be a good day." said Adam to no one in particular.

"Not if the sailor's ship is on fire," replied one of the men from the rear of the cab, bringing chuckles from the others.

09:00hrs, 25th October

The next day was cold, clear and calm as the previous night's sunset had promised. They had arrived back on the glacier at first light. The satellite connection had beamed the readings to the internet, so they could see the data that had been collected over breakfast. And that data had produced smiles on the men's faces. Now back on site, there was a palpable excitement between the men. Even Adam, the normally cool professional, had smiled broadly when they had confirmed the readings.

By lunchtime every reading and setting had been checked, rechecked and then checked again.

"Okay, get everything boxed up and check the seals. Once it's in place we won't be able to access it again."

For the rest of the afternoon the men dismantled the equipment before boxing it up and reconnecting it through heavily armoured cables. Once fully boxed the readings were all checked and everything adjusted to the minutest degree. When Adam was satisfied, the boxes were sealed and fast expanding foam pumped in to insulate the instruments from shock and heat. By the time they lowered the machine into the deep crevice the sun was close to setting.

"Let's get back to the hotel. I've arranged for the jet to pick us up tomorrow," said Adam. "Once we get home, if the readings are still stable, we can start phase three and in three months or so, this whole area will be one vast erupting volcano created by us." He smiled one of his rare smiles, although it was the smile a young elk might see from a wolf before it pounced. "Who says you can't predict volcanic eruptions?"

Just over a month later seismic activity started to be detected in the area with thousands of small earthquakes of magnitude 1–2 on the Richter scale. These continued to grow in size and become more regular over the following weeks until on 26th February 2010, unusual seismic activity was detected by the Icelandic Meteorological Institute. The activity continued to increase and in just two days in the first week of March, 2,800 earthquakes were recorded emanating from the centre of the volcano. Records later showed that the eruption began on 20th March, about five miles east of the main crater. After several days the eruption slowed and died down, until on 14th April Eyjafjallajökul resumed erupting, forcing 800 people to be evacuated from the path of the magma. Due to melt water from the glacier seeping into the volcanic vent, the eruption was explosive and violent, and ejected ash several thousand feet into the atmosphere which led to airspace closures and travel disruption in Europe for several weeks during April and May.

03:40hrs, 29th January 2011
12 miles south east of New Zealand

The *MV New Dawn* rode at anchor twelve miles off the coast, rocking slowly in the gentle swell. The lights of the coast were visible in the clear night, shimmering like jewels on the horizon.

The *New Dawn* was a 38,000 tonne merchant vessel.

Launched in 1972, she was past her economic best, but her three previous owners had spent enough to keep her well maintained and earning her keep. Although showing her age, she was still seaworthy and was neither remarkably well maintained for her age nor decaying beyond reason, so as to draw attention. In the age of the 100,000 tonne plus super container ships, she could not compete economically. But as a research vessel she offered an excellent working platform, stable and well equipped. Although registered to a flag of convenience, she was operated by an independent shipping firm, but was ultimately owned by one of the world's most advanced research institutes. The Grüssmire Gewerbe Institute had been a world leader in multiple forms of research for almost sixty years. Yet few had ever even heard the name. Rarely was any of their research published. Even more rarely was any of the research put into practice. But many of the advances in human knowledge were led by the institute and passed to its many worldwide subsidiaries. These were drip fed to avoid raising questions, often held back for years until the rest of the research establishment was on the same page before being released.

Adam stood by the port side hand rail admiring the night, almost lost in the vastness of the sky and its countless stars, the Southern Cross standing out above the coast.

The generator and whine from the midship derrick pulled Adam from his reverie. Looking around, he saw the large metal container being lifted from the deck. The disruptor they had left in Iceland was the size of two large suitcases, this one was the size of a family car.

"We are all set, Adam. Shall I give the order to lower the disruptor?" The tall bearded man looked as if he belonged at sea. His long, windswept dark hair and full, slightly unkempt beard, made him look like a stereotypical sailor. He had been in Iceland during the original research and had been project managing for the installation phase.

"All the checks done?" asked Adam.

Kendal Hummner nodded.

Adam took one more look at the large container.

"Drop it in, and make sure the position is accurate. The Iceland test is good, but we should have been seeing a major eruption by now. I want this test to go better."

Hummner nodded, he may be the project leader, but he was under no illusions as to who was in charge. He turned and indicated to the crane driver to lower away. Two of the crew held lines fastened to the corners of the large container to ensure it did not swing against the side of the large freighter. As it disappeared below the gentle swell, the two crewmen let go of the lines and the container sank into the depths.

It took ten minutes to reach the seabed, another twenty to ensure the position was correct, and another thirty minutes to establish all of the communication channels. All the time, Adam was watching the metal cable that was still attached to the crane at one end, the container at the other.

"All set Adam. Can we cut the lines?"

"No, bring up the comms buoy. I want to check that before we sever the link."

Two minutes later the dark grey float bobbed to the surface, a small metal dish pointing skywards. The communications buoy was barely visible even at thirty feet.

"Everything is working as planned," said Hummner as he scanned through the readouts on his computer tablet.

Adam pushed himself away from the deck rail. "Okay, retract the buoy and cut it loose." He turned and walked away. There was nothing he could do now, but hope that the equipment continued to work as planned.

Hummner spoke into his hand-held radio that was a direct link to the mini-sub several hundred feet below. It took another twenty minutes to disconnect the data umbilical and metal crane cable. As the sub started to ascend a quiet hum seemed to surround it, causing a resonance to vibrate the small portholes and internal equipment. The single occupant of the sub looked around in first curiosity and then worry as the intensity started to build. He blew air into the ballast tanks and the mini-sub started to rise faster. As he rose, the sound started to dissipate, the vibrations at first getting worse, but then dropping off quickly. At fifty feet, he adjusted the ballast to slow his ascent, using his thrusters to adjust his position, ensuring he was centred below the circle of high intensity floodlights that surrounded the ship's moon pool. As he surfaced, the dark natural environment of the ocean was banished by the high intensity lighting of the ship's middle hold that served as a launch and recovery site for the three mini-subs the *New Dawn* carried. Five minutes later, the sub pilot was out of the small craft and making his report.

Hummner listened to the man and then strode across to a workstation and checked the data recording from the submarine, nodding every few seconds before a half smile turned up the corners of his mouth. This he had to report to Adam.

Three decks up, Adam sat in the dimly lit research control room, watching the readings being recorded from the disruptor, now four hundred feet below the ship, being displayed in blue. These readings were projected against a backdrop of the predicted readings in red. In most cases the blue overlay the red. Adam looked up as Hummner entered.

"The sub picked up the set up calibration vibrations, exactly as you said it would. The records showed that another fifty feet down, and the sub would have imploded."

Adam sat impassively, the fact that he had been twenty seconds away from killing one of his team seemed to have had no impact on him.

"The graphs are all showing on track. If this goes well," Adam's tone made it clear that everything had *better* go well, "there should be a major quake in the area in around four weeks. Stay on station tonight, if everything is as predicted, set course for Japan in the morning. I want us on station with the next disruptor laid and running by the eighteenth of next month."

Hummner did a quick mental calculation. New Zealand to Japan was around 7,000 miles, passing between the Fiji Islands and Vanuatu would shorten that by about 300 miles, but they would still have to traverse past the Solomon Islands and Papua New Guinea before the long open stretch of the Pacific. The *New Dawn's* top speed was twenty-two knots, but they could not maintain that speed for 7,000 miles. Maybe a sustained twenty knots was possible. That would put them off the south east coast of Japan by the fourteenth or fifteenth. Three days to map the exact location, set up, launch and initiate. It was possible, if everything went well. If.

"We'll be there Adam."

"Make sure we are. If everything goes well I'll be standing down as project manager and handing over to you. If things don't go well…" Adam did not finish the thought. He did not need to.

"You know how important the Genesis Project is. We are about to enter a new era of humanity when everything changes," said Adam.

"Yes. I'll make sure everything goes according to plan." Hummner swallowed hard and tried to sound convincing.

The New Zealand earthquake was a magnitude 6.3 that struck the Canterbury region of New Zealand's South Island at 12:51 pm, 22nd February 2011. The earthquake was centred six miles south-east of Christchurch. The quake unexpectedly followed a previous 7.1 quake just six months earlier on 4th September 2010. Many scientists thought that the earlier earthquake had relieved pressure in the area and were surprised that such a major quake could follow so soon. Christchurch had the highest concentration of damage. This was exacerbated by buildings and infrastructure already weakened by the previous earthquake and its aftershocks. One of the unusual consequences of the second earthquake was widespread liquefaction which caused the ground to turn to a semi-liquid. Cars, structures and even some people sank into the ground which would then solidify as the vibrations passed, sealing the structures and innocent victims in a ground that was turning to rock. The effects of the earthquake were felt across the whole of the South Island and the lower and central North Island. In total, 181 people were killed in the earthquake, making it the second deadliest natural disaster in New Zealand's history. So widespread was the damage that a state of national emergency was declared which stayed in force until the end of April. The cost of the disaster was estimated at NZ$15-16 billion in property damage and repairs, loss of productivity and the cost of emergency services. The loss of human life was immeasurable.

On 11th March 2011 a massive earthquake struck Japan. At 9.0 it was one of the largest and most destructive of modern times and in the top five magnitudes since 1900. As well as the earthquake itself, the event triggered an extremely destructive tsunami with peak wave heights recorded of up to 128 feet. The quake was over in six minutes, but the after-effects would last for months with the cleanup expected to take years.

One of the worst effects was the damage and resulting meltdown at the Fukushima 1 Nuclear Power Plant, plus extensive damage to two others. This resulted in over 200,000 people being evacuated and the release of radioactive material into the atmosphere with the fallout being detected as far afield at the USA. Readings within the Fukushima Power Plant were recorded as 1,000 times normal. Over 4.4 million households were left without electricity and 1.5 million without water.

Shortly after the disaster, Japanese Prime Minister Naoto Kan said, "In the sixty-five years after the end of World War II, this is the toughest and the most difficult crisis for Japan."

So powerful was the earthquake and resulting tsunami, which inundated almost 200 square miles, that it is estimated the Earth shifted on its axis by as much as twenty-five inches. The actual power released during the quake was around 600 million times the energy release of the Hiroshima bomb.

As with the New Zealand earthquake, one of the worst phenomena was that of ground liquefaction. People, vehicles, roads, and even whole buildings simply sank into the liquid soil, often with little to show once the ground solidified.

The quake also triggered the eruption of the Shinmoedake volcano in Kyushu, and the rupture of the Fujinuma irrigation dam in Sukagawa causing massive flooding, washing away 1,800 homes and leaving around 4.4 million households without power.

In Ichihara, a 220,000 barrel-per-day oil refinery and in Sendai a 140,000 barrel-per-day oil refinery were set on fire. They were only extinguished ten days later after killing six people and totally destroying the storage facilities.

The overall cost of the disaster exceeded 400 billion American dollars, which would make it the most costly natural disaster of all time.

The Grüssmire Gewerbe Institute recorded all of the data with interest and considered it a good start and an indication of the disasters yet to come.

Chapter 7

Today
13:00hrs, 11th January

The flickering candles in the windowless circular stone walled room cast an almost romantic glow to the scene. That romance would be dispersed as soon as anyone cast an eye on the contents of the chamber. The walls were dark, possibly blue or black stone, in the candlelight it was hard to tell. There were semicircular alcoves around one half of the room with a deeper, more ornate alcove heading the room. Many of the ornaments, if that was the correct word for them, were glistening metal, silver and gold, but one stood out from the rest. Standing on top of a raised dais was the skull of some sort of horned beast. The bleached white bone reflected the flickering yellow light, casting eerie dancing shadows into the empty eye sockets. However, it was the people standing around the red painted pentagram on the floor that finally destroyed any semblance of romance. Five of the men were wearing dark hooded robes, their faces hidden in the shadows of the raised cowls. The sixth was wearing a white robe with red trim, arcane gold symbols running in two vertical rows down the front. The white robed figure had his hood pushed back, his bald head reflecting the flickering flames. In his left hand he held a thin bladed, curved knife. As he raised the knife he spoke unrecognised words, clearly some form of incantation. After a few seconds he fell silent. Lowering the knife he grasped the blade in his right hand and quickly pulled it through his palm. The rapid trickle of blood ran down his wrist until he lowered his hand and let the black looking blood run into the raised golden goblet that was held out by one of the other men.

After two minutes the goblet was half full and the white robed man squeezed his hand tighter until the blood flow stopped. He then stepped behind the dais and quickly wrapped a white cloth around his hand before stepping back to the circle. Saying a few words over the goblet he took it back from the other man and touched the contents to his lips, leaving a crimson stain and a coppery smell. He then walked around the circle of men and offered the cup to each in turn.

Returning to the dais, he looked up at the silver figure eighty-eight on the dark wall, the flickering light seeming to dance along the carved numbers, before reverently offering the goblet to the horned skull and returning back to his original position at the centre of the pentagram. Chanting unknown words, he removed the red stained white cloth from his palm and wiped away the remaining blood. He then held his hands up to the other men, demonstrating the now unblemished and undamaged palms.

Five minutes later the men were in the outer chamber, their robes placed in lockers. The bald headed man looked at each in turn. He was in his late fifties and his once muscular torso was turning to fat, but he was still an imposing figure.

"Good news. We have made progress."

"With the research? We've traced the genes?"

"No, not with the Messiah Project. With our other area of interest. We have a lead on the Knights."

"We know who they are? Where they are?" one of the other men asked. He was likewise in his fifties, but at five feet ten inches he was three inches shorter than their leader. His once honey blond hair was turning paler, heading towards white. His hook nose gave him the look of a predatory hawk. His eyes were the dead soulless black of a shark and he had the sort of stare that could turn a man's blood to ice.

"No, it's not that easy. We have a lead to one of their ex-members. With luck it will be the start we need."

"Bring him in, I guarantee I'll get the information from him." The man's dead eyes took on a sparkle as he contemplated the task. The other four initiates looked on, detaching themselves from the other men. Although the same rank within the brotherhood as hook nose, they knew better than to interrupt him and the Master while they were talking.

"By ex-member I mean dead. But we know where he lived. It may be that he has left information behind. And we are making progress with the research. Our founders had the right idea. Dispose of the undesirables and breed back to perfection. But they only had half of the tools they needed. They were efficient enough at extermination, but they did not have the benefit of the genetics research we have. Selective breeding is slow and unpredictable. With the identification of the human genome we now have the ability to breed scientifically. We will shortly have the gene sequence we need to breed back to the fifth race. And if we can track down the Knights and their treasure we will have the God Sequence." Bald head put his hand on hawk nose's shoulder.

"Relax Hans, we have waited over sixty years for this lead. The Knights have always guarded their secrets well. It is only by a fluke that we have come across this lead. I've dispatched someone to check out the information. He will get back to us shortly. And then we can start to take action that will change the world, and make us the rightful rulers."

14:00hrs, 12ᵗʰ January
Meltham, England

The day was cold. Snow covered the ground and heavy grey clouds promised more to come. Frozen snow covered the trees, bending the branches to breaking point. Some had already gone beyond that point. The garden ponds had not been free of ice for almost five weeks and the only private drives that were free of thick snow were the ones that had been cleared regularly. The roads were slick with compacted, frozen snow making driving feel the same as traversing a ploughed field.

The large silver Range Rover was parked in a side street that had not seen traffic for several days. The snow was fresh, white and crisp giving reasonable traction. The driver had slipped over from behind the wheel to the passenger side.

A second man was in the back. He was younger than the driver, in his mid-twenties as opposed to the driver's mid-forties. He was constantly looking around. Not nervous, more like hyperactive.

"Why are you sitting in the passenger seat? What if we need to get away quick?" the man in the back asked.

"We are here to wait for the old lady to leave. We aren't doing anything illegal so we won't need to make a quick getaway. With me here and you in the back, we are just waiting for the driver. It looks less suspicious."

"Well that's why you're the boss, Adam. I'll remember that when I'm the one in charge." Greg laughed at his own self-importance.

The driver caught movement out of the corner of his eye. Glancing at the dashboard clock he saw that the old lady was on time. Every Thursday she went for a meeting with the village committee. Even with a foot of snow on the ground, the English 'Bulldog Spirit' meant that the meeting would go ahead. He watched as the old lady walked away from the house and out of sight. Waiting five minutes, Adam stepped from the car and looked around, breathing in the cold, fresh air.

The cottage was set back from the road by about thirty feet, the front garden was surrounded by a picket fence that was not usually seen outside of 1950s films and advertising brochures for holiday lets.

"Wait here. Let me know if anyone approaches the house. Call me now and keep the line open." Adam stepped from the car and walked towards the picturesque cottage being careful of his footing on the slippery footpath. His mobile phone rang after a few seconds and he answered it, confirming he could hear Greg clearly and then placed the Bluetooth hands free clip over his ear. Adam walked steadily along the road and up to the old cottage as if he were a regular caller.

Approaching the house he made sure he stepped in the several footprints leading to and from the house, ensuring that his footprints would not stand out.

He would have preferred to go around the back of the house and enter through the back door or one of the windows, but the snow along the front of the house was fresh and unmarked and he did not want to leave any footprints to mark his visit.

Casually glancing around, he made sure no one was approaching and examined the door lock. It was a good quality lock, but old and probably worn making it easier to pick. A minute later the door opened and he stepped into the small hall, closing the door behind him. He quickly removed his shoes so as not to take any snow into the house, and stepped across the hallway.

The house was warm and welcoming. The front room still had several logs burning in the stove, although the vents had been closed to slow the combustion and reduce the heat. Where should he start? Where would secret information be kept? There was a large bookcase along the back wall. Maybe the best place to hide something was in plain sight?

Before he entered the room he took several photographs using a small digital camera. The man stepped over to the bookcase and started to systematically check each title. After several minutes he had turned up nothing from a visual search so he started to remove each book and flick through them before returning them to the same place. Quickly checking the room he found nothing of interest, returning each item to the same location. Back at the door he checked the photos to make sure everything was as it should be before moving on.

Greg sat in the driver's seat of the Range Rover, the rear mirror angled so that he could see back along the road and the entrance to the cottage. He felt he should have been in the house with Adam. He was wasted as a lookout. And Adam's idea of sitting in the passenger side to look less conspicuous, well that was his way, not Greg's. He was a man of action, that's what he was, and it was that action that would help him move up through the organisation. People like Adam, thinkers, well they were needed in any organisation, but men of action, their rightful place was leading the thinkers. Greg put his hands behind his head and stretched. Yes, he expected that he would start to move up in the organisation shortly and then maybe Adam would be answering to him.

Greg wound down the window and reached into his pocket for cigarettes. The packet was empty. Greg looked around, where had he put the other packet? He reached across to the glovebox on the passenger side. Lying across the centre console he rummaged through the paperwork, a packet of sweets he had bought at the service station, a high caffeine energy drink, there, at the back, the packet he was looking for.

He sat back up and lit the cigarette, drawing the smoke deep into his lungs. He then blew the smoke through the part open window. Adam did not like the smell of smoke in the car.

Sitting with his head back he glanced in the mirror. Oh shit, someone was walking up the footpath to the old woman's cottage.

"Adam? Adam? There's someone coming."

Adam heard Greg's voice over the earpiece, coughing and gasping. "Greg, what did you say?" There was a knock on the door. Adam froze, it was too late to leave.

"Adam, there's someone at the door."

Adam heard Greg's slightly panicked voice through his earpiece. *Thanks Greg, good surveillance.*

A second knock, at least it was not someone who was going to let themselves in by the sound of it. Adam edged to the door and looked along the passage leading to the front door. As he watched the letterbox opened and a card fell through. He then heard the crunch of footsteps heading away from the door. He took a deep breath and calmed his nerves.

"Adam, he's going on, I think it was the postman."

Adam watched as the figure retreated along the path and out of the front garden before resuming his search. He repeated the procedure room by room: the kitchen, utility room, small dining room, downstairs toilet. He took a photograph of each room and checked it before leaving.

Upstairs he started in the back bedroom. It was made up, several photos of a family group, mother, father and daughter. But the room looked too tidy, as if it had been cleaned away ready for use rather than actually in regular use.

Next was the study, a small but efficient workspace. Two filing cabinets held all the usual paperwork, receipts, instruction manuals, tax returns, insurance and car documents. All filed away in date and alphabetical order.

Last was the front bedroom. The wardrobes held the usual clothes and household linens. No papers, nothing of any use. Adam looked around and walked to the window, looking out at the snow covered trees and back garden, the hills forming a picturesque backdrop to the winter scene. Maybe there was nothing here to find after all. He took the camera from his pocket and examined the room, ensuring that everything was back in its original place and headed out.

Adam stopped and rocked back on his right foot. The floorboard was slightly loose. It was the type of thing that the resident would probably never notice. It had always been like that and was simply part of the house. He looked around. The carpet was laid wall to wall but was not fitted, not fastened down.

Five minutes later Adam had the carpet pulled back and the floorboard lifted. The space underneath held a small wooden chest. Opening the box he saw papers and journals. He removed the digital camera and started to copy the documents. This could be the key the order had been looking for, the key to secrets locked away for two thousand years. Adam frowned, the book looked like a handwritten story book.

Adam looked up sharply at a sound from downstairs. Standing, he walked quietly to the bedroom door.

"Adam? You up there?"

Adam could feel the anger rising. What the hell was Greg doing in the house?

As the two walked back to the car, Adam considered that Greg had lasted too long.

"Okay, let's go," said Adam as they climbed into the car.

Greg put the car in gear and accelerated away from the kerb too quickly. The Range Rover, even in four wheel drive, fishtailed away from the kerb and almost hit a car heading in the opposite direction.

"Stupid old git," said Greg. "Some people shouldn't be on the road."

"Just what I was thinking," replied Adam.

"At least the old lady in the house won't give us any problems," Greg said with a grin a few miles later.

"Why do you say that?" asked Adam.

"While you were poking around upstairs I searched the kitchen. The old dear drinks that fruit tea stuff. I injected poison into an unopened pack. When she drinks it she'll go to her maker."

Adam was barely containing his anger. "Why?"

"You said that killing her was an option, I used my initiative and took the option."

"That was only if she turned up while I was in the house. It was not your decision to make. What if the poison is discovered at an autopsy?"

"I used that stuff you showed me. You said it's undetectable."

"I said it's undetectable unless it is specifically tested for."

Thirty minutes and eighteen miles later, Adam looked up and into the back of the car. After a few seconds he turned back to the front and looked out of the side window.

"What's up, boss?" asked Greg.

Adam shook his head. "Nothing, I thought I heard something."

Greg bared his tobacco stained teeth in a wide grin.

"Must be your guilty conscience. Not something I suffer from. I can kill without a second thought."

"That could be a real problem, not thinking."

Adam again turned and looked in the back. "I think there's something wrong with the rear wheels. I'm sure I heard a grinding. Better stop and check to make sure there's nothing caught or any damage."

Greg pulled the silver car into a lay-by. It was a quiet stretch of road, quieter than normal with the recent heavy snowfall. Both the men got out of the car and headed to the rear.

"What's that?" asked Adam, bending and pointing under the back of the car.

"I can't see anyth…"

Adam swung the fist sized rock hard enough to stun Greg but not kill, hitting him square on the forehead. Greg slumped to the soft, snow covered floor, semi-conscious.

Adam took a bottle of water from his jacket pocket and a small tin box of pills. He removed several of the pills from the box and put them into Greg's mouth along with half the bottle of water. Greg was just conscious enough to swallow to avoid choking. The pills would be fatal in about thirty minutes.

Adam reached down and pulled the young thug to the side of the road. He then hit Adam again with the rock, the soft crack was the sound that Adam wanted to hear, not an immediately fatal blow, but definitely not good for his health. He them wiped the water bottle and put it into Greg's hand and laid it on the floor, where most of the content poured into the white snow. He did the same with the box of pills, putting them into Greg's pocket.

Walking back to the car, Adam pressed in the cigar lighter. After twenty seconds the small button popped out with a chime. He then took it back to Greg and opened his jacket and shirt, and applied the glowing red end to Greg's arm, breathing in the smell of seared flesh; it really did smell like pork. After a few seconds he stood back and examined his handy work. Greg had been a thug, not worthy of wearing the mark of the Order.

Looking around to make sure no cars were approaching, he rolled Greg down the short embankment and was satisfied to see him sink into the two feet of drifted snow at the bottom. The rock he tossed down so that it landed a few feet away from Greg's head.

Adam checked his watch, the old lady would be back home by now. It was too risky to do anything about the poison. He walked back to the Range Rover and drove away for fifteen minutes before turning around and returning to the lay-by. He was satisfied that he had only seen one other car on the road during that time.

Adam walked back to the top of the embankment and looked down. He was pleased to see vomit down Greg's chin, looking close, there was no sign of breathing. The snow was starting to fall, thick heavy flakes settling on the road and already starting to cover Greg's body. With some luck, it would be weeks before anyone found him.

"You may act without thought, Greg, but I don't. And I certainly won't be hearing from my conscience over you. Eight, eight."

Chapter 8

11:00hrs, 21st March
Western Massachusetts

The sunlight coming through the trees cast a stroboscopic effect across the face of the older man as he walked along with a determined stride. He was in his mid-seventies, but fitter than most people twenty years his junior. He still had the straight back and firm gait of his youth, although his hair now had more salt than its original deep pepper colour and his face was showing lines that he described as 'character'.

He had walked these roads and tracks for more years than he cared to remember, first as a young boy then as a husband hand in hand with his wife and then as a father with their delightful daughter. But now he was walking alone, not that he was lacking friends, there were plenty of people in the town that would have welcomed his company, but this was his time. A time he could just be at one with the countryside, especially at this time of year when the first signs of spring were appearing. Many people thought of Massachusetts, a part of the New England region, as a tourist destination for the autumn. But Robert P Jacobs preferred the fresh greens and early shoots of the spring rather than the startling burning reds, yellows and golds of the fall.

Jacobs' cabin was on the edge of the small town that had grown up around the old logging industry and now served one of the main hiking trails that criss-crossed the rural west of the state. He had been born and bred in the area, and after retiring from the Forestry Commission and Rural Affairs Department had leased several acres of the wilderness by agreement with the state so that he could be surrounded by the flora and fauna he loved yet still be close enough to civilisation to access his creature comforts.

He loved this time of year. It held the promise of new life and new hope. He had been out for almost four hours and the chill breeze was just starting to creep into his bones. He would be home in twenty minutes and looked forward to his afternoon hot chocolate and nip of brandy. But before heading directly back to his cabin he was heading into town to pick up his regular weekly supplies.

He walked along considering tonight's meeting. He was the treasurer of the local Wilderness Habitat Committee and the hot topic at the moment was the preservation of the Showy Lady's Slipper orchid, a rare flower in these parts. At around two feet tall with several coarse elliptical leaves it was easy to pass by until the flowers appeared in June and July. The flowers had white sepals and lateral petals. The lip petal, or slipper which gives the plant its name, is a pure white mottled with dark red. The Larch, Black Ash and Maple of the surrounding woods marked the ideal wet semi-swamp lands the orchid liked.

The committee was likely to suggest around the clock watches to ensure the plant's safety. But that in itself would draw attention to the area, possibly even tempting collectors to make the trip.

He stepped from the trees and looked left and right along the road. The highway had been cut through the forest years ago, and the loss of the wild habitat still annoyed Jacobs.

He heard before he saw a car approaching from the front. He stepped off the road onto the wide verge as the car slowed and pulled out to allow him plenty of room. The driver nodded and raised his hand from the steering wheel and smiled as he passed. Jacobs nodded, politeness cost nothing. He stepped back onto the road and set off again at a brisk pace.

The committee would want to set a rota for the guard duties. Well if they were intent on standing guard, Jacobs would volunteer for the night shift. It was likely that few, if any, would want to spend all night in the forest, whereas Jacobs often walked through the woods at night, quietly watching the wildlife that was not present during the day. It would give him plenty of opportunities to spot one of his favourite endangered species, the nocturnal Long-eared Owl. There was a breeding pair in the conifers near the orchid site. They had set up home only a few weeks ago and Jacobs had witnessed courtship rituals just last week.

He heard the sound of another car, this one coming from behind. He half turned and stepped onto the verge as the car, it was the same large dark blue car that had gone the other way a few minutes earlier, slowed and stopped beside him.

The driver lowered his window and smiled at Jacobs. "Excuse me, but do you know these roads very well?" he asked with an educated and slightly accented voice.

Jacobs smiled, he knew these roads and the area around better than most. He stepped off the verge and bent down to talk more directly to the man. He noted he had a Mediterranean complexion and eyes almost as black as his hair. He was probably in his mid to late thirties.

"Where do you want to be?" he said, bending to the window.

The man held up a map and pointed to a section near the top. Jacobs bent further, almost putting his head in through the window.

"In nomine Patris."

"Excuse me?" said Jacobs, not wanting to believe

what he had just heard.

With a sudden movement, too fast for Jacobs to register, the man's hand shot up and out, taking hold of Jacobs' coat as the car shot backwards. Jacobs was pulled from his feet and dragged along for fifty feet before the man let go and he fell to the floor.

Jacobs was shocked beyond reason. He could not understand what was happening. He needed to get home. He was scraped, cut along his legs, but he was not badly hurt. He started to stand, rising unsteadily to his feet. There was another car coming, perhaps it was someone who could help, maybe take him home.

The young black haired man watched as Jacobs rose shakily to his feet. He slipped the automatic gearbox into drive and accelerated along the road, hitting him square on the centre of the bonnet. Jacobs spun and hit the windscreen, sending cracks across the centre as his head struck the glass. The man slowed the car and stopped without skidding. He exited the car and walked casually back along the road to Jacobs' inert body. Bending, he quickly checked the old man and removed the keys from his coat pocket. He then walked back to the car and drove away.

Jacobs was only vaguely aware of his surroundings, he was numb and cold. Off to one side he heard the steady single tone of the Long-eared Owl as it called to its mate. He closed his eyes and let the darkness carry him away.

14:50hrs, 24th March
Oxford

The Red Lion was a traditional oak panelled pub, renowned for its good food and real ales. In days gone by the bar would have been filled with cigarette smoke and academics. The academics were still there, but legislation had outlawed the smoke some years ago.

Professor William Grace walked into the lounge and looked around. He was twenty minutes late and was hoping that his host would have had the patience to wait. He had received the enquiry and funding offer a few days ago, but this would be the first face to face meeting, or should he think of it as an interview?

As a professor of Biblical History he did not attract the funding of some of the more glamorous fields. So when the offer came it was too good to pass up. In truth he was not sure what to expect. Ten years ago he had officially retired from formal lecturing at the university when he turned fifty-five, the Dean and Committee had made him professor emeritus for life. He had no formal lecture programme, instead he kept his title and privileges and lectured when, and if, he saw fit. He had joined the college immediately upon graduating and had never needed to interview for a position. Even within the order, he had simply carried out research and kept their secrets, never needing to prove himself or compete. So the whole concept of 'having to prove oneself' was foreign to him. Still, if some company wanted to provide funding he was willing to accept it.

"Professor Grace." The smartly dressed man stood and offered Grace his hand, clearly he knew the professor by sight.

Grace took the man's hand, it was cool and dry, a good firm grip.

"Please professor, take a seat. Let me get you a drink."

"Thank you." Grace looked across at the specials board. Being a free house the pub always had at least three guest beers.

"I'll have a pint of Bombardier, please."

"I'll just get the drinks, have a look at the menu, and see what you want to eat. We'll order in a few minutes."

Grace watched the younger man as he walked across the busy bar. If this was an interview it was starting off well. And if drinks and dinner were so easy, maybe the sponsorship would be just as easy to secure.

"Here you go, one pint." The man set the glass on the table and sat down opposite Grace.

For the first time Grace noticed the man's voice. It was slightly accented, but very subtle. He was well dressed: black suit, crisp white shirt and thin, dark red tie. Grace knew next to nothing about fashion, but even he could see that the clothes were good quality. He put the glass to his lips and took a healthy mouthful.

"So, professor, care to talk me through your research." Again he made the question a statement, he was obviously used to getting his way. Was this the start of the interview? Grace had butterflies starting to form in his stomach. The young man took a long drink of his beer, his black hair standing out against the polished wood of the high backed bench seat.

"I thought you would know about the research before you made the approach," replied the professor. His palms were turning clammy and the butterflies in his stomach were flying around in agitation. If this was how people felt in interviews Grace was happy to have missed them for the last sixty-five years.

"My employers know a lot about your research. But if we are to sponsor you, we will expect you to present your research at times. A simple lecture as you would do at the college, but I'd like to see you talk one to one."

Grace nodded, so this was an interview. But at least he was talking as the expert, and he had lectured for years.

"Very well, where shall I begin?" said Grace as he pursed his lips. "Most people assume that the bible, that is the book that purports to talk about the creation of Heaven and Earth and the greater being that created them, and later His son that he sent to Earth to save our immortal souls, is one book, written by one author at the time of, or shortly after, the events. In fact, it was written by multiple authors, over several hundred years. The version we refer to now is actually a compilation of several earlier works and all of them are translations and re-workings of other books. Many say that the Jewish Torah is one of the most accurate bibles. Traditionally it is manually transcribed, word for word, letter by letter by a specially trained scribe." Grace paused, he was not worried about the lecture, he had given it a hundred times to different students. But the thought of an interview was still getting to him, he wiped his hands on his trousers and felt the same cold sweat starting to form on his brow.

"And the differences in the various bibles are less than distinct. The five books of the Jewish Torah are the same first books of the Christian Bible, Genesis, Exodus, Leviticus, Numbers and Deuteronomy. They are also incorporated into the Islamic Koran."

He was starting to feel sick, and he felt a tingling in his left fingers, as if someone under the table were sticking small pins into the outer layer of skin, not painful, but uncomfortable.

"So I suppose the only real way to determine the truth, short of time travel," the tanned young man sitting opposite gave a small laugh, "would be to find and translate actual texts from the time."

Grace looked at the dark haired man, he realised he had not introduced himself. What did he mean by the question? Was he fishing? Did he know something, or was it just a simple question?

"Obviously that would be the ideal. But research on what we do have can get us further than you may think.

68

By cross referencing bible texts, of all religions, with other historical texts, linking actual events, we can get a feeling for when they were written. That allows us to determine the dominant factors from the era and put a new slant on the writings."

"And what about artefacts, religious artefacts, items actually touched by or belonging to real religious figures? People or beings with real powers?"

The man had a half smile on his face and his dark eyes seemed to twinkle with amusement. The questions were too probing, too direct. It was as if he knew the answers already. But that was impossible. Grace raised his hands back onto the table and lifted his glass to his lips and took a deep drink, two mouthfuls, before lowering the glass back to the table with a shaking hand, the glass knocking against the oak table top several times before it settled.

Grace looked up at the man, he was finding it hard to breath and he had a pain in his chest. Maybe this was more than interview nerves. Were the years of fatty foods and no exercise finally catching up with him? Was this a heart attack?

"I'm sorry, I think I should go. I need to see a doctor." Grace put his hands onto the table and started to rise, but fell back onto the leather seat.

"Relax professor." The man reached across the table and patted Grace's hand. He then wiped his own glass and exchanged it for Grace's, placing the glass in the older man's hand. "It will be over in a few minutes. The pain you are feeling now will pass in a few seconds. Then you'll slip into a sleep and it will all be over."

Grace slumped back, the pain was fading and with it his strength. He watched as the tanned younger man stood and stepped around the table. He then bent and put his face close to Grace's.

"In nomine Patris, professor." The man straightened up and smiled as he looked down at the professor.

"No, no it can't be," Grace said weakly.

The man opened the front of his shirt and showed a small section of chest to the now pale man. Professor Grace's face took on a mask of horror before relaxing, pale and emotionless, only his eyes displaying the horror he felt. He watched as the man walked away, too weak to stand or even call out.

In the toilet, the glossy black haired man entered a cubicle and locked the door. He then poured the rest of Grace's beer down the toilet and pulled the old fashioned chain. Listening to make sure there was no one in the toilet, he left the cubicle and quickly washed and dried the glass, removing all trace of the drink and his fingerprints. He looked in the long mirror behind the hand basins and examined his face. He was clean shaven with smooth olive skin and looked like any other businessman you could find in the city. He ran his hands through his thick black hair to smooth it back into perfect position. He then placed the glass on the windowsill and left the toilet. Glancing across the bar, he saw Grace still sitting where he had left him. His eyes were open and he was sitting back relaxed, just another scholar on a lunch break.

12:50hrs, 26th March
Switzerland

Francois Bertrand bent his knees and dug his skis in as he came to an impressive stop. He took a breath and raised his goggles.

The impressive mountains stood out against the azure cloudless sky like white silhouettes. The packed snow reflected the dazzling sun in 360 degrees ensuring that the shadows were little more than a light blue/grey.

The skiers traversing the mountain cast plumes of ice crystals at each turn which cast the light into glittering rainbows.

It had been several years since Bertrand had been skiing, this was his second day in the resort and although the skill was still there his muscles were protesting. He bent slightly and massaged his thighs and calves. Looking around to make sure there was no one too close, he also massaged his buttocks which were burning from the last downhill run. But the aches and pains, even the burning buttocks were worth it for the sense of freedom and the views.

He took another deep breath, the air was like clear nectar, cold but sweet. And the view, it displayed the dramatic majesty of nature at its best and most raw. The season was coming to an end, much of the snow already having melted, exposing some of the more prominent rocks which stood out darkly against the crystal white snow.

Bertrand heard the regular swish of snow and ice kicked up from an approaching skier and turned to make sure he was not in the way.

The man was dressed in a one piece, yellow, green and blue skin hugging suit. Bertrand had to smile to himself, the young man, he could have been anywhere from twenty to forty, was not slim, but he was athletic and could carry off the suit. Bertrand had never been one to wear gaudy colours and even in his youth he had not had the body to show off skin-tight clothes.

The young man was clearly an accomplished skier and in control. Bertrand was not in the way and he turned back to the impressive view.

There was a swoosh from behind and the edge of a small wave of snow washed over Bertrand's feet. He turned to the gaudily dressed young man who had come to a dramatic stop only six feet away. He removed his goggles and dayglow yellow and green woolly hat revealing black hair and almost as dark eyes. Bertrand was surprised to see that he was probably in his late thirties, maybe early forties. Easily twenty years younger than Bertrand.

"Good morning." The young man greeted Bertrand in the international language of the slopes, but spoke English with a slight accent, maybe Italian?

"Good morning, lovely day," replied Bertrand.

"The view is very impressive. Have you skied here before?"

"Many times. But not for some years," Bertrand rubbed his thighs and smiled. "As my legs will testify."

The young man nodded. "Yes, my legs are starting to protest as well. But for such views I will put up with a little discomfort." The man looked at Bertrand's face, lingering for a few seconds on the scar running across the older man's eye before looking off to the distant peaks.

Across the valley the wind was blowing a constant stream of ice crystals from the peak of the mountain, the crystals forming a multi-coloured rainbow arcing from the peak to halfway down the top slope. The wind was gentle on their faces, but still held the sting of minus ten degrees and turned their cheeks red with the sting of the cold.

The young man replaced his dark green goggles and gaudy coloured hat before turning back to Bertrand. "Would you care to ski with me for a while, I'm heading across the slope down to the west?"

Bertrand turned to look across the expanse of crisp white snow and then back to the young man. "Thank you. I'd like that." Bertrand replaced his own orange glasses and waved his hand across the slope. "Please, lead on, but don't rush too fast, my legs are still protesting."

The young man straightened his skis and headed off straight down the slope for a few feet before angling off across the slope, zigzagging in a ploughing motion to control his speed. Bertrand followed with less speed and less ploughing, but covered the ground in a comparable time, if less dramatically.

As they crossed the slope a few scattered pine trees marked the edge of the wide run and the start of the off piste section. The snow here was finer and deeper, slowing but not stopping them.

After a few minutes the men were well away from the normal tourist trail. The views from this side of the slope were even more dramatic, the snow dropping away toward the edge of the cliff, the occasional dark rock standing proud, scoured bare of snow by the wind. Beyond the rocks the valley opened up four hundred feet below. The picturesque honey coloured timber chalets standing out against the white background looking like a model village set out in the wide valley below.

The young man slid to a halt, followed a few seconds later by Bertrand. The two men drank in the view for a few seconds, letting the scene wash over them, the sun bright and warm on their bare skin. The young man straightened his skis and headed off along the cliff edge, followed by Bertrand. As he rounded a large boulder he lost balance and slid out of control towards the edge and the four hundred foot drop. Bertrand dug in his ski poles and pushed off towards the fallen man. He pulled up short and, using his ski poles, unclipped his skis and stepped towards the motionless body, burying the base of his ski poles into the soft snow and leaving them standing. He removed his gloves and felt for a pulse in the man's neck, it was strong and steady and he was breathing. Bertrand reached over the man as if to turn him onto his back but paused. Was that the right thing to do?

With a low moan the young man started to turn onto his back and with shocking speed his right hand took hold of Bertrand's and his left shot up to the shoulder. The young man turned back to his side effortlessly levering Bertrand from his feet and over the edge of the cliff.

Bertrand was too shocked to cry out until he slammed into a rocky outcrop which shattered half of the bones in his body and bent his neck beyond breaking point, the scream dying in his throat.

At the top of the rock face, the black haired, olive skinned young man looked down on Bertrand's broken body. His face was expressionless, it was simply a job, a job that was for His greater glory.

"In nomine Patris," muttered the younger man under his breath as he turned away.

Chapter 9

13:20hrs, 3rd April
Afghanistan

The day was cold and wet. The rain had stopped an hour ago, but the sky held the promise of more to come. When the lead grey clouds did part, the sun was at best a washed out pale yellow and only served to cast an even more sorrowful light on the distant mountains.

The small convoy was heading to one of the forward reconnaissance posts and the troops were less than happy. They had been back from a five day patrol less than three hours when their VIP guest had insisted on being taken out, "by an experienced team that will tell it like it is". The base commander had offered the VIP a backup unit to take him 'in country', but he wanted a team, "fresh from the field and looking like they had seen action", insisting that he needed their views to be reflected on his return to the UK. But the MP's reputation had preceded him. Only recently elevated to his current cabinet position, he wanted to make a name for himself quickly and was not concerned who he needed to step on as he climbed the ladder. Several years ago, as a newly elected MP, he had carelessly said in the hearing of a reporter, "I don't care who I step on as I go up, because I don't intend to come back down to their level." That comment had haunted him for some years and had again raised its head following his recent promotion. But he felt that by being seen to side with 'our lads' in a war zone, and especially if he could get press coverage of himself in the thick of things, his public image would take a boost.

He wanted the best of both worlds. His vast family

fortune, education at the best of schools and Cambridge University and his reputation as a ruthless businessman allowed him access to the type of people who held power and influence. But he also needed to appeal to the public, the working class man. He needed to show he could get his hands dirty and 'mix it with our boys'. So committed was he to his image that he had insisted on leaving his protection detail back in the UK. That allowed him to publicly announce that he was saving money for the taxpayer and show that he was capable of looking after himself. The fact that he had insisted on having a dedicated armoured personnel carrier for his exclusive use and never travelling without at least one fully armed unit in tow was not for publication.

The PM had not been happy about the trip. There was a danger that the right honourable St.John Dalziel (pronounced Sinjon De-ell) was becoming more popular than the PM himself. But the PM knew that he could not afford a public split in the cabinet so had reluctantly allowed the trip, on the condition that Dalziel took at least one security specialist with him who could talk the language of the troops and their commanders.

And so Dalziel had arrived in Afghanistan two days ago with a photographer, a print journalist and a documentary maker with a camera crew. He also had Hugh Grantham, ex-SAS Major, in tow as his personal advisor. It had been made clear to Grantham that although he was a security expert, as far as anyone else was concerned, especially the reporters, he was simply there to advise the MP regarding military protocol. And Grantham was finding it difficult to remain civil when Dalziel clearly cared nothing for the men he was supposedly here to see and everything for his own image.

"When we stop, I want to get a photo of you with

the vehicles in the background and the troops on guard with their weapons on show." The photographer was looking out at the passing hills, weighing up the angles and best shots. "These hills would make a great background, emphasise the rugged country."

"Well if that's what you want," said Dalziel and leant forward to open the armoured hatch leading to the cab of the vehicle. "Driver, pull over here. We need to get some photos."

"This is not a good place to stop, sir. We have high country on both sides, an ideal ambush site," said Grantham, leaning over from the back of the Saxon personnel carrier and peering out of the armoured glass mounted in the narrow windows. "And you may want to refer to the driver as 'sergeant' not driver. He isn't a chauffeur he's a serving infantryman."

"And I outrank everyone here so I'll thank you to keep your advice to yourself."

"I thought that's why I was here, to offer advice on military matters," replied Grantham, his voice flatly expressing no emotion.

Dalziel leant forward and brandished his mobile phone in front of Grantham's face and said quietly, but with obvious menace, "With one call I could ensure that you never work security again. You wouldn't even get a job as a night club bouncer."

"Very impressive, sir. The best I can usually get with my phone is a pizza delivered, and they're usually late."

Clearly the MP was not used to people standing up to him and chose to pointedly ignore the remark. But he wanted his photos and two minutes later the small convoy pulled over. The troops exited the vehicles and quickly scanned the surrounding area. To Grantham's practised eye it was clear they were nervous at stopping in such a potentially dangerous spot.

"Time to stretch our legs, gentlemen. Just let me know where you want me." Dalziel exited the rear doors of the personnel carrier and looked around at the low hills and rugged countryside. The clouds were just parting and the weak sun was casting enough light to give some definition to the grey granite rocks.

Grantham looked around at the area and the positions of the troops. Satisfied with the men's defensive layout he headed back down the small column of vehicles towards the patrol commander, a young man, probably late twenties, thin and sinewy, sandy hair cut short, almost shaved. His desert camouflage clothing was stained from several days in the field and had clearly seen some rough use.

"Mr Grantham, how do you do your job?"

Grantham looked across at the small group surrounding Dalziel. The photographer was scanning the area with his light meter and setting up background shots, the camera crew, a camera man and soundrecordist were setting up to record a short interview and the reporter was chatting with Dalziel and taking notes.

Grantham turned back to the lieutenant, "Sometimes I wonder myself."

"At least you look at home here, and around weapons. I assume you've seen service?"

"Some," replied Grantham with a non-committal shrug.

Lieutenant Adams looked at the older man. Grantham was in his mid-forties, around six feet, short black hair with a hint of a natural wave and dark deep set eyes. He had a square jaw and a lean well muscled build. He appeared relaxed, but fully aware of his surroundings, clearly at home.

"I'd say Paras or Marines?" said Adams still weighing up Grantham.

"I did six years in the Paras."

"So you went on to Special Forces." Adams made it a statement.

Grantham continued to scan the surrounding countryside as if he had not heard the remark.

"I'll take that as a *yes*, then. I appreciate you pulling our guest up over his chauffer remark."

Grantham now turned and looked with fresh appreciation at the young officer.

"You've got the intercom rigged to be permanently switched on, you know that's against regs?" the half smile on Grantham's face made it clear he had no intention of commenting to the young officer's seniors.

"You know how comms play up in these dusty conditions." Adams looked past Grantham at the small group centred on Dalziel. "At least your cams look like everyone else's. His look as if they've been tailored. I suppose some people just look good whatever they dress in."

Grantham snorted his derision. "I was in his tent last night, he had three full sets hung up, all with designer labels on the inside. And they're not exactly canvas. At a guess, I'd say they're cotton. And I'd swear that one of them had strategically placed dirt put on to look good."

"You're joking." Adams was incredulous.

"I'm not." Grantham stopped and looked around sharply.

Adams looked from Grantham to the surrounding area, had Grantham noticed something he had missed?

"What…"

Grantham was already running when he cut the younger officer short. "Get the men…" The deep throated whoomp and breathy hiss announced the firing and flight of mortars.

"INCOMING." Adams ran towards the rear of the

nearest armoured vehicle and dove for cover as a second and then a third whoomp sounded from different directions.

Grantham was sprinting flat out by the time the second mortar was fired. "GET DOWN," he yelled as he headed towards the group with Dalziel. The photographer looked around and then up at the sound of the approaching bombs. He had spent time in war zones and reacted by throwing himself down and covering his head with his hands.

Ten feet from Dalziel, Grantham launched himself into a dive with his arms wide open, taking Dalziel and the camera crew down in one large group as the first mortar struck and exploded in a shower of metal, dirt and rock. The concussive blast made Grantham's ears ring, reinforced two and three seconds later as the second and third mortars struck. As the dirt and stones rained down around the small convoy, Grantham became aware of a quiet, strangled screaming behind him. He looked around and saw the reporter trying to simultaneously hold his throat, chest and stomach which had been lacerated from the initial blast.

Grantham raised himself to a crouch as Dalziel's hand gripped his arm. "Where are you going?" asked the MP in a shaky voice.

"The reporter's injured, he needs help."

"You're here to protect me, not them." Dalziel nodded to the camera crew and reporter.

Grantham pulled his arm free and, staying low, scurried over to the man and quickly assessed the wounds. All the cuts were deep and bleeding freely, but there was no rhythmic spurting which would have indicated a main artery had been severed. Grantham pulled the man's hands away and peeled back his clothing. The chest wound was superficial, the flesh and muscle was cut down to bone, but was not life threatening. The neck wound was across the front of the throat but had not damaged any arteries or the windpipe, again, nasty but not life threatening. It was the stomach that gave Grantham the most concern. The wound was not big, no longer than six inches, but it was deep and there was a twisted jagged piece of metal just proud of the surface. It was this metal that was slowing the blood flow and preventing the man from bleeding out quickly. It was also very close to the liver, it may even have caused damage to the organ.

"MEDIC," shouted Grantham. All members of the armed forces, especially Special Forces troops, were trained in basic battlefield first aid. But Grantham knew he was no expert.

Shots were now raining down from several positions onto the convoy, accompanied by the distinctive whine and chatter of the Russian AK47 assault rifle, the favoured weapon of terrorists around the world. Sporadic fire was also being returned from the troops in the convoy, their SA80 rifles making a crisper quieter sound, but without targets there were limits to their effectiveness.

Grantham took three large trauma pads from his pockets and got the reporter to hold one on his throat and one on his chest. Grantham then used disinfectant pads to clean around the stomach wound before applying the pad and fastening it in place.

The sound of scuffling to his left caused Grantham to look around as the troop medic slid to a halt beside him.

"Good work, sir. Let me take it from here." The medic quickly set up an IV bag and injected the reporter with painkillers. The reporter visibly relaxed as the drugs quickly passed into his system.

Grantham shuffled back to the small group of civilians as two new whoomps announced more mortars.

"INCOMING," shouted several of the troops together.

Grantham jumped on top of Dalziel and partly covered the camera crew as the latest round of mortars exploded. These were slightly long compared to the first three which had fallen short. The attackers were bracketing them. The next rounds, definitely the ones after, would have the range fully dialled in and they could then simply lob mortars into the stalled convoy, destroying the vehicles and men at their leisure.

The troops were again returning fire, but Grantham's experienced ear noticed a difference. Looking forward he saw that the lead vehicle, a Panther Command and Liaison Vehicle or Panther CLV, had taken damage to the front, the right tyre was shredded and the engine compartment ripped open. Just past the vehicle was the twisted body of one of the troops who had been taking cover adjacent to the solid lump of the EURO 3 engine.

"Do something, you have to save me. That's what you're paid to do." Dalziel again had hold of Grantham's arm and was half pleading, half demanding salvation.

Grantham roughly twisted his arm free and reached into his pocket. The mobile phone was not sexy or stylish, but it was rugged and designed for this sort of work.

"You know I said earlier that the best I could usually do with a phone was order a pizza, well there is something else I can do." Grantham pressed several buttons on the mobile and checked the connection.

"This is Mamba, seven, seven, Gridlock. Condition two, Alpha." There was a slight hiss of static then the connection went dead. Grantham checked his watch. He estimated he would have a call in thirty seconds.

Twenty-seven thousand miles away the signal from the phone was received by the geostationary satellite and passed on to its destination, Grantham's own home. But the code was recognised by the onboard software and automatically copied to a remote ground station. The station formed part of the doughnut shaped GCHQ at Cheltenham. The code was flashed through to the monitoring section where an operator accepted the code and entered it into his computer. Instantly the message came back to identify 'Mamba, seven, seven, Gridlock' as a valid code name. An operative in the field in Afghanistan with a VIP. 'Condition two' revealed that Mamba was under attack and needed assistance. 'Alpha' set the priority as immediate.

The operator entered a search for the coordinates of the phone's location that had been automatically recorded. The assets in the area were displayed and he selected one that could help the soonest. The details were flashed to the new target with 'Authorisation granted for full assistance'.

Grantham's phone rang and he checked his watch, twenty-eight seconds.

"This is Vixen One, go ahead Mamba."

"Vixen, we are taking fire and need your special abilities," Grantham had taken a small laminated map from his pocket and flipped through several pages before reading out a set of coordinates.

"Roger Mamba. Vixen is inbound one-twenty. Heads up at thirty."

"Who was that? What does one-twenty mean, one hundred and twenty minutes? We can't wait two hours. You have to get me out of here." Dalziel was clutching at Grantham as he spoke.

"There are more people to consider than just you."

"They aren't important, I am. Do something."

"I'm only going to say this once. With respect, *sir*, get your fucking hands off me and let me do my job." Grantham's voice was like ice, the tone capable of cutting glass and Dalziel visibly shrunk away, staring with wide eyes at the ex-SAS Major.

"Lieutenant, we have fast movers inbound, ETA two minutes."

Adams looked down the short length of vehicles and waved his understanding.

As Grantham turned he saw the body of the trooper to the front of the damaged Panther. There was a slight twitch of a hand, and he heard a quiet moan over the rattle of bullets from both sides. The man was still alive and coming around. If the attackers saw him they would pick him off before he could move.

"Lieutenant, cover fire, now." With the call, Grantham stood and started sprinting in a low crouch towards the fallen trooper. As he approached the end of the vehicle the shooting from the troops increased fivefold. They still had no direct targets, but the fire was designed to keep the enemy's head down rather than score a direct hit. Two troopers fired three grenades from the underslung launchers of their SA80 rifles, the dull explosions sounding a few seconds later.

Grantham skidded to a halt at the side of the young trooper, and realised he was the twenty-two year old American that was on detachment. He unceremoniously took hold of his shoulder webbing and started to pull him back towards cover. The attackers realised that the increase in fire was not finding its targets and had already started to take cautious shots again. Several bullets kicked up dust around Grantham's feet, the sting of stone chips cutting into his shins and calves. As he reached the front of the damaged Panther, a dozen shots peppered the vehicle's bonnet and windshield which shattered into thousands of spider web cracks as the thin security film held the pieces in place.

Grantham pulled the trooper into the narrow cover offered by the vehicle and called, "MEDIC," again.

A few seconds later he was joined not just by the medic, but by Lieutenant Adams who nodded his gratitude as the medic started work on the young American.

"Do you have smoke grenades?" asked Grantham.

Adams nodded, "Standard red, white and blue."

"Throw a red each end of the convoy. And get ready to move."

Adams moved away issuing orders to the troops as they returned fire, still looking for hard targets. Bullets from the rebels' AK47s still raining in and showering the vehicles with lead.

As Grantham sat with his back to the vehicle his mobile phone again crackled and the same voice as before came from the speaker.

"Mamba this is Vixen One, inbound thirty. Heads up."

"Roger Vixen. Look for red smoke to front and rear of column. Suggest a spread of fifty to one hundred metres north of column."

As Grantham finished speaking the ominous whoomp again sounded as the first of another series of mortars erupted over the continuous exchange of rifle and machine gun fire.

"INCOM…" The shout was cut short as the rear Saxon armoured transport erupted in smoke, the eight ton vehicle lifted ten feet into the air before slowly somersaulting and landing back on its side, swayed twice and toppled to its roof. The bodies of two troops cartwheeled twenty feet before hitting the ground with bone shattering force.

Five miles to the west, two Euro Fighter Typhoons

85

hugged the terrain, flying at no more than one hundred feet above the ground. Their forward looking radar and infrared coupled with visual topography recognition giving the pilots five seconds warning of the terrain almost one mile ahead. Flying at just over 600mph they would be on target in twenty-five seconds.

"Vixen two, form up on my left. Climb to three hundred and accelerate to mach one point one."

"Roger leader."

Vixen two eased to the right and formed up on his leader's left wing, separated from the other aircraft by seventy-five metres, fifty metres behind. The two aircraft rose steeply and fed in power as they accelerated, setting up for the attack run.

"Vixen two, full scatter pattern, set distance for three hundred metres. Drop on my mark."

"Roger one."

Both aircraft were carrying ground saturation ordnance, canisters of 'bomblets' that could be dropped from the aircraft and would disperse sideways up to fifty metres to each side of the aircraft along a path 300m long.

"One, I have a visual on smoke, ahead to your right."

"Roger that two, drop in ten."

The second mortar drifted over the convoy by forty metres, exploding in a shower of rocks, the concussive force from the explosive washing over the men. Grantham breathed a silent prayer to St. George and Joan of Arc, the patron saints that watched over soldiers.

The third mortar came five seconds later, landing ten metres short of the convoy, the blast sending white hot metal and rock fragments in and through two of the vehicles. Three of the troops called out as the shrapnel tore through them, all three swearing profanities and returning fire with renewed passion. A good sign, thought Grantham, the wounds had infuriated rather than disabled.

"Where are they? They should be here by now!" Dalziel was again pestering Grantham. "Maybe they've gone to the wrong coordinates. Call them again, call them."

"They'll be on final approach, they don't need me bothering them," said Grantham scornfully.

"But they aren't here, we would have heard them approaching."

"They'll be travelling at just over the speed of sound, so that they don't advertise their approach."

Two seconds later explosions erupted in a continuous roar as if the earth itself was being ripped apart. The explosions and concussive blasts continued for six seconds as the two aircraft blanketed 45,000 square metres of terrain with high explosives and shrapnel. As the sharp crack of explosions stopped, the deafening roar of twin jet engines swept over the scene. The deep base roar of the two Eurojet EJ200 jet engines quickly rose from a quiet background rumble to a heavy base roar that reverberated through the bodies of the troops as the two Typhoons roared past one hundred metres to the north of the small convoy.

As the two aircraft increased power and peeled away the gunshots that had been raining down on the convoy stopped, the silence was almost palpable as the deep base growl from the aircraft faded away.

"INTO THE VEHICLES, MOVE, MOVE, MOVE!" called Lieutenant Adams, the men jumping from cover, several helping those with injuries, two dragging the limp, lifeless bodies of the troops blown from cover by the last round of explosives back to the only remaining armoured troop carrier.

"Where are you going?" demanded Dalziel, his voice sounding distant, his eyes wide and his grip almost frantic.

"Get into the transport, we'll be moving out in a few seconds," said Grantham shrugging the MP's hand from his arm.

Running at a low crouch, Grantham headed for the two men manhandling the bodies of their comrades. He passed the first trooper, he was making good progress and was almost halfway to the transport and headed for the second. The trooper had hold of his comrade's webbing and was pulling the man across the rough terrain. But the downed soldier was much bigger than the man pulling him. Grantham skidded to a halt and took hold of one side of the body armour. Together the two men made swift progress and even started to catch the first.

After a few metres shots started to ring out from the raised ground. Grantham grabbed the fallen trooper's SA80 and returned a short burst then dropped to his knee and clicked the selector to single shot.

"Go, get to the transport," he called to the trooper who was still pulling the body along as quickly as he could.

As Grantham saw movement on the raised ground he adjusted his aim, putting the sights on the general area. Pausing, Grantham waited for a second until he saw the distinctive silhouette of head, shoulders and AK47 rifle. The rebel fired off several shots, two kicking up dust within six feet of Grantham. Grantham eased the trigger back, re-centred the sights and squeezed again. The shots ceased as Grantham noted the rebel slump forward and the rifle slide down the small rise.

Grantham stood and ran the remaining distance to the armoured transport and helped the troopers to unceremoniously haul the bodies into the back and then climb in themselves, slamming the doors shut as the engine fired to life and the vehicle lurched forward.

Several pings sounded on the exterior of the personnel carrier as the few remaining rebels fired shots at the retreating convoy.

Dalziel was cowering in one corner, pulling his legs as far from the two dead bodies as he could.

Lieutenant Adams looked up from his fallen men and across at Grantham. "Thank you. The troop owes you a lot, maybe our lives." He pointedly looked across at Dalziel. "Unlike some."

Chapter 10

13:00hrs, 3rd April
Leicester University

Richard Caley sat down at the computer and considered his options. He could carry on working for the next couple of hours and finish early. Alternatively he could have a late lunch and maybe bump into Jess Keeble in the refectory, although if he did that he would risk not getting back at all. Or, he could get the shuttle bus back to the dorm, grab a sandwich and get back here to finish off and be away by four o'clock. His stomach grumbled and he patted it. "Soon my lovely, soon," he said with a sigh.

Caley was a fourth year MGeol student, specialising in vulcanology and tectonics, the study of volcanoes and tectonic plates and their relation to earthquakes. It had occurred to him, more than once, that his studies satisfied the destructive side of his nature. Over the past three years he had taken part in field trips to several different areas: Tenerife to study pyroclastic rocks on the world's third largest volcano; to the Highlands of Scotland to examine the Moine Thrust zone and the Tertiary volcanic centre of Skye. But it was the trip to study economic mineralization and the environmental consequences of mining activity in Cornwall that evoked the fondest memories. It was there that Jess Keeble had first noticed him.

He sighed again and looked back at the computer. The fourth year of his master's degree was mostly taken up with his own research leading to his thesis, and he needed to complete this stage or risk falling behind. He was going home tonight for the weekend to attend a family wedding and then spend a week with friends over Easter skiing in France. If he could complete this set up, he could leave the computer to monitor the returns from around the world and the mainframe would analyse the results and map them into 3D visualisations. If they turned out well it would go a long way to proving his thesis was valid.

His stomach growled again, but he ignored it as he pulled his seat up and started to tap away at the computer. He accessed the historical data from some of the largest and best studied volcanoes and earthquakes and started to allocate them to fields in the database. After fifty minutes he paused and checked his work. He then spent another thirty minutes linking the fields to the key variables in the model before running a simulation with known test data.

As he watched the screen, running in simple 2D at a vastly accelerated pace, he saw the imaginary tectonic plates come together at the subduction zone and mesh together, forming a low ridge with no displacement. No, no, no. That was not right. He sighed, this was going to take longer than he thought.

There was a knock on the lab door and Caley called over his shoulder with annoyance, "What?"

The door opened and an attractive brunette head with deep brown eyes peeked in. "I thought I'd find you here. You missed lunch, so I brought you some chips and half a pizza. But if I'm disturbing you, I'll go."

The door started to close until Caley called out, "Jess, sorry. Come back."

Jess Keeble pushed the door open and came in displaying a dazzling smile. At 5' 6" she was slim and attractive with long, naturally wavy hair that she often spent hours trying to straighten.

"So I can come in?"

"Well, as long as you have food..." Caley smiled. The afternoon was looking up.

15:10hrs, 4th April
Meltham, England

The village church was a picturesque example of Edwardian architecture. The graveyard to two sides of the old building was lush and green, even the old headstones seemed to shine under the spring sunlight filtering through the beech and oak trees. The single bell was ringing a steady lament as the mourners passed slowly from the grounds, stopping briefly to talk and offer condolences to the woman dressed in a simple yellow summer dress and white jacket. The afternoon would be taken up with drinks, a buffet and chatting in memory of the deceased at the lady's favourite village public house.

Edwina Valentine had celebrated her seventy-fifth birthday only two months earlier. A spritely lady, she was regularly seen strolling through the village on her way to one of her regular classes or groups. Active in all of the village's social events, she would be missed by many, not least of all her daughter. One of her last requests was that mourners would only be allowed at the funeral dressed in bright colours. There to celebrate her life, not to mourn.

She looked up at the church, the sunlight streaming past the impressive tower and shining in dappled profusion across her high cheekbones and mahogany auburn hair. She sighed and her emerald green eyes held a slightly distant, wistful look.

Charis was not comfortable being the centre of attention. Her father had died while she was still young so, as the only remaining relative, she would be the host of the gathering for the afternoon. Her mother had been very popular in the village and the turnout was reflecting this.

After leaving school and starting university, Charis knew that she had her own life to live. Her mother would always be there, offering help and advice anytime it was asked for, and often when it was not. Within six months of starting university, her mother had the old family home on the market and four months later had moved half a mile to a smaller, more manageable cottage. The cottage had three bedrooms, one of which was reserved for Charis. But Charis had never been emotionally attached to the cottage having never stayed there more than a week or so at any one time. But Honeysuckle Cottage was now hers and she would have to decide what to do with it. Still, that was for later. Right now, she needed to get to the pub and host the gathering. She sighed again as the sun warmed her face.

"Okay Mum, let's get this over with."

17:10hrs
The Old Forge Public House

Charis looked around the room, there was still some of the buffet left, the triangular sandwiches were starting to dry and curl, the lettuce going decidedly limp. Most people were still here, chatting and laughing. At least it had not been a mournful event. In fact, Charis admitted to herself, it had not been as bad as she expected. To start with, everyone had been careful around her, not wanting to upset the only daughter of the departed. But once they realised she was not about to get over-emotional, the locals, many of whom had known Charis since she was a baby, had loosened up and started to tell stories about her mother, many of which she had never heard before. All in all, the afternoon had passed quickly and pleasantly.

She finished the last of the red wine, stood and looked around. Should she announce she was leaving? What was the social etiquette on this sort of occasion? Perhaps she could just slip out.

"Charis, it's nice to see you again. I think Edie would have been pleased with the turnout." The large florid faced man held out a ham sized fist to Charis, he pronounced it 'Kar-is'. So much for slipping out quietly.

"Thanks, Dan. I think she would have been more comfortable hosting the afternoon than me. I'm not sure what I should have done. I just sat here and talked to people, listened mostly."

Dan gave a throaty laugh, his jowls swaying from side to side, his eighty year old face still remarkably unlined.

"She would have been in her element, hosting her own wake. But you did good young lady. She would have been proud of you, as she always was."

"Oh, I don't know about that," said Charis. She loved her mother and knew the feeling was mutual. But neither of them had gone in for emotional or gushing compliments.

Dan shook his head and smiled. "She was not one to wear her heart on her sleeve, but she was always proud of you. Whenever she saw someone she hadn't seen for a few weeks, the conversation always opened with an update on how you were doing, what you were working on, where you were. Her pride was clear to everyone she met."

Charis smiled, not wanting to say too much in case the tears that were starting to sting the back of her eyes started to fall. But she need not have worried. Dan lent forward and engulfed her slim frame in a giant bear hug for several seconds.

"When you're ready, come and see me. I've got some things that Edie asked me to look after for you."

Charis looked at the large farmer in surprise. "What things?" she asked.

Dan pursed his lips and shook his head again. "Don't know what they are. A small chest, locked with a padlock. Edie just asked me to hold onto them in case anything happened to her. I was to make sure to give them to you. I'm not sure, but I got the impression they were your father's."

Charis was curious, she had always been 'Daddy's little girl' but if her father had left her something why had her mother not given her it before now?

"I'll call around tomorrow, if that's okay?"

"Of course it's okay. You're welcome anytime. And Bess has just had pups, so you can see them as well. Five weeks old today."

"Thanks Dan, I'll see you in the morning."

Charis walked from the village pub and looked up and down the street. She still was not sure whether she would make the village her home. At best she would only be here a few months of the year.

She had only arrived at the village this morning. She had gone straight to the cottage, dropped off her bags and changed for the funeral. But now here she was, in her mother's home, her home now. She closed the old timber door behind her and looked around. Her main suitcase was still in the hallway where she had left it this morning.

Walking into the traditional kitchen she went to the retro DAB radio and switched it on. She was not afraid of the house or of being alone in it, but for some reason she wanted noise, some sort of company that did not require an interaction. The radio was tuned to Radio 2 and at this time in the afternoon it was the drive time chat, designed to accompany workers on their way home.

The kitchen was in keeping with the traditional two hundred year old cottage, but somehow modern at the same time. The cooker had the look of a traditional Aga, but was in fact a double width electric cooker with double oven, four halogen rings and a hotplate. The cupboards and drawers were polished oak but with white painted panels and chrome and white handles. The worktops were gleaming white with dark green and brown veins. The mixture should not have worked, but together they reflected the tradition of the cottage and the use and practicality of the modern age.

In many ways the kitchen set the standard for the rest of the house. All of the decoration spoke of the traditional character of the cottage, but had been brought into the modern era with the sympathetic use of materials and technology. Her Mum had certainly liked tradition, but she had not been stuck in the past.

Looking through the cupboards, she spotted the fruit tea her Mum had liked. She had never been that keen on the flavour, but for some reason she fancied a cup now. Maybe it was just the memory of her Mum and her association with the drink.

Putting the kettle on, she reached up and took down one of the mugs from the cupboard. Mum had cups, but they were only for visitors. Taking the pack of tea down, she put it to her nose and smelled the fruity aroma. A chill ran down her spine and she turned suddenly. There was no one there, but she dropped the pack of tea and it spilled across the worktop and onto the floor. Charis smiled to herself. Maybe Mum was still protecting her precious tea. Oh well, she was not that keen on the taste anyway.

Charis walked back into the hall and carried her bags up to the bedroom, her bedroom, she was not yet ready to move into her mum's room.

07:40hrs, 5th April
Village of Standlake

Hugh Grantham had arrived home late last night.
Arriving back in the country at midday via RAF
transport directly from Afghanistan, he had to attend a
six hour debrief before he was allowed to return home
to the village of Standlake, just outside of Oxford,
where he had collapsed into bed for eight hours of
undisturbed sleep. Rising at 06:00, he had showered,
dressed and walked out into the crisp spring air where
he had run a punishing thirteen mile circular route
arriving back home seventy-four minutes after he left,
hot, sweaty and breathless, but strangely refreshed and
ready to face the world. And with the visit to
Afghanistan cut short, he could make it to the Oxford
Triathlon later in the week.

As he stepped from the shower again he heard the
old fashioned bell ringtone of his mobile signifying an
incoming call.

Grantham wrapped the large white bath towel
around his slim, muscular waist and picked up the
phone. As he did so he saw the call was coming from
the news crew that had been in Afghanistan only a few
hours earlier. He had asked them to let him know how
their wounded colleague got on.

"Hello?"

"Mr Grantham, it's Doug Scott. I just wanted to say
thanks again and to let you know that Mickey's doing
well. The Doc says he should make a full recovery,
although he'll be immobile for a few weeks. His wife
says thanks as well. Actually she said a lot more than
that, but I don't think I could repeat it all." The
connection was clear but had the distinct flat sound of

97

someone speaking on a mobile phone in the open.

"You're welcome. I'm just glad I could be of some help."

"You may want to watch the eight o'clock news. It's the first airing of the footage from Afghanistan. You come out very well, which is more than I can say for our right honourable friend."

"I thought I made it clear that I didn't want to be seen in the reports." During his time in the SAS, and in the few years since, Grantham had made enemies that would love to see his face and track him down.

"Don't worry, Mr Grantham. You can't be identified. I personally made sure of that. After all, I've seen what you can do and I don't want to get on your bad side."

Grantham's voice softened. "Thanks," he said.

Two minutes later he had the TV on and was watching the news.

The screen showed an attractive blonde female news reporter, her hair turned under in a fluffy bob which made her look younger than her late thirties. She was wearing a demure blouse and jacket that managed to be businesslike and show off an enticing cleavage at the same time. Behind her was the image of the MP Grantham had recently accompanied to Afghanistan in one of his designer camouflage uniforms.

"The right honourable St.John Dalziel returned home yesterday after his recent trip to Afghanistan to see the troops. Mr Dalziel, well known for speaking up for the man in the street, despite his own privileged background, was criticised in the press shortly after being elected when he commented that he did not care who he stepped on. During his recent trip, Mr Dalziel came under fire when the patrol he was accompanying was ambushed. We go over now to Doug Scott who also returned home yesterday with Mr Dalziel. Doug."

The image changed to Doug Scott standing outside of a palatial set of wrought iron gates. The Dalziel coat of arms was prominently displayed behind Scott's shoulder.

"Thank you, Stacey. Yes that's right. Me and the crew returned home yesterday from Afghanistan where we had been shadowing the MP on his recent visit. That visit was cut short after the convoy was attacked and several troops killed or injured while protecting Mr Dalziel. We have here some footage we shot while under attack."

The report cut to the view of the convoy just before the attack. Dalziel was standing at the back of the transport talking to Doug Scott about the wonderful job the British troops were doing.

"These men, and women of the British Army are a credit to the country. Every man, woman and child owes them a debt of freedom. If I had my time over again I would like to think I could serve the country in the same way. A more direct form of service in the military than the behind the scenes service of a politician." Dalziel stopped speaking as a shout sounded from somewhere off camera. Dalziel and Scott looked around before a second later the camera started spinning and the two men fell sprawling to the floor. The picture showed the arms and legs of several men, scrabbling in the dirt as first one, and then a second explosion ripped through the convoy, shouts erupted as dirt and rubble rained down around the men.

The scene again changed, the camera angle was askew, but clearly showed Dalziel cowering behind the troop transport. A trooper, someone in camouflage but not carrying a weapon, was rising from the cover of the transport. Grantham realised this new figure was himself seen from behind.

"Where are you going?" asked the MP in a shaky voice.

"The reporter's injured, he needs help."

"You're here to protect me, not them." Dalziel nodded to the camera crew and reporter. Grantham pulled his arm free and moved out of view of the camera.

Again the scene changed. Dalziel was still cowering behind the troop carrier but could be seen from the side. There was the sound of repeated gunshots in the background and the camera was far from steady. All that could be seen of Grantham was his arm where Dalziel had a hold of it.

"Do something, you have to save me. That's what you're paid to do."

Grantham roughly twisted his arm free and reached into his pocket.

The scene changed again. Grantham smiled to himself. The picture and scene were substantially the same. If this had been a film or TV show no one would have thought anything of it, simply a different camera angle on the same scene. But Grantham knew that the film crew had only been using one camera. The last cut had hidden a gap of maybe thirty seconds when Grantham had called for air support.

Dalziel was again clutching for Grantham.

"There are more people to consider than just you," said Grantham.

"They aren't important, I am. Do something."

"I'm only going to say this once. With respect, sir, get your – bleep – hands off me and let me do my job." The bleep had been put in to prevent offence to the viewers.

The picture changed back to Scott still standing outside of Dalziel's home.

"The visit had been intended to aid in the MP's continued rise. Instead it has shown Mr Dalziel's true colours. He came back from the adverse publicity a few years ago. But it is difficult to see how he can recover from this. Back to you, Stacey."

The image cut back to the studio and Grantham used the remote control to switch the screen off. He smiled to himself again, a few images had probably ended a rising star's career as an MP. Scott had said he did not want to get on Grantham's bad side, Grantham admitted the feeling was mutual.

08:20hrs, 5th April
Meltham, England

Charis walked out into the large back garden of the cottage and looked around, drinking in the fresh country air. The grass was covered in morning dew that sparkled in the early sun. The garden was enclosed on three sides by hedges neatly trimmed to exactly six feet six inches; her mother had been very keen on the accuracy. Taller would have blocked some of the light, shorter would have been less private. Beyond the hedge was the open expanse of the Peak District National Park, one of the main reasons her Mum had moved to the western side of the village. It took Charis ten minutes to wander around the garden filling the various bird feeders with an assortment of seeds. The stream running across the back of the garden supplied water for the animals' drinking and bathing.

After spending some time simply absorbing the peace and quiet of the garden, Charis locked the back door and climbed into her black Honda Civic. She was on the way to see Dan, and perhaps more importantly, the puppies.

Dan's farm was a few miles the far side of the

101

village, a pleasant fifteen minute drive. While she drove the roads she had known for years, she wondered why her Mum would give Dan something to look after. Why not simply keep it at the house? In fact, why not simply give it to her when she was here?

The drive leading up to the farm was every bit as rough and potholed as she remembered. At 300 years old, it was dark by modern standards, but it was homely and comfortable. The kitchen was always a little warm in summer due to the constant heat coming from the old fashioned wood burning range that was never out. But today it was welcoming and cosy. And best of all, offered a comfortable warm atmosphere for the seven Border Collie puppies.

Dan was as welcoming as ever, but it was difficult for Charis to focus on anything other than the seven fluffy black and white bundles that had free range in the kitchen and welcomed the chance to make a new friend. For fifteen minutes she played with the pups, until eventually they started to slow down and curl up near the stove for one of their regular naps, a fluffy mass of soft black and white fur.

"So, which one would you like?" asked Dan.

Charis smiled but shook her head. "I'd love one, but I travel too much and I'm regularly away from home. It wouldn't be fair on the dog. And these are working dogs, keeping them in the house wouldn't be fair..."

Dan gave a hearty laugh. "Aye, you're right it wouldn't be fair. But you're welcome anytime. I'll have them for a few weeks yet. Are you staying for a while?"

"I'm not sure, a few days at least. I don't know how long it'll take to get things sorted. I don't even know what I'm going to do with the house."

After a large mug of tea with a liberal helping of chocolate biscuits, the two sat talking about Edie for some time. Eventually Dan stood up and left the room, returning a few minutes later with a small chest.

"I still don't see why Mum would give this to you. If she wanted me to have it, why not just give it to me?"

"I can't say. She just asked me to look after it and make sure you got it if anything happened to her."

"When did she give you it?"

Dan rubbed his ruddy cheeks and looked off to the distance. "It was shortly after last Christmas. A week or so after you went back. A few days after the break-in."

"What break-in?" asked Charis.

"You don't know? Well you were here for Christmas, remember we had that heavy snow for the week? Well you'd been gone for a couple of days and while Edie was out someone broke into the house. At least she was convinced that someone had broken in. There was no damage and nothing missing, but she insisted that things had been moved, disturbed. If it had been anyone but your Mum I'd have put it down to a senior moment. Anyway, the next day she brought this box over and asked me to look after it."

Charis took the key Dan was holding and undid the lock. Opening the small chest, she looked inside. Folders, envelopes and notebooks. As she lifted the folders she saw some paintings and drawings she had not seen for years. She had done them while at primary school. Her father would read her bedtime stories and she would draw the characters the next day. They mostly consisted of knights with swords, fighting dragons or on horseback. She was surprised that her mother had kept them for all these years.

She lifted the drawings out and placed then with the folders on the table. One folder caught her eye. It was older that the others, faded with age, but not ancient, not like some of the books and papers she examined at

103

work. She opened the soft cardboard flap. It contained a few sheets of paper. With surprise, she recognised her father's handwriting on the papers and her mother's on an obviously much newer piece of paper.

As she read, disbelief crossed her face. This had to be some sort of joke. This was beyond belief, it was more like a story her father would have made up while she lay in bed. If this was even partly true it could change the world and accepted history.

Chapter 11

19:30hrs, 7th April
The Red Lion, Oxford

Grantham walked into the old public house and looked around. He liked the atmosphere, a mixture of old world warmth and modern lighting that enhanced the character without being garish or too dark. Best of all there was no jukebox blaring out noise that the youngsters would call music. He had been recommended the public house as one with character, good food and real ale. By the smell and look of the place he was not going to be disappointed.

Grantham had arrived in the city yesterday and got an early night to prepare for today's event. He was in Oxford for the annual triathlon. Run and sponsored by a local businessman, it had become a favourite with the University students, and there was heated rivalry between the various colleges.

The race had been run that morning and Grantham had clocked a very respectable time of 2 hours, 38 minutes. Not quite in the Elite league, although he was pleased to have beaten several of the slower Elite athletes, but a very good time for an amateur. The race was run over the Olympic distance with a 1.5km open water swim, a 40km bike ride and a 10km run. He had done well in the swim, exiting the water fourth in his class. But as usual it was the bike that had cost him time and position. While in the SAS it had been easy to maintain general fitness. Swimming and running were essential requirements for the Regiment, but the SAS had never found the pushbike to offer practical transport in a tactical advance to battle. So Grantham's technique in the middle section of the race was pure brute force and ignorance. He had dropped seven places by the changeover, putting him eleventh in his class. But the 10km run was his speciality. He had made up eight places to finish third in his class and only one and a half minutes behind the class winner.

He had arranged to meet an old army comrade in the pub. Both men had served together in the SAS until Bert 'Digger' Sheldrake had got too close to an IED and lost the bottom half of his right leg. Invalided out of the army, Digger had kept in occasional contact with Grantham and shared a quiet pride when his former second in command had been promoted to Major, the rank Digger had retired with.

Grantham had arrived ten minutes ago and ordered a pint of the Old Bull, a crisp, hoppy bitter that was almost a light lager but with a longer lasting, creamy head. He had just sat down when his mobile phone rang and Digger told him that he would have to miss the evening due to a plumbing emergency at his daughter's house.

Looking around the bar Grantham considered eating here or going back to his hotel. What the hell? Digger had recommended the food and he was already here. He sat back against the high backed leather seat and examined the menu. There was certainly a good choice. But one dish particularly caught his eye. Braised calves liver, with garlic mash, buttered fresh vegetables and onion gravy. Okay, that decided it, tea tonight would be eaten in the Red Lion.

He took another drink of the beer and with a little surprise noticed that he had almost finished the crisp bitter. He must still be slightly dehydrated from the triathlon this morning. Either that or the beer was going down easier than he thought.

Leaving the almost empty glass at the table to hold

his place, he walked across to the bar to order a second and his food. While he was waiting for the barman to finish serving another customer, he glanced around. The bar was maybe half full, most people were in pairs or small groups. The average age of the patrons was probably early forties. The lack of jukebox and the presence of real ales probably kept the younger element of the city away. As he looked around a particularly stunning woman walked in looking a little lost. She stood near the entrance for a few seconds looking around before walking across the room to the bar. She stood 5' 8" in two inch heels. Long dark brown hair with a hint of red, trailed over her shoulders with what looked like a natural wave, was set off against a yellow blouse. Her figure was slim and athletic, the black skirt stopping just above the knee showing shapely muscular calves that hinted at a distance runner. She had high cheek bones and a slightly pointed chin with a clear, apparently flawless complexion. But she was one of those women that were far more than the sum of their parts. She had that certain something that could draw attention and turn heads even when she was not trying.

As she crossed the bar she caught Grantham's eye and he smiled before he even realised. She smiled back, a polite rising of one side of her lips, but the eyes stayed disconnected. Oh well, thought Grantham, you cannot win them all. The way she was looking around probably meant she was looking for someone specific, lucky man.

As she arrived at the bar, the landlord returned and Grantham placed his order. As he finished he turned to the woman, close up he could see that her complexion was indeed flawless with just a hint of freckles across the nose and a delicate blush to the cheeks, a definite English rose complexion.

"Could I buy you a drink?" he asked.

The woman, she was probably in her mid-thirties, looked at Grantham with her sparkling green eyes and smiled, this time showing perfect teeth, and shook her head.

"Thank you, but I'm not stopping long."

"That's a shame. I could have done with some company while I eat."

"Maybe another time."

Oh well, thought Grantham again, if she is not interested there was nothing he could do. At least he had a good meal to look forward to.

"There you go, sir. I'll add it to your food bill." The barman placed the new pint on the bar. "I'll bring the food across when it's ready, about ten minutes."

Grantham returned to his seat and finished the first pint and took a small mouthful of the second.

The woman was chatting to the barman as he poured her a glass of red wine. Grantham got the impression the conversation was not simply small talk. She was asking questions and the barman was answering. But he was too far away to tell what was being said.

After a few minutes another two men came in and headed for the bar, standing next to the woman. As they ordered drinks one started to talk to her, probably asking her if she wanted a drink as she held up the still almost full glass of wine and shook her head. But the man was not ready to take no for an answer and seemed to be persisting. Once they were served the two men left the bar, both glancing back at the woman, and took seats in one of the comfortable booths that lined the walls.

Glancing around the bar, Grantham noticed several of the men were looking the woman's way, she was certainly a head turner. Another man had walked in and was standing at the bar, tall, blond and lean. For some reason Grantham's attention was drawn to him. He was standing towards the far end of the bar, well away from the woman and had not even glanced at her. Maybe that was what had caught his attention, his indifference to the woman. Grantham smiled to himself, maybe he was more the blond man's type.

Grantham checked his watch, the food would be here soon and he could feel the call of his bladder. Glancing around he saw the sign for the toilets and headed off to make room for the meal, and another pint, maybe two.

As he returned from the toilets he saw the two men were again at the bar, this time one either side of the woman. Both were talking to her, more like talking at her. She clearly was not interested and stood to leave the bar stool she had perched on. But one of the men took hold of her arm, not hard but it was clearly unwelcome.

"Come on, gents. The lady already said no to a drink. It's a free country. Why don't you take a seat and I'll bring another round across for you."

Without thinking, Grantham walked across to the bar, placed his hand on the woman's shoulder and bent to kiss her cheek. The woman had not seen him approaching and was too surprised to react to the kiss.

"Sorry I'm late, darling. Are these friends from work?"

Grantham looked from one man to the other, with a pleasant, slight smile and open expression on his face.

"Eh, no. We were just chatting while I waited for you." Good girl, thought Grantham, she had recovered quickly and played along.

Both men were eyeing Grantham, sizing him up as if determining their chances.

At an even six feet, with a lean muscular build, broad shoulders and what Hollywood would describe as a chiselled jaw, Grantham was clearly in far better shape than the two average height and build men.

"Thanks for keeping her company guys," said Grantham, maintaining the smile. "Shall we grab a table?" he said to the woman.

With a liquid grace, she slipped from the stool and walked across the room to Grantham's table. As they walked, Grantham placed his hand on her back, a clear sign of possession to the two men who he was sure would be watching.

Sitting at the table, Grantham casually looked the woman in the eye as he leant forward.

"Thank you for being my Lancelot," she said.

Grantham smiled at the reference. "You're welcome, how could I ignore a lady in distress? But if I'm Lancelot, that makes you Guinevere. And that means we end up lovers."

It was the woman's turn to smile. "You know your Arthurian legends."

"History, well parts of it, is an interest of mine." He clinked his glass against hers. "Hugh Grantham, by the way. Although if you want to continue to call me Lancelot, I've answered to worse."

"Nice to meet you, very nice under the circumstances," she hesitated, as if wanting to go on but not sure if she should. "I'm Charisma Valentine."

Grantham smiled again, but consciously stopped the smile turning to a grin or a laugh. "Now that sounds like a name from legend, or maybe the name of a heroine in a novel."

"It was always a source of embarrassment when I was growing up. But now I've become very protective of it and only hesitate to tell people it because I don't want to defend it or get annoyed with them if they make fun of it. But if you can accept being a knight, I can go along with being the heroine."

"How did you come by the name? Parents I

110

suppose?"

"The first time my Dad saw me, he said I was full of charisma, and the name just stuck. But I'm either Charis or Val to my friends."

There was a natural break in the conversation as the barman approached the table with Grantham's food. He also put a plate of lasagne in front of Charisma and a large plate of thick cut chips between them.

"I thought you'd be staying for tea as you've joined your friend." The barman pointedly looked across the room at the two men who were still at the bar, but had stopped watching the booth. "The lasagne is vegetarian, just in case you don't eat meat. The chips are on the house."

For a couple of minutes Grantham and Charisma tasted their meals, Charisma announced she most definitely did eat meat, but that the lasagne was very tasty. Grantham was also complimentary of the liver.

"You said you're interested in history, is that something to do with your job?" asked Charisma.

"Not directly. I was in the army for a few years and studied historic battles and conflicts, especially tactics. That got me interested in history generally. Although my knowledge is very patchy. I know a lot about specific sections, but could fall down on what a lot of people would think of as general knowledge. What about you? History an interest or is it just the romance of the Arthurian legends?"

Charisma weighed up the man sitting opposite before replying. He had dark brown, almost black hair and piercing blue eyes that looked intelligent and wise with an almost wicked glint. The only slight flaw to his looks was a small scar on his right temple. Actually she admitted to herself, the scar added to his looks rather than detracted.

"History is an interest and a job. I specialise in

Biblical History." At the enquiring look on Grantham's face she continued. "It has little to do with religion. I study the historical contents of religious history, specifically looking for historical data, stuff that is documented as fact that can be related to events that are described in religious texts. Most people would be surprised at how similar a lot of religions are and how many historical events can be found in the bibles of different religions."

"I know what you mean. A lot of people assume there are big differences between Christian and Islamic teachings. But the differences are subtle."

"One of your interests?"

"Some of my time in the army was spent in Islamic countries. I always thought it a good idea to understand the locals as much as I could. That includes their beliefs. What historical correlations have you found?" Grantham wanted to turn the talk away from his own background.

Charisma considered her reply before answering.

"You know about the ten plagues?"

Grantham nodded. "From the book of Genesis, God sent the plagues down on the Egyptians until the Pharaoh released the Hebrew slaves."

It was Charisma's turn to nod. "That's right. Well there has been some research done to see if there could be a scientific explanation to the story. It's a long explanation but there is evidence that the first plague, the river of blood, was a Burgundy Algae Bloom, like a Blue Green Algae. That destroyed the oxygen in the water and led to the tadpoles turning into frogs early so they all appeared at once. The frogs died and the lice flourished without the frogs to predate on them, same with the flies. The lice and flies carried disease to the cattle and the dead animals brought plague to the humans. About the same time there was a volcanic eruption on the island of Santorini. The ash brought hailstones and darkness. The plague of locust was just a natural phenomenon."

"Very impressive," said Grantham, "But what about the death of the first born?"

"You do know your history. Well, the first born got the best and most food. With all the disease about, the grain and meat was tainted and the first born got the most so they succumbed first. By the way, the story told how the Angel of Death passed over the Hebrew houses, hence the term Passover in the Jewish religion." Charisma took a sip of her wine and finished the last of the lasagne.

"Your turn, what did you do in the army?"

Grantham took a mouthful of the Old Bull to give him a few seconds to think. He was not just going to blurt out his whole history, but he suspected that she was too perceptive to simply accept that he was a member of the catering corps.

"Well, I spent a few years in the Paras. Since retiring a couple of years ago I've been doing a bit of freelance security work."

Charisma looked Grantham squarely in the eye as if looking into his mind, looking for lies or deceit, her emerald green eyes seeming to penetrate his soul.

"Why do I think there's more to your history than that?" Before Grantham could answer, she seemed to think of something else. "What type of security work do you do? Bodyguard work?"

Grantham wondered where this was leading, it did not seem like simple curiosity.

"I've done some bodyguard work, but it's not what I normally do. I usually simply advise on security issues."

Charisma pursed her lips, which made her look as if she were pouting. She then lifted her glass and finished

113

her wine. "I'll get another round of drinks." She stood and walked across the bar.

As Grantham watched, he considered that the view from behind was as good as the front. He looked across the bar and saw the two men glance at her, but look away. They had apparently written her off as a lost cause. Good.

When Charisma returned with the drinks she sat down and looked Grantham in the eye again. "Are you going to finish that last chip?"

"How could I take the last chip from a lady? Mind you, I wouldn't give up the last chip for just anyone."

Charisma stabbed the chip with her fork and ate it while clearly considering something.

"If you were doing bodyguard work, how much would you charge?"

Grantham sat back and looked Charisma in the eye, considering his response.

"Do you need a bodyguard?"

"Maybe. My dad died when I was a teenager. Mum raised me, helped put me through University. But she passed away recently. Just after Christmas Mum thought that someone had broken into her house. Nothing was taken, but she asked a family friend to look after some bits and pieces for me. She also left me a note with some names on. They were all people that Dad had known years ago. One of them, the Prof, Professor William Grace, helped me when I was at University and pulled a few strings to get me my first job. He was in the same field of research, Biblical History. I haven't actually seen him for a few years, but we've kept in touch by letter, he was a bit of a Luddite when it came to computers and e-mail. The others I've not been in touch with for a while. But, when I tried to contact them, all three had died."

"Well I'm sorry to hear that. But these things

114

happen over the years."

"They all died within four days of each other, all in different countries, all apparently accidental deaths, more or less. But unless you can help, I think I may be next."

Chapter 12

20:30hrs, 7th April
The Red Lion, Oxford

"I admit that three people who knew each other dying in such a short time is unusual, but coincidences do happen. That's why the word exists," said Grantham as he took another drink of his beer. This was his third pint he reminded himself, and he suspected he had better keep a clear head. He sat back so that he could get a better overall view of Charisma and read her body language.

"And just because someone is paranoid doesn't mean they aren't out to get you."

"Okay, tell me about the men who died."

"Well, Robert Jacobs, he worked with Dad. He visited a few times to see Dad and once or twice after he died. He always sent birthday and Christmas cards but we haven't been in direct contact for several years. For the last few years he's been working as some sort of park ranger, he's American by the way. He retired a while ago and lived in Massachusetts. He took an active role in conservation, wildlife and nature, it was a real passion of his. He was killed walking home in a hit and run accident."

Grantham simply nodded as he absorbed the information.

"Then there was Professor William Grace. He was a friend of the family. He was often there when I was growing up. He kept in close contact after Dad died, helped to get me into university and, as I said, get me my first job in research. He studied Biblical History. He died of a heart attack in this very pub, that's what I was talking to the landlord about, to see if he could tell me anything that wasn't in the official report."

"Did he?"

"Well, he told me he died in the seat you're sitting in."

"Thanks, that's made me feel better." Grantham shifted in the seat.

"He came in and sat with another man for a while. Then the other man left and after a while, when the Prof hadn't moved, the barman came across to see if he was okay and found him dead. Official verdict was heart attack. He was overweight and broke out in a sweat at the thought of exercise. But in his last letter he sent me he said he may be getting funding from a private company to do some research, but he didn't go into details. He did say that he felt someone had been looking into his history, he assumed because of the potential funding, but maybe it was something else."

"Did the police track down the other man?"

"Not that I know of, but I'm not family, so I'm not sure how much they would tell me."

"What about the third man?"

"That was Francois, Francois Bertrand. He also worked with Dad. He was big in finance. He was French but worked in Switzerland, at one of the big banks I think. He was a regular visitor when Dad was alive. He visited regularly for a few years after Dad died, I think he helped Mum sort out finances and the like. We still saw him occasionally, maybe every couple of years or so. He visited Mum last summer while he was over here on business, but I didn't see him, I was away in Africa at the time. He died in a skiing accident. He went off piste and fell to his death."

For a minute Grantham sat and absorbed the information, Charisma sat back and sipped her wine, allowing Grantham time to think.

"You said that your Dad worked with Francois and Robert. What did your Dad do?"

"Well remember I was only young when he died. But as far as I knew he was a troubleshooter for a procurement and import company. Basically, if you had a business and needed raw materials from abroad, you could go to the company Dad worked for and they would act as the go-between. Buying the materials and importing them. If there was a problem with the supply or transport, Dad would go over and sort it out. When he was in the army he was based in Africa and the Middle East, so that was the area he specialised in."

At the mention of the army Grantham's interest was piqued. "What did your Dad do in the army and how long was he in?"

"He was in logistics, supplies and stuff. I think he was in for about ten years. He was a soldier when Mum met him and when they got married. But she refused to have kids until he left the army. She said raising a child was the job of a couple. So Dad left and a couple of years later I came along. Dad still travelled a lot with work, but at least he was only away for a few days, maybe a week or so, and he wasn't being shot at, well usually."

"What do you mean usually?" asked Grantham.

"Well sometimes he would have to go to areas where there was local trouble. Once or twice he came back with minor injuries. But they didn't do business in war zones."

"And Francois and Robert did the same job?"

"I'm not sure. I assumed Francois was to do with the finance, as far as I remember Robert did the same job. I think they often consulted on the work. But..." Charisma paused, obviously thinking. "Francois never came to Dad's funeral. We didn't see him until about six months later. When I did see him again he was hurt.

He had a permanent limp and he had lost an eye. I never put the two things together before, but maybe he was hurt when Dad died."

"Were these three men in the army?"

"I don't know. I suppose Robert had the same sort of military bearing as Dad. Francois always seemed a bit more laid back. I can't imagine that the Prof ever did anything physical, so I doubt he was ever in the army. Remember Robert was American and Francois was French, so they wouldn't have been in the same army as Dad."

Grantham considered what Charisma had told him. He had always been a good judge of people, when they were telling the truth and when they were concealing something. It had saved his life, and others, on more than one occasion. He was sure that Charisma had been open and honest about the men's background, but he was equally sure she was still hiding something. It was time he asked the main question.

"I still say it could have been a coincidence that all three died in a short time." He held up his hand to stop Charisma interrupting. "But even if they were killed, why do you think you could be next?"

It was Charisma's turn to sit back and weigh up Grantham. Could she trust someone she had met less than two hours ago?

"Okay, I need to give you some background first or the actual answer won't make sense." She considered how to start for a few seconds.

"Although Dad went abroad a fair bit, he was home more than he was away. I don't think Mum would have allowed it to be the other way around. When I went to bed either Mum or Dad would read to me. I loved stories about adventure and derring-do. My favourite stories were the ones that Dad would make up. He made them seem so real. Tales about knights and

119

dragons. How the knights had gone on the Crusades, fighting for good against evil. How later they protected travellers making pilgrimages to the Holy Land. How they had recovered holy relics and items of great value and taken blood oaths to protect them."

"It sounds like you're talking about the Knights Templars," said Grantham.

Charisma looked at him with a mixture of curiosity and maybe a little suspicion. "You know about the Knights Templars?"

"There's been plenty written about them and on TV in the last few years. But I've known about them for a long time. Remember I said I'd studied military history? Well the Knights Templars are considered as one of the first Special Forces groups. They were well trained in multiple weapons, battle hardened and fought as much with their intelligence as with their muscle. They were often a small elite attachment of a larger army. Well respected by their supporters and comrades and feared by the opposition."

Charisma nodded at the assessment. "Do you know how they got their name?"

"I know a lot about their tactics, not so much about their history. After the Crusades they started protecting the pilgrims making their way to the Middle East? A king, not sure who, allowed them to set up base at the ruins of King Solomon's temple. The Templar part of the name came from the temple they used as a base?" Grantham sounded less sure of this.

"Pretty good. The King was Baldwin II of Jerusalem. He gave them space for a headquarters on the Temple Mount, in the Al Aqsa Mosque which had been captured during the first Crusade. The Temple Mount was above what was believed to be the ruins of the Temple of Solomon so the Crusaders referred to the Mosque as Solomon's Temple. It was from here that the

Order took the name of Poor Knights of Christ and the Temple of Solomon, or Templar Knights. That was around 1119. They were a poor order financially, but as you say, well respected and feared. But they gradually grew in power and influence and their organisation spread. Some say they found a vast treasure in the ruined Temple and that they used this to build their power base. They also created the first credit card or cheque. Travellers could deposit money with one group of Knights and be given a credit note which they could cash with a different group of Knights. That way they didn't have to carry cash. The organisation eventually became so wealthy that they were lending money to royal houses across Europe. That was their downfall.

"King Philip IV of France was in debt to the order so on Friday 13th October, 1307, he arranged for the Templars in France to be arrested, tortured into giving false confessions, and then burned at the stake. He also used his influence with Pope Clement to get him to issue the papal bull Pastoralist Praeeminentiae, which instructed the Christian monarchs in Europe to arrest all Templars and seize their assets. Some say it's this date, Friday 13th October 1307, which gave rise to the superstition of Friday 13th being unlucky, it certainly was for them."

"Is it true they found a vast treasure?" asked Grantham.

"There's never been any concrete proof. The Templars never admitted or denied anything. But they did have a fast rise to power and were certainly wealthy as an organisation, if not as individuals. But that may have been through good management." Charisma sat back and took another sip of her wine.

"Is that the end of the history side of the story?"

Charisma thought for a moment before nodding slowly.

"Okay, so what's the modern day part?"

Charisma was clearly still thinking as she turned the glass between her fingers. She leant forward, and her green eyes took on a deep glint as she watched Grantham while speaking. "The note that Mum left, she felt that she should warn me." She watched Grantham closely. "Dad was a troubleshooter, but not for an import firm. He was a modern day Knight Templar, the organisation still exists, albeit secretly. The stories that Dad told me were true, at least the ones that didn't involve dragons. The Knights have been guarding secrets and relics for hundreds of years." Charisma stopped and waited for Grantham to absorb the information.

"I told you that Dad died years ago. Actually he died while working away for the Templars. He was killed trying to recover a holy relic of some sort, Mum didn't know what. Dad had only told Mum what he had to, and only told me stories that seemed like fiction. But Mum was always worried that the past would catch up with us. She wrote down what she knew in case anything happened to her so that I could be forewarned just in case. Once I'd taken in the news I started to do some checking, not that there was much I could check. But when I called Dad's old friends I found they had died. And for the last few days I've had the feeling I've been followed, but I admit that may be my imagination."

Grantham nodded slowly, absorbing the information before speaking. "If we accept that the Templars still exist, who would want to kill any of them and why?"

"I wondered that. In the information mum left she mentioned an organisation called the Ahnenerbe. They were…"

Grantham cut her off. "The Ahnenerbe Forschungs und Lehrgemeinschaft. The scientific, historical and

122

archaeological arm of the Nazi SS. Hitler and his generals, particularly Heinrich Himmler, searched the world for holy relics that could bring them power. The Ark of the Covenant, the Spear of Christ, the Holy Grail, the list was almost endless. If the Templars were protecting relics I can see that they would be natural enemies."

"Well, if they killed Dad, maybe they are still around today and killing the Templars?" Charisma sounded less convinced with this than she had earlier.

"As well as looking for holy relics, the Ahnenerbe had another mission. They wanted to create, or in their view re-create, the master race. I can't remember the exact details, but they believed that the world had been populated by several different races. They believed that one particular race, the Atlanteans, had psychic powers and were destroyed in the flood that destroyed Atlantis. They maintained their abilities and developed into the Aryan race that were the direct ancestors of the ancient Greeks. Hitler had the vision of recreating the Aryan race and regaining their lost abilities and rightful place as leaders through selective breeding. He also used the extermination camps to rid the world of undesirables."

"You know more about them than I do," said Charisma.

Grantham shrugged and finished his beer. "I studied the Second World War in some detail. I found the Nazi views fascinating, totally mad and definitely evil at times, but fascinating. And I don't find it hard to believe that the Ahnenerbe still exist, or some descendant of the organisation. A lot of the leaders disappeared after the war and were never found. And people who hold such radical views don't just fade away. They re-group and find another way to advance their cause." Grantham considered what Charisma had told him. She seemed to be telling the truth. And she was asking for his help.

"Do you know how the Knights are organised?"

Charisma looked confused. "In what way?"

"Well you say they're a secret organisation. I know there's been a fair bit written about them, but that's all historical or fictional. Assuming they do still exist as an organisation, do you know anything about their set-up?"

"Not really. Historically they had one leader, a Grand Master, and then regional commanders and then knights. They made up about ten percent of the force. The rest were made up of foot soldiers, sergeants and squires. But why does that matter?"

"What you've just described is a typical military set up, even a business organisation. But that's not how secret groups work. If they want to remain truly secret they compartmentalise everything. One person or group is given a task and they don't know who other groups or members are."

"I've heard that in relation to terrorist groups, cells, right?"

"That's right. But if the Ahnenerbe find members of the Templars, wouldn't they want info, to find out where the relics are? Wouldn't they capture them rather than just hunt them down and kill them?"

"That makes sense, but if they didn't kill them who did?"

"Well, still assuming you're right and the deaths weren't accidental, then someone who wanted to keep the secret rather than let anything leak out."

Charisma looked Grantham directly in the eyes. "You mean Templars killed other Templars to stop the secret coming out?"

"It wouldn't be the first time an organisation has turned on its own members to keep secrets."

"I feel even more scared now than before. If they

could do that to their own, what will they do to me if they know I've got information?"

"Well, as your Lancelot, I'll just have to protect you from the black knights, won't I?"

Chapter 13

08:00hrs, 8th April
Forty miles east of Hohenau, Paraguay

Landlocked Paraguay is bordered to the southwest by
Argentina, to the northwest by Bolivia and to the east
by Brazil. Hohenau, two hundred miles to the north of
the nation's capital, was founded on 14th March, 1900
by German colonists. As a district it has the country's
second highest standard of living, only beaten by the
capital, Asunción. The area is surrounded by cultivated
fields and farms and has little light industry and no
heavy manufacturing. The air is clear and calm in this
sub-tropical haven that attracts few visitors.

However, forty miles to the east, in the sprawling
open countryside, was one of the largest and most
advanced genetics laboratories in the world. It was
Grüssmire Gewerbe that had been the first to apply
genetic engineering to crops, twenty years before the
public had even heard of the idea. In the early 80s
Grüssmire successfully cloned the first mammal, a
mouflon, a type of hardy wild sheep. By the time Dolly
the sheep was publicly heralded as the first official
mammal clone in 1996, the institution had been cloning
rhesus macaques, chimps, and orangutans with a
success rate of over 80% for a decade. But it was Adam
that was the jewel in their crown. The only survivor of
100 subjects, he had not only been cloned, but had his
DNA engineered. He was the first step back to the fifth
race.

Little was known about the firm outside of its own
workforce. Each worker signed a non-disclosure
agreement before receiving a contract. No jobs were

advertised, every employee from the cleaners up had been asked to join the firm before they even knew that a job existed.

Background checks and ongoing monitoring of the employees' public, private and personal lives would be the envy of any country's intelligence service. The pay for every member of the institution was twice to ten times the industry standard. Those employees that had any questionable dealings were sidetracked and quietly dismissed. Once they left the firm, all ties were cut with the remaining staff. They moved away from the area and were never heard from again. Not only were the laboratories equipped with the best cutting edge technology, but much of that technology had been created by its own research wing. It would be years before any of the hardware was even known about outside of the firm.

The large complex was landscaped with open picnic areas and a perimeter running track just inside the high security fence.

The large conference room could sit twenty around the deeply glossed mahogany table, with seating for a further forty around the sides. Large plasma display screens were suspended at the centre of each end and side wall. Small touch screen control units were mounted in front of each seat at the table. The glass panelled wall looked out over the complex and to the woodland beyond. The chrome and LED lighting could be adjusted to any colour and any intensity to produce each and every mood possible.

Today, only six people were in the room, the CEO and his five deputies. These were the people who had inherited the company's seventy-five year quest to reproduce the finest race that had ever walked the face of the Earth.

"Guten Morgen, meine Herren. Karl, how goes the

Genesis Project?" the man sitting at the head of the table asked.

A small man sat forward and seemed to grow in stature. His manicured hands folded into each other and rested on the table, his almost polished, rosy cheeks seemed to glow in the lights. He was clearly confident that his response was going to be to the CEO's liking.

With a couple of taps on the controls set within the table, a large screen dropped down from the end of the room displaying a world map. Ranging around the Pacific Rim, the coast of Africa, across the North Atlantic, throughout the Far East and through the Mediterranean region were several hundred blue lights and a handful of red.

"Most of the disruptors are in place and are proving to be reliable, that's the blue lights. The rest should be in place within two weeks, the red lights. We then have several days of testing to carry out and some calibration. But we are almost three weeks ahead of schedule." Karl von Papen sat upright with a smile on his face. This had been his project from the beginning and many had said it could not be done. Some of those people were sat around this table.

"That is good news. And I will have pleasure in spreading the word to those who doubted the validity of the project." Eigel looked pointedly around the table.

"And when Genesis is complete it will allow us to repopulate the world with our own people. Speaking of which, what of the Messiah Project?"

When not dressed in his immaculately tailored suit, as befitted the CEO of the world's most advanced, and secretive, genetics research laboratories, those around the table referred to him as 'Master'. During the black right masses they knew and accepted that he quite literally held the power of life and death over them.

"It is going very well, Hans. The latest line of

research is looking very favourable. By the use of the correct techniques, it appears that once the genome is split, we can induce a tendency to recombine. A chemically split section of DNA readily joins with any newly introduced foreign DNA, recombining to form a new genome."

Hans Eigel nodded his bald head, the thick neck seeming to be an extension to his massive shoulders.

"What of the introduction of the new DNA to the host cells?"

This time another of the men around the table spoke up. At thirty-six, he was the youngest of those present. His thin build and slicked back, black hair, black goatee beard and small rimless glasses gave him the look of a World War Two German scientist. In fact, he had been born and raised in America, where his German father had emigrated after the Second World War to carry on his own rocket research following the German defeat in 1945. Over the years, Michael Spielmann had grown tired of the restrictions the Americans placed on his research and had readily accepted the offer from Grüssmire Gewerbe when it came.

"We have overcome many of the problems. We can clear DNA from the host cell and implant the new DNA with a high degree of success. But there is still a high percentage of rejection when we use the recombined DNA, but we are progressing. Much of what we are learning now will serve us well when we have the target DNA."

Again, Eigel nodded his head, the LED lights shining from his seemingly polished dome. "Speaking of the target DNA, how goes the search?"

"We have several leads, but we have lost our link to the Knights." Joseph Adler's eyes were a dead soulless black as he looked at the leader of the group. "The three members have suffered accidental deaths." He snorted through his hooked nose at the thought that 'accidental' had anything to do with the men's deaths.

Eigel slammed his huge meaty hands down on the polished table. All except Adler visibly jumped at the sudden eruption. Eigel cast his eyes around the table, each man was studiously avoiding his gaze, except Adler who met his eyes with his own black soulless pits.

"When did this happen?"

"While you were away. I have already taken steps to mitigate the situation."

"And you didn't think it was worth a call to keep me informed?"

"The first death seemed like a genuine accident. It was only when the second occurred that we became suspicious. By the time we got anyone to the third contact it was all over. There was nothing you could have done."

"I need to be kept informed. Of everything." Eigel took a deep breath and visibly calmed himself, the calm intensity was no less frightening than the anger. "What have you done?"

Adler sat back as he looked at the CEO. "I instructed Adam to find the girl, the daughter of the original target. She is starting to ask questions. I suspect that she knows more about the Knights than she should. Adam can bring her in and we can extract the information."

It was Eigel's turn to sit back, smiling slightly as he shook his head.

"Joseph, you are very good at what you do, but you are too single-minded." Eigel was the only person who could talk to Adler in that tone.

"If the girl knows something, if she is looking for the Knights, it would be better to let her find them and track her. Tell Adam to observe and follow her. No direct action, yet."

14:00hrs
Corsica

Corsica, the Island of Beauty, although a region of France, lies only 56 miles from the Italian mainland whilst sitting 110 miles south west of the Côte d'Azur, France and just under 7 miles north of Sardinia. The population is predominantly French but with a good proportion of Moroccan immigrants, native Italians and Portuguese.

The island is known as the most mountainous in the Mediterranean. At 114 miles long and 52 miles wide it has more than 200 beaches, and mountains cover two thirds of the area with a fifth covered by beaches.

The small town square was bathed in spring sunlight, the old stone buildings with slatted shutters casting sharp shadows and splashes of colour. The temperature was in the low seventies and the humidity comfortable. In another two months the square would be deserted at the start of the mid-afternoon siesta. But now, in April, the temperature was not hot enough to demand a break and there were several people still going about their business.

The man looked across the square and noted with approval the two old women walking steadily between shops dressed in the traditional black dress that reached from neck to floor. As he crossed the square one of the old ladies dropped the bag she was carrying and several oranges spilled from the torn bottom. The man diverted his route slightly to avoid the fallen fruit and casually walked on.

Slinging his bag over his shoulder, he crossed the road and headed between the old two storey buildings. The shadows cast a refreshing coolness as he walked along. Two minutes later he came to the car he knew would be waiting for him. Bending down, he felt along the top of the front left tyre and removed the key. The car was an older model Fiat 127, white as was traditional to reflect the sun, clean and well cared for. Climbing in, he started the engine and listened to the small motor come to life and settle down into a steady whine.

Ten minutes later he was outside of the town and pulled over, just off the side of the road. The beach and crystal clear azure sea stretched away to his right, the mountains climbing to dramatic 6,000 foot peaks to his left.

This section of the road was straight for over two miles and he had stopped in the middle. Looking off along the ancient Roman road, he noted that no other traffic was in sight. He reached back into the car and took out the bag he had been carrying. He placed the bag on the ground and removed two old, battered number plates. He quickly placed sticky pads on the car's own number plates and pressed the new plates in place. He then took a wide roll of car pin-striping tape from the bag. It had three rows of colour, the green, white and red of the Italian flag. This he placed on the bonnet of the car, off centre to the left, in line with the driver's position. Trimming it to length, he placed another section across the roof and a third down the back. He then climbed back into the car and placed several eye catching stickers in the rear and side windows and another in the windscreen that made the screen look as if it had a bullet hole towards the centre top of the passenger side.

Standing back, he examined his handiwork. It was a common make and model in these parts, and anyone seeing it would remember the embellishments.

He drove on for another thirty minutes before

turning off the main road and heading for the village. The road, it was little more than a dry track, rose steeply into the hills and was well worn, well travelled by visitors from the town.

The small village was little more than a sparse collection of buildings. A large building that looked like an old town hall dominated one end of the street and looked out along the small row of buildings, a cafeteria, small general purpose shop, a farm supplies and old fashioned blacksmiths with forge. Two cantinas completed the small collection of buildings.

The man pulled the car up to the rear of the large building and noted only three other cars. He walked to the rear doors, which opened as he approached. A large man, six feet two of half fat, half muscle stood holding the door.

"Bonjour, monsieur, comment ça va?"

"Eh, salute." Michael was born and bred in southern France, but spoke Italian with a natural southern accent that even a native Italian would be hard pushed to spot as a fake. He raised his hand to his face, gently rubbing his recently grown and roughly trimmed Vandyke beard.

"Ah, Italiano. Benvenuto, come stai?" How are you?

"Eh, well, thank you." The man sounded nervous, bordering on scared.

"Who shall I say is visiting?" the large man smiled, probably at the other's discomfort.

"Dominic, eh, this is my first time," he said, with obvious embarrassment.

The large doorman smiled, almost a leer, "Don't worry, it's not the girls' first time."

Michael smiled self-consciously and followed the large bull like man.

The corridor opened into a large room decorated with silk drapes, thick, but well worn, carpets and

133

several couches strewn with large silk and fur cushions.

As he entered, the bull announced in French accented Italian his name, and pronounced that he was a visitor from Italy. His little ruse was working.

Three women, little more than girls, straightened up on the couches and eyed the dark skinned, lean and handsome young man. He was different to the usual overweight, old men that usually visited the establishment. For once maybe they would enjoy their afternoon's work.

An older woman walked into the room from behind a row of silk drapes. Although a little overweight, she looked quite attractive, dark brown hair falling just to her shoulders, long dress, open at the top revealing a generous cleavage. But as she drew closer, Dominic could see that much of the beauty was only make-up deep. Her smile, although wide, did not touch the eyes, an insincere salesman's smile.

"Good afternoon, Dominic. I'm Sophia, how nice of you to visit our home. What would you like today?"

"Eh, well, I'm not really sure." Michael looked around the room, looking at each girl in turn before looking back to the older woman.

"Well, if you are not sure, may I suggest Daniela? She is well versed in…everything. So you could try different things?" Sophia indicated one of the girls, who stood from the couch and walked across the room. She was of average height, but the long legs made the blonde appear taller. She was dressed in a short black skirt, high heels and black stockings, the skirt revealing the stocking tops, with an almost see-through filmy red blouse that made it clear she was not wearing a bra. As she approached, Michael noted that she too was no stranger to cosmetics, although her obvious beauty did at least extend to her skin.

"Daniela will look after you, she is very

experienced."

Michael nodded, was the woman's experience with goodness knows how many men supposed to attract him?

"But first we need to get the boring business out of the way." Sophia smiled her best salesman's smile. "As you are a first time visitor, I will give you a discount. Shall we say three hundred Euros? For an hour?"

"Eh, well...if I paid four hundred Euros could I have two of the girls?"

Sophia laughed. To Michael's surprise it sounded genuine. "So you do know what you would like... As you are new, for four hundred you may have two of the girls. Ellana."

Ellana stood and walked across the room. She was a little shorter than Daniela, but with more ample curves. She wore white shorts, half unbuttoned with a bare midriff and a white bikini top that did little to hide her ample bosom. Her long black hair, too black to be natural, fell across her shoulders. Several strands hung across her face which she either did not notice or chose to ignore.

Leading him by the hand, Daniela led the way through a side door and along a corridor, several doors led off to the sides. But they passed these and headed for the last door which was slightly ajar.

The room was red. Every surface was red with splashes of gold. The walls were painted a dark red with fan lights projecting upwards from eye level. The floor was covered by a well worn Ferrari red deep pile carpet. The unmade, ruffled bed was covered in red and gold satin sheets.

As she walked into the room, Ellana reached behind her neck and untied the strap. The bikini top fell away with virtually no movement of her obviously artificially enhanced breasts. Michael noticed with some curiosity that one nipple was noticeably higher and off centre compared to the other. He could see a small pale scar to the left and top of her ribcage.

Ellana walked up to Michael and reached up, putting her arms around his neck and pressing her lips to his, her tongue slipping between his lips. He could smell the cigarette smoke on her hair and taste it on her lips. He put his right hand on the small of her back and slowly moved his finger tips up her spine into her black hair. He slowly wound the hair around his fingers, pulling it tight. Ellana gave a small gasp at the gentle pain as Michael pulled her head back. With one swift motion he drew his left hand across her exposed throat, let go of her hair and stepped back. The knife was so sharp that Ellana did not realise her throat had been severed through to the back of her trachea, until she took a breath and her lungs filled with blood. The carotid arteries sprayed bright red blood around the room, which blended with the vivid decoration.

Michael turned to Daniela, who still stood with a vacant half smile. She had opened her see-through red blouse and allowed her short black skirt to fall to the floor, revealing the black stockings and suspender belt. With two quick steps, Michael stepped up to her and thrust the eight inch blade into her lower abdomen and pulled it sharply upwards until it ground against her sternum. Still with the vacant expression, she looked down at the spilling viscera. Her expression slowly faded from vacant to horror. She started to take a breath, her mouth opening to form a scream that died in her throat as she slumped to the floor.

Michael picked up his bag from where he had dropped it and headed back into the corridor. As he passed each door, he pushed it open and checked the room. They were all vacant, each decorated in similar garish tones. As he reached the main reception area, he opened the door and stepped smartly through. Sophia was sitting on a large comfy, high backed chair. She glanced up as he entered.

"Finished already? I told you my girls were good. I'm afraid there are no refunds for speed." The smile had turned into a knowing grin. As he approached the chair, her smile faded as she saw the blood splatter on his arms.

She stood and started to step around the chair, trying to keep it between them.

"Hugo, HUGO!" she screamed.

Michael feinted around one side of the chair and then sprang the other way as Sophia moved to avoid him. As he reached her, she turned and tried to move away. But Michael caught her hair and pulled her back. With practised ease, he snapped her head to one side and let her inert body fall to the floor.

The third girl, who had still been sat on the couch when he entered, stood and ran towards the entrance. As she reached it, Michael's left arm shot out and the knife arced across the twenty feet, hitting her high up in the back. She stumbled, her right arm going up and over her shoulder, reaching for the knife. As she tripped, the door opened and her head collided with the edge, causing her to bounce back and fall onto her side.

Hugo, the large doorman came rushing through the door. He paused, looking down at the fallen third girl, and then glancing around the room. Seeing Michael, he started walking towards him. He stopped when he saw the lifeless form of Sophia on the floor, before looking back at Michael and starting to advance with a snarl.

Michael simply stood waiting for the large man to approach. As he got to ten feet away, Michael moved with speed, spinning anti-clockwise, pivoting on his right foot, curling his left leg in close to his body to increase his angular speed and then snapping it out as he completed the turn. His left heel connected with Hugo's cheek as he completed the roundhouse kick. Continuing his turn, he planted his feet on the floor as he hooked his left arm around the back of the larger man's neck and pulled him over, off balance, and threw him over his hip.

The room shook with the force of Hugo's landing and Michael followed him down, his right elbow smashing into the man's face. Michael rolled away and sprang to his feet. Hugo was clearly shaken and stunned, but he was far from down and out. With effort, he was rolling upright and climbing unsteadily to his feet.

Michael waited for the man to stand and then unleashed a vicious straight kick with his right foot, followed in one fluid movement with a snap kick with the left. The man staggered, hit the wall and bounced off. With a last gasp of hope, Hugo swung a huge meaty fist at Michael's head. He was so surprised at the fight left in the big man, he only managed to pull his head out of the way of the crushing blow at the last second. Hugo's meaty fist collided with Michael's shoulder with such force that his collar bone was taken to the point of breaking, the muscle surrounding the shoulder would be deeply bruised for several weeks. Hugo was fading fast, but Michael had learnt his lesson. He threw a right jab, which stopped just short of Hugo's jaw. Hugo reacted slowly, but managed to pull his head back and raise his hands to his face, exposing his abdomen. Michael threw a vicious left right combination to the man's solar plexus and just under his right ribs.

Hugo slumped to his knees, gasping for air but unable to breathe in. Before Hugo could try for a second breath, Michael straightened the fingers of his left hand and drove them into Hugo's throat. Hugo gave a shudder and collapsed gurgling to the floor.

Michael looked around, the third girl was still breathing. He walked over to her and retrieved the knife. The wound was deep but not fatal if she got medical treatment to stem the flow of blood. He bent to one knee and drove the knife through the girl's back and into her heart.

Michael went to the main door and made sure it was locked. He then quickly checked the rest of the building. Sophia had a live in cook and cleaner, plus Hugo for security. But Wednesdays were always slow so the cook and cleaner were given the day off, along with most of the girls.

Heading down to the cellar, Michael found the gas bottles used to power the heating and cooking. There had to be some tools around to change the bottles. Tucked behind the gas bottles was a red metal toolbox. Opening it, he found the spanner to disconnect the tubes to the bottles. Two minutes later he retreated to the top of the stairs and reached into his bag. The small incendiary device was little bigger than an old fashioned video cassette.

Making sure the doors were locked behind him, he drove the old Fiat from the car park and headed through the small town and up into the hills. Five minutes later he checked his watch and pulled the car over and walked off the road to the edge of the cliff so that he could look down on the village. Less than a minute later there was a flash from below and he watched as the old brothel disintegrated into a pile of rubble. A couple of seconds later the deep growl of the explosion rolled up the valley and washed over Michael. Half of the building had been immediately destroyed, the remainder was ablaze, flames licking at the old beams of the structure.

An hour later, having taken the temporary markings,

stickers and number plates off the car he pulled back into the town and parked the car where he had collected it from. He then walked to the old church just off the main square. The church was the largest building in the town, the twin towers dwarfing most of the other structures. The interior of the church was cool and dim. The primitive, but impressive, stained glass window cast multi-coloured shadows and beams of light across the rows of pews.

Michael paused at the head of the aisle, bent his knee and crossed himself. He then walked to the middle of the church and sat down on one of the hard wooden pews. Saying a quick prayer, he again crossed himself and walked to the confessional.

"Forgive me Father, for I have sinned. It has been a week since my last confession."

The voice from the other side of the carved wooden screen was relaxed and well modulated. Not bored, but familiar with the process from years of experience.

"What are your sins, my son?" asked the priest.

"Earlier today, I was crossing the square and an old lady dropped her bag of fruit. Instead of helping, I walked on, ignoring her efforts to recover the fruit." Michael was speaking in his native French.

"Have you any other sins?"

"I have had unpure thoughts. I imagine what I would like to do to sinners. And just this afternoon, I saw two scantily clad women…I felt lust."

"Did you act on your feelings of lust?"

"No Father."

"Very well, say a Hail Mary and ask for the Lord's forgiveness. Go in peace."

"Thank you, Father." Michael crossed himself and said a short prayer.

"And how are the latest plans working out?" asked the priest.

"It's all complete. Madam Sophia will not be sinning, or enticing others to sin again." Michael handed the car key to the priest.

"Well done, Michael. God is proud of you. Are you ready for your next trial?"

"I am always ready to do God's work, Father."

"The girl, the daughter of the Knight? It appears she is seeking out the Knights and others have her under surveillance. She must not lead the Ahnenerbe to the Knights."

"Don't worry, Father. She won't lead anyone anywhere.

Chapter 14

02:00hrs, 10th April
Paris, France

The last few days had been unusually warm, but tonight it was definitely cold. A ground frost would be turning the old city white by the morning. The rain had stopped two hours earlier, and the ground was mostly dry with just the odd puddle reflecting the lights of the ancient city that attracted millions of tourists each year.

The Range Rover HE Sport was parked at the side of the road near the Jardin du Forum des Halles, a small public garden on the north bank of the river. Four men sat in the car, bundled up against the cold and light wind, a wind whose chill factor was taking the temperature below freezing.

"Are we ready?" asked the man in the front passenger seat.

"As we're going to be, unless you can turn the temperature up," said one of the men in the rear as he looked out of the tinted windows at the cold night.

The first man looked out at the light traffic and satisfied himself that there were no people around. As he raised the small radio to his lips he saw a police car turn at the end of the street and head their way. A few seconds later the police car passed the dark green Range Rover and went on its way. Gold One let his breath out and started to breathe again.

"Gold to Bronze, execute."

Three miles away, a van with the livery of the Paris Power Company stopped and two men stepped from the rear doors, slammed them shut and walked away as the van drove on. Five minutes later they crossed behind the metal fencing of the electricity sub-station, looked around carefully to check the CCTV cameras, and dropped to the floor. Two minutes later they had cut through the mesh and were inside the compound. In another two minutes the charges were set and they were back out through the fence.

Back at the Range Rover the radio came to life. *"Bronze is set, on your command."*

"Very well, Bronze, hold. Silver, are you ready?"

"All set Gold."

"Okay, get us into position," said Gold One to the driver.

The large 4x4 pulled away from the side of the road and headed south, crossing the river and entering the Île de la Cité, it turned east along the small island and stopped.

Our Lady of Paris, better known as Notre-Dame Cathedral, was floodlit from both above and below. The illumination was designed to show off the architecture better at night than during the day, and better now than when it was built over eight hundred years ago by Bishop Maurice de Sully.

"Bronze, go, go, go." The command was said clearly and quietly.

For several seconds nothing happened, until suddenly the lights of the city started to go out, section by section. As the lights on the island flickered and faded, the passenger and two men in the rear of the Range Rover opened the doors and quickly exited the car.

A mile away, the rear doors of a grey van opened and three figures, all dressed in black from their balaclavas to their Globaltech cross-sport trainers, exited the van and ran along the Quai François Mitterand to two different locations. Silver One stopped at a four by two foot inspection chamber and placed a small cigarette box at each end with a two kilogram lead weight on top of each. Silver Two and Three stopped at a heavily barred wrought iron gate set into the wall of the old building. With quick, practised movements, the two men threaded a dull white rope through the bars and around the locks. Two and Three looked back at One and gave the ready signal.

Silver One checked his watch. The electricity to the city had been off for thirty seconds, another thirty and the generators in the building would kick on and the security system would start to reboot.

He took shelter behind a litter bin and pressed send on his mobile phone. The two simultaneous explosions sounded dull as the small shaped charges of C4 blasted downwards into the inspection chamber, destroying the heavy duty locking mechanism. He ran the ten feet to the now open chamber and tossed a fragmentation grenade into the pit. He then sprinted on to meet up with Silver Two and Three, reaching their position as the grenade exploded and shredded everything in the pit.

"Go," he said.

Silver Two pressed send and the detcord wrapped around the gate exploded with a cutting force of several tons concentrated along the ten millimetre width of the cord, neatly cutting through the iron it was wrapped around.

The three black clad men ran through the gate, pushing it closed behind them. To a casual glance it appeared to be undamaged. They stopped below a ladder fastened to the side of the wall, the bottom rung set ten feet above the ground. Silver Three locked his hands together and boosted Silver Two up to the ladder.

Silver Two climbed hand over hand up four rungs until he could get his feet on the bottom of the ladder. He then unclipped the latch holding the ladders above the ground. With a clatter the rungs dropped down and all three men quickly climbed to the roof. The three men set ropes and harnesses to air vents and handrails.

The city was dark for well over a mile in each direction, the stars standing out clear above them, clearer than was ever seen above the city of Paris since the blackouts of World War Two.

The three ran over to one of the doors that dotted the roof and placed charges on the key points before taking cover in the shadow of the stone structure. As the explosives shattered the door, Silver One looked out across the darkened city, the full moon reflected off the still wet roofs. He looked down into the large open frontage of the building, and onto the point of the glass pyramid that fronted Le Louvre museum.

"Silver entering," he said over the radio.

Gold One acknowledged the message with a click of the radio as his team stopped in the corridor of the Treasury of Notre-Dame de Paris. The treasury, which also housed the sacristy rooms used by priests in charge of the church, was far newer than the main cathedral, having been rebuilt and modernised in the 19th Century. Sitting to the south of the main building it is linked by two covered arms. The treasury holds the treasures of the cathedral that are on display at certain times in the cathedral, and security is not simply provided by locked doors and alarm systems. The building is also guarded by the Knights of the Holy Sepulchre, one of the original five orders of knights. But these days the knights did not go around in robes, carrying swords, they carried modern weapons and used electronic surveillance.

"Gold One, this is Gold Two, systems disabled. All clear."

Gold One again clicked the radio. He and Gold Three pulled infrared goggles down and checked the corridor before heading off towards their target.

There was light ahead, the irregular swaying of a torch beam. Gold One and Two stopped and flattened themselves against opposite walls. A second torch beam joined the first, two guards. Five seconds later the guards rounded the corner and stepped into the corridor, their torch beams scanning the walls, floor and ceiling.

Two quiet thuds echoed along the old stone walls, the shots erupting from the guns carried by Gold One and Two. The torches dropped to the floor as the guards went down. The two Gold team members rushed forward and checked the guards. Another two quiet thuds rang out as they delivered the coup de grâce.

"Gold One, two guards down."

The emergency lights in the corridors of Le Louvre flickered to life as the Silver team exited the staircase leading from the roof. The cables and equipment destroyed in the outside inspection chamber would stop alarm bells ringing in the nearby police stations, but internally the alarms would be reinitiated in another thirty seconds.

Quickly extending two telescopic stands, the men placed them in the doorframe and propped the door open.

The three members of Silver team split up and headed for their targets. The best known works of art were housed in various galleries, every piece in the huge museum was not only collectable but worth a small fortune, and one piece was as good as another for their requirements.

Gold One checked around the corner of the corridor and indicated for Gold Three to advance. Checking behind before every move, Gold Three saw a torch beam approaching from around the corner. The guard had to have seen the two bodies of his colleagues and would raise the alarm any second.

Gold Three indicated the threat and ran quickly and quietly back towards the corner. As he approached the corner, the torch beam wavered and fell to the floor and became still.

"Gold One, this is Gold Three, third guard down, approaching from your six."

Gold Three quickly jogged back along the corridor and joined up with Gold One as Gold Two arrived from the opposite direction. All three were standing in front of a large, ornately carved door. The electronic locks had been disabled, but there was still the old fashioned deadbolt which Gold One was already picking. With a loud, hollow click, the lock disengaged.

Gold One and Two entered the room while Gold Three stood guard at the entrance.

The room had a vaulted ceiling of granite and sandstone, there were no windows and only one door. As they entered the room, the two men took off their night goggles and lit small LED lanterns.

Several glass cabinets lined the old walls, but it was the centre display that was their focus. Standing six feet high and two feet on a side, the bottom half of the case was oak and cast iron, the top appeared to be glass. In fact, the glass was two inch thick, laminated ballistic acrylic, impervious to any bullet up to and including a fifty cal. The acrylic was not the weak point. Instead, the case's weakness was the apparently solid base. The locks had been updated a few years ago, but the surround was original. The oak and cast iron were solid, but worn. The joints between the two materials had parted slightly as the old timber gradually dried out over the last four centuries.

Gold One bent down and removed the small rucksack from his back. He quickly put on a double filter gas mask and close fitting safety glasses before carefully removing a small rigid plastic container. He opened the padded container and withdrew a small plastic bottle and dropper. With care, he filled the small dropper with the clear liquid. This he applied to the joints between the locks and surrounding cast iron. The iron started to hiss and bubble, a faint green vapour rising into the air giving an acrid smell to the room.

"Don't get too close to the smoke, remember, the hydrofluoric acid vapour will eat through your lungs in seconds," said Gold Two.

Back at Le Louvre, the alarms were sounding. As soon as the artworks had been touched, the alarms had started to ring. Silver team had quickly removed three paintings from their frames, rolled them into tubes and retreated back to their entry point.

Once the alarms were triggered, all the entrances and exits were automatically sealed by dropdown gates. But the gate at their entry point was still raised by two feet where it had struck the metal stands the team had placed earlier. They quickly crawled under the gate and ran up the stairs to the roof. By now the guards would have realised the alarms and landline telephones were not connecting to the outside and would be calling the police from mobile phones.

All three of the team ran to the ropes they had secured earlier, quickly clipped them to their harnesses and stepped over the roof to abseil to the ground next to the van as police sirens sounded in the distance. Silver One checked his watch, almost a minute faster than expected, the guards had been quick to act.

The acrid smell in the room had driven Gold Two and Three into the corridor while Gold One watched the bubbling and hissing locks of the cabinet. As the bubbling subsided he stepped forward and hit each lock several times in turn. Each gave a hollow breaking sound. With a final hard blow one of the locks gave way and it fell away in several charred pieces. Within seconds he had the other three locks out of the frame and lying on the floor.

"Give me a hand," he called and Gold Two came in.

Between them, the two men lifted the glass top from the case and set it on the floor.

"Lights," called Gold Three from the corridor.

"Go," Gold One nodded towards the door and Gold Two ran out, pulling his night vision goggles back into place as he went.

There were two torch beams coming from around the corner. By now they had to have seen the fallen guards.

Gold Two and Three stopped and pulled two fragmentation grenades from their belts, pulled the pins and tossed them down the corridor before quickly taking cover.

The two torch beams disappeared as the twin explosions echoed through the old building followed by the shattering pops of dozens of razor sharp steel shards erupting down the corridor along with the pained cries of the two guards. The agonised cries of one of the guards died away quickly, but the other seemed to go on in an endless series of tortured screams. Gold Two and Three ran forward, their short, bullpup automatic FN P90 submachine guns held forward. As they rounded the corner, Gold Two centred the red dot laser target on the chest of the screaming guard and pulled the two stage trigger half back. A single 5.7 x 28mm bullet shot from the short urban machine gun and silenced the screaming man. As he scanned the corridor for the second guard a shot rang out and slammed into Gold Two's shoulder, knocking him off balance and twisting him against the wall. His finger jerked fully back on the trigger and the gun fired ten shots on full auto before he recovered. The bullets stitched a neat row of holes in the wall and ceiling, the shell cases emptying into the collector bag.

Gold Three crouched down and sprayed the corridor with automatic fire. At 900 rounds per minute, the small bullets formed an almost solid curtain of metal. As the echo of the shots subsided, he scanned the corridor for the shooter. There, a flash of movement against the wall. Before Gold Three could centre the sights on the movement three shots rang out, the first shot hit Gold Three in the leg, the second hit the edge of his ribs and slammed him into the wall, the third left a hot crease across the side of his neck.

Gold Three returned fire on full automatic, the guard jerked against the wall and fell to the floor.

Gold Three crossed to Gold Two and checked his condition. The bullet had been stopped by the bullet-proof vest at the shoulder, leaving a bruise but no permanent damage. As he helped his colleague to his feet, Gold Three staggered back slightly against the wall, reaching out in time to stop himself falling. Gold Two took hold of his arm and lowered him to the floor.

Gold Two quickly checked Gold Three. The neck wound was bleeding freely, the bullet having nicked the jugular. Gold Two quickly removed a medi-pad and pressed it to the wound. The vest had stopped any real damage to the ribs. As soon as he got to the leg he found the real problem. The first bullet had hit the inside of the right leg, severing the femoral artery. Gold Two raised the night vision goggles and turned on a small LED torch. The blood was covering the floor, pooling under Gold Three's legs. The flow from the wound was already dying down, his blood pressure dropping through the floor. Gold Two looked at Gold Three, his face was white and clammy with the look of putty. He was already unconscious. He would be dead in seconds.

Silver Two stopped the van at the end of the road. There was the odd car driving along the wide boulevard, but it was the approaching flashing lights from the police cars that he was waiting for.

"Okay, get ready…GO," shouted Silver One.

The van pulled out in front of a car, deliberately cutting the car up, the driver responding by swerving and leaning on the horn. The approaching police car changed lanes and followed the quickly accelerating van. The driver of the van stood on the brakes and turned a sharp left onto the Pont du Carousel, crossing the River Seine and turning right to head west. The police car was been joined by two others, all displaying flashing red and blue lights and blaring sirens.

Gold One was fastening the straps on the backpack, securing the thornless crown of thorns he had recovered from the case. Gold Two came back in and quickly told him what had happened.

"Okay, let's go."

The two men exited the room at a quick jog, turned left and headed back to the corner where the guards and Gold Three lay. Gold One stopped and retrieved the plastic flask from his pocket. With care he quickly poured a dropper full of the hydrofluoric acid on Gold Three's hands and face. The acid immediately bubbled and burned through the flesh to the bone. Gold Three was not known on any criminal database, but removing the fingerprints and face would only help to confuse the authorities. Thirty seconds later, the two men ran out into the cold night, pausing long enough to take a breath of the clear air before running back to the waiting Range Rover.

"Where's Three?" asked the driver.

"He won't be joining us, go," replied Gold One.

The driver put the car in gear and pulled steadily away, not wanting to draw any attention to the vehicle or men inside.

"Were there any calls?" asked Gold One.

The driver nodded. "Two to the police, one to the Sepulchre HQ."

"You intercepted them?"

"Of course. No mobile phone or radio signals are getting in or out of a four hundred metre radius. I answered the calls, as far as the guards know, help is on the way. I told them, sorry the Sepulchre HQ told them, to hold fast and protect the Cathedral and not to engage the intruders."

"I wondered why so few guards came at us."

By now they had crossed to the north bank of the Seine and were heading east out of the city along the Quai de la Rapée. Flashing red and blue lights were approaching from the front at speed. The three men in the car held their breath as two police cars flashed past.

"Looks like the diversion's working," said Gold Two from the rear of the car.

"Of course it is. Anyone messing with the national treasures is attacking the nation. The French take their artwork very seriously."

Gold One and Two started stripping off their black outer clothing, stashing their weapons and equipment in two kit bags. Two minutes later they were dressed in dark blue jeans and casual shirts. They would dump the bags in a few more minutes.

"Gold is clear," said Gold One into the radio.

"Gold is clear." Silver One heard the voice in his earpiece.

"Gold team is clear, let's end this," said Silver One to the men in the van.

By now there were at least five police cars following the van. The closest had closed to fifty metres.

"Okay, get ready with the spikes, after the next corner."

The two men in the back lifted two heavy boxes from the floor of the van, pulled the tape off the top and peeled back the flaps. As the van braked sharply and turned right with squealing tyres, the men threw open the back doors and tipped the four pronged tyre spikes out of the van and onto the road. The road was narrow, with parked cars on both sides. As the police car careered around the corner, closing the gap to forty metres, the driver never even saw the dozens of spikes lying in the road. The two front tyres and one of the rears burst, sending the car skidding out of control to slam into the side of three parked cars, coming to rest across the street, effectively blocking the road as the next police car rounded the corner and also hit the spikes, losing control and ramming heavily into the rear of the first police car.

The van accelerated along the street, leaving the police cars behind, at least temporarily.

"Okay, where are we?" Silver One watched the sat nav and checked the map. They had several escape routes worked out depending on how the decoy chase had gone. Now was the time to make good their getaway.

"Head for RV two," said Silver One.

As they reached the end of the road the van took the right turn at speed, the tyres skidding across the cobbles, the van heading the wrong way along the wide one-way street before braking hard, swerving around an oncoming car and turning left. As they made the turn, red and blue lights appeared from several streets back. The police had detoured around the collision and finally made it back to the chase, but Silver team had opened the required gap.

The van was accelerating hard, the turbocharged engine now delivering the full three hundred brake horsepower that the driver had until now been holding back. A quick right, short sprint and another right and left. The road was slick under the heavy tree covering and the van drifted sideways as the wide tyres sought grip. A screech and jarring crunch from the rear as the van clipped a parked car sent the back of the van fishtailing for fifty metres before the driver finally got it back under control.

"The police helicopter should be here any minute, keep an eye open," said Silver One to Silver Two and Three as the men scanned the sky around the buildings.

At least two of the police cars were keeping pace, but there was still over a hundred and fifty metres between them and the fleeing van. At the end of the straight the van was travelling at over 90 mph and braked hard, drifted out to the right and took the left turn on three wheels.

"Okay, one mile, get ready," said Silver One to the men in the van. "Bronze, ETA one minute."

"Roger Silver, Bronze is in place."

As the van accelerated hard along the boulevard, the turbo gave a counterpoint whine to the deep base growl from the big V8 power plant, the sound echoing off the buildings spaced along the wide road.

The van braked hard, the ABS the only thing stopping the wheels from locking up as the right turn forced the van to drift sideways before straightening up for the short straight. The van pulled out to the left and overtook a slow-moving articulated wagon before cutting back to the right and taking a side street in front of the cab. The brake lights of the artic glowed red as the lorry driver tried in vain to avoid hitting the smaller van.

The first police car rounded the corner just in time to see the van cut in front of the wagon and collide with the front. The police driver smiled to himself, the road they had taken was a long straight leading to the river, but it was a dead end, a cul-de-sac.

The van slowed as the rear spun out of control and slammed hard into the parked cars, bouncing off one, straightening, overcorrected and T-boned into another.

The police car screeched to a halt at the corner. The articulated wagon had stopped across the end of the road, effectively blocking the road to the police. As the second police car arrived, followed by a third, the driver of the first police car jumped out and ordered the lorry driver to move the wagon.

The four men from the van exited the wrecked vehicle and ran from the road, between the parked cars, across the wide verge and footpath into an alleyway between the old buildings.

Silver One stopped and pulled what looked like a small calculator from his pocket, punched in a number and looked back at the van. A small pop sounded from the van as a small incendiary device under the bonnet detonated, smoke and small flames licking around the grill and vents.

As the lorry pulled away from the junction, the first of the police cars squeezed through the widening gap, the driver smiled when he saw the van had hit hard against the parked cars. He then noticed the growing flames around the front of the van. Were the men still in the van? He scanned up and down the street, there was no sign of anyone, but a few of the curtains were pulling back, the locals curious as to the noise and police lights and sirens.

The men from the van ran through the interconnected alleyways, crossing the next street and ducking back into the alley across the other side.

In the cab of the articulated wagon, Bronze One keyed in a code on his mobile phone. This time a larger explosion erupted as the second incendiary ignited the petrol tank. The resultant explosion lifted the back of the van and sent flames erupting into a thirty foot fireball. A second smaller explosion ruptured a container strapped under the van sending white teargas into the flames.

The regular fluttering whup-whup of rotor blades sounded from above and an intense white spotlight lit the street, centred on the burning van as the police helicopter arrived.

The police cars stopped short of the burning van, already calling for the fire service and starting to shout for people to move back from their windows. As the teargas spread, the police officers were forced back, none of them able to get closer that seventy feet, their eyes stinging and tears falling freely down their faces. They backed up further, coughing and rubbing their eyes, making the stinging even worse.

Silver team arrived at the second street away from the crashed van and split up to two different cars, a five year old Renault Scenic and a six year old Citroën Picasso. Neither were the typical getaway cars, but both would see the Silver team safely out of the city.

Silver One paused as he heard a voice over his in-ear speaker.

"Silver One, this is Bronze One, all clear. The police can't get to the van to check for bodies. See you back at base."

Chapter 15

08:00hrs, 11th April
Oxford

Grantham sat down at the breakfast table and looked around the room. As well as himself, there were six other people in the room, two couples and two singles. One couple had the casual, easy comfort of a happily married partnership, the other looked slightly nervous, but happy. Either newlyweds or a couple on a first date away, maybe having an affair. He was wearing a wedding ring, she was not, probably the affair. The two singles were both men. Grantham paid closer, but casual attention to them. They both appeared to be businessmen. One was in his late fifties, he looked like he had been everywhere, done everything and had a wardrobe full of tee shirts. The other man was younger, with his back to Grantham it was hard to determine his age. He was dressed in a dark business suit and white shirt, eating a healthy bowl of cereal with fresh fruit, toast and a third cup of black coffee before getting ready to rush off and conquer the world.

"Good morning, sir. Would you like tea, coffee?" the waitress was young and bright, dressed in the traditional black skirt, white blouse and small white apron.

"Coffee please," replied Grantham with a smile.

"The breakfast is self service. You can help yourself when you're ready. But if there's anything you would like that isn't out please ask. We have most things."

"Thank you, I'm just waiting for a friend, she should be down in a minute."

After their meeting in the pub, Grantham had

suggested they take some basic measures to protect Charisma, moving hotels, not using her credit or charge cards, including any store cards, and definitely not calling family or friends or telling anyone where they were. At first Charisma had questioned if all the precautions were necessary. But after Grantham explained how easy it was to find and track someone she agreed, especially after Grantham pointed out the best way to cope with trouble was to not let it find you in the first place.

Grantham and Charisma had spent the last two days researching the background of the Templars, holy relics and German research, particularly from the Second World War. The internet was awash with information, but much of the best data had come from the outstanding libraries of the colleges of Oxford University.

Grantham had also put some calls in to a contact he had within the British Intelligence community, but with mixed results. The deaths of the three Knights were officially accidental. With no new evidence it was not possible to reopen the cases, at least officially.

"Good morning. I wondered where you'd gone until I found your note." Charisma sat down at the table opposite Grantham and flashed her stunning smile.

"I thought you'd appreciate having the room to yourself while you got ready." When they checked into the hotel, Grantham said that a couple would be less suspicious than two singles. And that way they could use Grantham's name and credit card without having to give Charisma's name. What he did not say was that the credit card was secure and monitored, if anyone checked on it for any reason he would be notified within minutes, and any info they could get would be dead ends.

Charisma was dressed in her usual stretch jeans,

coupled this morning with a white England rugby shirt.

"Anything new?" she asked as she brushed her auburn hair behind her ear.

"Some of my contacts have agreed to look into the death of the Professor. The two that happened abroad are more difficult."

The young waitress came and poured Charisma her coffee and gave her the same spiel about breakfast. Once she was out of earshot Grantham went on.

"Also, several of the Ahnenerbe escaped after the war and for years there have been rumours in the intelligence community that they continued their work."

"Which work? The search for holy relics, world domination or the resurrection of the master race?"

Grantham shrugged. "Probably all three."

"It sounds like that film, what was it called, the Odessa File?"

Grantham nodded. "The film was based on a book by Frederick Forsyth which itself is based on a true story. Although the book is more accurate than the film. Odessa stands for Organisation der Ehemaligen SS-Angehörigen, which translates as Organization of Former Members of the SS. The book and film tell the story of the tracking down of Eduard Roschmann, the so-called Butcher of Riga. Mind you, after the film was released, the publicity brought about the downfall of Roschmann."

"He actually existed?"

Grantham nodded. "As I say, the story was based on reality. He wasn't prosecuted though. He was arrested by Argentinean police, but skipped bail and fled to Paraguay. He died there a couple of years later."

"They let him out on bail?"

"Who'd have thought that a Nazi mass murderer couldn't be trusted to stay around for prosecution?

Have you turned anything up?"

Charisma pursed her lips, making her look almost petulant. "Well, yes and no. I found something a bit...odd. But I'm not sure what it means, if anything." She reached down to the bag she had placed on the floor and took out a red, hard backed book.

"This is Dad's story book. While he was away, he used to write stories and read them to me when he came home. I used to know most of them off by heart and would ask for my favourite ones time after time." Charisma paused with a faraway look for a second. "Dad never let me have the book. He always said it was his job to write and read, and mine to listen. I'd forgotten about it until Mum left me it with his other stuff. I've been re-reading the stories." Charisma handled the book almost reverently, it was clearly precious to her.

"The stories are still great, just like I remember. And they're all of the same style, maybe a bit...basic I suppose you could say, but they were aimed at a young girl. From my research I see now that at least some of the stories are based on actual recorded events. But I found one that's out of place. It's the last one. Dad must have written it on his last trip. It isn't like the others, the style's different. And it's short."

Charisma flicked through the book and passed it across the table. Grantham scanned through the story and then carefully turned to several other pages and read them. Finally he turned back to the last story and read it in detail.

Eventually the Knights became persecuted and hunted. The church feared their power and knowledge, knowledge that could topple kingdoms and fell the establishment of Rome.

In order to protect themselves and their treasure the

Knights retreated to the new land where He had walked before and took the secrets they guarded with them. Many of the bravest knights swore to protect the secrets, but the danger did not come from a physical threat as had been present in the old country. Instead, the threat was of a different nature, one of solitude and isolation from family, friends and homeland. Those that stayed knew they were unlikely to see their homes and families again. But they had sworn a holy oath to God and would give their lives to protect that which they held dear.

Over the years, they built a new home, a new land, a new country. The secrets were passed from one knight to another. To protect those secrets, only five knights at any time held the knowledge. But in order to keep a record, where all men are free and brother loves brother, the key was cast clear and sound in one of the land's new treasures. So it was that liberty would pass the key to stow.

"You're right. It is different to the others. Not really a story even, more a sort of description. Obviously it refers to the persecution and retreat of the Knights Templars."

The two finished their coffee, both in thought.

"So, what do we do now?" asked Charisma.

"Well, I'm going to have breakfast," said Grantham as he stood and walked to the table, returning a few minutes later, his plate loaded with a full English breakfast plus a few extras.

"Aren't you eating, breakfast is the most important meal of the day?" asked Grantham.

"While you were stacking your plate, I've ordered kippers and Eggs Benedict."

Charisma's food arrived five minutes later and they ate in silence.

"There is something we could do," said Charisma as the plates were cleared away.

Grantham looked at her and waited.

"We could go to America and check with the local police who investigated the car accident that killed Robert Jacobs."

"Why Jacobs? We could just as easily go to Switzerland and investigate Bertrand's death."

Charisma shrugged. "One's as good as the other, I suppose. But there seems more to investigate with a car accident than a fall off a cliff."

Grantham sat back and smiled. "Why not?" He picked up his phone and made a call to check on flights and times.

"Okay, we're booked on the ten o'clock flight from Heathrow day after tomorrow. So, you've got today and tomorrow to finish off the research. Have you got your passport?"

Charisma shook her head. "It's at my Mum's house, my house."

"Okay, we'll call there and pick it up, along with any clothes and stuff you need."

Ten minutes later, the young blond haired businessman collected his computer tablet from the table, disconnected the pen sized directional microphone and walked from the room, already making a call on his own mobile phone.

14:00hrs
JTAC HQ, London

The office was small, but efficient, the majority of the work was done on computers, laptops that rarely, if ever left the office. They were fully encrypted and password protected, but the most sensitive material was not committed to electronic memory. Paper may not be modern or cutting edge, but it had the advantage of only being readable by someone who was physically present.

Phil Everett stood up and walked across to the window overlooking the River Thames. Their office may be small, but it had one of the best views. As the office door opened, he turned from the window, the sun appearing from behind the heavy grey clouds made his dirty blond hair appear halo like around his head.

William Windsor entered the office and nodded to Everett. Both men were of similar average height and build with nondescript blue/grey eyes. Windsor's hair was a mousy brown rather than a dirty blond, but they could be brothers rather than simply colleagues.

"Anything new from the border patrols?" asked Windsor.

For some time JTAC had been monitoring both legal and illegal border crossings between several African and Asian countries thought to be training or housing terrorists.

"Just the usual updates, there's some new rumours about a threat originating in Pakistan, and a flag from South Africa. It seems as if some group has been probing deeper into UK security than is normal."

Windsor crossed to his desk, sat down, logged onto his computer and scanned through the list of e-mails and communications.

"How deep are they probing?" asked Windsor as he clicked to open a file.

"Not deep, the interest has only been rated a two."

"I've got the report back into the death that Hugh Grantham asked us to look into, Professor William Grace in Oxford. Mmm…" Windsor scanned through the report, mentally noting various points.

"All those grunts and moans sound interesting," commented Everett.

Windsor nodded slowly before looking up.

"Well, glancing through the report it looks like there is something to the claim of foul play. The body was exhumed and the toxicology report has shown trace amounts of Amelic Acid, Astringyne and Curare."

Everett looked surprised. "They're used to paralyse and simulate a heart attack, fast acting, fatal and very difficult to find in an autopsy, unless it's specifically tested for."

"Grantham asked us to test for substances that would not normally show up."

"He was right. So, what now?"

"Not sure," replied Windsor. "It's not our jurisdiction, not a terrorist threat. Although, it's not exactly your run of the mill murder. We should at least inform the police…"

"You don't sound convinced," said Everett.

"It's just that it's Grantham that asked us to look into it. And he isn't exactly your run of the mill member of the public. If he's involved, even second hand, things seem to have a way of getting serious very quickly. He has a talent for rooting out trouble."

Everett chuckled. "Yes, finding trouble and making that trouble wish it had stayed hidden. What's wrong?"

Windsor had opened another folder that had caught his eye and was scanning through the summary.

"Grantham asked me to do a background check on the girl's father. John Valentine. He was some sort of troubleshooter, died in the late eighties. Well, according to this, Captain John James Valentine retired from the SAS in 1974 after serving with distinction in several conflicts. He then acted as a consultant for the security services, specifically MI-6. Starting in 1983, he dropped off the active radar for a couple of years. He surfaced again in 1985, in Israel. Mossad had some question as to his activities. In 1987 he was suspected of being involved in smuggling in Egypt. A year later he was in Ethiopia, queries about suspected theft from some sort of religious storage area. He died in Berlin on 9th November 1989 during the fall of the Berlin Wall."

Windsor scanned further through the report. "The investigation into his death turned up some questions as to why he and his friend were there. His friend was Francois Bertrand whose death in Switzerland Grantham also asked us to look into..."

"Bloody hell, when Grantham decides to get involved in something he doesn't do it by halves, does he?"

"There's another odd thing as well. Although he'd been questioned several times about being in the wrong place at the wrong time, he was always released and on his way in a few hours." Windsor paused as he read a little deeper. "The longest he was questioned was overnight, by Mossad."

"I don't imagine that was fun."

"Mmm, but it does beg the question, who was looking after him?"

Everett walked back to the window, clearly thinking to himself. "Organised crime? Terrorist organisation?"

"That was my first thought, but no organised crime syndicate spreads that far. And do you know of any that have that pull with Mossad?"

"Good point. Same goes for terrorist organisations. And look at the areas he's been linked with, they aren't crime centres or terrorist hot spots, well Israel has internal problems, but they rarely attract foreign interest. So who does have that pull?"

Windsor looked up. "There are some groups that can exert that sort of pressure."

"You mean national security services. I'm assuming not any of ours?"

Windsor did not immediately answer as he read

more from the computer.

"You haven't heard the best bit yet." Windsor turned the screen around so that Everett could see it.

The report had several sections blacked out, redacted. Whilst this was not unusual in service personnel records, it was unusual for their private life after leaving the service to be redacted. But it was the added note at the bottom of the page that really caught Everett's attention.

Person of interest, see me soonest.
C

The text was in dark green. The only person in the British Security services to use green ink, or green electronic text, was the head of MI-6, known as C.

"It looks like we're involved whether we want to be or not."

Chapter 16

08:00hrs, 13th April
Heathrow Airport

As usual the airport was busy with businessmen, couples and families, all busily passing through the terminals on their way to all corners of the globe. The atmosphere was bright, airy and crowded. Armed police circled the buildings both discreetly and overtly. Some were there for all to see, their uniforms, flak jackets and MP5 sub-machine guns displaying a restrained, potentially deadly force. But there were far more behind the scenes, officers watching the CCTV monitors, looking for the abnormal, the passenger that looked unusually nervous, looking around to see if they were being watched. Other armed officers were held in reserve, ready to attend any part of the huge complex at a moment's notice. Yet other officers mingled with the crowds in plain clothes, observing, listening and watching.

As they headed for one of the executive lounges, Grantham casually glanced around, weighing up the security services. He knew that there would be a small detachment of SAS troops stationed at the airport, held in strict reserve for major incidents. He had done several weeks duty over the years, sitting around and doing nothing.

"After you," said Grantham, holding the door open for Charisma.

The lounge was an oasis of calm from the hustle and bustle of the public areas. It almost had the atmosphere of a library. After helping themselves to drinks, Grantham going for fresh orange and sparkling mineral water, Charisma going for a medium white wine, and a small selection of savoury snacks and muffins, they took a seat near one of the large picture windows from where they could look out over the airport and across to one of the runways.

"So, what's the plan?" asked Grantham.

"Well, I've tracked down the sheriff that dealt with the car accident, he was a bit reluctant at first, but he's agreed to talk to us. We have to give him a ring once we get there and he'll meet up with us."

"Okay, well..." Grantham stopped as he felt his mobile phone start to vibrate in his pocket. Taking it out and checking the display, he saw it was a withheld number. Very few people had his number and even fewer who would have a withheld number.

"I'd better get this. I'll just go out into the corridor." The lounge was supposed to be a quiet area and mobile phone conversations were frowned upon.

As he headed for the door, Grantham answered the phone and said, "Hold on." Once in the corridor, he selected a quiet corner with only a staff door at the end.

"Grantham." The voice on the other end did not introduce itself, but Grantham recognised the voice as William Windsor.

"Are you free to speak?"

"I'm by myself, what's wrong?"

"Go to scrambler."

Grantham was surprised at the instruction. Windsor obviously had something confidential to talk about. He pressed in the code and listened to the three seconds of screeches and scratches as the two telephones synchronised. As soon as the phone went quiet Windsor started speaking.

"We've got the results back from the new autopsy on Professor Grace. It was definitely murder."

"Poison to look like a heart attack?"

"Amelic Acid, Astringyne and Curare. Less than five minutes from first ingestion to unconscious, fatal about three minutes later."

"Professional hit."

"Very. We've opened a case, investigating as we speak."

Grantham paused, JTAC, the Joint Terrorism Analysis Centre was established in 2003 as a terrorism investigation and assessment branch of the British security service. Although not one of the better know security institutions, like MI-5 and MI-6, JTAC had links to all of the European security services along with direct control of a dedicated SAS unit referred to as Sierras. It was this unit that Grantham had led as a Major in the SAS until he retired and started to work for JTAC as a private 'contractor'. JTAC as an organisation were not known to do charity work for anyone who asked them for a favour, so if they were opening a case then they knew more than they were letting on.

"What aren't you telling me?"

There was a pause from the other end, but Grantham could hear Windsor take a breath and sigh.

"Well the hit was professional, which is enough to make us suspicious...and the girl's father was on a watch list. He'd been connected with some questionable dealings and locations."

"Anything proven?"

"No, but we had to meet C. He knows more than he was saying, as usual. But there is, or was, interest in him. There was suspicion that he was a foreign agent, but he was never tied to a specific government or organisation."

"Can you send me the details?"

"I'll do it as soon as we ring off. We've also got some info about the French guy, Bertrand. He was a

169

member of the French Foreign Legion, served with distinction, but it's difficult to get any more than that, you know how tight lipped the Legion is." There was another pause from Windsor. *"There is suspicion about the girl as well. Simply because of her connection to the father and now that she's asking questions."*

A member of the airport staff came around the corner and passed Grantham, his footsteps silent on the plush carpet. Grantham paused in his conversation with Windsor, quickly weighing up the other man. He was of average height, slightly overweight, dark skinned, probably Indian ancestry, he walked with a slight limp and stoop, probably in his mid-fifties. He nodded to Grantham as he passed and opened the staff only door. The door closed quietly behind him.

"If she had anything to hide would she be making things public?"

"Does she know who you are, your connections and that you asked us for help?"

"No...she knows I work in security and that I've asked some of my connections for help, but she doesn't know who," replied Grantham.

"It'd be best to keep it that way."

Grantham paused, considering what Windsor had said even though it did not feel right. "I'll play it by ear."

Windsor knew better than to argue with Grantham, especially when he was not actually working for them.

"Anything else?" asked Grantham.

"Not at the moment. I'll keep you informed."

Grantham hung up and a few seconds later his phone chimed to announce the arrival of a file. He opened the message and quickly scanned through the contents before closing it and putting the phone back in his pocket.

A minute later he was back in the lounge, sitting

next to Charisma.

"Anything interesting?" she asked.

"Mmm. Well, Professor Grace was definitely murdered. The new autopsy has shown poison." Grantham kept his voice low to fit the quiet surroundings.

"Why wasn't it picked up at the first autopsy?"

"It's a type of poison that's very hard to detect. It was only found because they were specifically looking for poison that would mimic the symptoms and outcome of a heart attack. And it's not available at the local Boots the Chemist. It's a special concoction of poisons that professional assassins use. Especially assassins that work for state security and don't want their handiwork discovered."

"You mean...he wasn't just killed...he was assassinated by a...a spy or something?"

"Well 'spy' isn't the right word. A spy is a non-professional who passes information to a competitor. Someone who works for a security agency, like James Bond, is referred to as a security officer or an agent. And I'm not saying a foreign security agency assassinated the professor. But someone with training who knew what they were doing was at least involved."

Charisma was obviously having difficulty taking it all in. Even though she had first suggested that Grace had been murdered, this was getting away from her.

"But why? What threat could an old Oxford professor be to anyone?" she asked.

Grantham shrugged, "It may be to do with information the professor had rather than any direct threat he posed. The authorities are starting an investigation. For now, we can't do anything. Our best bet is to see what we can find out about the death of Robert Jacobs."

For a few seconds they both sat there, lost in their

171

own thoughts.

"The flight's ready for boarding," said Grantham, looking up at the large screen displaying the various flight times.

Down in the public lounge, two men sat casually side by side, chatting and appearing the same as everyone else. But what they were discussing was far from a normal topic of conversation in an airport departure lounge.

"You will be remembered for this. People who do God's work are themselves blessed. People who die for God, they are immortal in our thoughts and prayers."

"Thank you, Michael. I will not fail you."

"I know you will not fail me or God. You are the chosen. This is a great honour. I wish I were going in your place, but my destiny lies in another direction."

The two men sat in silence for a moment, heads slightly bowed, before Michael looked up and nodded to the large departures board.

"Your flight is boarding. Business class will board first. Good luck David. God will be with you." Michael stood up and held his hand out to the other man, taking David's right hand in his and cupping it with his left he shook it warmly. His face was no longer clean shaven. Instead he had grown a thick, black Vandyke beard and his hair was a salt and pepper mix of black and grey. The effect was to age him at least ten years and add an air of class to his already swarthy good looks.

David nodded and gave Michael a half smile, his teeth slightly crooked but looking white compared to the black beard that covered most of his face, a bright almost feverish light behind his eyes.

"Tonight you will feast with God."

David took a deep breath, nodded and turned away, heading for the departure gate.

Michael watched him go. He would gladly give his life to further the Lord's cause, but he was not suicidal and had no wish to martyr himself just yet. After arriving in England, Michael had set about tracking down the girl. He had several contacts, but finding her had been harder than expected. Putting a simple trace on her credit card had tracked her to a hotel in Oxford. But she had checked out and had not used her credit or debit cards since. He had little choice but to put a watch on places she may go. This had thankfully paid off when she had turned up at her mother's old cottage yesterday. There was a slight complication due to the man accompanying her. That made an accident harder to arrange. But they were travelling to America and an air accident, especially one that was the result of a terrorist attack, was unlikely to be connected to her directly.

But Michael believed in planning for all eventualities. He knew that an individual without explosives would find it difficult to down an aircraft. So, just in case David failed, Michael would travel to America tomorrow. If need be, he would deal with the girl and her partner himself.

Grantham stretched out is six foot frame in the ample seat, Charisma sitting at his side next to the window. Whenever possible, Grantham travelled business class. First class was prohibitively expensive, economy or standard class too crowded. But business class provided extra room, more comfort and pleasanter surroundings without bankrupting him. They had already been welcomed aboard with a selection of drinks, Charisma choosing champagne, Grantham going for the fresh fruit juice and mineral water, preferring to stay well hydrated.

Charisma excused herself to make use of the toilet

before they had to be seated for takeoff. Grantham was becoming surer of Charisma, but he had one more check he wanted to do. Reaching into her bag he took her mobile phone out and connected by Bluetooth so that he could download her memory and directory, he would check them later. With a few presses of buttons he closed the connection and put the phone back in the bag.

As the Airbus A330-300 pushed back from the stand, Grantham checked his watch, one minute early. He casually glanced around the cabin at their fellow passengers, they were mostly couples, three seemed to be travelling alone. There were several businessmen, at least one woman who looked and dressed as if she owned a large company, and a couple of small family groups. No one looked out of place, although at least three looked a little nervous, which was not uncommon on aircraft.

Charisma took her seat just as the safety announcement started and Grantham gave the cabin staff the courtesy of watching them perform their duty, even though he probably knew more about the workings and exits of the aircraft than they did. One of the regular drills the SAS performed was storming an aircraft that had hostiles – tangos – aboard.

The airbus turned onto the runway and lined itself up with the distant end lights. The pilots would be making their final checks. After thirty seconds the engines wound up to full power, still remarkably quiet, another good reason for flying business class.

As the brakes released, the aircraft accelerated along the runway. Grantham checked his watch, for years he had timed the takeoff runs of the aircraft he had flown in. At thirty-nine seconds the nose lifted and the large aircraft climbed quickly and smoothly into the air.

After seven minutes the aircraft started to level out

and the seatbelt sign pinged out. Grantham stretched again but kept the seatbelt on. He knew firsthand the damage that could occur if an aircraft suddenly lost height. Several years ago he had been on a Hercules making a rapid exit from a small South African country when the pilot had to take evasive action. Two of his men who had not managed to get their belts on had been thrown about like rag dolls, both suffering broken bones. Still, hopefully this flight would not be as eventful.

For ten minutes Grantham read through the details that Windsor had sent regarding Charisma's father.

He had served eight years in the Royal Marines before transferring to the SAS in 1966. There were several missions listed in various hot spots and several redacted incidents, one lasting several months. Although there were no details, to serve that long he had to be either undercover or on a surveillance mission behind enemy lines. He had met Edie, Charisma's mother, in January 1972 while on security detachment at Boscombe Down research facility. Edie had been a peace protestor – there was a side note regarding her protest activities, a few marches and banner waving, nothing committed. They had dated for eighteen months before marrying in September 1973. He retired from the Regiment in 1974 as a captain with a full pension. Officially he became a security consultant, several large firms were listed that he advised regarding their internal and international security. He started to work freelance for MI-6 in 1975. Most of the work with MI-6 was blacked out. Grantham smiled to himself. This was reading much like he imagined his own record would. His MI-6 record stopped around the end of 1983 along with his private security services. The next entry was a problem in 1985. He was arrested and detained overnight by Mossad, Israel's security services. He was suspected on some sort of unspecified security concerns. Released the next day but escorted to the airport and onto a flight out of the country. In 1987 he was suspected and questioned, but not arrested, while leaving Egypt. He and Francois Bertrand were driving across the border when the border patrol stopped their car. Several religious items were found, but they had licences for the export and were allowed on their way. It was only later that the licences proved to be fake, but by then it was too late. In 1988, there was a break-in at a church. Bertrand and Valentine were in the town and were questioned when a witness gave descriptions of two men seen entering the church at night. A priest, the guard, was found asleep in the church, but nothing was missing and the priest had no memory of anything. Actually the odd thing was that the priest appeared to have lost several hours memory, not even remembering coming 'on duty'.

Grantham looked up from the report, there were several drugs, some in gas form that would cause someone to lose several hours of their memory. But why break in and not take anything? Grantham considered this. He had been on jobs where the idea was to get access to information but leave no trace of the break-in, record the information rather than take the documents. But what could be stored in a church in Axum, Ethiopia that would be of interest to an ex-SAS and MI-6 officer? Grantham mulled over the name, Axum. It had a slightly familiar ring. He was sure it was not a military connection. Ethiopia became well known during the famine in the early eighties. He shook his head, he could come back to that later.

The last entry recorded Valentine's death in Berlin on 9th November 1989, the night the Berlin Wall finally came down. He had been there with Bertrand. Both men were injured in an attack, Valentine passing away before receiving medical help. Bertrand surviving, but at the cost of the sight of one eye and severe blood loss. He had been hospitalised for two weeks.

Windsor had attached a note to say that the investigation would continue with the backgrounds of the other three men who were killed being looked into.

Grantham looked up and around the spacious cabin. Everyone was either reading, watching a film or using a laptop computer. There was the vague smell of food coming from the galley several rows behind their seats.

Grantham had some questions for Charisma, but for now, he did not want her knowing how much he knew about her father.

"Charisma, did your dad have any connection to Jerusalem?"

Charisma looked up from the laptop she was working on.

"Not that I know of, but he did work in Africa and the Middle East, so he may have some connection to the sacred city. Why are you asking?"

"Oh, it's just something that was in Francois Bertrand's background. He was questioned in Jerusalem by the police. If your dad worked in Africa, I assume he visited Egypt?"

"Oh yes, several times. He often brought souvenirs back for me. I still have the stone he brought me back from the foot of the Great Pyramid."

Grantham sat back and looked around the cabin. He had a prickling sensation at the back of his neck. He did not believe in the paranormal, mind reading, precognition and the like. But he did believe that the human mind would sometimes pick up bits of information subconsciously which would then manifest as a sense of unease or, in his case, raised hairs on the back of his neck. He had more questions, but he did not want to make Charisma too suspicious.

177

Five minutes later, the cabin crew started to serve lunch. A choice of chicken curry, poached salmon or stuffed mushrooms. The tray also contained cheese and biscuits, a chocolate pudding and a cup and saucer for tea or coffee. A dark red cotton napkin contained the cutlery and condiments. Grantham chose the curry, Charisma went for the poached salmon.

After a few minutes, when they had both finished their chosen main course, Grantham commented on the unusually tasty airline food, Charisma agreed.

"Does Axum in Ethiopia mean anything to you?" he asked.

Charisma snorted. "You're joking. I've been trying for years to get to St. Mary's Church in Axum."

Grantham looked blank.

"The Church of St. Mary in Axum supposedly houses the Ark of the Covenant, the chest that carries the stone tablet that held the original Ten Commandments. You know, the one in the first Indiana Jones film."

"That's where I know the name from. I saw a TV programme on it a few years ago. Don't the priests show off the chest once a year in some ceremony?" Grantham asked through a mouth full of excellent chocolate mousse.

"Well these days it's a replica. They say that the original is too old and delicate to bring out into the open. Only one priest has access to the chest. He dedicates his life to care for the Ark. He never leaves its side. He lives and sleeps with it. Food is taken to him so he has no need to leave the treasury building that's part of the church. I've applied three times to have access to the Ark, well teams I've been in have. But all requests are always met with a polite but firm refusal."

"What do you mean, they use a replica?" Grantham

had the prickling sensation on his neck again.

"Every year, the priests would parade the Ark through the village. No one could get to the Ark, it was in a case carried at shoulder height. But for years now they have used a replica for the parade. If they would allow access we could determine the age and type of timber it's made from, maybe even tell where the trees grew. Just a visual examination could answer countless questions."

"Doesn't legend say that just touching the Ark could cause death?" asked Grantham.

Charisma nodded. "The Ark holds the power of God. Scientifically speaking, it's been speculated that it's some sort of storage battery. The gold is a good conductor, the wood a good insulator. And the hot dry desert air could cause a static charge to build up."

"When did they swap the original for the replica?" Grantham added the last of his cheese to a cracker.

"Well they still have the original inside the treasury, they just don't bring it out." Charisma pursed her lips in thought. "Well, the original has not been used while I've been working in biblical history. I've seen photos from the parade in the seventies. That was the original. So I'd guess the replica started to be used in the eighties or nineties."

"Could they have started to use the replica in 1988 or '89?"

"I suppose so." Charisma shrugged. She handed her tray to Grantham. "I know how much chocolate mousse is left so don't even think about taking any." She cautioned as she opened her laptop. With a few clicks and a lot of scrolling Charisma found what she was looking for.

"The last time the actual Ark was displayed in Axum was in early 1988. The year later there was no parade. From 1990 the replica has been used."

179

Grantham considered this as he handed the tray back. Could John Valentine, ex-SAS captain and freelance MI-6 officer, and ex-French Foreign Legion officer Francois Bertrand have broken into the church in Axum and stolen the fabled Ark of the Covenant? And if so, why? For money? Power?

"It's odd you should ask about Egypt and Jerusalem as well. They are both places that have been thought of as the home of the Ark at one time or another."

Ten minutes later the trays were cleared and Grantham sat back considering the information. Charisma had gone back to her laptop. After a few minutes, Charisma tuned to Grantham.

"I've been thinking about the last story Dad left. I still think it's more a riddle than a story. You know the part that says 'In order to protect themselves and the treasure, the Knights retreated to the new land where He had walked before and took the secrets they guarded with them'? Well it got me wondering what that could mean, especially the part 'He had walked before'. You only capitalise the word 'he' if you're referring to God or Jesus or some other deity. So I think it's referring to somewhere that Jesus had already walked."

"So, what? The Middle East, Israel? Nazareth?"

"Well Nazareth didn't actually exist at that time. The title Jesus of Nazareth was probably a corruption of Jesus the Nazarene, Nazarene being a tribe rather than a place. Actually the name Jesus was a British invention. The actual name is more likely to have been Yehoshua or Yeshua. Anyway, I was thinking a bit further afield. Have you heard of the Silk Road?"

Grantham nodded, "The trade route to the Far East?"

"It was in use 1,000 years BC. It covered the route from the Mediterranean, through the Middle East, including India and Nepal to China. Well the Bible covers Jesus's birth, the visit to the temple and the money changers when he was about twelve or thirteen and His teachings and ministry when he was about thirty. But where was He as a teenager and in His twenties? There's evidence that he spent at least some time in India."

"Really? I never heard that before."

"Well it's mostly conjecture. But there is some circumstantial evidence. In the late eighteen hundreds a Russian reporter, Nicolai Notovitch, was travelling in the Kashmiri region of India."

"I like their chicken," said Grantham with a grin, for which he received a withering look.

"He had an accident and was taken to a monastery where he was cared for and given shelter. When he thanked them, they told him that as a European, they considered that he shared their religion. Nicolai was puzzled, saying that he was not a Buddhist. But the lama – no I don't mean a talking alpaca – said that the greatest of the Buddhist prophets, Issa, was the founder of the Christian religion. The lama read the story of Issa to Nicolai from two large books and Nicolai made notes. The story told how Issa was born in Israel and came to India when he was fourteen. For fifteen years he travelled widely to all parts of India, Nepal and Tibet, learning the teachings of Buddhism and gained a reputation as a prophet and healer. Later, he returned home to Israel to help fight the oppression of the Jewish people. When Nicolai returned home to Russia he turned his notes into a book, which he tried to publish. But the church leaders, especially the Vatican, opposed the publishing and he was eventually imprisoned as a danger to society and exiled to Siberia, without a trial."

"Mm, interesting. Is there any evidence?" asked Grantham.

"Others have travelled to the area and heard the same story. The monastery claims to still have the two books, but refuses to let them be tested. By appearance they look old and the writing is in a dialect that died out centuries ago. Plus, in the bible, the stories of Jesus when he is in his thirties show he is already an accomplished speaker. And many of his teachings are similar to Buddhism, all men are equal, we should live with nature and only use what we need, etcetera. He had to learn that somewhere. Plus some of the stories in Christianity and Buddhism are the same, you know the story of the old woman who gave her last two coins to the church being worth more than all the gold that the rich could give? Same story appears in both religions. If it's true that Jesus learnt his later teachings from Buddhism, and Buddhism is documented almost five hundred years before Christ, then it could be argued that Christianity is essentially an offshoot, or sect, of Buddhism."

"I bet the Pope and his Cardinals don't like that."

"You're not joking. They won't even contemplate the idea. They're afraid that it would devalue their faith and leadership."

"And their monetary worth and income."

"There's one more thing. When Christian missionaries arrived in Kashmir, as well as the nice chicken," Charisma looked pointedly at Grantham, albeit with a half smile, "they found that the locals were already familiar with much of their teachings and were using rosaries. They also found the Roza Bal, a shrine with two tombs. One is well known as the resting place of Mir Sayyid Naseeruddin, a Muslim saint. The other tomb is recorded as the resting place of Yuz Asaf which translates as Jesus of Nazareth. Mir's tomb faces north-south as is the Muslim tradition. Yuz's faces east-west as per the Jewish tradition. There is also a carving of a pair of feet, that's quite common in the tombs of saints, but these footprints show the marks of a crucifixion, and crucifixion was not know of in India."

Grantham sat for a few seconds absorbing the information. "So you're saying that the body of Jesus was taken to India and buried after he rose from the dead?"

"I'm not saying anything. I'm just reporting research and theories. But after the resurrection what happened to Jesus's body? And why was the body taken from the cross at all. The bodies of the crucified were left on the cross to rot and act as a deterrent to others. Plus crucifixion was slow and painful, as much torture as execution. Some victims would last days. If Jesus was taken down early then perhaps He didn't actually die. That would explain the resurrection and why He would have to leave the area, perhaps the country, and why He may have gone back to India where He had already spent half His life." Charisma shrugged. "It's a theory," she said.

Grantham sat back, lost in thought and drifted off to sleep, letting his mind wander. Suddenly he was awake. He did not move, but his eyes roamed around the cabin. The passengers were carrying on as before, the engines were a muted roar, nothing seemed out of place. But Grantham had a prickling sensation at the back of his neck again. And this sensation was one he had definitely experienced before. This one signified imminent danger. Something was most definitely wrong.

Chapter 17

13:00hrs, 13th April
Western Atlantic

Grantham kept his head back against the headrest and looked around. The aircraft appeared to be flying okay. The cabin crew, two of them, were going about their business. One, an attractive redhead, was heading forward to the cockpit with the pilots' meals and drinks on a tray, the other, a brunette with a touch too much make-up, was serving drinks to a couple across the far side of the cabin. They did not seem to be bothered by anything. Most of the passengers were in their seats, drinking, reading or watching the small TV screens set in the backs of the seats in front. The businesswoman was working on her laptop, two men were making notes while reading what looked like reports.

Unconsciously, Grantham's hand went to the seatbelt buckle and pulled it up. He lifted his head from the headrest and stood up, looking around. The brunette stewardess had finished serving drinks and was walking back towards the galley. The redhead was at the cockpit door. She knocked and took a step back so that the pilot could see that she was alone before they opened the doors which, since 9/11, were always kept locked. Looking back towards the rear of the aircraft, he saw everything was as he expected. Families and couples were filling almost every seat. Two children were playing in one of the aisles getting in the way of the good natured cabin crew who were just starting the rounds with the duty free. Several people were queuing for the toilets. As he noticed the small queue, the prickling on Grantham's neck intensified.

Scanning back through the business class cabin he did a quick inventory of the passengers, replaying the images from when they first came aboard. One was missing, the man with the beard who had looked nervous. He looked around, no sign of the man in the cabin. The toilet was engaged, he could be in there, nerves getting the better of him.

The cockpit door opened and the redhead stepped forward, pushing it wider as she delivered the tray of food and drinks.

Grantham was moving towards the front of the aircraft before his conscious mind caught up with his body. He was still seven steps from the cockpit door, when the toilet door burst open and the bearded man slammed his body into the cockpit door before the stewardess could close it completely.

Grantham started to run. The man was already in the cockpit, something was in his hand, a weapon? A detonator? The redhead was sprawled over the rear of the pilot's seat, with the food and drinks spread across the floor and splattered over the instruments.

The man raised his hand and slashed down, once, twice, a third time. The co-pilot had turned at the sound of the door crashing open, and was wrestling with the bearded man. Blood was flowing freely from his hand and arms and gushing from a deep wound in his neck.

Grantham reached the cockpit door as the man turned towards the pilot and the redhead. The knife was slashing down again, the man appearing frenzied as Grantham's hand shot out and intercepted his wrist, pulling it down and to the left, using the man's own movement to assist the block rather than trying to overcome his momentum.

For the first time, the man noticed Grantham and turned his attention to the new opponent. He was not big, but he was fast and agile. His hand, holding the

185

dull cream, bloodstained blade, slashed upwards towards Grantham's face. But Grantham was just as fast and had been expecting the move. He pulled back, allowing the knife to slash harmlessly inches in front of his face. Still on his back foot, Grantham again pulled his head back out of the way as the man slashed down and then up again. His movements were fast, almost frenzied, but the width and height of the small area outside of the cockpit restricted his movements.

Timing his move with the man's attack, Grantham stepped inside the man's reach, blocking his next slash with a solid stiff arm that jarred the other's arm and shoulder. In one swift movement, Grantham wrapped his left arm around the man's and lifted his lower arm up, forcing the man's arm straight and making him stand almost on tip toe to prevent his arm breaking. At the same time, Grantham lifted his right knee up to slam into the man's left side, just under the rib cage. With more room, Grantham could have reached higher to break ribs, but a winded opponent was a good start.

The man slumped slightly and gasped for breath and Grantham pulled his head back to deliver a vicious head-butt aimed for the man's nose. Delivered correctly and with force, the blow would stun the man and force blood into his eyes, temporarily blinding him.

But before he could deliver the blow, an arm wrapped around his neck and pulled Grantham back into the business class part of the cabin. For the first time, Grantham became aware of the near panic in the cabin. Many of the passengers had moved back away from the commotion, screams and near panic were starting in the economy cabin as the passengers became aware of a problem. But without details they were starting to make up their own details involving guns, explosives and hijacking.

Grantham slammed his right elbow back into his

new attacker's ribs. A satisfying snap and gasp from behind evidence that the blow had found its mark. Grantham grasped the left arm that was around his throat, his right hand gripping the thumb and bending it back, loosening the hold further, his left hand gripping the arm just above the wrist as he bent forward and to the side, pulling the man over his shoulder in an effortless judo throw.

As the man hit the floor, clearly winded and in pain, Grantham followed him down and pulled his right arm back to deliver a crushing blow to the throat. But he hesitated, the man was one of the passengers who had been sat near Grantham and Charisma, and did not have the look of a professional or a frenzied attacker. He was probably just a well meaning passenger. Grantham pulled the blow and hit the man square on the jaw, hard enough to stun, but not hard enough to do any permanent damage.

Looking up, he saw the attacker looking around the cabin, the knife held before him in an underhand grip, ready to strike. Grantham was surprised to see that the man was ignoring him, as if searching for something or someone. With a start the man almost jumped forward, heading for the seats in front of Grantham, the seat where Charisma was sitting. Grantham reacted without conscious thought. Still crouched next to the other passenger, he stretched out and brought his right leg up in a snap kick to the man's jaw, the blow staggering the attacker and forcing him to collide with, and bounce off, the opposite row of seats.

Grantham risked a quick glance around. The passengers were clearly panicked, but no one was coming to help the attacker. Looking back, he was relieved to see the man trying to get back into the cockpit, but the stewardess was putting up a gallant fight with the door. As he moved, the attacker turned on Grantham and brought the knife up to attack again.

Grantham was still crouched down and lashed out with his right leg, connecting with the man's kneecap which gave a satisfying snap. The man stumbled and Grantham, using the momentum from his kick, stepped in low past the man's guard. As he turned his back to the man, Grantham took the arm with the knife across his right shoulder and blocked its downwards strike while his left hand gripped the man's wrist, twisting the arm through ninety degrees. Using the man's top heavy momentum, Grantham executed a shoulder throw, but as the man hit the floor, instead of following him down he snapped his hand back, snapping the man's wrist and elbow. Reversing his hold, Grantham twisted the man's arm through 180 degrees and felt bone scrape against bone. To Grantham's surprise, the man gave a scream of rage rather than pain or fear. Grantham dropped down and allowed his full weight to transfer to one knee which landed into his solar plexus. The man's breath exploded out and Grantham slammed a steel like fist into his face, breaking his nose, upper pallet and several teeth.

The man went limp and Grantham pulled his hand back to deliver a fatal blow. Grantham's combat instructor's word flashed through his mind – "If you put an opponent down, finish him. A wounded man will fight with fury and fear and come back at you now or in the future." But Grantham had also been instructed in intelligence gathering and he knew that a live prisoner could be questioned and was worth more than a dead one. All this flashed through his mind in the time it took to raise his hand into a killing blow. From this position there were four obvious targets, a straight finger blow to the eye socket, ramming the fingers into the brain, a punch to the throat, crushing the larynx and windpipe, the nose was already broken so a sharp uppercut would ram the bone into the brain or he could deliver a crushing blow to the temple.

Grantham lowered his hand and stood up from the man, then bent and turned him over, removed his belt and tied his hands behind his back. Two stewards had come forward and were trying to calm the passengers. Their efforts were helped by the fact that the disturbance in the forward cabin had died down.

Grantham stood and turned back towards the cockpit, scooping up the knife as he went. He was surprised to see that the door was still slightly ajar. As he approached and pushed it inwards, he could hear the Captain on the radio.

"This is Foxtrot Three Two Seven, Heavy. I am declaring an Alpha Tango Two alert. Requesting priority approach and landing."

"Roger Two Seven. What is the nature of the emergency?"

Grantham knew that an Alpha Two alert meant that the aircraft had a potentially fatal problem that was temporarily under control. A Tango alert meant a terrorist attack.

As he entered the cabin he saw why the door was open. The pilot was running diagnostics on the instruments to ensure the aircraft was still airworthy. The stewardess was attending to the co-pilot, trying to staunch the flow of blood from his wounds. Grantham dropped the knife behind the door, out of harm's way.

"Let me," said Grantham as he approached. The pilot was still describing the incident but looked around, a trace of alarm on his face at the sound of the new voice.

"I've had first aid training," said the stewardess.

"And I've had battlefield training and dealt with worse wounds than that on several occasions."

The stewardess looked across at the pilot, who

nodded and indicated for her to stand back.

Grantham stepped up to the co-pilot and quickly assessed his wounds. His blond hair was plastered to a clammy forehead, he was pale and gently shaking. Some of that would be emotional shock, but most of it was due to physical shock that came with heavy blood loss. The stewardess had been trying to apply several pads taken from a first aid box to different parts of his body. Grantham carefully removed them and put them to one side so that he could assess the wounds. A deep cut to the bicep, bleeding freely but starting to clot. It was debilitating but not life threatening. Another slash down the front, a long cut through the crisp white shirt, but not deep. However, the third wound was potentially life threatening. The blade had gone deep into the right side of the co-pilot's neck. As Grantham looked, not only was the blood flowing freely, but he could see the regular pulse of the carotid artery and the solid mass of the clavicle bone. Another millimetre and the man would already be dead.

"I need some superglue, more pads and disinfectant. And a metal knife or spoon. Also some cable ties to secure the attacker. And someone needs to check on and secure the passenger that's unconscious out there." Grantham nodded back towards the cabin.

"I can get the stuff from the main galley," said the stewardess.

"No, you can't go out covered in blood. I'll call back and get one of the others to bring the stuff, and a change of clothes for you," said the captain. "And what happened to the other passenger?" he asked, looking at Grantham.

"Well, he sort of got in the way. I don't think he was connected to the attacker, but I'd feel better if he was restrained until we can land and hand everything over to the authorities."

The captain nodded and called to the rear, asking for the provisions and making sure someone would restrain, but care for the passenger.

"Talking about the authorities, you know they'll take you in for questioning?"

Grantham nodded. "I know. If you don't mind I'd like to make a call?" he held up his mobile phone.

The captain looked from Grantham to the phone and back. "Well, strictly speaking mobiles should be switched off, and I don't think you'll get a signal up here."

"This is a satellite phone, it'll get a signal anywhere, almost. And don't worry, it's completely shielded, it won't affect the instruments.

"Fair enough, make the call while I talk to the passengers."

The pilot adjusted the radio settings, took a deep breath and pressed the transmit button. "Ladies and gentlemen, this is the captain speaking," his voice was steady, calm and measured, almost bored. "As I'm sure you're all aware, we have had a little disturbance up here. One passenger panicked and decided he could fly the aircraft better than us. Thanks to another passenger he has been subdued and is now restrained. There is no damage to the aircraft and we will be landing in about forty minutes. Please remain in your seats so that the crew can get some order back. Thank you."

Grantham looked at the captain, he estimated he was in his mid-fifties, a thick mass of silver grey hair and dark blue eyes gave him the appearance of a competent and solid person. Exactly what every passenger wanted to see in a pilot.

"Do pilots practise the almost bored tone of voice?" asked Grantham with a smile.

"Some of us do, it reassures the passengers. You should hear my stifled yawn when things get really hairy," the captain replied with a grin. "I'd like to know how he got that knife on board." He nodded to the floor where Grantham had dropped the weapon.

Grantham had packed the bloody pads into the co-pilot's neck but blood was still seeping out between his fingers and the younger pilot had stopped moaning at the pain, that was not a good sign.

"The knife's ceramic. Harder than steel, sharper and keeps an edge better. The manufacturers put steel fibres into them so that they set off metal detectors, but if you know the right people, or wrong people depending on your point of view, you can get virgin ceramics without the steel fibres."

"You seem to know a lot about it. Is that the military training?"

Before Grantham could reply, the satellite phone cheeped to indicate it had locked onto a signal and he put it to his ear. The voice on the other end already knew who was calling and pleasantries were not required. Grantham quickly explained the situation before disconnecting.

"Is that someone who can vouch for you with the authorities?" asked the captain.

"Something like that."

"Well for what it's worth I'll vouch for you as best I can. But I wouldn't make any plans for tonight."

There was a knock on the cabin door and the captain checked the small screen before unlocking it.

A male steward came in carrying a small holdall. He closed the door and opened the bag. The cabin was getting crowded with three standing people, but Grantham reached in and took out what he needed before handing the bag to the stewardess.

After taking in the scene and asking a few questions, the steward made his way out of the cabin.

"I'll change into these then," the stewardess looked

around the cockpit at the pilot and Grantham, a little unsure.

"Don't worry, Cheryl, we won't look. You go ahead. And there are some disinfectant wipes in the locker up there. They aren't as good as a shower, but they'll get the blood off."

Grantham held up the spoon the steward had brought and dipped the handle in the disinfectant and then took a lighter from his pocket. Making a couple of quick adjustments, he flicked the lighter open and applied the small, fierce blue flame that looked more like a mini acetylene torch than a cigarette lighter to the tip of the spoon handle.

"That doesn't look like a normal lighter," said the captain.

Grantham ignored the remark and took the now soaking pads from the neck wound.

"This is going to hurt," said Grantham. He touched the tip of the now hot spoon handle to several spots inside the wound. The co-pilot moaned and fresh beads of sweat broke out on his waxen looking face. Grantham dabbed at the wound with a fresh pad. He heated the handle again and applied it to another couple of spots before cleaning the wound again. The blood was still seeping from the walls of the wound, but the heavy bleeding had stopped. He poured a little disinfectant into the wound which brought a new groan from the young man before he used a fresh pad to mop up the liquid and blood.

Grantham applied a thin film of superglue to one edge of the deep cut and held the sides together for a few seconds, before repeating the process and slowly closing the wound. He then wiped the wound with the antiseptic and fastened a pad on top.

"I think he'll be okay. Get him to hospital and they can get some fluids into him. By tomorrow he'll be back to normal, well on the way."

"Thanks for all you've done. I'll see that the airline knows what you did as well as the authorities."

After cleaning himself up, Grantham exited the cockpit and felt every eye on him. At first several of the looks were clearly fear or suspicion, but these quickly changed to respect and thanks. Most of the passengers in business class had seen what happened and realised that Grantham was one of the good guys.

As he sat down next to Charisma she leant over and kissed him on the cheek. "My hero. It seems as if you are always there when needed, a true white knight."

Grantham smiled to hide the slight blush. Taking down a target was nothing new, doing it publically and getting thanks was.

"We'll be landing in about thirty minutes. When we do, the police will come in hard and fast. They'll take the attacker off and then allow the medical team into the cockpit," at the look on Charisma's face Grantham lowered his voice. "The co-pilot was injured. He's been patched up and should be okay, but he needs to get to hospital. Anyway, everyone will be taken in for questioning. Most will be out in a couple of hours. They'll probably keep me overnight, ensure they know who I am and check out my story. As you're travelling with me they'll do the same to you. Although you'll probably be out a lot quicker than I am."

"They should be giving you a medal, not questioning you."

"Look at it from their point of view. There was an attack on the aircraft. The attacker got into the cockpit and injured the co-pilot. It could have been an attempt at a hijack, or an attempt to bring us down. It could even have been a panicked passenger who just lost control."

"You don't believe that."

"He was too organised to be acting out of panic, although he was quite frenzied. And the knife…"

"What about the knife?"

"I don't want to tell you too much. When the police question you, be as honest with them as you can. We met a few days ago, I was coming to America on business and asked you to come along. Tell them what you know about me. Be honest about yourself, but don't tell them about your suspicion that you're in danger. That could make you look paranoid, or worse."

"What do I do once I get out?"

"Get a taxi, cab as the Americans call them, and go to the American Grand Plaza hotel and book us a room. Unfortunately you'll have to use your own credit card, but we can move once I get there."

"You seem to know the area, have you been to the hotel before?"

"I've done some work in Boston a few years back."

"Security work?"

Grantham looked evenly at Charisma without saying anything.

"Okay, I get it, best I don't know."

"You catch on quick."

There was the customary ping and the chief steward's voice came over the PA, confirming that the seat belt signs had been illuminated and that they would be landing in a few minutes.

The descent was smooth and direct. As they approached the airport, Grantham noticed out of the window that there were several police cars along the perimeter. Although they were too far away to see details, Grantham suspected that at least one of the vans was a SWAT unit. He did a quick calculation, at least three snipers would be on high ground, ten ground troops would surround the aircraft, probably with armoured vehicle back up. As they came over the threshold, they would be followed along the runway by chase cars and, once they had slowed, they would be led to a secure area of the airport, an area deliberately set aside for potential hostage situations. As soon as the aircraft stopped, the vehicles would park in front and behind the wheels to stop it moving. Stairs would be wheeled up to the aircraft and police would storm it with guns at the ready.

Grantham sighed, things were about to get interesting.

Chapter 18

09:20hrs, 14th April
Leicester University

Richard Caley opened the lab door and entered the room. As usual he was the first to arrive. There were no planned teaching sessions until this afternoon, and anything before 10:00am was mostly too early for students. Caley walked across the lab, favouring his right leg, keeping the weight off the ankle as much as he could.

The week skiing had been brilliant. The snow, the last of the season, had been deep and crisp due to a late freeze and fresh falls on the first three nights. He had even picked up a snow tan, well, a snow pink glow which with his light blond hair and blue eyes was about as best as he could do in the tanning department. On the final night all eight of the group had gone to a local concert. Deciding to make the most of the last night, they had walked the two miles back to the chalet, a walk that had developed into the snowball fight to end all snowball fights. As they got to the chalet, he had run up the steps, slipped on the second and fallen to the snow, where the rest of the group had bombarded him with snowballs. But, apart from a dent in his pride, he had come off unharmed. However, the next day, as they entered the airport, he had tripped over his own feet and twisted his ankle, much to the amusement of the rest of the group.

With a small degree of relief, he sat down at the computer terminal and placed his foot on an upturned waste bin while the computer booted up.

After logging onto the computer, then the network

and finally the internet, he started the download of the data his model should have collected while he was away. While waiting, he considered yet again changing his password. When he joined the university, the IT department insisted that he select a password that had at least eight characters. As a joke, he had selected 'SnowWhiteAndThe7Dwarfs'. The IT department, appreciating the humour had allowed it and it had been the same for over three years.

While he was waiting for the download, his mind started to drift to Jess. He had spoken to her every day while he was away, but it was ten days since he had seen her and he was looking forward to this afternoon.

There was a beep from the computer that pulled him out of his reverie. Caley scanned through the database and the links. Everything looked as if it had downloaded okay. All of the cells were populated and the links live. The model was ready to run. Selecting the appropriate programme, he hit 'download' and sat back, watching the egg timer symbol and the blue bar slowly creep across the screen – 12 minutes remaining.

Caley stood and hobbled over to the rear of the lab, into the office and the small fridge that held bottles of water and soft drinks that were reserved for staff and fourth years only, and woe betide any pre-fourth years that dared to help themselves.

While he was in the office, Caley logged onto another computer and checked his e-mails. There were several messages from fellow students, including another two offers for him to play drums in another new group. He deleted the junk mail and checked out a couple of geology websites before sending some short replies. Checking the clock, he saw that the download should be almost complete. He logged off, picked up his bottle of cola and limped back to the main lab.

The download was just completing as he sat down.

With a few key strokes he selected the 2D graphics mode and set the simulation running.

A map overlay appeared on the screen showing the north west Pacific. As he watched, the time clicked forward, one day every five seconds, the subterranean earthquake starting to show signs of life. He sat and watched for several minutes as the sea floor rose and the waves spread out. He paused the simulation and made a note of several data points. He minimised the simulation and called up a list of actual data. His simulation had used actual data up to the start of the quake and had then run the simulation based on his own algorithms. He wanted to see how close his predictions were to the real outcome.

Five minutes later, he had a smile on his face. The predictions were not perfect, he did not expect them to be on the first run, but they were closer than he could have dared hope.

Okay, now to run the simulation backwards. If the programme worked as he hoped, he could be on the verge of having a programme that could predict earthquakes far earlier than ever before.

He watched the simulation scroll back to the start and then head back in time. The waves rolled back from the land, across the ocean and centred to the east of the Japanese main island.

Caley switched modes so that the changing data was displayed visually on top of the photographic image. A roughly circular edge of vibrations appeared out at sea, as the time ticked back, the circle gradually contracted towards the epicentre. Across the bottom of the screen, a separate display showed the readings for the relative subsurface S and P Waves and the shallower Love and Rayleigh Waves.

The secondary, or S Waves, only transmittable in solid substances, were not present in the ocean waters surrounding the island, but the waves were deep under the seabed and showed a gradually varying amplitude and wavelength as the time ticked back. The primary, or P Waves, followed the same pattern as the S Wave, but recorded compression and dilation rather than vertical and horizontal displacement.

The Love Wave followed a pattern similar to the S wave but displaced the ground only in horizontal planes at right angles to the direction of travel. The Rayleigh Wave also displaced the ground, similar to waves in the sea, the ground rippled vertically up and down. It is the Love and Rayleigh Waves that cause damage to buildings and structures.

Caley paused the simulation and checked the readouts. There was something wrong. The epicentre was well known, not only had it been detected with instruments, but submersibles had been down for visual confirmation. But the simulation was showing something different. Not only was the centre off by well over fifty miles, but it was showing low power S and P Waves radiating from a fixed point. Most earthquakes had a fixed centre, the epicentre, but the waves generally propagated over a long split or convergence zone. And the simulation was showing other frequencies gradually dropping in intensity for several days before the earthquake struck. They were little more than background noise. But these were at frequencies that had nothing to do with earthquakes, and they certainly could not be natural.

Caley sighed and sat back, if he could not get the simulation correct with a known incident, what chance was there for it to work as a prediction tool? He sat forward and closed the simulation. Opening the database and links on one screen and the programme parameters on the other he started the laborious task of debugging the system. It was going to be a long day.

Grantham looked up as the cell door opened and Detective first class Yeman looked in.

"Okay, Grantham. You're free to go."

Grantham stood from the low, hard bench bed in one fluid motion and walked towards the door where Yeman stood back and allowed him to exit the cell and walk ahead of him along the corridor.

The night had gone as Grantham had expected. Once the aircraft came to a halt, armed police had quickly entered the cabins. It was not quite an assault, but it was not far off. While ten officers kept watch on the seated passengers, three others almost carried the suspect from the aircraft, closely followed by two each with Grantham and the passenger who had gotten involved.

The trip to the police station had been fast and accompanied by the sound of sirens and blue lights. As soon as they arrived at the station, Grantham had been almost thrown into a cell and the door slammed shut. He smiled and lay down on the hard bed. It was a classic interrogation technique. Put the prisoner in solitary where he can worry about what was going to happen. But two hours was barely long enough for Grantham to settle in and get a catnap.

After two hours he was escorted, roughly, to the interrogation room where the lights were bright with no outside windows. Over the next four hours all of the standard techniques were used. Good cop, bad cop, threats of imprisonment and persuasion with being let off and treated as a hero. Offers of food and drink, publicity and fame or continued interrogation. Questions were repeated in subtly different ways to trip him up, questions would follow a track and suddenly

201

change course. One officer would sit back and take notes, saying nothing for long periods before suddenly coming up with a question designed to shock. Quiet pauses designed to make Grantham fill in the spaces with explanations. After a short break, during which Grantham watched the officers drink coffee and eat sandwiches, another officer came in and handed a thin folder to the two interrogators. After glancing through the folder, Yeman started asking Grantham about his military career. So far Grantham had been open and honest, to a point, but they had concentrated on the incident on the aircraft, only briefly covering his background. But with the folder they would have a better idea of his history, at least a sanitised version of it.

For another hour they had tried to get details from Grantham, but he had stuck to the basics, when he had joined the forces, basic military career, and no mention of the SAS or his work for the security services since his retirement. But there were gaps in the records and the two detectives were clearly suspicious.

Grantham had gone along with the questioning, answering calmly and in as much detail as he could. Never losing his temper, showing annoyance or fear and most definitely never showing amusement, even though the interrogation techniques were predictable and good by police standards, but amateur compared to those he had been trained to withstand. Finally they had taken him back to the cell and slammed the door, leaving him alone for the rest of the night.

"You have friends in high places, who know people over here who can command our chief."

Grantham did not respond to the comment, he assumed someone from JTAC had finally made a call to vouch for him.

"Do you want to tell us who you really are? British

intelligence? Military intelligence? MI-5? MI-6?"

"Nothing so exciting. As I said, I'm a private security consultant."

Yeman opened the door leading from the cells and led Grantham to the custody sergeant's desk. While Grantham was inspecting and signing for his belongings, including his luggage which had been collected and searched, Yeman stood to one side, weighing Grantham up.

"You know, I have a cousin in the SEALS. You remind me of him. Nothing fazes you, you're polite and easy going, almost laid back even when being questioned. But there's a sense of danger underneath. I got the feeling that our interrogation had no effect on you, as if, like my cousin, you had been trained to withstand interrogation techniques that we couldn't even think of."

"Your cousin sounds like a good guy. But like I say, I'm just a private consultant, nothing as glamorous as a SEAL."

"Sure. Okay, you're out of here. You've got your passport back, but I'd prefer if you let us know if you leave the area."

"Will do, detective. I don't suppose you could give me a lift could you?"

"Don't push your luck, Grantham," said Yeman, although there was a trace of a smile.

Grantham turned towards the exit, but paused and turned back. "Detective Yeman, do you know how the pilot's doing?"

Yeman looked at Grantham as if still trying to weigh him up. "He's doing okay. He was given blood and the wound was cleaned. With luck, he'll be flying again in a couple of months. The doctor said that you saved his life. If you hadn't sealed the wound like you did he wouldn't have made it to the landing.

Apparently they were very impressed."

Grantham shrugged, "Everyone in the Paras learnt basic first aid, you never know when your mate's life may depend on it. I'm glad I could help."

"Well you did a good thing."

"Careful Detective, that was almost a compliment." Grantham held up his hands. "I know, I'm going."

"I'm surprised you haven't asked about the attacker," said Yeman.

Grantham shrugged. "You won't have got anything out of him yet. The doctors will have been treating him overnight, probably won't let you speak to him until this morning. But when you do speak to him, I doubt you'll get much. He struck me as a fanatic, not a terrorist with a cause who wants publicity."

"So now you're a psychologist as well?"

"I've seen that wild look before. He's some sort of zealot. If you challenge his views, lay down the law, attack his beliefs in any way, whatever they are, he'll just treat you as an infidel. He'll treat you as beneath him, not worthy of an explanation."

Yeman looked sideways at Grantham for a second. "What, so I should sympathise with him? Go along with his cause?"

"That's difficult until you know what his cause is. But it's worth a try. Show you're curious, a seeker of knowledge. He may even treat you as a novice and start to explain things. Do you have any idea who he is?"

"We've run his prints and got nothing, from here or Europe. The only identification is a tattoo he's got on his chest." The detective opened the thin folder he was holding and took out an A5 size photograph and passed it to Grantham.

"Best guess is some sort of religious crest," said Yeman.

The photograph showed a shield in front of a cross.

On the shield were crossed swords. Beams of light radiated from the points of the cross.

"Can't say I've seen it before, but I agree, it looks religious."

Yeman sighed and shook his head. "I can't read you Grantham, and I don't like that. But what you say about how to get through to him may have some merit."

Once on the street, Grantham called a cab and headed for the airport where he collected a hire car and drove back into Boston and the American Grand Plaza hotel. He had stayed here a few years ago and remembered the layout. The hotel had an underground car park which was manned and only useable by guests and staff. As he turned in, the attendant stepped out and asked his name. Grantham explained that his partner had already checked in, but he had arrived late. The attendant checked Charisma's details and gave Grantham a pass for the car park before raising the barrier.

Ten minutes later, Grantham knocked on the room door. It was 8:20am. He was not sure if Charisma would be up after the flight and questioning.

The door opened and Charisma stood there wrapped in a red silk kimono decorated with black and gold dragons, her wet hair shimmering in a halo backlit by the light from the room. She wore no make-up, but her complexion was flawless and clear. She had obviously just stepped from a hot shower as evidenced by the gentle pink flush to her cheeks and the kimono clinging to her obvious curves. Grantham could not fail to be taken aback by her beauty.

"Room service, madam?" asked Grantham with a smile.

Charisma smiled and reached up on tiptoe to kiss him firmly on the lips before wrapping her arms around him in a short hug. As she unfolded from him, she stood back to let him into the room.

"Do you always welcome room service like that?"

"The police said they were charging you with terrorism and that the next time I saw you, you'd be in court being sentenced to life."

"They said that to make you talk, to scare you."

"It worked. So what happened?" she asked.

"Let me order some breakfast and I'll tell you."

Grantham ordered a full breakfast with toast, coffee and a large jug of freshly squeezed orange juice, all to be delivered in thirty minutes. He then quickly told her what had happened, leaving out the fact that someone had vouched for him and hastened his release.

"Have you any idea what it was all about? Did the police tell you anything about the attacker, what he was after?"

"They don't really know anything about him." Grantham said with a slight hesitation.

"But you know something."

"Well, I don't know, but when he came into the cabin…well he seemed prepared to attack you."

"Why do you think he wanted to get to me specifically? I could just have been there, just a coincidence."

Grantham shrugged. "I don't like coincidences."

Charisma was taken aback. The thought that someone wanted to kill her was bad enough, but that they were willing to take down an aircraft full of people, that was unthinkable.

"I know that I asked you to help me because I thought someone was after me, or following me, or something. But to be faced with it as a fact…"

"Well, I am your Lancelot." Grantham gave her is most gallant smile in an attempt to lighten Charisma's mood.

"And I am so pleased to have found you."

Grantham stood and stretched, he was practised in going long periods without sleep, and in truth the night had not been that tiring. But he felt grubby and sweaty.

"I'll get a quick shower before the room service gets here."

Charisma stood and came to Grantham before he could get to the bathroom.

"I mean it. I really appreciate what you did. Taking on a crazed attacker like that..." She reached up and kissed him again. Longer this time. Grantham could not fail to notice the feel of her body through the robe, pressing against his own.

"Do you want company in the shower?" she asked.

Grantham smiled. "If I realised that was the reward, I'd have arranged a life or death struggle on an airliner over the Atlantic sooner." He smiled as he took her hand and headed for the bathroom.

Chapter 19

23:40hrs, 14th April
Basilica of the Holy Blood
Bruges, Belgium

Tucked away to one side of the old Bruges city square, the Basiliek van het Heilig Bloed, the Basilica of the Holy Blood, housed one of the most revered, yet least known, holy relics. Legend has it that after the crucifixion, Joseph of Arimathea wiped blood from the body of Christ and preserved the cloth. The relic remained in the Holy Land until the Second Crusade, when Baldwin III, the King of Jerusalem, gave it to his brother-in-law, Count of Flanders, Diederik van de Elzas. When he arrived in Bruges in 1150 the Count placed it in a chapel he had built on Burg Square.

Historically, the first records to mention the Holy Blood in Bruges dates from 1256. The real story seems to be that it came from Constantinople, which was known to have had an extensive collection of relics including the Holy Blood.

Constantinople was sacked by the Crusader army of Count of Flanders Baldwin IX in 1204, during the Fourth Crusade. Baldwin IX probably sent the Holy Blood to Bruges shortly thereafter. The cloth is housed in a crystal vial, sealed inside a glass tube with golden crowns at each end. Studies have shown that the crystal vial bears many similarities to crystal originating in the Constantinople area.

Snugly located in a back corner of Burg Square, the Basilica of the Holy Blood consists of a Romanesque lower chapel and a Gothic upper chapel. The surrounding buildings are at odds with the ancient architecture, which seems to make the Basilica shrink into the background as if trying to hide its early origins.

The three men walked across the square, just three men coming toward the end of a night out in the old city, three men in a small crowd of twenty of so walking between pubs or back to their hotels.

As they approached the Basilica the three men headed down an adjoining alley, narrow enough to force them into single file. The last man paused in the shadows a few feet into the alley and checked behind. No one was paying them any attention. The few people about in the square were going about their own business. He turned back to the inky blackness of the alley and joined the other two as they rounded the rear of the church.

The rear was only lit by the reflective illumination from the street lights and the soft white glow from the half moon. The first man approached the rear door, an old solid oak construction reinforced with iron bands.

The security here was nothing compared to the last job the men had done together at the Notre-Dame, Paris. Rather than advanced security systems and a small army of guards, the Basilica relied on stout doors and heavy duty locks. There was an alarm system, but it had been installed twenty years ago and should pose few problems.

"Five minutes," said one of the men, checking his watch.

The men pressed grey putty into the lock and metal bands where the hidden hinges would be. Inserting the small detonators, the men stood back and took cover around the corner.

"Two minutes."

The men stood quietly, waiting patiently.

"Thirty seconds, check the square?"

One of the men jogged back along the alley and

again stood in the shadows, looking out at the square. After a few seconds he turned back and flashed a mini spotlight.

A few seconds later, the town square clock started its wind up to the hour. The men waited as the first chime rang out, then the second and the third. As the fourth chime sounded and reverberated around the square, echoing off the surrounding buildings, the man holding the detonator turned the top and sent a small electrical charge to the detonator. The explosion was a muffled thud that seemed to be contained in the small courtyard behind the Basilica. The man standing along the alley checked the square and turned back, blinking his torch twice to indicate that all was well.

Again on the sixth and eighth chimes the muffled explosions rang out. The men waited until the full twelve chimes ended and the echoes died away, leaving a silence that was almost touchable. The men walked back around the corner to see the door still in place but bearing three distinct holes. One of them reached in and felt along the door frame until he found the magnetic contacts. With practised ease, he connected a small, but strong magnet to the contacts and quickly checked the rest of the frame before standing back.

The other two men placed short crowbars against the door and pried it slowly inwards. As soon as the gap was large enough, the men eased through and clicked on their head lights. The front man, who appeared to be in charge, held up his right hand and stepped forward, shaking an aerosol can. As he sprayed the contents into the air, the droplets drifted down highlighting the previously invisible laser beams that criss-crossed the hall.

"They've upgraded the system," said the leader with a smile.

"Not enough," replied one of the others.

The electronic trip wires were easy to avoid once they could be seen. Two minutes later they were in the main Romanesque chapel, the Chapel of St Basil. Built in the 12th Century by the Count of Alsace, it was dedicated to St Basil the Great to house the holy blood relic.

Their lights barely reflected from the bare stone floor and walls. All the time checking for more laser trip wires, they methodically made their way to the front of the church. As they reached the choir stalls, the three men turned left into the smaller Chapel of Saint Yves.

After a thorough check of the entrance, one of the men went across to a small wall cabinet. The lock took less than twenty seconds to pick. The door opened to reveal the alarm control box. This took a little longer, but after less than four minutes he turned and nodded, the alarm was off.

The smaller chapel was more ornate and colourful than the Chapel of St Basil. They quickly made their way across the chapel to the side and looked up at the large dais that held the holy relic. The altar's white marble seemed to glow under their lights.

The leader reached out and carefully checked around the container that housed the relic, checking for traps and trip wires. He found nothing to give him concern and turned his attention to the apparently old lock. After a few seconds of exploratory probing, it became evident that, whilst the case may be ancient marble, the lock was state of the art. The leader stood back and indicated for one of the other men to take his place.

"When the going gets tough, management hand over to the grunts," said the man with a grin.

It took almost ten minutes and several different tools before the lock clicked open. The man stood back and let the leader step up.

"Time for management to take the credit…as usual," he said.

After a few seconds, the leader slowly lifted the lid just high enough to see under the lip. With no sign of anything, he lifted it up and off revealing the crystal and gold tube holding the cloth with the brown stain. He lifted this out and placed it on the cloth-covered flat surface to the front of the dais and stepped back indicating for the third man to step up.

As he stepped back, the leader checked his watch, 00:21. "Nine minutes to the guard's rounds," he said quietly.

The man at the front had already removed what looked like a cross between a sci-fi laser gun and a supermarket barcode scanner from his bag and proceeded to point it at the ornate container. The machine beeped and the man looked at a display on the rear before resetting it and trying again. After three more tries he stepped back and looked at the other two men.

"It's not human blood."

"Is it close?" asked the leader.

"Only if He was closely related to a pig."

"Mmm…question is, was the church duped or are they being very cunning?"

The leader checked his watch, 00:24, and stepped up to the reliquary. "Set up for the guard," he said. He then looked more closely at the box that had held the relic, tapping the sides and bottom. Twisting and turning anything that he could get a grip on.

"Guard!" said one of the men from the entrance.

"Switch the alarms back on and take cover." The leader pocketed the fake relic and put the lid back down on the box before stepping around the large dais and crouching down behind, a silenced matt black pistol in his hand.

Once the men switched off their lights, the small chapel was plunged into darkness. The only light entering the room was through the two stained glass windows.

After a few seconds footsteps could be heard at the far end of the main chapel. There was a pause while the guard automatically accessed the alarm system and disabled several sectors so that he could walk his rounds.

The flashlight swept around the chapel, pausing on the large reliquary and then again on the marble balustrades of the front altar. From his position at the side of the dais, the leader could see that the light was resting on the black clothing of one of the men that was lying on the raised floor of the altar, behind the low balustrade. He raised the pistol and prepared to stand and take aim, but as his legs tensed the light moved on. The guard walked back into the main chapel, whistling a tuneless melody. Five minutes later the men heard the main doors close and the keys turn in the lock.

"Get the alarms," said the leader. He stood and turned back to the reliquary, his lips pursed in concentration.

The marble box that held the relic was part of the large altar. The leader reached out and pushed and pulled the box. It did not move. He put his hands on the sides and lifted upwards. With effort the box came free. He lifted it and placed it to one side. Under the box, recessed twenty millimetres into the marble top, was a dull brass ring that looked as if it had not seen the light of day for many years. Carefully he lifted the ring. With a click a panel on the front of the reliquary sprang open. He bent down and peered in. A wooden box was nestled in the small opening. With care he removed the box and placed it on the marble top and lifted the lid. A six inch long glass vial sat on a dark blue velvet lining. He lifted the vial from the box and handed it to one of the other men.

Two minutes later the man nodded. "Human, well almost."

"How almost?"

"Ninety-seven point three. The other two point seven is unknown. Probably just corrupt over time."

"Maybe, but the sample we recovered from Notre-Dame gave the same reading. Okay, clear up, let's move out."

18:00hrs
Western Massachusetts

After a very memorable shower and breakfast, Grantham and Charisma had slept for several hours before ordering a late lunch from room service. Checking out at three o'clock, they had loaded the bags into the car and headed west for a meeting with Sheriff D. B. McClure.

Charisma had called the sheriff while they waited for room service to deliver lunch and had arranged the meeting to discuss the apparent car accident that had killed Robert P Jacobs in March. It was not the first time Charisma had been in touch with the sheriff, so it was with only a little reluctance that he had agreed to see the pair.

The sheriff had given them the grid reference so they could meet at the location of the accident. The road was wide and ran through a forested area.

"That's it, we're at the grid reference," said Charisma watching the sat nav.

Grantham pulled to the side and off the road, there had been one accident here, no point in tempting fate. As he pulled off the road his caution was shown to be justified as a cherry red American Dodge saloon, a V8 by the sound of the roar from the exhaust, sped around the bend and disappeared into the distance.

"So, while we wait, have you turned anything else up about the so-called accidents?" asked Grantham. Charisma had been researching the accidents as best she could by using the official reports and what other pieces of information she could pick up.

"Well, I have found something, but I'm not sure what it means. Do you ski?"

Grantham smiled. As a member of the SAS he had spent months training in all climates, including the Arctic. He had even taken part in three biathlons; cross-country skiing and shooting.

"I've done some skiing. What have you found?"

"Well Francois Bertrand died when he had a skiing accident. He fell four hundred feet from the ski run. But when I read the report, the skis and ski poles were found at the top of the cliff where he fell from."

Grantham pulled his eyebrows together as he tried to imagine the accident. After several second he said, "How were they found, spread out or all in one place?"

"The report said the skis were together with the poles sticking in the ground."

"Do you have any photos?"

"No, the police wouldn't send the full report. They only agreed to send a description of the accident when I insisted I was a close family friend and that he didn't have any close family."

"In a skiing accident the skis are designed to come off so they don't twist the legs and body as the skier falls. The poles may stay with the skier if they have them on wrist straps, although most skiers won't use them for the same reason the skis break away. So I'd expect the skis and poles to either go over the cliff as well or be left behind but spread out over a pretty big area, definitely not to stop side by side with the poles a few feet away. That sounds more like Bertrand stopped and removed his skis and put the poles down."

"That's what I thought. Looks like the sheriff's here." Charisma nodded to the front where a white and blue police cruiser was pulling up in front of them.

The sheriff was a short thin man, completely bald with a ruddy red complexion and glasses. He was not what came to mind when you thought of an American sheriff.

Grantham and Charisma stepped from the car and, after brief introductions and handshakes, Sheriff Daniel Baldwin McClure talked them through the events of the accident as best as could be determined.

"So, there was nothing suspicious?" asked Grantham.

"Officially it was a clean hit and run. We ran through all the procedures," McClure shrugged. "Nothing more we could do."

"You said officially. What about unofficially," asked Charisma.

"I spent the first twenty years of my career in Chicago. Five years as a beat cop, five in homicide and ten in organized crime. As a force we got some excellent results. But no matter how well we did, how big the busts were, there was always a queue of criminals ready to take the place of the ones we got off the street. That's why I moved here, somewhere I thought that I could make a difference. Anyway, I saw injuries like Mr Jacobs had several times when I was a beat cop. Hit and run accidents, injuries to the legs, thorax and head. But when I was in major crimes I saw a variation of the injuries." The sheriff paused, looking off along the road as if watching the accident in his mind's eye.

"There were scuff marks on the tops of his shoes

and his knees. In my opinion he was dragged for a short distance before being run over."

"And that couldn't have happened in a simple accident?" asked Charisma.

Sheriff McClure shrugged. "Anything's possible. But I've seen those signs before when I was in organised crime, when someone has been pulled around by a car to torture them. Of course, the injuries and scuff marks to your friend were smaller and less serious, I don't think he was tortured, but they were the same marks."

"Did you investigate the crime?"

The sheriff looked at Grantham as if weighing up the comment to see if it was a criticism or a simple question. He seemed to decide it was just a question.

"I did what I could. Asked around for background, questioned as many locals as I could. I got in touch with as many body shops as I could find, there had to be damage to the car, there were traces of paint and glass found on the body. But nothing turned up. I even got in touch with the State Police and asked them for help in tracing the hit and run car..." he shrugged again.

"You didn't find anything useful?"

"Well, if the body had been found with gunshot wounds or a knife sticking out of it, there would have been a five man forensics team, a ten man detective squad, at least half of which would be seasoned officers. There would be TV and radio appeals and almost unlimited uniformed officers to help with the groundwork. But with a hit and run... It was lucky it was me and one deputy taking an interest."

"The moral being, if you want to commit murder, do it with a car and not a gun or knife."

"You got it, Mr Grantham."

"Well thank you for your time Sheriff," said

Charisma.

"Thanks Sheriff." Grantham held out his hand and the two men exchanged firm handshakes.

"Sorry I can't be of more help. But I'm sure it was not a simple accident. If you turn anything up, let me know."

Ten minutes later Grantham and Charisma were back in the car and heading towards a local town they had passed erlier to find a hotel for the night.

"What do you think?" asked Charisma.

"The sheriff seems to know his job. If he's suspicious then I'd say he has good reason. But I'm not sure what we can do. If he couldn't turn up anything, I don't see that we will. And it was interesting what he said about committing murder with a car. It's not exactly an assassin's normal weapon of choice, but it is effective."

"So you think we're looking for a man who killed all three of Dad's friends?"

"I don't know if it's one person, man or woman, or a group. But I agree that all three deaths are more than suspicious."

"Man or woman? Surely you don't think a woman could have done any of this?"

Grantham glanced across at Charisma with a half smile. "You know the old saying, the female if more deadly than the male. You know the old joke about the CIA assassins?"

Charisma shook her head.

"The CIA needed some new assassins, so they advertised amongst the police, army etc and got dozens of applicants. After several weeks of testing they'd narrowed the candidates down to three, two men and a woman. One at a time they took them into a room and told them they had one more test. Pass this test and they were hired. So the first man came up and they gave him a gun and told him to go into the next room and kill the person inside. He goes in and everything is quiet for five minutes and then he comes out and hands the gun back. 'I couldn't do it' he said 'it's my wife and we've been together for ten years'. He goes out and the next man comes in. Same procedure, he takes the gun and goes into the room. Ten minutes later he comes out in tears. 'It was my wife, she's given me two lovely daughters and I love her, sorry I can't do it'. He hands the gun back and goes out. In comes the last candidate, the woman. She takes the gun and goes through the door. There's a pause of a few seconds and then a shot rings out, followed by two others. Then there's some screaming and shouting, lots of banging and finally it goes quiet. A few seconds later the door opens and the woman comes back out looking a little dishevelled. 'It was my husband' she says. 'And you bastards gave me a gun with blanks in. I had to break up the chair and beat him to death with the broken leg.' Like I say, the female if more deadly than the male."

Chapter 20

08:00hrs, 15th April
Grüssmire Gewerbe HQ

The chrome and glass conference room was cool despite the temperature outside already climbing into the high eighties. The lighting along the rear wall was turned to a cool blue fading to green to complement the air conditioning. The full glass wall looked out over the open ground and the forest beyond, the sun was rising behind the trees allowing those in the room to look at the burning orb through the branches without injury.

Eigel looked at his watch for the third time in as many minutes before glancing around the high gloss mahogany conference table. He was not used to being kept waiting. The meeting was a regular weekly update and this morning Michael Spielmann was late.

"Maybe we should start. I'll bring Michael up to date later," said Adler, his eyes their usual dead black, but with perhaps the smallest of glints at the thought of bringing the younger man 'up to date' and no doubt pointing out the error of his ways.

Eigel opened his mouth to speak as the intercom buzzed. He took three long strides over to the table and depressed the button. "Yes?" he said.

"Sir, Mr Spielmann has just passed the outer gatehouse." The voice was the crisp female voice of Eigel's secretary.

Eigel glanced at his watch. The outer gatehouse was two miles from the front of the building along a wide sweeping drive that wound its way through the dense woodland. No doubt Spielmann would be riding his ridiculous motorcycle. The one he was always eager to point out was the 'fastest production bike in the world', a hangover from his days in America where the bigger, the faster, the more powerful the better.

Eigel saw the dark blue motorcycle break the cover of the trees, already braking for the turn into the underground car park. Eigel glanced at his watch, around fifty seconds to cover the two miles from the gatehouse, a ridiculous speed.

"Let us start, Spielmann can catch up later."

Eigel looked around the table. The other men nodded and started to update Eigel on their research. A few minutes later the double glass doors slid noiselessly open and Spielmann walked in, a little breathless. The voices quickly died down as all eyes turned to the younger man, still dressed in his gaudy red, green and white one piece leathers.

"Sorry I'm late," Spielmann glanced around the room at each man, quickly looking away from the dead stare of Adler.

"Even though you have often told us how fast your motorcycle is, you still manage to arrive late. I trust you have a good reason?"

Spielmann swallowed before nodding. "Yes sir. I was working at home, analysing the latest results from the last batch of genetic recombining. We have made a large step forward. The best I've achieved before is just under five percent. This batch was a fraction over fifty. That is high enough to make the process more than practical."

"The process is stable?" asked Eigel.

Spielmann hesitated. "It appears so. But I'll need more time to be certain. Another week should confirm the results and give us baseline stability."

Eigel eyed the younger man. Perhaps he did have reason for being late. Still, he could not simply let his off so easily. Without acknowledging Spielmann further he turned to one of the other men.

"What of the search for the donor DNA?"

Adler turned his black eyes away from Spielmann and towards the Master. "The sample from Belgium looks promising. It shows the same irregularity as the sample from Notre-Dame. We'll have it in the lab by this evening. The test will not take long to compare the samples."

Eigel sighed, he was a scientist of notable standing and far from an idiot. But the cutting edge genetics were a little beyond him. He understood the concept, but the details were fuzzy.

"The sample from Notre-Dame, I thought it was corrupt. You said it was only ninety-seven percent human. I thought that chimp DNA was ninety-eight percent human. Surely ninety-seven percent is less than chimp?"

Adler's gaze never wavered, no emotion showed on his face. "It was actually ninety-seven point three. The two point seven percent that was not human was not any other animal or plant. It was...more than human. It was human on steroids. Superhuman if you like. A new DNA that has never been seen before. A DNA branch that," he shrugged, a mighty expression for Adler, "should not exist."

The implications were not lost on the rest of the men around the table. For years they had been following the aims of the Führer, to delete the weak mongrel blood that dominated the current human race and replace it with the bloodline of the Aryans, a race that had phenomenal mental and physical powers. And the last pure blood of the Aryan race was a man that had died, had been executed, two centuries ago. The son of God, at least, the son of a race that should be worshipped as gods. Once their genetic research started to show promise, they needed donor DNA from the last of the pure bloods. And there was no shortage of sources. There were hundreds of churches, monasteries and retreats that claimed to have samples of blood belonging to the son of God. But the majority, and they had obtained many examples, were most definitely not that of a two thousand year old saviour. Many simply proved to be normal human blood, some animal and a few simply some form of coloured mineral extract. Until recently, the search had proven fruitless. But now, in the space of a week, they had two samples showing the same genetic variation, a variation that should not exist. If they could extract the DNA and insert it in an unfertile egg, they could return the Aryan race to its rightful place as rulers and dominant species. And with their other project almost ready for implementation, they could wipe out the majority of the current human inbreeds and delete the opposition.

Eigel was the first to break the silence. "How long before we can be sure?"

Adler considered for a few seconds. "A day to compare the samples. Another to map the genome. We should have a definitive answer by the end of tomorrow."

"And if it's positive?"

"We could start the re-hydration and then extraction of donor DNA in...two days. First implantation in a week."

"It is a sign from the fifth race themselves. First the Genesis Project is finalised and now this, we find the donor DNA for the Messiah Project."

The men around the table sat considering the implications until Eigel spoke up.

"Back to work."

The men stood up, still mostly lost in their own thoughts and visions of what was to come.

Adler strode to the side of Spielmann, the physical

comparison between the two men was marked. Adler solid and greying with the look of a predator. Spielmann taller, thin and dark haired with glasses that made him look like a Second World War laboratory geek.

"Herr Spielmann, take a walk with me to my office, we should discuss your punctuality."

14:15hrs, 16th April
Leicester University

Richard Caley pushed the computer keyboard away in frustration. This was not going well. He had spent the last two years designing the programme: at best it was a waste of time, at worst the programme was going to be the nail that pinned his reputation to the wall for everyone to laugh at. He had only slept six hours in the last sixty. The rest of the time had been spent trying to find the problems and correct them. Caley grimaced at the thought. He had not even got close to finding the problems let alone fixing them.

The readings could not be correct, they could not exist. But the predictive element on known incidents checked out. The predictions were correct when run from the test data he entered. The predictions based on that data were correct. But when he went back in time to before the start of the test data there were impossible readings. Maybe the test data was wrong. But no, it could not be wrong, he was using data collected from actual incidents.

Caley slammed his fist on the desk. This was going nowhere. He could not reason the problem. He had no idea where to start. He had been going around in circles for the last two days, checking things he had checked a dozen times already.

"How's it going?" Caley jumped in his chair, he had

been so focused on the problem he had not heard Jess enter the lab.

"How's it going? It fu..." Caley paused and took a breath. "It's not going at all. It's got me going in circles. I've checked everything I can think of. I've checked things I know it can't be."

Jess looked at the blank computer screen, obviously lost in her own thoughts. After a few seconds Caley turned to her. "I know that look. What are you thinking that I won't like the sound of?"

Jess pursed her lips, perfect lips thought Caley with a slight smile. "Well...if everything you can confirm is correct. And you can't find a problem...are you sure there is a problem?"

Caley shook his head, the frustration barely contained.

"The readings just can't be. Earthquakes, tsunamis, volcanoes, they're all natural events. The field waves, standing waves and oscillations this heap of crap is showing do not exist in nature, you know that. The Lithosphere cannot propagate these sorts of waves. If I present this in my thesis I'll be a laughing stock. If I don't present it, I have nothing. Either way I fail, and the last four years have been a waste of time and money." Caley stopped talking as his breath ran out and he realised he had been almost shouting. He took several deep breaths, calming his breathing. After all, it was not Jess's fault. He looked up at her again.

"Sorry... Didn't mean to shout. But...what? You've got that look again."

"You won't like it."

"Oh what the hell? I'm all out of ideas. Nothing you can say now can make it worse?"

"Well, there is someone who you could ask for help."

"Who?...No, no, no. I can't call the professor."

225

"She was very impressed with you. You know she said that you should call if you needed any help or advice. She even offered to help when you qualified to find a job, point you in the right direction with contacts."

"That's why I can't ring her. She was great to me. But if she sees this mess," Caley indicated the computer with a sweep of his hand. "She'll realise how wrong she was and what a close call she had in getting her name associated with such a loser."

Jess bit her bottom lip for a second. "Actually you don't need to call her. I rang her this morning. She'll be here in an hour or so. She said she was looking forward to seeing you again."

Caley groaned and let his head fall to the desk.

The taxi pulled up in front of the main building. The rain from the April shower was just starting to dry on the concrete sets and thin wisps of water vapour rose into the still air as the sun dried the ground. The back door opened and the passenger stepped out, a lady 'of a certain age'. Of average height with silver grey hair she had the look of the archetypal grandmother. But it was not just her looks that had earned her the nickname Miss Marple. Any of her former students could attest that Professor Billie Lee had a mind like a steel trap. She could easily lull the less wary into believing that she was a lovely, polite, gentle old lady only to bring them back to reality with an insight that did not seem possible.

As an Emeritus Professor of Geology, she was these days largely retired. But she liked to take an interest in the students who showed real promise, if they had an interesting thesis all the better.

As she walked through the foyer heading for the labs she received several nods of acknowledgement from staff and senior students, and noted several students who avoided her eyes.

As she approached the lab door she could hear slightly raised voices, one male, and one female.

"Actually you don't need to call her. I rang her this morning. She'll be here in an hour or so. She said she was looking forward to seeing you again."

"As I am," said the professor. "And I won't be an hour, I'm here now. I got a taxi instead of the bus. Although I have to say, I'll be pleased when my car is repaired."

Professor Lee walked into the room and saw that the only two people there were Richard Caley and his girlfriend Jess. The professor reflected that when she had met the two last year she had been very impressed, more than impressed. They had shown some of the best promise she had seen in years. They both had a real feel, a real insight for the subject. And Richard's idea for the detector, well it was potentially world changing. But it was Jess that had called her, and that showed not only intelligence but maturity.

"So Richard, I understand you have a problem with the detector? Giving incorrect readings or some such. Ah." Professor Lee held up her hand. "Before we start, I feel the need for a strong coffee. I brought these to go with it." The professor took a cardboard box from her bag, placed it on the desk and opened the lid to reveal a half dozen assorted cream cakes.

"I'll do the coffee," said Jess with a smile as she stood and headed for the staffroom at the rear of the lab.

"Thank you, dear. Well now Richard, bring me up to date."

Caley sighed, he really had no choice now so he may as well make the best of it. For several minutes he recapped the basics of the programme. As Jess came back with a tray of drinks and a plate of biscuits to accompany the cakes he was finishing the briefing.

"The programme isn't giving wrong results, well not exactly. If I use actual data and run the programme forward it gives a result that is very close to the actual outcome. But if I then run it backwards, to a time before the start of the data, it gives results that can't exist. It's showing waves that can't happen in nature. And if it does that, how can I base my dissertation on the detector? The whole idea is that the detector will detect the earliest signs of an earthquake, tsunami, volcano," he shrugged. "Whatever the incident is, and give a prediction of the outcome with a timeline and intensity."

"And if it's looking for a wave form that can't exist, then it won't detect what it's looking for and so won't predict anything," said Professor Lee, summing up the problem.

"That's right," said Caley with a sigh.

"Well, let's have the coffee and some cake. Then you can show me the results that can't exist," said the professor with a smile as she reached for the box.

Ten minutes later, after a drink, cakes and some idle small talk they all set down their cups as if signalling the start of round two.

Caley took out several pages of A4 paper with data closely printed in neat columns. Leafing through the pages, he pulled several out and handed them to Professor Lee.

The professor scanned through the pages. Gradually the amiable expression on her face changed to one of concern. She turned back to the first page and started to read through the data in more detail, her expression growing more serious as she read.

At first Caley thought she was just disappointed with the results, but as her expression turned more to what appeared to be worry he started to think there was more wrong with his work than he thought.

After a full ten minutes Professor Lee placed the papers on the desk and looked up, her expression looking more serious than he had ever seen on her normally openly pleasant face.

"I need to make a call. Do you mind if I share this data with a colleague?"

"Err, well no. I suppose that's okay. What's wrong?"

"Let me make this call and I'll tell you more."

The professor pressed several buttons, obviously making a call from her speed dial directory.

"Hello, this is Professor Lee. Can I speak to the Minister please?"

Caley looked from the professor to Jess. Was she talking religious minister or political? Either way, he had no idea why or who she could be calling.

"Hello Howard, nice to speak with you again." The professor's voice held a hint of its usual good humour, but her expression was still serious.

"Something has come up. I need to see you as soon as possible." It was clear that whoever was on the other end of the phone was trying to put the meeting off.

"I'm sorry, Howard, this can't wait until you get back. I need to see you before you go. This is about an E.L.E. Red Dawn." There was a short pause, obviously what the professor had said had an impact.

"Yes, tomorrow will be fine. I'm going to e-mail you some data as well. Yes...We will see you there...Who? Oh I suppose you need to clear them for security. Yes, they are both students, Richard Caley and Jess Keeble. Leicester University." After saying her goodbyes she replaced the mobile phone back in her bag and looked at the two youngsters.

"I suppose it's my turn to explain," she said. "Do

you know what Bletchley Park is?"

"It was the British code-breaking centre during World War Two. They broke the German code that led to the capture of the Enigma machine. Wasn't there a film about that? U-571?" replied Jess with only the trace of a smug grin as she looked across at Caley.

"That's right. Although the Enigma was before my time. And the film was a travesty of inaccuracy. The U-571 was a German U-boat that actually sank off Ireland in 1944. The Royal Navy captured the first Navy Enigma machine in 1941 when HMS Bulldog captured the U-110. There were actually fifteen machines captured, and all but two of those were captured by UK forces, one by the Canadians and one, in 1944 by the U.S. Navy. But we had been reading the codes for years by then. Mind you, the film wasn't a complete loss, Matthew McConaughey wasn't too bad." Billie smiled before continuing.

"Anyway, during the war, my husband flew Lancasters. He was involved in the raid that destroyed the German battleship Tirpitz. He received the DFC, the Distinguished Flying Cross. So, after the war, he was often away on duty, and I've never been one to stay at home simply doing the housework so I joined Bletchley Park."

"You were a code-breaker?" asked Caley.

"I worked in intelligence, code-breaking was part of it. A lot of what I did is still classified. The actual name of the organisation was the Government Code and Cypher School or GC&CS. It was made up of Naval, Military and Air Sections, plus MI-6."

"Wow," was all Caley could say. Jess simply stared at the professor.

"Eventually the GC&CS become GCHQ. That's the modern day British communications centre. I was there for several years. Eventually I left and did my degree and PhD in geology, something I'd always been interested in. But once you've worked in the security service you never really leave. I've been an advisor to the intelligence service and the government through various ministries for years. Red Dawn is the codename for a threat we have considered possible for years. Tomorrow I'm taking you two to meet the Minister for Defence, Howard Thomas. There'll probably be some other people there as well from the intelligence community. I think what you have stumbled on with your detector is a threat to the security of this country, possibly the world."

Chapter 21

08:30hrs, 17th April
Grüssmire Gewerbe HQ

The large candles flickered in the still air of the room, casting light that did not quite reach the rear of the alcoves. Multiple shadows danced across the walls, the flames casting shimmering starbursts of light from the gold and silver surfaces of the room's adornments.

The men gathered in the room were again wearing their dark cowled robes, their faces hidden in the shadows.

The Master stepped behind the raised dais, his white robe standing out against the black, red and white swastika on the wall behind. He reached down below the dais, his head coming level with the horned skull. As he stood upright, he raised his arm above his head, the candlelight reflecting from the gold and silver blade.

Since Adler had spoken with Spielmann about his punctuality two days earlier, the younger man had been in early each day. But the Master still felt the younger man needed putting in his place.

"Let us give thanks and praise." The light flashed from the blade as the Master stepped from the dais and walked to the centre of the painted pentagram.

The other disciples had their heads bowed, a soft chant gently filling the room.

The master held the blade up, as if showing the polished golden dagger to the room itself.

"We give thanks to the past and seek guidance from the future so that we may prosper in the present."

The smell of incense drifted around the room,

giving a heady feel to the atmosphere.

The Master walked around the circle of disciples, stopping at each as they stood on the points of the pentagram, the dagger touching them on each shoulder before moving on, until he came to the last of them.

"The past, future and present demands a blood sacrifice. In the name of Thule we honour our ancestors."

The disciples gave the required response, waiting for the Master to give the required blood sacrifice from his own hand. Instead, the Master waited for the men to look up.

Spielmann looked up at the Master standing in front of him. The Master looked back steadily, a slight smile on his face.

"Herr Spielmann, a sacrifice is called for." The Master held the knife before him, the edge of the wickedly curved blade glinting in the candlelight.

Maybe it was Spielmann's imagination, but he felt sure there was a hint of red in the reflection. He had seen the Master on many occasions draw the knife along his palm, collect the blood as it dripped into the goblet and then wipe away the blood from his hand, leaving no trace of the cut. But how could *he* do that? He was no master, he was a simple disciple.

Spielmann hesitantly raised his hand, his palm upwards. There was a hint of a smile on the Master's face as he drew the razor sharp edge along Spielmann's palm. The knife was so sharp that there was little sensation, but Spielmann still flinched as the thin line of red appeared and spread across his palm. The Master held the golden goblet out and indicated for Spielmann to direct the steady flow of blood into it. After almost a minute, the Master judged the amount of blood in the goblet to be sufficient and gave a white cloth to Spielmann to wipe his hand.

Spielmann gasped as the disinfectant seeped into the wound. He was not surprised to see that the blood slowed, but did not stop. The wound certainly did not disappear.

As the Master drew the ceremony to a close, the men headed to the changing room. Spielmann was the first to leave, intending to head for the medical centre to get some stitches.

"I think Herr Spielmann will remember the lesson for some time," said Adler with a wicked grin.

"It may also keep him off his infernal motorcycle for a few days until his hand heals," replied Eigel, his large frame and flabby cheeks shaking with laughter.

"The young always disrespect their elders, it is the way of life. So sometimes the elders have to remind the young why they are in charge."

Adler nodded his agreement before adding, "I can always remind the young man in more direct ways."

"No Joseph," Eigel pronounced the name as Yosef. "Herr Spielmann may be a little disrespectful and full of himself, but he is a gifted geneticist. And we will need his expertise when the Messiah Project comes to fruition."

"Mmm. I still think it should be if, not when," said Adler.

Eigel's smile faded, there were few that could question his vision and live, Adler was one of the few. "You've seen the results of the latest samples. Both have the same genetic abnormality. It appears that they came from the same host. There is only one conclusion. The host was a man who lived two thousand years ago. That man was known as Jesus and was the last of the Aryan race. A race of gods by today's standards. With his blood and modern genetics, we can recreate the original masters in all their glory. And when Genesis wipes the Earth clean of the impure races that have overpopulated it and bled it dry of its resources, we can rebuild the world with a new race. And we will be the masters of that new world."

09:10hrs
New York

After the disappointment in Massachusetts, Grantham and Charisma were at a loss to know what to do next. They had considered travelling to Switzerland to investigate the killing of Bertrand, but in reality they knew what they would find, that the death had appeared as an accident, case closed. In truth, they did not really know where to go or what to do next. Rather than go straight home, Grantham suggested that they spend a few days in New York. In order to keep the right side of the law, they had visited the police to report a change of address. While there, the police told Grantham that the airline attacker had been charged and remanded to prison pending trial. Grantham would be called as a witness, but it was likely to be several weeks, maybe months. It was true that in America, as in England, the wheels of justice occasionally turned slowly.

Once registered at a decent hotel they had spent the afternoon and evening sightseeing. Charisma had insisted on visiting Macys and Bloomingdales before seeing Central Park. Here Grantham had taken the lead and hired a horse drawn carriage for the twenty minute drive through the centre of the green island in the city. The highlight of the day had been the after dark visit to the Top of the Rock, the observation deck of the Rockefeller Center. The glass walled, open air observation deck looked out across the expanse of the city, mostly looking down on the rest of the buildings. Looking out across the city, the lights twinkled like millions of fireflies with the more distant illumination being diffused by the slight mist which added a ghostly feel to the scene.

Now, after two full days in the city, they were trying to decide what to do next over breakfast. They had both opted for the breakfast buffet. A vast selection of food, everything from cereal and fresh fruit to a wide selection of meats and vegetables and a station for freshly made omelettes. But it was the condiment bottles that had really caught Charisma's eye. The miniature bottles were exact replicas of the larger versions but only held around three tablespoonfuls.

"We can't just give up," said Charisma.

"I agree, but I'm not sure what else we can do. Professor Grace was definitely murdered. The police are looking into it, but if someone can do such a professional job I doubt that there'll be much for them to go on. The sheriff suspects foul play in Robert Jacobs' death, but again, without some new evidence he seems to have run into a dead end. The report we have from Switzerland seems to have circumstantial evidence that the death wasn't the result of a simple fall. But even if we go out there we aren't equipped to carry out a criminal investigation. Especially when the crimes span three countries and two continents." Grantham paused as he spread butter on his wholemeal toast. He sat back looking around the dining room at the other dinners. He had no reason to suspect a threat, but his natural instinct was to sit with his back to a wall so that he could see the room and any approaching trouble. There were twelve other guests in the room, plus three circulating staff, none of them looked familiar. Most were couples, one group of four friends laughing and joking and two single men. One was a grey haired, well dressed man in his late fifties who looked as if he were on his way to a business meeting.

The other a dark complexioned, almost Mediterranean looking man with black hair and well trimmed beard who was seated at right angles to them and working on his laptop. For some reason Grantham was drawn to the man. He had the vaguest feeling he had seen him before. But the man was paying no attention to them.

There was a 100" wide-screen TV mounted at the end of the room tuned to a 24hr news channel, currently showing highlights of last night's basketball games.

"Could we try to track down other members of the Knights?" asked Charisma after a few minutes.

Grantham contemplated the question for a few seconds. "Where do we start? Have you any other names, contacts from your Dad's past?" Grantham considered what he knew about her father's background. There were maybe some leads he could track down, but did he want to go down that route? True to his word, William Windsor had texted him yesterday with the backgrounds of the three dead men.

Professor William Grace had the fullest and shortest background of the three. A first class student, graduating with an honours degree in Biblical History. He had spent his time lecturing to students and generally being well regarded as an expert in his chosen field. He had travelled extensively in Europe and the Middle East. There had never been any flags raised against his name.

Francois Bertrand, raised in a small village several miles outside of Marseilles, academically sound. He had worked in his father's finance firm until 1984 when he had left to join the French Foreign Legion where he served with distinction. Although not easy to access, his record was impressive with no missing sections. He had successfully commanded three hostage rescue raids without the loss of any hostages and only two minor injuries to his men. A good record. He had a three month leave of absence in late 1988 before leaving the Legion in early 1989. He had dropped off the grid for over six months before emerging again in Berlin on the night that John Valentine had died. Again, dropping off the grid for several months he had emerged as a financial advisor specialising in international finances and offshore accounts. Although he had never been directly connected, he had been in the same country when several 'incidents' had occurred that had raised questions. Oddly, all of the 'incidents' had some form of religious connection, although not always the same faith. Several questions had also been raised regarding the funds that he handled as part of his financial works. Suspected of money laundering, he had been investigated three times and cleared each time, although without ever identifying his clients.

Robert P Jacobs, American, bit of a tearaway in his teens, minor problems with the law which lead to him joining the American army, the Rangers no less. Good service record. Saw action in several trouble spots around the world. Received two purple hearts after being injured in the line of duty. Later on he was seconded to Special Forces field training as an instructor. He took a three month break in 1982 before retiring with a full service pension in 1983. A three month break? Similar to Francois Bertrand. After leaving the Rangers he seemed to more or less disappear. Actually 'disappear' was not the word. He just faded into the background. After a year he joined the forestry service, appeared to spend most of his time in the outdoors. There were often extended holidays in his forestry service, one ending in hospitalisation for three weeks with unspecified injuries that kept him off work for almost two months. Retired from the forestry service in 2003 and moved to Massachusetts where he lived quietly until his recent death.

The three month gap in Bertrand's and Jacobs' service prior to leaving the army had bothered Grantham, it was a coincidence and he had learned over the years not to simply dismiss coincidences. He had checked back into John Valentine's records and sure enough there was a three month gap in his service history nine months before he left the SAS. And when he did leave, he didn't start any new work for almost ten months. And that was not a coincidence, it was a pattern. The trouble was, he did not know how to make anything of it. He had contacts in the SAS who could track down the background of former members. He also knew a couple of US Rangers who could do the same. But he was not sure that background so far back would be much use. What he needed to know was what happened during the three months gap and then the several months after they left the service.

Looking across the table at Charisma, Grantham could not help but be taken aback by her stunning green eyes set off perfectly by her dark hair. It was time he came clean with her about her father. Well, almost clean, he need not say that he had the information before they left England.

"I got some more info last night from my contacts."

"Anything that would help?" she asked.

Grantham shrugged. "Some interesting coincidences, although I'm not sure how useful the info is. But I need to tell you some stuff about your Dad, he wasn't quite who you thought he was."

Charisma looked interested, maybe a little worried. For ten minutes Grantham told her about the background he had on her father and the coincidences with the others.

"Actually, I'm not that surprised. Somehow Dad working in logistics never seemed quite right. I always put it down to a little girl idolising her Dad, but him being in the SAS, well it sort of seems right. Do you have details of any of the missions he went on? If mission is the right word."

Grantham had a few details, and could get more. But there were reasons that these things were kept secret, even from the family. He told her a few of the basics, some of the trouble spots John Valentine had served in, but kept the few details he had to himself.

The two of them sat back and considered what they had just discussed. The television was still showing the various American sports. The picture cut from the smiling face of an all-American 'jock' with black hair, perfect white teeth and a tan that was just a shade too orange to be natural, to highlights of last night's baseball game between the Philadelphia Phillies playing in red and white and the blue and white of the New York Mets. The sound was turned too low for Grantham to hear, but there were captions across the bottom showing what the voice-over was saying. Grantham was idly reading the captions, it appeared the Phillies had beaten their close rivals by one run, as the caption said 'not much brotherly love between these two teams'.

Grantham continued to watch the screen, but was not paying any attention. Something else was creeping through his mind, something from a few days ago.

"Have you got your Dad's story book?"

"Not the actual book, but I've got it copied." Charisma took some folded papers from her pocket and handed them across to Grantham. He opened the pages and read the last page several times. For a few minutes he tapped away at the keyboard of his mobile phone, and then he sat back with a smile on his face.

"I think I know where your Dad is leading you."

Chapter 22

14:45hrs, 17th April
Victoria Tower Gardens, London

Billie Lee, Richard Caley and Jess Keeble strolled through the lush green gardens overlooking the River Thames and Lambeth Bridge. Billie paused and checked her watch before sitting down on one of the garden's benches.

"Shouldn't we be getting to the meeting?" asked Caley.

Billie smiled at the young man. "We've got a few minutes to spare, and I think I should explain a few things before we get there. Firstly, the people you'll meet will be the directors and deputy directors of several of the intelligence agencies. There's likely to be some military and science representatives as well. The chairman of the meeting will be Howard Thomas, the Defence Secretary. And it's likely that most of them won't give their names."

"So how do I refer to them? And I still don't understand why we're meeting these people."

"If they ask you questions, and they will, just talk to the person asking the question. You don't need their names. And what they want is to discuss your detector."

"But it doesn't work," said Caley dejectedly.

"But it does work, Rich. It just doesn't work as you expected it would. But it does detect something," said Jess.

"Jess is right. But I'd best not say anymore now. It's not my place and a lot of what will be discussed is classified on one level or another. Just remember, they are interested in what you can tell them, but don't make stuff up. If you don't know something, say so. If you're speculating, make it clear that you're speculating so they don't think you're stating facts. And try to relax. You aren't in trouble. The worst that can happen is that they thank you for your time and you never hear from them again."

Billie checked her watch. "We had best be going. We don't want to be late. That's Thames House, over there." She indicated the large grey stone building on the far side of the park.

The building was designed by the Principal Architect of the Government's Office of Works, Sir Frank Baines. It was built in 1929-30 on a derelict site and acquired by the Government in the late 1980s. It was extensively refurbished and modernised before being refitted with the latest technology and security and becoming home to the security services in 1994.

The building was tall, majestic and seemed to perfectly blend the old solid stone walls with the modern dark mirrored windows

The walk through the park took less than two minutes. As they approached the entrance, Billie took the lead to climb the stairs.

The foyer was bright and airy with marble and polished wood giving the impression of age beyond its eighty plus years. To the uninitiated, the only sign of security was the thirty something female receptionist sitting off to one side at an old looking desk, in keeping with the surroundings. However, looking more closely, the trained eye would pick up three CCTV cameras and notice that each of the three doors and one lift leading from the foyer was secured by key card locks. What was not visible were the four armed guards monitoring the CCTV cameras behind one of the doors and the automated detectors that every visitor passed through that were built into the frame of the main entrance. Those detectors could pick up metal and explosives along with certain high density plastics and scanners that could 'see' through clothing. These scanners had been in operation for at least five years and were now being introduced at airports.

Billie Lee stepped over to the smiling receptionist and handed her what appeared to be a credit card. "I'm here to see Howard Thomas." Although the Secretary of Defence was not based here, he would be registered as a visitor who was chairing a meeting. The receptionist scanned the card through a reader and looked at the details on her screen.

"And your two guests?"

"Richard Caley and Jess Keeble," Billie turned to the other two and held out her hand. "Have you got your passports?" She had already made sure they had their IDs when they met up. Billie handed the dark red passports to the receptionist who scanned them and looked closely at the two younger visitors before obviously reading from the screen for a few seconds.

"If you would like to take a seat," the receptionist indicated several chairs against the wall. "There will be someone here to collect you in a minute."

The three walked over to the seats and sat down.

"When someone comes to collect us, they'll probably take us through to an office and give you some paperwork to sign," said Billie. "That'll be the Official Secrets Act. You can take your time reading it if you want, but what it all boils down to is that if you reveal anything you learn today, even who you have talked to or where we are, you could be liable to prosecution. And that could mean a fine or imprisonment. And don't think 'it won't happen to me' because believe me, it will. These people do not play games with security."

"I thought you said the worst that could happen was that they would ignore us," said Caley.

At the look of worry on the two younger faces, Billie added, "Don't worry, just don't talk about this to anyone and you'll be fine. They aren't likely to reveal anything particularly important to you anyway."

As Billie finished speaking, a thirty something man of medium height but with shoulders that would put an ox to shame crossed the marble floored foyer and walked up to them.

"Mrs Lee, Miss Keeble, Mr Caley, if you would follow me." Without waiting for a reply he turned and walked across the foyer to the far side, heading for a door on the same wall as the lift.

The three followed the man, who looked as if he would have to turn sideways to get his shoulders through the door.

Once in the room, Caley and Jess sat in the seats indicated by the man. He opened a folder that was on the table and placed several yellow pages in front of Caley and Jess.

"Read these and sign where the tabs are," he indicated the bright orange tabs which pointed to dotted lines in several places.

The two younger people scanned through the pages, picking up various points. The documents were not quite written in legal jargon, but they were close enough to be difficult to understand without concentration. After a few minutes both Jess and Richard looked at each other and almost shrugged before turning back to the pages and signing and dating where indicated.

The man, he had not given his name, checked the documents and handed one copy back to Caley and Jess and placed one set of each into the folder.

"You've just signed the Official Secrets Act. You

are legally bound by the documents. If you reveal anything that you learn today, at any time in the future, you will be prosecuted to the full extent of the law. Understand?"

The two youngsters just nodded, the man looked as if he could pick them both up in one meaty hand and squeeze them until they popped.

"Good," the man smiled and his whole face lit up, softening the previously stern, almost mean appearance to something approaching a big cuddly teddy bear.

"Okay, wear these and follow me." He handed over two ID badges with their faces on one side and the word VISITOR emblazoned across the bottom. How had they got their faces on the badges so quickly? wondered Caley. As they followed the man out, he saw that the professor was also wearing an ID badge, but hers matched the man's, most definitely not a visitor's badge.

Leaving the room, they turned left and stopped at the lift doors. The man scanned his ID card and the doors slid open noiselessly.

Stepping out on the second floor, the man led them along a hushed corridor. The carpet felt expensive and seemed to suck all the noise from the air. Pausing at a door, he knocked once and opened it, standing to one side to allow the visitors in and closing the door behind them.

The room was large and bright, the walls were covered with light coloured wood panels. The large windows extending from the ceiling to three feet from the floor had a tinted look to them and Caley realised they would be the mirrored windows he had seen from the outside.

The table was a large oval capable of seating thirty comfortably. But for now there were only seven men and one woman at the table. As they entered, the man at the far end stood and walked around to greet them. He obviously knew Billie as he went straight to her and bent to kiss her on both cheeks. He then shook hands with Caley and Jess and introduced himself as Howard Thomas, UK Secretary of Defence.

Of equal height to Caley, he was heavier set, a build that spoke of too many lunch meetings and not enough exercise. His hair was dark, but thinning, his eyes a mid blue-grey but piercing, as if he were looking through rather than at them.

After showing them to their seats, about a third of the way down one side, facing the others, Thomas asked if they would like drinks. Billie asked for a tea, Caley and Jess declining.

"Well, let's get down to business, shall we? I won't bother introducing the others around the table, I'm sure you won't remember their names anyway. But between them, they represent the Armed and Special Forces and the intelligence service."

Caley looked around the table. Five of the men were dressed in dark suits and white shirts with varying coloured ties. Two of them were wearing uniforms. His father, who was now a fireman, had served in the Royal Navy and would recognise the ranks and service ribbons, but Caley was no expert of military uniforms. One was clearly an Army uniform and one Air Force and from the amount of coloured ribbons, shiny studs on epaulettes and braid on the sleeves, they obviously senior in rank. The one woman brought a splash of colour to the gathering. She was in her late fifties, same as the men. Dark hair just starting to show grey, her jacket was bright red over a black blouse.

Thomas continued, "After Billie called yesterday, we looked into your backgrounds. I understand you are both Geology students?" He phrased it as a question but continued without waiting for an answer, although both

246

Richard and Jess nodded.

"And it is you, Mr Caley that has made a breakthrough with your detector."

Caley was at a loss for words, he opened his mouth but no sound came out as he looked around the table, finally looking at Professor Lee.

"I haven't explained anything to the young couple, Howard. I thought it best to leave that to you," said Billie.

"Mmm. Well, where to begin? You have signed the Official Secrets Act?"

Caley and Jess both nodded while muttering a quiet, "Yes."

"Okay. Well there are many potential threats to the security of this country. Obvious ones like terrorist, financial threats, even denial of service, if you've heard the term?"

"Isn't that where someone brings down the Internet? Denies access to the service?" asked Caley.

"It's a bit more than that. Basically crashing the Internet service and computer operations to the whole country. It may not sound that serious, but the country would grind to a halt. Every service, telephones, power, water, transport, everything would stop. But there are a lot of other threats that most people never think of. But that's one of the things that we're paid to do." He swept his hand around the table.

"One of those things is a threat that we always thought of as theoretical only. Something we considered, but could never see how it could be done in practice. Until now," Thomas paused to let the comment sink in.

"It's long been hypothesized that if you could generate enough force you could trigger a landslide, volcano, earthquake or tsunami. But we've never been even close to being able to generate enough power. In the nineties someone came up with the idea that if you could find the natural resonance of the media, the rock basically, then you could do that with far less power."

"But a rock, err sorry. I didn't mean to interrupt." Caley looked a little embarrassed as he looked around the table.

"No, please continue, I'd welcome your thoughts," Thomas seemed genuine.

"Well. The natural frequency of something pure, like a crystal glass, can be determined. If you match the frequency, the power builds up until the glass shatters. But a rock is a more complex item. It won't have one natural frequency, it could have dozens, and they could vary depending on the direction of the approach of the waves. You'd need a lot of different transmitters. Or a transmitter that could vary its signal until it found the right one." Caley's voice gradually trailed off as he considered what he was saying. "And that's just one natural rock. The Earth, the ground that you would have to energize would be infinitely more complex."

Thomas nodded in agreement, a half smile on his face. "You obviously know your subject, young man. I see Professor Lee was correct."

"Well that was more physics than geology. And it about exhausted my knowledge of natural resonance."

"Well you are correct. However, some experts," Thomas glanced at one of the men sitting around the table, "have speculated that if you could produce a series of signals that varied fast enough, the power could be low and still make the oscillation build up over time until something gave and..." Thomas spread his hands.

"The power would...dissipate suddenly...maybe, well, shattering the rock. Or causing a sudden...slip. That could result in an Earthquake or eruption," said Caley hesitantly.

"Quite. As you know, Professor Lee contacted me yesterday and sent me the data from your experiment. I passed that data to several other people," he indicated the same men sitting across the table, who nodded and smiled at Caley and Jess.

"It looks like your detector has picked up a signal that we thought of as theoretical. We are not sure how the signal could be produced, but by detecting it, you've shown it exists which means someone has found a way to create it."

"But, what signal? You mean the background noise that the detector sort of predicted if you work back in time?" asked Caley.

Thomas picked up a remote control from the table and clicked a couple of buttons. A white screen lowered from the ceiling at the end of the room and a projector set mid-way came to life. With the repeated press of a button, Thomas flicked through several slides before stopping at a graph.

"Do you recognise this?" asked Thomas.

"It's a readout from my detector," replied Caley. The screen was showing an X and Y axis with various notations and a thick 'S' shaped line flowing across the screen.

"And this?" said Thomas as he changed slides.

"Err, well it's similar to my readout. But...different?"

"Actually, it's not different, just more accurate." Thomas looked across the table. "General, would you care to take over?"

So, all those pips on the shoulder meant the army officer was a General, thought Caley.

The General, his name had not be mentioned, looked slightly less than pleased. "Do you know anything about directed energy beams?" he asked.

"Not really. Aren't they something to do with

lasers?" asked Caley.

"Yes, but that is like saying is a pistol a gun? Directed energy beams are concentrated energy projected over a distance. Lasers are just one type. But there are others, including acoustic." The general reached across the table and took hold of another remote control and flicked the screen back to the slide of Caley's data.

"This is your data. The only real mistake you made was to restrict the representation to data you expected. What the detector picked up, or predicted backwards was outside of those parameters. So it made the best compromise it could. This," he flicked forward to the next screen, "is what the readout should look like. We've tweaked the analysis and this is what you should have."

The image showed a similar 'S' curve to Caley's readout, but instead of a thick black line, the line was made up of multiple coloured lines. Caley could make out at least a dozen different colours merging into one line. As he looked at the screen, the general changed slides, this one showed a blown-up image of the line. Caley was wrong, there were not a dozen coloured lines, there were what? Hundreds?

The signal was a combination of almost a thousand individual signals.

"But, that can't be natural," said Caley.

"It isn't. What you're looking at is what has been speculated on for some time. As Mr Thomas said, generating one signal to create an incident would take too much power. And there isn't one natural frequency to tap into. But, if you could generate hundreds of signals at the same time, you could affect hundreds of components, ultimately creating a cascade affect. Actually, this signal is more subtle than that."

The general changed slides again, an even closer

view of the signals. This showed the lines twisting around each other, but it also showed that the lines were broken.

"A natural harmonic works like a swing. If you sit on a swing you don't start it going by one massive push, you keep adding energy by small increments at just the right time. That's how this signal works. A small nudge of a specific frequency which is absorbed by the ground. The signal then stops and a different frequency is generated. That's what the breaks are in the lines. Once all the frequencies have been cycled the first one starts again. If the switching can be done fast enough, the first signal won't have dissipated by the time it cycles around again. Like the swing, the signals gradually build up, until..."

"Until...the energy is enough to cause the earthquake or eruption?" asked Caley tentatively.

The general nodded.

Caley looked around the table, the faces were sombre. Several of them looked as if they were deep in thought.

"So what do you want me to do?" asked Caley.

"Actually, you've already done the hard part, or the clever part. You've developed the technology to show the threat is real. With your permission, we'll make use of your technology and take it from here ourselves," the Minister finished with a smile.

"Well, yes. I suppose I can't really say no, can I?"

"Of course, you will be paid a royalty for the use. I suggest you patent the software before it becomes public. To protect your investment. And I will of course arrange an endorsement for your thesis. That should go down well with the examination board." A politician's smile again.

"Err, thank you." Caley smiled now. "It was only a few days ago that I thought I'd ruined my chances with the degree."

"Hardly. Although I must remind you, we do take the Official Secrets Act seriously. You can not divulge anything that you've heard today, and that includes putting anything in your thesis. The endorsement will be glowing, although non-specific in detail." Thomas stood and extended his hand to Caley and Jess. It was obviously a polite dismissal.

"If you would wait in the foyer, Professor Lee will be down shortly, we just need a quick word."

The door opened and the huge bear of a man who had shown them up appeared. How had he known when to come in?

As the door closed behind the two younger people Thomas turned back to the table, the smile gone, to be replaced by a serious look.

"Professor, you were one of the leads when the E.L.E. threats were identified," Thomas glanced around the table. "It was before most us were in our current roles. Would you run us through the highlights? We have, of course seen the reports, but a first-hand résumé would be useful."

Billie Lee looked around the table. She had met most of the people before in one capacity or another. The head of the armed forces, General Clive Simmonds, and his deputy Air Marshal Colridge-Stewart. The head of MI-5 and C, the head of MI-6, not M as in the movies, Michel Fortnum the head of JTAC. The rest were senior advisors of one form or another.

"E.L.E.s, Extinction Level Events, can be natural disasters such as meteor impacts, or manmade events such as a nuclear war or a fatal pandemic. They threaten large sections of the population, maybe the entire human race. Potentially all life on Earth." Billie paused and looked around the table, she had their attention.

"What we are potentially looking at here, is a worldwide disaster by earthquake, tsunami and volcanic eruption. You've all seen what happened in New Zealand with the earthquake, Japan with the tsunami, the disruption caused by the Icelandic volcano. All those incident together would not be a drop in the ocean if a caldera erupted. Or if a mega tsunami were triggered."

"Where could these happen? Could they affect the UK?" asked Air Marshal Colridge-Stewart

"There are several caldera around the world, one of the best know is the Yellowstone caldera in America. But tsunamis, they could happen along any of the tectonic plate join lines. If anything, we are lucky in the UK, we don't have any direct threats. But that's not to say we won't be affected. The Icelandic volcano spewed several thousand tons of ash into the atmosphere, and you know the disruption that caused. A major caldera won't be throwing tons of ash into the air, it will be throwing thousands of cubic *miles* of ash into the air. One caldera has the potential to destroy life across half to two thirds of the Earth. The only survivors, including humans, would be the ones that could move from the affected areas. And even then, with crops and animals dying, there won't be enough food and power production to support more than thirty percent of the current population."

Billie looked around the table, the figures were in the report, but hearing them stated as fact had clearly shaken most of those present.

"But the event wouldn't be...well, it wouldn't be an extinction event?"

Billie looked across to Air Marshal Colridge-Stewart. "The majority of the world population wouldn't agree." Billie sighed. "The truth is no one really knows for sure just how bad a caldera eruption would be. There hasn't been an eruption in mankind's lifetime. One theory says that the extinction of the dinosaurs was caused by a caldera eruption."

The people around the table looked from one to the other, everyone looked as if they had questions, but no one knew what to ask. After a few seconds Michel Fortnum, head of JTAC spoke up, the spelling of her first name evidence of her Greek ancestry, as were her Mediterranean complexion, glossy black hair and almost as dark smoky eyes.

"If a caldera eruption is potentially an extinction event, and young Mr Caley's device has picked up man made signals that could trigger an eruption and tsunamis and earthquakes, why? How could anyone profit from the destruction of all life on Earth? Surely they would suffer as much as anyone."

Before Billie could reply, Thomas spoke up.

"You of all people, Michel, should know, there are certain fundamentalist groups and religious fanatics that would love to see the end of mankind, a cleansing of the Earth. But that isn't what we think is the motive here. Professor, correct me if I'm wrong, but major eruptions and the other things work in two ways. Direct and indirect. Direct would be the death and destruction caused by the incident, people killed and property destroyed by the wall of water of a tsunami, by the fire and magma from a volcano, the falling buildings of an earthquake." He looked across at Billie, who nodded. "But the immediate effect would be nothing compared to the longer term consequences."

Billie took up the story. "The ash that was thrown into the air would blot out the sunlight. It would be permanent night for one to two years. During that time pretty much all plant life would die. Without plants, animals would die. Scavengers would survive a little longer by living off the carcases. But that would only be months longer. If anyone was prepared enough, preferably with underground bunkers with enough supplies to last two years or more, and enough expertise and facilities to start afresh when they came out, they could survive and start a new world order."

Again, Thomas took over the briefing.

"Most western countries, plus Australia, Japan and China, have such bunkers. In the UK, we could support five hundred people for three years. Plus there're supplies of crop seeds that would be grown in artificial underground bunkers, along with a limited supply of animals. But things would be vastly different when the survivors came out. They may have survived, but they probably wouldn't have prospered. Although they haven't admitted to anything, we think the Chinese and Japanese have provision for several thousand. Once they came out, they would be in a very strong position to take over whatever they wanted."

"Do you think the Chinese or Japanese are behind this?" asked one of the advisors.

"No," replied Thomas. "They have some radical views, but even they wouldn't willingly destroy all life."

"So, who would?"

Thomas stapled his fingers and tapped them against his pursed lips. "As a best guess, some radical but very advanced organisation. They would have to have very advanced technical knowledge and vast resources. It's also unlikely that they would be linked to any recognised government."

"So, no particular country?" asked the advisor.

"Very unlikely. Even the most radical government wouldn't take these steps. No, this is someone else. Some organisation that we haven't considered. But we are certainly going to consider them now. We need to find the transmitters and who has planted them and stop them. Michel, I want JTAC to coordinate the task force." Thomas held up his hand to stop the expected objections from the heads of MI-5 and MI-6. "The Joint Terrorism Analysis Centre has access to your organisations and the equivalents in Europe. They may not have the direct resources, but they are ideal to coordinate the work. And I expect you all to make whatever resources they require available. You won't be out of the loop, but JTAC will coordinate." Thomas looked around the table, some of those present were not happy, but they nodded their reluctant consent.

"And Professor, I would like you to be on board to act as senior advisor, someone who can pull the technical information together and offer insights." He looked around the table again. "Okay, let's get on with this."

Chapter 23

12:25hrs, 17th April
New York

"Are you ever going to tell me what this is all about?" Charisma slapped Grantham on the arm in mock annoyance, well mostly mock annoyance.

Grantham smiled, he had strung her along enough. "Okay, but I'd rather have checked some things out first before I got your hopes up. Here," he handed Charisma the paper with the last story that her father had written. "It suddenly came to me his morning when the sports news was on. But there're still some things I don't get. Look, here." Grantham pointed to the paper and different sections of the text.

Eventually the Knights became persecuted and hunted. The church feared their power and knowledge, knowledge that could topple kingdoms and fell the establishment of Rome.

In order to protect themselves and the treasure the Knights retreated to the new land where He had walked before and took the secrets they guarded with them.

Many of the bravest Knights swore to protect the secrets, but the threat did not come from a physical threat as had been present in the old country. Instead, the threat was of a different nature, one of solitude and isolation from family, friends and homeland. Those that stayed knew they were unlikely to see their homes and families again. But they had sworn a holy oath to God and would give their lives to protect that which they held dear.

Over the years, they built a new home, a new land, a new country.
The secrets were passed from one Knight to another. To protect those secrets, only five Knights at any time held the knowledge.

But in order to keep a record, where all men are free and brother loves brother, the key was cast clear and sound in one of the land's new treasures. So it was that liberty would pass the key to stow.

"The first part's pretty obvious from what you told me back in England. The Knights became financially very rich, which led to power and the King of France and the Pope wanting rid of them."

"That's right," said Charisma. "King Philip IV of France and Pope Clement persecuted them, captured and tortured them. But a sizeable number escaped."

"But did the Templars have something that threatened the church?"

Charisma shrugged. "There have been rumours over the years, but nothing that's ever been substantiated. I suppose it's possible."

"Okay, well the next part looks like it's saying that the Knights left their homes and went to another land. But the Knights were made up of many different nationalities. Predominantly English and French, but most European nations were represented in their ranks. So they had no one nation, no one home to leave. I think it means they left Europe all together." Grantham was clearly getting into the story he had been researching all morning.

"That makes sense. Especially here, where it says 'a new land where He had walked before'. That could

258

mean India and the Silk Road route through Asia."

Grantham nodded. "I remember you talking about the Silk Road on the flight over so I've been looking it up. Basically you said it made sense with Jesus being missing from the bible for several years and returning as an experienced preacher."

"Right, plus the story of Nicolai Notovitch and others who have travelled the area reporting that Buddhist monks have similar values and tales that are similar to bible stories."

"But that still didn't sound right. It would still have been a known land that they could have returned home from. But this part in your Dad's story seems to say that returning home would have been difficult."

"Well maybe it was dangerous more than difficult," said Charisma.

"Maybe, but this part seems to say it was a new land, not just to the Knights, but a new land altogether."

"Well, if you tell me your theory, maybe I can help."

Grantham sighed, he thought earlier that he had a way forward, but the more he thought about it, the more the idea seemed wrong. "Okay, but don't laugh. I'd got it into my head that maybe the new land the Knights had gone to was America." Grantham shrugged, "But the more I think about it, how could it mean America? Could Jesus have even got to America two thousand years ago?"

Charisma had a faraway look of concentration on her face, her brows drawn together, lips pursed. Grantham let her think for a few seconds before asking her thoughts.

"Well this isn't my field, although there is a bit of crossover. You know who discovered America?"

"In fourteen hundred and ninety-two, Columbus sailed the ocean blue. I remember the rhyme from school. Although it's now thought that he wasn't the first to discover America, just the first to really publicise the fact."

"That's right. There's plenty of evidence that the Chinese were sailing the Pacific and Indian Oceans for hundreds of years before Columbus. It's also thought that the Vikings made regular visits to America over a thousand years ago. Even as far back as 600 BC the Israelites were using the Pacific and Indian Oceans." Charisma paused, a curious look on her face. "So you're thinking that the new land the riddle refers to is America?"

Grantham looked a little embarrassed, but shrugged and nodded.

"That may not be so far-fetched. A lot of the Native American tribes have stories and traditions that are remarkably similar to those in the bible. Many of the tribes refer to a pale face healer who came across the sea. At least one, I can't remember which tribe, tell tales of a traveller who brought medicine and knowledge to them. They call him Cheezoos, the God of the Dawn Light. Some even say that the Pale God had marks on his hands and that his symbol was the cross. And geneticists have sampled many of the tribes' DNA and found that there is European DNA that was introduced two thousand years ago."

"Couldn't the DNA have been introduced in the last three hundred years?" asked Grantham.

"Apparently not. The geneticist can tell roughly when it was introduced, and that was two thousand years ago. So, enough of the history lesson. Are you going to tell me what you have worked out?"

"Okay. Here," Grantham held out the paper with the riddle. "Where it says the secrets were passed from Knight to Knight. That's just standard security. But here, 'all men are free and brother loved brother' could

260

be the Land of the Free, America, and the City of Brotherly Love, Philadelphia."

"Why didn't I see that before? It's obvious now. But then what? What happens when we get to Philadelphia?"

"We try and work out what the last few lines mean."

Chapter 24

11:00hrs, 18th April
Quantico, Virginia

The alarm bells rang out from the sandstone building, the shrill ringing punctuated by gunshots. The doors to the bank burst open and a man in a blue ski mask ran from the building. His right hand was holding a sack, his left a large, vicious looking gun. He ran from the building, across the sidewalk and into the path of a car, causing it to skid to a halt. The man aimed the weapon at the driver.

"OUT, GET OUT!"

The driver opened the door and the man pulled him from the car, throwing him bodily across the road.

"FREEZE, FBI." The man turned and aimed the .45 semi-automatic back at the chasing agent. The agent squeezed the trigger to hear a loud click as the hammer fell on an empty magazine.

The bank robber smiled under his ski mask and pulled the trigger three times. The gun roared with the release of the three large calibre bullets and the FBI agent fell to his knees, his own gun clattering to the floor as three red stains splattered across his chest.

The robber jumped into the car, his foot jamming down on the accelerator as the car squealed away leaving long tyre marks on the tarmac.

Three more gunshots rang out from the bank before the bells fell silent. The watching crowd standing across the street, many of them wearing FBI windcheaters, looked on in interested silence. A few seconds later the car returned and stopped in front of the bank, the robber stepping from the car and raising his ski mask as two men were led from the bank in handcuffs by FBI agents. The robber with the blue ski mask watched as the men were led out. As they stepped onto the sidewalk he started to slowly clap his hands together.

"Not bad, but you lost one agent to a rookie mistake. Never forget to count your shots. Always know how many shots you've fired and how many you have left." He walked over to the agent he had shot and helped him up.

"Those bloody pellets hurt," said the agent as he rubbed his chest, spreading the red dye further.

"Not as much as the real thing," replied the instructor now wearing the ski mask as a hat. "Okay, debrief in the bank in ten minutes."

"Very impressive. Realistic as well. I can see the value of the whole town." The man stood an even six feet, his broad shoulders, athletic build and solidly straight stance marking him down as a professional soldier. His accent though made him stand out from those around him. Most of the spectators spoke with various American accents, his was clearly English Geordie.

"Thank you sergeant, oh, sorry, sergeant *major*." Dean Sharp, the man leading the small group across the road smirked at his own continuing joke. Sergeant Major Henry 'Mac' Maguire ignored the remark.

The small group of six men following Sharp were British SAS on a week-long exchange. The idea was that the SAS would come to the world famous FBI training facility to exchange ideas and experience with the senior FBI instructors. 'Teach and be taught', as the invite had said. Unfortunately the head FBI instructor seemed to have taken an instant dislike to the SAS men, saying at their welcome that American troops had to work harder to get promotion thus the British ranks were less valuable that the American equivalent. Although not openly hostile, he had made a point of constantly undermining the men, questioning their expertise and deliberately referring to them by lower ranks than they held. To their credit, the SAS troops had not risen to the bait, which seemed to frustrate Sharp and make his teasing worse.

They had arrived yesterday and spent the morning being welcomed by the facility director, attending a series of briefings and sitting in on lectures.

The whole facility sat on almost 400 acres of Virginian countryside. Housing classrooms, assault courses and offices, the gem in the crown of the facility was Hogan's Alley. A town built by the FBI specifically for the training of law enforcement officers from all corners of the country along with most branches of the military. It was not unusual for the facility to also welcome foreign visitors who would both train and teach.

"I think you'll like the next visit. It's a large single building, used to house hostages and allow various forms of assaults to be undertaken."

As the group approached the building, they could see it was a three storey, mostly brick built building. Around 120 feet by 80 feet, 29,000 square feet, more if there were any sort of basement or attic. Other buildings, mostly just fronts built around scaffolding, flanked the building so that the whole area seemed like an urban street.

When they were still 100 feet from the front of the building a siren sounded and several trainers in bright orange fluorescent tabards with FBI emblazoned across the back directed the group to a section behind wide ballistic glass.

"This should be interesting," said Dean Sharp. "The group about to enter are using live ammo, that's why we're behind the glass. They're the FBI Hostage Rescue Team, on their 120 day training cycle. They train every day plus attend lectures, refresher courses etc." Sharp turned around and looked at the wall behind them that held a series of times.

"Three minutes forty-six, that's the current best time for a full building clearance and exit with two unharmed hostages with a full brief and floor plan. Five minutes forty, that's for the same but going in blind without a briefing or floor plan. The hostages are dummies of course due to the live ammo."

One of the SAS group snorted and turned away. Sharp was not sure what the man meant by the noise.

"Even if they don't get a brief, don't they get to know the building over time?" This came from Sergeant Jez Stinger, the second most senior of the SAS group.

"We thought of that corporal," again Sharp had a grin on his face at the putdown. "All the walls and doors inside of the building can be moved and rearranged. A building team can rearrange the whole building in three hours. They never run the same building on different visits."

"That's like our killing house at Hereford. Only we use rubber walls and move them around. Your set up would be more realistic. And a hell of a lot bigger."

As the men watched, an armoured van pulled up at the bottom of the street and disgorged six men all dressed in black one piece suits with black helmets and visors pulled down. Five of the men were carrying modified Heckler and Koch MP5s chambered for either 9mm or 10mm rounds with forward mounted pistol grips. At their sides they carried holstered Springfield Armory's 1911 pistols. One of the men also had a Remington 870 12-gauge shotgun over his back.

"They're all qualified for fast rope and air and

maritime assaults. But today they're going in on foot," said Sharp.

Mac nodded but kept his eyes on the FBI HRT.

"We had an HRT group training with us last year. They were very good," said Mac.

By now the HR team had advanced to the entrance to the building, checking to see if it was open. At a nod from the leader, two of the group swung a solid looking battering ram and slammed open the double doors.

"GO, GO, GO," the leader of the group shouted and the men rushed the front door, streaming through as one group.

Shots, bangs and flashes could be seen and heard from the inside as the HRT swarmed through the building, clearing each room in turn. Their progress could be followed from the outside by the noise and flashes coming from the different rooms.

"How do you monitor their progress and offer resistance?" asked Mac.

Sharp indicated down the street. "There are a group of operators down there. They monitor the inside via CCTV and can bring up dummies and bad guys to pose as opposition. And the dummies shoot back with paint balls so we know if anyone has been hit. And the operators can only see what's on their monitors so they don't get warning of an assault. They only see and hear what the monitors tell them including some that look out the windows. And they can't jump from one camera to another, they can only swap at the pace a man can run. And they can only have as many monitors working as there are bad guys and as they get neutralised, they get less and less monitors and operators. It's a real contest between the assault team and the operators. By the way, the operators are all SWAT qualified, not just computer geeks." Sharp laughed, "You want to see their scores on Urban Combat games."

"Do the operators ever win?" asked Jez Stinger.

"Oh yes. It depends on who the assault team is. Obviously some are better than others." He looked pointedly at the group of SAS troops. "The HRT suffer losses about one in three times. About one in ten they fail completely. They don't have it all their own way."

As he finished speaking the HR team came through the front door, carrying two dummies. Sharp turned to the wall behind them. Six minutes fourteen seconds.

"No record this time. So in your *expert* opinion, what do you think?"

"They're a good team. And it may not be a record, but I'd say that looked a pretty good time," said Mac with sincerity.

"No observations that could perhaps improve their performance, after all, that's why you're here, to give your *expert* opinion."

The constant jibes were starting to wear thin, even on Maguire's thick skin.

"Well, if you want my honest opinion, the two point men that opened the door were a little slow clearing the opening. They made themselves targets for almost a second. And when the team were clearing the house they were too regular with the progress." Mac took pleasure as he saw the smile slip from Sharp's face.

"The progress was fast and thorough, but a bit predictable. If the Tangos had monitored the progress they could have set explosives on a timer and retreated, or waited for the team to enter a room and know how long they had before they came out and be waiting for them."

"Anything else?" asked Sharp with obvious annoyance.

"Don't forget the exit boss," this came from Danny Fathom, the most junior of the SAS team, who turned away with a grin as Mac looked at him.

"When they exited they relaxed as they came through the door. If there had been a Tango left at one of the windows he could have taken at least half of the team out with one burst. If we could see the CCTV footage, we could give you a more in-depth analysis." Mac kept a steady innocent look on his face.

"Do you think the famous SAS could do better?" Sharp was obviously not pleased with the frank analysis.

Two of the SAS troops opened their mouths to respond, but Mac spoke up first.

"We aren't here to compete. Just learn as much as we can and offer a few tips if possible. The team was very good."

"What, our facility not good enough for you? Can't lower yourself to take part? Or are you all talk, I've always suspected the SAS reputation was based on a few specific jobs without any great experience. I heard that an SAS team got captured as they got off the helicopter in Libya in 2011. Not exactly a shining endorsement."

There were a couple of snorts from the SAS team and at least one stepped forward to answer Sharp.

Mac held up his hand to stop any of his team. "Most of our operations never get publicity. I can't comment on the capture in Libya, but sometimes a team has to be sacrificed. If the opposition are expecting an assault it's best to give them one they can stop while the real assault goes off unchallenged."

"Maybe. But that isn't an answer. You were scheduled to do a day of attacks later in the week. Why not now? Surely the SAS are up to an unplanned assault. Aren't the SAS always ready?"

Mac looked Sharp coolly in the eye, maybe it was time to bring him down a little.

"Okay, but we'll need our gear. And I have to warn

you, we aren't known for being building friendly. I hope your insurance is paid up."

"Don't worry. The FBI probably has a maintenance budget larger than your operational funding." Sharp turned to one of the instructors in an orange fluorescent tabard and indicated for her to come over.

"Agent Kenny will take you back to the barracks to collect your gear."

"No need for us all to go. Jez." Sergeant Jez Stinger stepped forward. "Jez, go with the agent and collect the assault gear. Back here in thirty."

"Full gear, Mac?"

"Oh yes."

"What about Mark?"

Mark Smedley was the only missing member of the team. He was the 'fly boy' a specialist in helicopters and fixed wing aircraft. He could fly anything as well as being a full member of the assault tem. He was spending the day with the FBI helicopter assault team.

"No, we won't be doing an aerial assault. Mark can sit this one out. Let him play with the FBI's toys."

Jez Stinger walked briskly away with the female FBI instructor.

"I'll take you down to the staging area at the end of the street. You see the broad yellow line across the road at the end? The exercise starts as you cross the line, but the time only starts as the first man enters the building and stops when the last man comes out, the exercise ends when you cross the line again."

"Dan, you'll be the hostage."

"Oh come on, Mac. I'm always the hostage." Danny Fathom was clearly unhappy at the order.

"Stop whinging, Danny. It's your turn. But maybe Agent Sharp, sorry *Special* Agent Sharp would keep you company?"

Sharp looked at Mac, obviously not sure what he

was being asked.

"When the SAS train back at home, we use live ammo but put one of the team into the building. That way it sharpens our aim and gets an informed opinion from the hostage's point of view. So, would you be a second hostage?"

"You want me to go in there with live ammo flying around?" the incredulity was evident in Sharp's tone.

"Well you'll have a vest on. Of course, if the FBI doesn't have the nerve..." Mac let the sentence hang.

Sharp looked around, not sure that his earlier needling of the British troops was the best idea he had ever had, but was unwilling to lose face.

"Okay, I'll be one of the hostages. Just make sure your aim is bloody good."

When they got to the end of the road, Special Agent Sharp left the SAS men to talk and went into the control room to brief the operators and set up the exercise.

Twenty minutes later Jez Stinger arrived back at the end of the street, the large 4x4 obviously full of equipment.

Sharp came out of the control room and walked over to the assault team. He was now wearing a bulky bulletproof vest usually worn by the HRT.

"You can get changed over there." Sharp indicated a low concrete building.

Mac nodded. "Dan, you stay here with Mr Sharp and explain what will happen as a hostage."

Mac led the way to the building, each SAS trooper carrying an assortment of equipment and bags.

"Listen up," said Mac. "Once we're in the building we're operational. And that building is unknown status."

"You think they'll be listening?" asked Jez.

"I would be."

270

By now they were at the entrance to the building. Mac kept walking and headed around the corner.

"Remember team three's accident in the killing house about three months back?"

"With the frag?" said Sergeant Ken 'Snake' Dunhelm

"Yes. I want to repeat that as we assault the building. And Bird, I want you in position." Mac nodded and used his eyes to indicate a building across the street to Corporal John 'Bird' Sparrow.

"Can we do that?" asked Bird.

"No one has said we can't. But that's why I want the frag incident. That'll distract them so you can exfil."

The men entered the building and started emptying the bags and checking equipment, now using hand gestures to indicate their status.

Fifteen minutes later the men exited the building and walked over to Sharp who was still standing outside the command centre with Danny Fathom.

Sharp noticed the movement from the corner of his eye and turned to face the approaching SAS assault team. He was used to seeing all sorts of men, dressed in all modes of uniform. The SAS, dressed all in black and carrying their weapons at the ready were not dissimilar to the FBI HRT. But something was subtly different. Whereas the HRT looked like a professional assault team ready to take on any obstacle to achieve their goal, the SAS looked like they would simply destroy any obstacle and walk over it. Maybe it was the full face respirators that made them look meaner, or the way they held their weapons, but something appeared distinctly deadly about the SAS team. Not for the first time in the last half hour, Sharp wondered why he had agreed to be a hostage.

"Okay, well, the short briefing." Sharp sounded distinctly uneasy.

"There are at least two hostages, unknown number of bad guys, but at least six, possibly as many as ten. Bad guys are known to be armed and ready to use weapons, some of which are assault automatics. They're using the building as a base so they've had time to set things up. Any questions?"

"Primary objective?" This came from Jez Stinger.

"Primary objective is hostage rescue, secondary is capture of terrorists."

"Okay, let's kill something," smirked Bird at the look on Sharp's face. This surprised the rest of the SAS men as John Sparrow was normally the quiet member of the team.

"Right, five minutes, you two," Mac looked at Sharp and Danny Fathom, "had better get into position."

Mac ran over last minute instructions and assignments before pulling his full face gas mask down and clicking two switches to activate the comms.

By now a large crowd had gathered to watch the assault. Word had quickly spread around the facility that the SAS were going in and it seemed like everyone wanted to see the best of the best either give a lesson or fall flat on their face.

One of the instructors gave a thumbs up and the SAS crossed the wide yellow line at a fast run to the nearest car. Using hand signals rather than voice communications, Mac directed the men to cover the distance to two box vans sitting outside of the building they were to assault.

Mac and Jez ran at a low crouch to the front of the building, stopping either side of the railings fronting the building's entrance. As they stopped, two short bursts of automatic fire rang out from the SAS team behind them.

"Tango one, down."

"Shit," the operator sitting at the computer screen pushed back from his station as the screen went black and simulated blood dripped down. "The lucky bastard just took out the lookout on the second floor."

The operator had been using CCTV to watch the street from the inside of the building, one of the 'terrorists'. He had intended to time the response with the SAS entering the building, but the SAS had seen the dummy with the camera and taken it out with two bursts of automatic fire.

Mac covered the buildings opposite, while the rest of the team covered the target building. Jez took the Remington 870 shotgun from his back and fired four shots at the double doors. Each round carried a small explosive charge and took out the hinges and almost half of the doors which fell into the building. Before the doors hit the floor, Mac pulled his arm back and threw a green cylinder with a black rim towards the opening. Rather than going through the opening the grenade bounced off the top of the stone doorway and bounced into the street.

"GRENADE," yelled Mac.

Everyone watching the start of the assault recognised the fragmentation grenade, a weapon that was packed with high explosive and enough metal and plastic fragments to ruin everyone's day. The crowd dropped to the floor, either behind some solid object or covering their heads with their hands.

At almost the same time as Mac threw the frag grenade, Jez pulled the pins on flash-bangs and hurled two through the door opening where they exploded with a huge crack and intense white light.

Another operator in the control centre was shocked to see his screen turn white and his ears fill with static. He knew the signs, the SAS had used flash-bang grenades on the hallway. It would take about ten seconds before his view started to return, another thirty or so before he started to get stereo sound back through his headphones. He pressed the trigger and fired a burst of automatic rounds, the computer controlling the machine pistol in the building would pick a direction, or several, at random to fire the high velocity paintball rounds. It would be pure luck if he managed to hit any of the troops, but it was worth a try. The smile on his face vanished as he saw the top of his screen turn red and blood start to flow down. A second later his console went dead.

Mac and Jez burst through the open doors less than half a second after the flash-bangs exploded. Scanning the large open foyer, it looked like the building had been set up as a hotel. They both saw a figure on the stairs, an automatic rifle pointing off at an angle. Both men fired a three round burst at the same time, all six bullets finding their target, which bent double. They assumed that was the sign that the target had been neutralized.

Before the echo of the shots had died away two more SAS troopers came through the door and automatically took up covering positions behind Mac and Jez.

"Tango two, down," said Jez over the radio as Mac kept a mental count. Two bad guys down, how many left?

"Bird?" said Mac as they scanned the area.

"Ten seconds," came the reply.

As the dummy frag grenade bounced into the street and the observers dove for cover, Corporal John 'Bird' Sparrow had peeled off from the assault and ran across the street, behind the opposite building and up the fire escape. He was now setting up on the second floor flat roof and would have his sniper rifle ready in ten seconds.

With hand signals, Mac indicated their route. It was an educated guess, but he knew that Sharp would not want the SAS beating any records, so he suspected that the hostages would be as far away as possible from the entrance, which meant second floor, far end of the corridor.

The SAS men started to climb the stairs in pairs, each man covering the other, Mac and Nick Perkins at the front, Jez and Snake bringing up the rear and covering the bottom floor. As they reached the first landing and turned back on themselves, Jez chambered a gas canister into the grenade launcher fastened to the bottom of his MP5, a custom made attachment, and fired it down onto the ground floor.

The men sitting at the terminals smiled as their second colleague pushed back from his dead screen. They were ready for this, looking forward to the challenge of taking on the SAS. Two early casualties taken so quickly was not a good start, but they had a few tricks left yet.

Two of the operators were puzzled as their screen started to simulate running water, making the picture blurred, and they could hear coughing and choking in their earphones. The SAS were using tear gas.

Mac and Perkins stepped from the stairs onto the first floor corridor. Six doors each side of the corridor, two open on the left, one on the right. Mac indicated for Perkins to take up position as Jez and Snake passed and continued up the stairs. Mac and Perkins readied flash-bangs and tossed them into the first two rooms and followed into the first. The room was empty, no targets, no hostages.

"Bird on line. Tango three and four, one, two." Bird was in place and had spotted two targets on floor one, second room.

"Bird, fire at will, but only on the floor we are assaulting."

"Roger that. X-rays two five."

X-rays - hostages, were in the fifth room, second floor, as Mac had suspected.

In the control room the men were watching their displays intently, two of them still having trouble focusing due to the effects of the tear gas. Flash-bangs went off, shaking two of the units but causing no ill effects, the grenades going off in the next room. One of the operators readied his weapon, as soon as the door opened, he would open fire before they could throw in the flash-bang. He indicated for his partner in the room to take up position to one side of the door. Before he could complete the thought his screen went red and the console died. He looked around in time to see his partner's screen do the same. How had they done that, they had not even opened the door?

Four operators down in fifty seconds.

"Tangos three and four down," reported Bird.

Mac and Perkins headed back to the stairs, pausing to check up and down the stairwell before firing two tear gas canisters along the first floor corridor.

Jez and Snake had paused at the landing between the first and second floors, ready to advance. Mac gave the signal and they climbed the stairs, staying to the outside and covering all areas with broad sweeps of their weapons.

"Tango five, two landing."

Even through their masks and head gear Mac and the others heard the double tinkle of glass as Bird's two sniper rounds crashed through the windows and took out the single dummy in hiding behind the packing cases on the second floor landing.

"Tango five down. Tango six and seven, two, two. Tango eight and nine and X-rays one and two, two five. No clear shots."

Mac indicated for Jez and Snake to cover the rooms to the left, he and Perkins took the right. In unison, both pairs of troopers kicked open the first two doors and threw flash-bangs into the rooms each side of the corridor.

In the control room the remaining operators monitored the sound and shock waves of the flash-bangs. The troops were clearing the second floor. They had just thrown flash-bangs into the first two rooms, both empty but that had signalled where they were, they should be entering the second room in about ten seconds. One of the operators covering the second room looked across at his partner and grinned, nodding at the thought of being the ones to take down at least two of the SAS troops.

Jez and Snake followed the flash-bang into the first room and swept the area with their MP5s, no targets. As the explosions ripped through the first room, Mac and Perkins kicked open the door of the second room and entered at speed, stepping to each side of the door so that they were not framed in the open door. Quickly scanning the room they both saw a target and fired a three round burst at each. Both targets twisted and slumped, one firing off a sustained burst of paint balls which went wide and covered the floor.

The control room operators grinned at each other and turned back to the consoles in time to see the door to the room slam open and the SAS troops enter. Both of them snatched for their controls as their screens turned red. They should have had at least another five seconds, how had the SAS got in there so fast?

"Tango six and seven down," reported Perkins.

Mac and Perkins stepped back into the corridor at the same time as Jez and Snake. Mac gave a few hand signals and Jez and Snake continued to clear the rooms, left and right as Mac and Perkins jogged down the corridor to the fourth door on the right. Bird had said the first and third rooms on the right were empty. Let's hope he was right, thought Mac.

The third room was indeed empty and Mac signalled for Perkins to ready the gear.

Jez and Snake cleared the next two rooms, both empty. The last on the left was different. The flash-bang went in and Jez and Snake followed. The room was half filled with cardboard boxes, several had been blown away due to the flash-bang, leaving a target across the room. Snake brought his MP5 around and fired a sustained burst on full auto and at the same time felt a hard hit on his leg. The target went limp and doubled over.

"Tango ten down," said Snake.

Jez sprang to one side and covered the other side of the room. Another target was swinging its gun in his direction. Jez fired a sustained burst and saw it double over, the paint balls going wide.

"Tango eleven, down. Snake?"

"Okay Jez, flesh wound to left leg."

"Okay, stand down, ready for extraction."

Any shots that actually hit the target were classed as 'fatal' if to the head or chest, 'debilitating' if to the body other than the chest, or 'weakening' if to the limbs. A weakened victim could only move at half speed and could not take further part in combat.

Snake simulated a limp as he exited the room. Jez flattened himself to the side wall to cover his exit. He was not surprised to see three of the boxes fall forward as Snake reached the door. The room was obviously a trap. Jez fired off a second sustained burst, hitting the target and sweeping the area to each side before exiting to the corridor.

"Tango twelve down," reported Jez.

The control room was a quiet seething mass of suppressed anger and frustration. The three latest operators to see red were pushing back from their stations.

"I got one, I'm telling you I got one of them."

Several other operators were still at consoles, two sitting together and discussing strategies. Four others gesturing to positions on the bottom floor, setting up flanking positions and preparing trip wires on grenades ready for the SAS team as they came down the stairs to leave the building. Ten operators down in two minutes fifty-five seconds. But they had to get out yet.

Mac listened to the reports from Jez and was not surprised to hear that there were at least twelve tangos. He had not expected the estimate of six to ten bad guys to be accurate after everything Sharp had said.

"Ready, Mac," reported Jez.

"GO."

Jez kicked the last door on the right and stepped back out of the line of fire, not even throwing flash-bangs. At the same time Perkins pressed down on two detonators.

The two shaped rope charges detonated, one blowing a ragged hole in the wall between the fourth and fifth room, the other destroying a large section of the exterior wall and window.

The two control room operators who had been discussing tactics saw the door to the room crash open and they opened fire on full automatic. But no target materialised in the doorway to launch flash-bangs. Almost instantly there was a flash and concussive blast from the left which they could feel through the force feedback of their chairs and hand controls. Before they had a chance to turn, both screens went red.

"I don't believe it, the door was a bloody decoy. The bastards have come through the walls."

Twelve down, three minutes twenty seconds.

Mac and Perkins peered through the dust and picked out their targets, Mac allowing his red laser designator to flash across the eyes of Special Agent Sharp before each fired a single shot, aware that the hostages were in the room. The two dummies slumped forward and Mac and Perkins stepped through the opening.

"ARE YOU GUYS MAD, YOU COULD HAVE KILLED US." Sharp spat a string of expletives for several seconds before seeming to run out of things to say.

By now Mac and Perkins had freed the two faux-hostages.

"Can you fast rope?" asked Mac to Sharp.

"What?"

"Can you fast rope?"

"Yes, but...why?"

"Put these on." Mac gave Sharp a pair of heavy duty leather gloves and led him and Fathom back through the hole into the next room. As they stepped through they were just in time to see Snake disappear over the rim of the hole in the exterior wall. Jez was already on the floor outside covering the other's exit.

"Danny, go." Fathom stepped over to the rope and rappelled rapidly down.

"Sharp."

"I'm not going out there. That's not in the rules."

"You didn't say it wasn't in the rules. So you either go or I'll knock you out and carry you down."

Sharp only paused for a second, the men still looked menacing and he had no doubt that Mac was capable of backing up the threat. He pulled the gloves on and stepped through the opening.

Mac watched him clear the gap and nodded for Perkins to follow on the second rope and then swung himself over the edge and rapidly slid down the first, only slowing himself ten feet from the floor.

As Mac and Perkins landed, Jez was already helping Snake along the street at a quick jog. Perkins herded Fathom and Sharp along the street as Mac covered their exit.

Ten seconds later Mac crossed the wide yellow line at the end of the street to a huge round of applause from the gathered crowd. The SAS men made safe their weapons and removed their masks.

The senior controller came from the operations centre and handed Sharp a note. He read the note and looked up at the SAS men.

"Did you have a sniper?"

Mac nodded. "Bird, up there." He indicated the rooftop opposite where Bird was standing, his L96A1 AW 7.62mm sniper rifle held at an angle away from his body, the butt stock on his hip.

"How did you get him up there without anyone knowing?"

"He hung well back across the street when we started the approach. I had a slight accident with a fragmentation grenade at the entrance and everyone took cover, Bird crossed to the ladder and climbed up.

281

The grenade wasn't primed. Bird directed us from there and took out several tangos, that's how we refer to targets. With visual he could see through the windows and with infrared he could detect the heat signature of the motors of the targets. They were obviously different to living people so we knew where the hostages were and headed for them rather than clearing the whole building."

Sharp actually looked as if he had grudging admiration of the men.

"Well, it's not exactly orthodox, and not what we were expecting."

"Predictability in this game gets you killed real quick," replied Mac.

"And you weren't exaggerating about not being building friendly." Sharp looked at the damage to the building and then down at the paper again before looking back up and holding out his hand.

"Congratulations Sergeant Major, you just broke the record. Five minutes twenty-four."

Chapter 25

11:50hrs, 18th April
Outside of Philadelphia

Grantham slowed and turned into the rest stop. The journey from New York to Philadelphia was an easy eighty miles, especially in the luxurious BMW 550i, but they had taken a scenic route, which had added another forty miles, to see some of the most amazing sights of blossom they could have imagined.

"I've always wanted to see the colours in autumn, but now I've seen the spring colours...wow. They're something else," said Charisma as they climbed from the car and headed for the small collection of shops and cafes.

"I was here a few years ago and we spent two weeks in the woodlands. If there is one thing America has in abundance, it's space."

"You were camping?"

Grantham smiled at the thought. "You could say that, mind you there was a group of US Marines trying to track us down." At the look on Charisma's face he smiled again. "Don't worry. We were on a military exercise. For a week they hunted us, then for the next week we hunted them. We didn't have a lot of time to admire the countryside, but I do remember how stunning it was."

As Grantham and Charisma walked into the small arcade of shops, a late model cherry red Dodge Charger turned into the park, its V8 engine burbling with restrained power and pulled up well away from the BMW but within the line of sight. The driver sat back watching the BMW and considering his options.

Michael had flown in the morning after Charisma and Grantham and had immediately hired the car at the airport and driven to Grantham and Charisma's hotel. His instructions had been amended. His superiors felt another attempt on the girl's life would be too suspicious. So for now he was to watch and follow the two of them. If killing the pair was his only task he had already had several occasions where he could simply have gunned the pair down and driven away. But it was correct, an obvious murder would attract an investigation, and the two had been asking questions of the authorities who may put two and two together and suspect that his earlier killings may have been less than accidents or natural causes.

Tracking the pair had not been easy. There was only one transaction on the girl's credit card, when she booked into the hotel while Grantham was still in police custody. He had tried to track Grantham's cards, but his contacts had spotted that any searches were automatically tracked and reported. For that to be the case, Grantham must have friends within the security services. And if that was the case he was someone Michael would have to take seriously. But it seemed like God was smiling down on him. He had arrived at the hotel just after lunch to stake it out, less than an hour before they left. He had followed them west, quickly realising that they were heading for the site of his killing of Robert P Jacobs in March. The couple had stayed in a small Mom and Pop hotel for the night, allowing Michael time to place a tracker on their car so he could track them without having to stay in visual range.

While they were staying in New York, God had again smiled down on his servant and had arranged for Michael to occupy the room next to Valentine and Grantham. This allowed him to listen in to their conversations by the use of an electronic version of the glass against the wall. He had used similar technology to listen in to their conversation at breakfast yesterday when it seemed they had some sort of clues leading them to the Knights Templars. This allowed him to track and listen in to the couple, but most of all it had given him time to plan.

18:30hrs
La Palma, Canary Islands

The sea breeze blowing across the volcanic island was refreshing, taking the edge off the heat from the still strong sun in the blue, cloudless sky. The island rose steeply from the blue of the Atlantic Ocean 400 miles west of Morocco. A favourite destination for holidaymakers, the island's peak rises almost 8,000 feet above sea level with the base of the island plummeting to 13,000 feet under water. With a population of 90,000, the island's main industry, and source of income, is tourism. Within the scientific community, the island is also famed for its twelve internationally renowned observatories.

The small team of three stood back and watched as the fourth man tapped away at a tablet computer. The connection established within seconds and data started to feed into the small computer. After a few minutes the man made a few adjustments and the results started to match up to the predictions. They would monitor the results locally for the next twenty-four hours to ensure there were no hardware problems. This was far easier on land than checking the sensors they had placed out at sea, which were the majority. Recovering the sea bound ones varied from difficult to impossible.

Heinrich Hummner smiled at the thought of the last twenty-seven months. It had been a long hard project.

He had travelled the world with the team, both land and sea, placing the disruptors at predetermined locations. Hundreds of them. And they were now down to the last handful before they all came on-line. Things had not always gone smoothly. There were several times he feared for his position, possibly his life. But he had always managed to pull things around and he had received not only good feedback, but a promotion and pay increase with the promise of a substantial completion bonus.

"Okay, everything's looking good. Pack up the equipment. We will head back to the town and check everything overnight and in the morning."

13:50hrs
Philadelphia

Grantham stepped from the car and handed the keys to the parking attendant along with a ten dollar bill.

"Thank you, sir. Is there anything in the trunk?"

"Two cases."

The attendant opened the boot and lifted the cases out and placed them onto a trolley. Refusing the offer of help, Grantham pushed the trolley from the parking area into the hotel reception.

The weather had turned distinctly warm on the drive down from New York. Whereas the Big Apple had been cool, dull and overcast with frequent light showers, Philadelphia was bright, hot and distinctly summery.

Grantham looked around the large open reception area, the floor and walls were muted cream and brown polished stone which gave a bright, airy, cool feel, a nice relief from the heat outside. Registering took less than two minutes and the receptionist handed over two credit card room keys and quickly ran through the facilities of the thirty floor hotel.

"And lastly is the Cricketers' Restaurant." The receptionist indicated the double glass doors across from the reception. "The restaurant specialises in English cooking, it may give you a taste of home."

"Thanks. But we can get English cooking at home. I was hoping for a Philly Steak."

The receptionist smiled. "They serve the best in town, with any accompaniment you wish to add."

Grantham checked his watch. "Could we book a table for five o'clock?"

The receptionist tapped at the computer for a few seconds. "Five will be fine, Mr Grantham."

"Do you have any brochures for local attractions?"

The receptionist indicated to her left. "There's a large rack of brochures and magazines just outside of the deli."

Grantham nodded his thanks, flashed her a smile, and turned to the bank of lifts to the rear of the lobby.

Five minutes later Grantham and Charisma were in their fifteenth floor room. Charisma spread out on one of the two king sized beds while Grantham started to unpack the two cases.

"So, what now?" asked Charisma when Grantham finished and put the cases away into the bottom of the large closet.

"Well for a start I suggest we go downstairs and gather as many leaflets about Philadelphia as we can get. Then we take them into the bar and get some drinks before dinner."

"Good grief, have you seen that?" Charisma was standing at the almost wall-sized glass window looking out across the street.

Grantham walked across and looked out. Across the street was a large building, at least thirty storeys. Half way down the building, just below the level of their own room, were two window cleaners swinging from ropes attached to multi-point harnesses and bosuns' chairs. Large white buckets of water were suspended behind the chairs and they were expertly swinging from side to side, dragging the squeegees over the surface of the windows.

"Rather them than me," said Grantham.

Charisma turned to Grantham and looked him up and down. "I thought you were a big tough Para, used to jumping out of aircraft at thousands of feet."

Grantham smiled. "I didn't say I couldn't do it. But jumping out of a perfectly serviceable aircraft never seemed natural. Anyway, if you want to eat I'll just have a quick shower."

Charisma went to the wardrobe and selected a clean top and threw it onto the bed as she turned back to select new jeans. The top flew too far and landed on the bedside table causing a slight clatter as it knocked things over. She crossed to the small cabinet between the two king sized beds and picked the notepad and pen from the floor and Grantham's thin gold watch with the elegant black face. Before she realised, she was reading the inscription on the back. With a frown she placed the watch back on the table and got changed.

A few minutes later Grantham emerged from the bathroom, still naked from the waist up, towelling his short wavy, almost black hair.

"Good shower, very powerful," said Grantham.

"I'll try it later. The SAS motto is 'Who Dares Wins' isn't it?"

Grantham nodded.

"When Dad came back from being away for a few days, Mum would often ask him 'Did you win?' and Dad would always reply 'Dared and won' which I now realise was a play on the SAS motto."

Grantham nodded again, not sure where this was

going.

"I noticed the inscription on the back of your watch, the winged dagger and the inscription 'You Dared and Won'. Are you in the SAS?"

"I was, I retired a couple of years ago. I've been freelance since then."

"Why didn't you tell me before?"

"I prefer not to broadcast my past for several reasons. And when we found out about your Dad it didn't seem right. To be fair, I didn't actually lie to you. And it's not a winged dagger, although that's what most people think. It's actually Excalibur surrounded by flames."

Charisma was clearly weighing up Grantham. After a few seconds she seemed to come to a decision. "Okay, I'll accept that." She walked over to him and, reaching up, she put her arms around his still damp neck and kissed him. "Fancy helping me work up an appetite?" she asked with a flirty smile. "And by the look of it, that shower wasn't cold enough."

Ninety minutes later they were in the hotel restaurant. The room was cool and comfortable, with thickly padded bench seats and high backed leather chairs. There were prints on the walls of typically English scenes: cricketers playing on a village green, the English Rugby Union and League teams, several of the royal family, including a picture of Prince William and Kate from their wedding day, rolling green countryside and Stonehenge. Several prints of London showing black taxis, red busses and Beefeaters. Wall lights with imitation candles in old style sconces and even a large inglenook fireplace at the far end of the room, albeit without a lit fire.

They had put the leaflets to one side while they ordered food and drinks.

"So, after all the research and training you've done, do you actually follow any recognised religion?" asked Grantham.

"That's something I've struggled with for years. There is almost unlimited evidence, but the vast majority of it is either circumstantial or hearsay. There are places and events that exist or are so well recorded they can be taken as true and correct. But, well...none of those things are actual proof. But after a while, the volume of circumstantial evidence starts to become overwhelming."

"So you do believe in something."

Charisma paused with handful of salted peanuts part way to her mouth and shrugged. "I don't know. What about you?"

Grantham smiled, "Religion isn't something I've given a lot of thought to, at least what I believe in. I've seen it cause lots of suffering all over the world, lots of death and destruction."

"That's not religion, it's religious followers, zealots."

"Subtle difference. I will say that there are no atheists on the battlefield. As soon as the bullets start to fly everyone discovers religion."

Both of them were lost in thought for a few seconds.

"Okay, putting formal religion aside, what do you think of the Ahnenerbe beliefs in the Aryan race of supermen?"

"There is some anecdotal evidence of different races having inhabited the Earth, and I don't mean our ancestors."

"I thought the Aryan race was just fiction?" said Grantham.

"It probably is. But you've heard of the ancient Greek and Roman myths of Gods coming to Earth and mating with humans? Their offspring were giants and demigods. Well in western religion, particularly the Jewish bible, angels came to Earth. The first were the fallen angels. Some mated with humans resulting in offspring of giants. But what if the giants weren't physical giants but mental giants, highly intelligent or with special mental powers?"

"That assumes that angels exist, and by extension God or Gods."

Charisma shrugged. "I'm just stating research and possibilities. But from what I understand, the Ahnenerbe believed that Jesus was either the son of God, or was the offspring of God and a human host. Jesus could have been a 'giant', the last of the Aryan race. And they want his DNA to breed back to a better, more pure form."

Grantham looked across the room and saw their waitress bringing a tray of food and broke out into a smile.

"You're going to enjoy this, I can feel my arteries clogging at the thought of it."

The waitress set two plates of steaming Philly Cheese Steaks in front of them with a large bowl of fries and a large pitcher of iced water.

Charisma looked at the huge pile of food in front of her.

"So this is shredded steak, onions and cheese fried together with added mushrooms."

"And I've got the same but with peppers and mild chillies instead of mushrooms." Grantham scooped up the large roll in two hands, a lot of the filling spilling onto the plate, and bit into the large sandwich, a closed lip grin spreading across his face as he chewed the melt in the mouth filling.

Charisma took a few seconds weighing up the best approach, even considering the knife and folk before giving a small shrug and following Grantham's lead and simply diving in with both hands. For several minutes they ate in silence apart from the occasional satisfied sigh and groan.

After five minutes Grantham pushed his empty plate away and sat back, tapping his stomach. "Wow. That was as good as I remember. How are you doing?"

Charisma put down the small handful of sandwich and also sat back. "I can't finish it, more's the pity. That is fantastic." She sighed and reached for her glass of still cold Budweiser.

For several minutes the two chatted and unconsciously dipped into the large bowl of fries until they too were gone.

"I suppose that being in the SAS you got very close to the other men, more like a family?"

Grantham nodded, "Not just in the SAS. You get the same in any profession where you have to depend on the people around you, military, police, fire brigade etc." Grantham smiled at some memory. "Mind you, like all families, it doesn't always go smoothly."

"That sounds like the start of a story," probed Charisma.

"Well, a few years ago we were in CQB, that's Close Quarters Battle, and one of the lads managed to get himself captured. I came into the room and the bad guy had his arm around Snake's neck using him as a shield and was pointing a handgun at me and then Snake and then back at me. He shouted that if we didn't let him go he'd shoot me and then Snake."

"So what did you do?"

Grantham grinned but also managed to look a little sheepish. "I shot the bad guy."

"I thought you said he was using this Snake as a shield?"

"He was, Snake was shorter so I shot him through the shoulder and the bullet went through Snake and into the bad guy's chest."

Charisma shook her head in part wonderment and part incredulity. "Did it kill Snake?"

Grantham shook his head. "No, Snake was okay after a couple of weeks R and R. Although he never lets me forget that I actually shot him."

"Why was he called Snake?"

Grantham actually laughed this time. "It's for the reason you can imagine. When we got new recruits in, he'd wait until after an exercise and they were queuing up at the toilets and then he'd go behind them and ask them to 'pass this forward'. I've actually heard grown men almost scream in shock."

"Mmm...I think I'd like to meet this Snake," grinned Charisma.

Grantham put a hurt look on his face. "Okay, you take half of the leaflets and I'll take the other half," he said .

"I think we can be a bit cleverer than that. We're not looking for quickly changing exhibits. We need something that's permanent. Probably historic."

Grantham nodded and started to sort through the leaflets, putting aside temporary art exhibits or festivals.

The remaining leaflets he split up and started leafing through his half.

Independence National Historical Park the most historic square mile in the U.S.A., it was here that a group of colonists first got together to plan their independence from the King of England.

Independence Hall built between 1732 and 1756 as the Pennsylvania State House, this is the site where the Declaration of Independence, modelled after the Magna Carta, was first adopted and the United States Constitution was written.

Franklin Court, the site of Benjamin Franklin's

house.

Betsy Ross house, the home of Betsy Ross who made the first American Flag.

Suddenly Charisma sat forward and gripped Grantham's hand.

"Look, this has to be it. Here, look at the last part of the clue, and look at the names on this leaflet. This is where we need to go."

Chapter 26

11:10hrs, 19th April
MoD London

They had been in the room for three hours, it felt like three days. After the initial meeting yesterday afternoon, they had discussed the approach and implications late into the night. Food and drinks had been brought in, and they had only broken just before midnight. Billie Lee had stayed in one of the small guest rooms provided in the basement of the building, usually referred to as cells by the guests, and had been back in the meeting room by 08:00 that morning.

For the last ten minutes, Billie Lee had sat back listening to most of the others arguing over the perceived threat and their planned response.

"Gentlemen!" Billie Lee raised her voice and snapped the word to get attention. The arguing died away quickly and all faces turned towards her.

"As far as I can tell, there seems to be some disagreement between you as to just how much of a threat this is?"

Several of the others looked around the table at each other, some, the military officers, slightly uneasily at the fact that Billie Lee had taken charge.

"Even after what you told us yesterday and what is speculated in the reports," General Simmonds indicated several volumes on the table, "the threat seems a little remote."

Billie Lee looked around the table, pausing before answering.

"The facts and figures are all in the report. But let me give you a few examples that aren't spelled out.

74,000 years ago there was a massive eruption of the Toba volcano in Sumatra. That eruption brought the human race to the point of extinction, there were as few as two to five thousand humans that survived. But that probably still seems a distant event. In 1783 Iceland's Laki volcano put so much ash into the air that six million people died due to crop failure. There are around 1,500 active volcanoes around the world with fifty eruptions every year.

"La Palma in the Canary Islands has been rumbling away for years. There is speculation that if the volcano has a major eruption, a third of the island could fall into the sea. That could result in a tsunami hundreds of feet high travelling at just under the speed of sound. The Canary Islands would be wiped out. The wave would hit Portugal, Spain, France and England less than an hour later. Three hours after that the wave would hit the eastern seaboard of North and South America and destroy everything from one to ten miles inland.

"If Mount Fuji in Japan erupted again it could wipe out Tokyo and its thirty-five million inhabitants. Only twenty years ago, satellites found a potential new super-volcano in Bolivia. Since then it has been growing at two centimetres in height every year over an area of forty-five thousand square miles. That means that magma is flowing into the magma chamber one cubic metre every second of every day.

"The relatively small earthquake that affected New Zealand in February 2011 measured 6.3 on the Richter scale, and shook the ground for seventy seconds. Every second of that time the earthquake released the equivalent power of ten tactical nuclear weapons.

"Now what we are discussing here is not the eruption of one volcano or one tsunami or one earthquake. If some organisation has developed a way of triggering these events, they could trigger dozens, maybe hundreds of events across the whole globe. It is no exaggeration to say that the whole of life on Earth is under threat. The fact that there are no truly active volcanoes in the UK would not matter if there was so much ash in the air that sunlight were blocked out for a year, or if a giant wave wiped out all life and property for several miles inland along the whole of the coast. This threat is real." Billie Lee sat back and let the information sink in. All those around the table either looked at each other or down at the polished table top, seemingly lost in thought for several seconds.

"Eh, we've been discussing the effects and likelihood of this happening and our response. But shouldn't we ask how it could be done?" This came from one of the younger men at the table. He was in his mid-thirties, fair haired and clean shaven. As was the fashion these days, he wore an open neck pink shirt with white collar under a chunky grey jumper that made him look more like a salesman than an IT expert working for GCHQ, the British electronic surveillance and communication agency.

"We covered that earlier Mr Barrett. A combination of hundreds of frequencies being projected together and gradually building up to eventually tip the balance to an eruption or earthquake," replied Air Marshal Colridge-Stewart with an edge of impatience in his voice.

"Sorry sir, I didn't exactly mean that. I understand the theory of how the effects can be delivered. What I meant is how would all the devices be coordinated? If they were to set off multiple devices the most devastating effect would be to set them off all at the same time. But if I understand the theory correctly each device would not only send out a multitude of frequencies in order to build up an eventual chain reaction, it would have to monitor the effects and make constant adjustments. No two locations would react the

297

same, so the time to build up the effect would vary. From Richard Caley's predictions that would take days if not weeks."

"Okay, well you're our communications expert Mr Barrett, how would you coordinate the devices?"

"Well...two ways come to mind. You could set them off with a deadline and they would work towards it autonomously, monitor their own performance and feedback and adjust to achieve the goal at a preset time. But that would be dangerous. If anything went wrong or things didn't progress as planned you could get the effects spread out over time rather than one massive effect."

Barrett sat back and locked his fingers behind his head, obviously more comfortable talking about his own subject. "The best thing to do, the only practical thing, would be for each device to communicate with a control centre which could monitor and adjust each one."

"What form would the communication take?" asked Air Marshal Colridge-Stewart, his uniform still looking crisp and clean even after three hours.

Barrett leant forward, glancing around the table as he spoke. "It would have to be digital, but the exact style could vary. It could be as simple as a mobile phone signal, using anything from ETSI to EGPRS. They could use a specific protocol, even short burst package data like our subs use. Record the data then send it out in a microburst to limit detection and location."

"Talking of submarines," said Billie Lee as she tapped some keys on one of the wireless keypads that were scattered around the table. "Many of the fault zones and key points of pressure are sub-sea. The New Zealand and Japanese earthquakes were both centred off the coast. I assume the device that causes the disruption would have to be close by. Could a device communicate from the sea floor?"

"Y.e.s...." Barrett dragged the word out. "We communicate with submarines and sub-sea bases. But it would be more difficult for a fixed device. Submarines surface, at least just enough to raise their antennas. We can send ultra long wave signals to them from shore. Undersea bases generally communicate with support vessels on the surface, usually via fixed cable and they relay the communications."

"So, how would an undersea installation communicate?"

Barrett sat back and thought for a few seconds.

"Several ways come to mind. One," he ticked the points off on his fingers. "The most reliable method would be via a direct hard wire to shore. But that would be a big undertaking, to lay a cable to shore. So two, have a surface ship or even a submarine on station and allow that to relay the data. But again, it's a bit impractical to have a ship, or especially a sub, permanently on station. The best way, three, would be the most convenient. Have a built-in antenna that could be wound out to the surface and withdrawn to, say, fifty feet to avoid any shipping. The communications could be burst or standard data stream."

"And could GCHQ track and trace them?"

"Well the signal would simply be lost amongst millions of other signals. Without knowing the signal characteristics the signal would be next to impossible to find."

"So it can't be done." General Clive Simmonds sat back looking dejected at the dead end his questions had come to.

Barrett smiled and sat forward. "I didn't say that, General. If the signal is emanating from land, especially a populated area, it would be lost in the

299

general clutter. But at sea there is much less chatter. And if the professor can give us the likely hot spots we can quickly check them and see if any signals are coming from the general areas."

10:00hrs
Philadelphia

The sun was hot and growing hotter. The concrete footpaths were reflecting the glare and making everyone without sunglasses squint in the bright light. Grantham and Charisma had only travelled eighty miles from New York, but by the feel of the weather they could have travelled eight hundred miles south.

The previous night's revelation had dawned when they saw the leaflet for the Liberty Bell. Housed in the Liberty Bell Centre, across from its long term home in Independence Hall, the Centre was purpose built to cope with the often large crowds. The Bell fitted in with the last part of John Valentine's puzzle '*the key was cast clear and sound in one of the land's new treasures*'. But it was the final part '*So it was that liberty would pass the key to stow.*' That clinched it. The bell was originally cast in London by the firm of Lester and Pack in 1752, but, following the bell cracking, it was twice recast by local craftsmen John Pass and John Stow.

After arriving early, Grantham and Charisma had walked across the street to the Independence Visitor Centre. This two storey high brick and glass building housed gift shops, a central cafe and ticket office. They browsed the gift shop for several minutes before purchasing tickets and heading for the cafe. After a leisurely cappuccino and triple chocolate cookie, they headed out of the centre and crossed the wide street to the purpose made Liberty Bell Centre that had just opened.

Although only just after 10:00, there was already a small queue waiting to get in. As they entered the hall, there was a security check with bag search and metal detector. Once through the security area they headed around the centre which was busy, but far from crowded. Most people were at the far end of the long gallery where the bell itself was housed. Grantham and Charisma took their time, deliberately browsing the sides, picking up history and information on the bell.

As they approached the main exhibition there was a small throng of people around the symbol of liberty. Small, narrow metal handrails ran both sides with white ropes across the ends to prevent access to the bell, although the public could still get within three feet. The walls were grey concrete and the end wall was made up of glass panels to let in as much light as possible. Grantham smiled slightly when he saw the glass. It was multi-layer anti-ballistic glass, nothing short of an RPG round would even scratch it.

Grantham and Charisma waited patiently, shuffling forward until they were next to the bell. Grantham was examining the bell with a detached air of scrutiny, Charisma seemed to have more a sense of wonder at what the bell represented.

"Here," said Grantham, pointing towards the top of the bell.

There were two lines of text circling the bell, *'Proclaim Liberty throughout all the land unto all the inhabitants thereof,'* from Leviticus 25:10, underneath which was *'By Order of the Assembly of the Province of Pensylvania for the State House in Philada'*. It was some years later that the now accepted spelling of Pennsylvania was adopted.

Just below the main inscription were the names they were looking for, Pass and Stow. The crack ran up from the bell mouth, stopping just short of the names.

Charisma looked from the bell to Grantham and back again, a hesitant smile on her face.

"It all fits, but what now?" she asked.

Grantham looked at the bell for a few seconds before photographing it from every angle.

"I'd like to know what happened to these two gentlemen," he pointed at the names on the bell.

As he backed away from the bell, several waiting Chinese tourists stepped in, posing politely for multiple photos.

"Let's see if we can find some more information about them."

It took some searching, the displays in the room covered every aspect of the bell's history. Its commissioning, design, its relevance to society, tours it had been on. But after thirty minutes, Charisma finally asked for advice from one of the attendants who was happy to point them in the right direction.

John Pass and John Stow were locals who earned a steady living as blacksmiths and foundry workers. The bell was originally commissioned in 1751 by the Philadelphia Assembly from London firm Whitechapel Foundry. The bell was delivered in 1752, but not hung until 10th March 1753. Unfortunately on the first ringing the bell cracked.

In order to solve the problem, the two local men were tasked with melting down and recasting the bell. During the process, Pass and Stow added one and a half ounces of copper per pound to decrease its brittleness. Once recast the townspeople were unhappy with the sound, and after receiving much criticism Pass and Stow melted the bell and tried again. In June 1753 the bell was again raised into place, a momentous occasion for John Stow, it being his 55th birthday. However, in November, the speaker of the Assembly, Quaker Isaac

Norris wrote that he was still displeased with the bell and requested that Whitechapel cast a new one.

Unfortunately once it was delivered from England, it was agreed that it sounded no better than the Pass and Stow recast bell. So the 'Liberty Bell' remained where it was in the steeple, and the new bell was placed in the clock tower to sound the hours.

"Here, this could be worth something," Charisma pointed to an entry in a large ledger with yellowed pages.

Grantham bent over, trying to angle the light and view to get the best contrast. The entry was a memorial to John Stow. It gave a brief description of his history and the part he played in the Liberty Bell. It ended with the funeral and memorial and his burial in city cemetery on Pine Street.

Grantham and Charisma looked around for another half an hour, but could not find any more references to either Pass or Stow and certainly nothing to connect them to the Knights Templars.

"Let's go back across the road to the Visitor Centre, they had some history books and I'm sure I saw something about the churchyard when I was scanning through them earlier," said Grantham.

Ten minutes later they were back across the road, scanning through several racks of book shelves.

"Can I help?" asked a young blonde girl with a dazzlingly white smile. She was the exact image of the American girl next door.

"We were in here earlier and noticed a book about Philadelphia, I think it was history? I noticed a piece about a cemetery I think. But I can't remember which book it was." Grantham returned the smile.

"Mmm... We have several books covering the city's history." The blonde looked along the shelves.

"This one...this one...and this one. I think there are a

few more along the far wall. If you have a look through these I'll go and get the others." She gave the same dazzling smile and placed the three books on a small side table that had some spare space.

Grantham flicked through the pages with Charisma watching closely. The first two books did not look familiar and he placed the second one down as the blonde returned with several others.

"I think these are all we have that cover history, this one is very popular, it covers history and the present."

Grantham glanced down at the cover. "That looks familiar." He took the book and flicked through to the centre where there were several pages of photographs. There, that was the image of the cemetery he had seen. Something to do with the making of a film.

"This is the one, thank you very much."

"You're welcome. Don't worry about these, I'll return them and maybe organize the books into some sort of order. Have a nice day."

"Thank you for your help." Grantham held out a ten dollar note, tipping in America was expected for good service.

"Oh, no. We don't work on tips here. But thank you very much."

"Okay. Is there a charity box that I could donate to?"

The blonde gave a dazzling smile and pointed towards the till. "We have a collection jar for war veterans, if you want to give something that would be very much appreciated."

"A very worthy cause. Thanks again."

Five minutes later they were sitting in the cafe, Grantham with a large Americano, Charisma with an even larger Cappuccino with chocolate dusting in the shape of the Liberty Bell.

"Here, this is the piece I saw earlier." Grantham

scanned through the article picking out pieces of interest.

"It houses 3,000 bodies, souls as they put it here...Mostly from the eighteenth and nineteenth century...Burials started in 1764...Most of the graves are nine feet deep with four interments per grave, usually family members...There are also a hundred vaults with two to ten bodies in each...During the civil war most of the stonemasons joined the military or fled the city so some of the graves went unmarked...The last interment was in 1958 for a University student who was murdered in a hate crime...There's a memorial garden...In 2004 a shootout scene was filmed there for the film National Treasure...The churchyard is open every day except national holidays...Information is available about those buried there by written request, or, there is a public record held at the church which you can browse through."

"So nothing about John Stow?" asked Charisma.

"Not directly. There is a list of the type or class of people buried there, everything from a signer of the U.S. Constitution to lawyers, doctors, sea captains, craftsmen and tradesmen."

"So what do we do? Go to the churchyard?"

Grantham considered this for a few seconds.

"I can't think of anything else, we've no further clues to go on."

Upon checking the map in the book, they saw that the cemetery was less than half a mile from the Independence Visitor Centre.

After finishing their drinks, they set off for a pleasant stroll through the older part of the city. The streets were considerably narrower, the buildings mostly two storey with the occasional three storey towering over its neighbours. Rather than the gleaming white stone of the newer part of the city, here the buildings were mostly red brick and timber, although the same sense of cleanliness was still in evidence. The sky was a clear light blue and the temperature had risen even further.

The churchyard was an oasis of green surrounded by old brick buildings. Several trees were covered in soft pink cherry blossom casting welcome shadows from the mounting heat. The purple lavender was just coming into flower, standing out against the succulent green grass and the headstones glowed white in the bright sun.

"So where do we start?" asked Grantham.

"There's probably a registry somewhere, how about over there?" Charisma pointed at the chapel and started heading across the grass.

Five minutes later they were in a small stone room at the rear of the chapel. A large hard backed book stood on the marble topped desk. Charisma seemed completely at home in the surroundings, in her element. She opened the heavy front cover and looked at the first two pages, working out the filing system. The entries went back to the late 1600s and although the book looked old, the paper was firm and crisp. It was obviously a copy of the original. After turning a few pages Charisma looked up at Grantham and smiled.

"It's indexed by date, name and plot number. So," she turned several of the large pages and ran a finger down the entries. "Stow, John. Died 2nd May 1807. Plot number G27."

Charisma looked across at the wall, a large scale map of the grounds was hung to one side. "Here," she said, pointing at the map.

Both Grantham and Charisma squinted as they left the cool dark of the church and stepped out into the warm sunlight. A few minutes later they were looking down at the gleaming headstone.

John Stow
02.05.1807
Rest in Peace

Absent in body, but present in spirit
Lev 34-12/18

For two minutes Grantham and Charisma looked at the headstone. Grantham then walked around the stone twice. On the second time he bent down at the rear and examined the stone in detail before coming back to the front.

"Okay, I'm beaten. Unless it's worn off, the only markings are what we can see on the front." He squatted down and looked at the front.

Grantham looked a little troubled, his eyebrows pulled together. "The inscription on the front is still pretty clear, it looks like it's the only markings that have been put on." Grantham shook his head. "Sorry, short of digging up the body, I don't see there is anything else we can do."

Charisma was still looking at the front of the stone, a slightly puzzled look on her face.

"That quote, 'Absent in body, but not in spirit', it's a fairly common inscription on grave markers. The 'Lev 34-12/18' indicates it's from Leviticus, chapter thirty-four, in verses 12 to 18. But Leviticus only goes up to the mid-twenties, and I'm sure the verse is not from Leviticus anyway."

Grantham took his mobile phone out and took a photo of the headstone. He then accessed the internet. "You're right. The quote is from One Corinthians verse 3."

"Can I borrow your phone?"

Charisma tapped away with her own internet search.

"I thought so. I did some research over the internet a

few years ago and accessed the US Library of Congress in Washington. That reference, Lev 34 -12/18 looks like the way they reference books in the library. I think we need to go to Washington DC."

Chapter 27

16:00hrs, 20th April
Grüssmire Gewerbe HQ

The meeting had been very productive. Hans Eigel sat back and clasped his hands across the paunch of his stomach. At 6'2" he was still an imposing figure and held complete authority over the entire Grüssmire Gewerbe, an organisation that commanded some of the world's most cutting edge technology and scientific advances.

The discussion today had centred on their two main projects. And those projects would change the world. For the past fifty years the company had spent billions of pounds and countless man years developing the projects which were now approaching their climax.

"So, the Messiah Project can move on to stage two?"

"Yes sir." Michael Spielmann nodded and removed his rimless glasses and polished the imaginary smudges away, a nervous gesture that the master recognised but chose to ignore. The man's right hand was still wrapped in a bandage following the ceremony a few days ago. Spielmann replaced his glasses and ran his fingers through his slicked back hair and down his small goatee beard.

"The implanted DNA is proving to be incredibly stable. Far more so than any we have tried before."

"And there will be no problems moving the samples to the shelter?" asked Eigel.

Spielmann shook his head. "The enclosures are self-contained at this stage. As the embryos grow they will become more delicate. But for now, for the next few weeks, they are secure in their containers."

"And the embryos are definitely stable and viable?"

"Of the thirty we implanted we lost one on the first day. The rest are all stable and viable. The growth rate is at the top end of normal. We have enough stored DNA for fifty to sixty more embryos if need be. But once the current embryos reach term we will have enough genetic material to build the new race."

"Good. Arrange for them to be moved to the shelter as soon as convenient." Eigel turned to another man along the table. "And Genesis, everything is on track?"

The man sat forward and smiled. "All the sites are responding within predicted limits. Once you give the word we can start to modify the signals and tie the effects together," said von Papen.

"And what is the time limit once the disrupters are aligned?"

"It will take two to three days for them to come into line. Once they do, we can progress as slowly or as fast as you want. It would take a minimum of seven days. There is no maximum, other than the power limit of the disrupters themselves, which is around twelve months."

Eigel sat back and looked around the table, finally his gaze settled on von Papen. "If we bring the disrupters into alignment will there be any outward signs?"

Von Papen thought for a few seconds. "To bring the disruptors into alignment we will have to increase the power and resonance. That could lead to some minor local tremors. But they would be very minor, noticeable but minor, and considering the locations, not out of the ordinary."

"Very well, bring them into alignment, but do not progress to the final stage."

Von Papen nodded and beamed.

"Any other business?" asked Eigel.

"One item," Joseph Adler spoke without leaning forward or bothering to look up. "The Templar's daughter. Adam has kept her and the man under surveillance. They have left Philadelphia and arrived in Washington. They are progressing, I think they may be getting close."

"Adam is still watching them?"

"Yes."

"Bring her in, dispose of the man. Once we have the world we can force her to reveal everything to us. If possible, we can take up the chase then."

Adler looked up at this, a hint of a smile touching the corner of his thin lips at the thought of a new young subject he could work on.

17:50hrs
Washington DC

Michael sat in the open park and looked around in the spring warmth at the crisp green grass, the blossom on the trees and the families enjoying the warm spring weather. He had been following the man and woman for the last three days. He had passed up several chances to dispose of them, but it was not his place to question the way of the Lord. He may be a general in His army, but he did not interpret God's message, he simply followed His orders. He checked his watch, time to report in.

The call was answered on the third ring.

"Father, it is good to hear your voice." Michael slipped back into his native French like slipping on a warm coat in winter.

"And you my son. What have you to report?"

"The girl's search goes on. She has arrived in Washington."

"You have recorded all of her trail so far? How she

311

has found her way and what has led her there?"

"Yes Father. I have the clue from her notebook that led them to America and then to Philadelphia. I followed them to the grave site and recorded what they saw, which grave they visited."

"The bell maker."

"Yes Father. And that has led them to Washington, although I'm not sure as to what specifically led them here. I think clues are running out. The end may be in sight."

There was no immediate answer, but Michael could hear the old priest's breathing and the chiming of a bell somewhere nearby. The old priest must be in his study. It would be 01:00 in Corsica. Michael had not considered the time difference when he had made the call. But God did not keep office hours, why should his servants feel the need to?

"Very well. We cannot allow the girl to find the Knights. Finish her and the man, but make it look like an accident."

"I will not let you down Father."

"You never have Michael. More importantly, you have never let God down. God speed Michael."

Chapter 28

15:00hrs, 20th April
MoD London

The morning session at the MoD's Emergency Response Group, as the multi-agency task force had become known, had been of little real value. The discussions had consisted mainly of how the country could combat the possible threat from a coordinated attack of volcanoes, earthquakes and tsunamis. The conclusion had been that defence, once the events were triggered, was impossible. It was agreed their best bet was to stop the attack before it went too far. They needed to find the devices and stop them.

They had broken for lunch at 13:00 with the intention of being back by 14:00. But shortly before they were due to return, they had received a text message from Danny Barrett, the GCHQ liaison, saying that he had some information but would not be back for another hour.

"Ah, Mr Barrett, nice of you to join us. I hope this will be worth the wait?" The sarcastic comment came from Air Marshal Colridge-Stewart, the deputy head of the UK military who seemed to look down on anyone who did not wear a uniform, and many who did.

"I think so, sir," said Barrett as he tapped away at one of the keyboards, searching for a file, opening it and sending an image and several tables to the large screen at the head of the table.

"As you know, for the last couple of days we've been monitoring several dozen areas that Professor Lee provided us with to see if we could pick up signals from the devices. It took some time to get things set up, but this morning we picked up signals from some of the locations. They were microbusts so not easy to track. What we can tell is that the signals were data transmissions, not voice, and after some analysis we found they followed a certain loose pattern."

"What do you mean by 'loose pattern'?" The question came from Michel Fortnum, Head of JTAC and coordinator of the task force.

"An automatic transmission by a computer will follow a set pattern so that the computer that receives the data knows what to expect, what order things will be in. But the actual data that is transmitted will vary from one time to another, so the actual data streams will have a pattern but each will vary slightly. That's a loose pattern." Several people around the table nodded.

"Anyway, the signals were from these points." Barrett indicated the large screen. As they watched, dozens of flashing red circles appeared. These were followed by a handful of flashing blue squares.

"The red circles are the high risk locations supplied by Professor Lee. The flashing blue squares are the data transmissions we first picked up. Once we found these and analysed the signal we came up with the loose patterns. That allowed us to search back through the stored data from the last few days and we found these." Another twenty of so light blue squares appeared.

"These are all transmitter sites?" asked Michel Fortnum.

"Well, they're data transmissions from sites suggested by the professor and they all follow the loose pattern so they are all data transmissions that are very likely to be from and to the same system." Barrett shrugged. "I can't say for definite what they actually are, but in probability they are signals from the transmitters."

"That's very good, well done. So now we can

destroy these things," said Air Marshal Colridge-Stewart, rubbing his hands together at the relish of action.

"It's unlikely to be that easy Air Marshal," said Billie Lee. "The transmitters will not be just sat out in the open, especially the ones underwater, which by the look of it make up the majority of the locations."

"So for the ones on land we send in a search team and demolition team, find them, destroy them. The ones underwater we use the navy, submarines if necessary."

"All of those locations are on foreign soil or territorial waters, many of them in areas where we would not be welcome," said Michel Fortnum.

"So we deal with the ones we can, in friendly countries and worry about the others later." The condescending tone in the Air Marshal's voice was clear.

"Actually, sir, even the ones in friendly countries won't be easy to find. The locations are not narrowed down to anything less than a mile, some two or three times that. If we were close by we could narrow that down, but we would have to be on site and wait for the signals and then triangulate them over several transmissions. At best it would be over a week at each location and the ones at sea would be harder to track, we would need ships on site and they would have to sit there for many days. And even submarines would need to be on the surface to detect the transmissions."

Air Marshal Colridge-Stewart gave a dismissive grunt.

There was a quiet knock on the door which opened halfway and a young woman's blonde head looked through the opening and around the room.

"Sorry to interrupt, Daniel, could I have a quick word?" She stood back from the door.

Daniel Barrett stood up and exited the room, closing

the door behind him.

Billie Lee looked at the large screen at the end of the room and then walked over and looked closer.

"Anything wrong?" asked Michel Fortnum, head of the Joint Terrorism Analysis Centre.

"No, not wrong, just a little odd. I notice that the signals seem to be fairly evenly spread around the world, all coinciding with known risk spots. But there seems to be none in South America and very few off the coast."

Michel Fortnum looked at the screen and nodded. "You're right. Maybe they haven't been placed yet."

"Or maybe whoever is behind this doesn't want primary effects in the region."

"Primary effect?" asked Michel Fortnum.

Before Professor Lee could reply, the door opened and Daniel Barrett came in.

"We have new data just in," he said as he walked back to his seat. He tapped away for a few seconds as Professor Lee and Michel Fortnum retook their seats and looked at the screen.

The screen showed a simple bar graph, the columns spread from left to right, rising to just under half way up the screen.

"This shows the amount of data transmitted over the last three days. You can see that each column is a different height indicating different amounts of data. But all are within fifteen percent of each other. Now this," Barrett tapped a few keys. "This is the amount of data we have picked up in the last three hours." Each column grew and rose almost to the top of the screen. "We've seen a five hundred percent increase in data over the last three hours compared to the last three days."

"Can you tell where the data is going?" asked Michel Fortnum.

The image on the screen dissolved and was replaced by a 3D image of the earth from space. As they watched, images of satellites appeared around the Earth, semicircles radiating from them down to the Earth with single data streams rising from the transmitter positions.

"Just over three hours ago, we detected a data stream rising from a commercial ground station in Costa Rica to this satellite." One of the satellites flashed and the view zoomed in on the thin strip of land between North and South America.

"This was then transmitted to the other satellites and relayed to the ground." The view on the screen zoomed out to show the whole globe and the circling satellites.

"After a few minutes the transmitters came to life and broadcast data back to the satellites and back down to the ground station. This two-way conversation has been ongoing for the last three hours."

"So the command is talking to the devices and they're replying. Do we know what it means?" asked Air Marshal Colridge-Stewart.

Barrett noticed the 'we' when there was possible good news and the 'you' on occasions when there was negative news. Still, thought Barrett, you did not get to be deputy head of the UK defences purely on your own merits.

Barrett shook his head. "We can detect the signals, but we can't decode them. It's clearly a two-way exchange of information, but we can't determine what the message is."

"I assume you're trying to rectify the situation by decoding the data?"

Barrett smiled. "Of course, sir."

"Mr Barrett, satellites and communications are not my area of expertise, but would I be correct in assuming that the data signal from the command must be somewhere close by the transmitter?" asked Professor Lee.

Barrett pursed his lips and considered the question. "Well close is a relative term. It could still be hundreds of miles away. Technically it could be thousands of miles if you arranged a ground based cable or radio transfer. The best way, from a technical point of view, would be via fibre optic cable. But laying a fibre optic cable for hundreds or thousands of miles is impractical for private use by anything other than a multinational communications company or a major government."

"I'd have thought that anyone with the capability of producing a device that could create earthquakes could simply transmit commands to the satellites from their own compound."

Barrett smiled, barely keeping the sneer from his voice. "Yes Air Marshal, but then we would be able to track them back to their base."

Professor Lee spoke up before the two men could start anything either of them would regret. "So it's likely that the command originated from somewhere within a relatively short distance of the ground station, which puts it in the southern part of North America or the northern part of South America?"

"More than likely."

"I'd say South America," said Billie Lee. "South America would be easier to hide in and by the look of the distribution of the transmitters they would be avoiding the primary effects damage." Remembering her earlier conversation, Professor Lee looked at Michel Fortnum.

"Primary effects are the initial physical effects of an eruption or quake. The violent shaking, the lava or pyroclastic flow, even the volcanic bombs. They would probably be inland as well to avoid the effects of a tsunami."

318

"But I thought you said that this sort of event would potentially kill all life on Earth regardless of where you were?" said General Clive Simmonds, head of the UK military, taking a rare part in the discussion instead of preferring to sit back and let others do the discussion and then sum up at the end.

"That is the case in the long term. But if you are preparing for this sort of event, as we have said that most countries have, with some sort of bunker, the last thing you want is for the bunker to be obliterated with a 450mph pyroclastic flow or be blown to smithereens by supersonic volcanic bombs."

"So you think that the base of operations is in Costa Rica?" asked Simmonds.

Professor Lee shook her head. "Costa Rica and Panama are barely one hundred miles wide, they would be virtually wiped out if tsunamis hit them from both the Atlantic and Pacific. Nicaragua is barely any better. I'd say it would have to be more inland, Columbia or Brazil, and well away from the coast."

"That's still a large area," said Air Marshal Colridge-Stewart with a distinctly sarcastic note to his voice.

"I agree Air Marshal," said Professor Lee. "But in the last hour we have gone from somewhere in the world to somewhere in around ten percent of the world, that's a ninety percent improvement in one hour."

Touché, thought Barrett with a smile.

Chapter 29

10:00hrs, 21st April
Washington DC

In 1800 the US Congress voted to create a library to house research materials and works of artistic merit. For eighteen years the Library was housed in various buildings including the Blodget's Hotel at 7th and E Streets. However, in 1818 funds were appropriated to move the Library back to the Capitol. As the Library quickly grew, the contents expanded beyond the capacity of the Capitol's North Wing so Charles Bulfinch, the Capitol's architect, drew up plans for an expansion into the building's centre. After a disastrous fire on Christmas Eve, 1851 destroyed much of the building's 55,000 volumes a new Library was planned using 'modern' fireproof materials. The new Library opened its doors in 1853, but again it was apparent that due to the vast growth of its collections, the Library of Congress needed a separate building. After thirty years of planning and construction the Jefferson Building was opened to the public in 1897. Wanting to set a new standard in American architecture, the building was based on the Paris Opera House and was widely regarded as unparalleled in national achievement. The centre of the building is dominated by a gold-plated dome which caps the largest library building in the world. Today, the building represents a unique blend of art and architecture and is recognized as 'the best decorated building in the US' and a national treasure. The Library of Congress now houses just short of 100 million items, including 25 million books on 540 miles of shelves.

The weather in the nation's capital was even warmer than in its previous capital of Philadelphia. Grantham and Charisma had taken a leisurely drive, the 150 miles south along the I95, arriving late the previous afternoon. This morning they had risen early and taken a cab to the Library of Congress.

The library is a white, stone building with impressive columns and arches and a huge central golden dome. Grantham and Charisma strode past the ornate iron cannon bollards, in reality anti-ram raid bollards buried two metres into a mass concrete foundation, and strode up the thirteen steps to the large open plaza that covered the front of the impressive building.

As they entered the cool interior of the Library it took a few seconds for their eyes to adjust from the bright spring light of the outdoors. Grantham stopped a few feet in and looked around.

"Wow..." was all Grantham could get out.

Charisma was equally awestruck, her mouth dropping open slightly and her eyes wide.

The interior of the building was grey-veined marble with fresco reliefs and alcoves with busts and works of art. The floor was polished brown marble with a gold circle pattern and the Presidential seal. Around the walls were matt black metal benches for visitors to sit and take in their surroundings. Two ornate staircases rose either side of the large room leading to the upper level and multi-arched ceilings in gold, black and white. The gold appeared to be gold leaf rather than simple paint. The ground floor (first floor as the Americans referred to it) had Ionic columns with the upper levels having the more ornate Corinthian columns. Dozens of circular windows lined the upper floor, drenching the whole area in light.

After a few seconds of staring around, Grantham

and Charisma came to their senses.

"I'd heard how impressive the Library is, but this...? They call it the most beautifully decorated building in the US. I can see why."

"I didn't think there were any buildings of this style in America," said Grantham.

"It was built to rival the best that Europe had to offer."

"They succeeded."

Still looking around, they headed up the grand staircase to the registration office. Before setting off, Charisma had booked them into the system and registered their details, all they needed to do was present their passports and sign the applications and they would have their temporary library cards.

Twenty minutes later, newly equipped with their library cards, Grantham and Charisma walked into one of the impressive reading rooms.

"Not much like the reading rooms in the local library I used as a kid," whispered Grantham as he leant in to Charisma.

The room was easily 150 feet in diameter. The walls were light coffee-coloured marble with rose tinted, veined marble columns. Reading desks were placed in concentric circles around the room. The floor was a mottled grey slate in the centre with regular inlaid images of open books surrounded by laurel leaves. The outer circles were cream-coloured marble with dark brown diamond shapes. The desks were a dark red/brown timber in what looked like perfect condition. The whole room rose to a huge dome three floors above, with the ground floor being double height. Around the ground floor were a series of arches leading to rooms and wide corridors containing countless books. The first floor had rows and rows of arches with the third floor showing a stone handrail and close columns, and impressive larger than life statues looking into the centre of the room. Above this the large arched stained glass windows led to an impressive dome.

The centre of the room was dominated by a raised two layer wooden dais with four librarians working around the first layer. As they walked towards the centre, Grantham realised that although they were walking on stone floors, their footsteps seemed to be swallowed by the room rather than bouncing off the walls and ceiling. Clearly as much thought had gone into acoustics as had gone into the lighting and appearance of the interior.

As they approached the dais, one of the librarians looked up and smiled. She was everyone's image of the archetypal librarian. Of indeterminate age, something over late thirties and below seventy, she had grey hair in a perfect bun on the top of her head and gold rim spectacles.

"Hello, I'm Mary, may I help you?"

"We're looking for a book," said Charisma.

"Well you've come to the right place," the librarian waved her hand around the huge room. "We have over 90 million items to choose from, although they aren't all books."

"The thing is, we don't know what book," said Charisma.

"Well all our books are cross referenced by title, author, publisher, date published, where published and key words. Do you have any information?"

"We have a reference number."

"Even better, as long as it's valid, that will be specific to one book."

Charisma handed over a slip of paper with the reference from John Stow's gravestone.

"It looks like one of ours. We may look like an historic building, but everything is computerised and temperature controlled." As she spoke, Mary tapped away at the computer well hidden behind the timber up-stand of the circular desk forming the outer ring of the central dais.

"Here it is, Tax Codes and Excise Duty of the New States, by Temple, K. Published 1807."

Grantham nodded and smiled his most ingratiating smile at Mary. "That sounds like the right one. May we see it?"

Mary checked their newly issued cards and nodded.

"Take a seat. I'll be a few minutes."

Grantham and Charisma chose a seat along the back wall, well away from anyone else.

"Tax codes and excise duty? It's not what I was expecting," said Charisma, sounding a little crestfallen.

"What were you expecting? The Secrets of the Knights Templar and their Hidden Lairs?" Grantham's grin was almost ear to ear.

Charisma gave a half smile. "I suppose not."

"Anyway it has to be the right book. Author K Temple, published in 1807, same year as John Stow died."

A few minutes later Mary seemed to materialise at their side and set down a large book. Tome would have been a better description. It was almost 24" high, 12" wide and easily 2" thick. Although spotlessly clean and well preserved, it looked like the type of book that you should blow dust off before opening.

"Please wear these cotton gloves when you handle the book. We give them to all readers if the books are more than one hundred years old. They are clean, when you hand them back in, they go straight in the wash."

Grantham and Charisma waited while Mary walked away and they put on the gloves. Charisma opened the book and scanned through the first few pages. It was exactly as she was expecting, dry descriptions, facts and figures. Skipping a few pages, she carefully skipped through the book. A few diagrams caught her eye, but nothing seemed relevant.

Once she finished looking through the book Grantham took over. Instead of looking at the content of the pages, he looked at the thickness of the pages, the cover, front and back. He checked for any loose pages and closed the book looking for any gaps. Nothing showed up as unusual in any way. He opened the book and turned to the contents page, everything looked as you would expect. He checked several locations with the contents and the actual page, everything seemed to match.

Grantham sat the book on the spine and allowed both covers to gently open with guidance from his hands to see if the book opened to a specific page, but the pages seemed to open perfectly naturally and more or less in half.

Grantham left the book open on the desk and shrugged.

"I'm sure this is the right book, but I don't know what else to do. If we could take the book out we could cut open the covers or x-ray it to find anything hidden but..."

When they registered they had to leave any bags in lockers, they were not allowed to bring anything in that would be big enough to hold a book. Although with the size of the book that sat open on the desk in front of them, the bag would have had to be a fair size suitcase, preferably with wheels.

"Could there be a code hidden in the actual writing?" asked Charisma.

"I suppose so, but it would have to have been written with that in mind, you'd need a key to look up page, word and letter. And we don't have anything like that."

Grantham sat back and looked around for a few seconds, admiring the ornate architecture of the impressive room before looking back down at the book.

Grantham's eyebrows came together as he looked at the book. As with a lot of very old books, the pages were sewn onto webbing with the spine separate to the pages. The spine was naturally bent away in a semicircle and gaping open slightly. Grantham lifted the bottom of the book and peered down the open spine. There was something in there.

"Have you got a pencil or tweezers?" asked Grantham.

Charisma shook her head. "Everything like that is in my bag in the locker. But..." Charisma stood up and walked to the centre dais, returning a minute later with a spiral bound book and pencil with the Library of Congress seal and title on it.

Grantham took the pencil and inserted the rubber end into the spine and carefully pushed up against what appeared to be a folded sheet of paper. After a couple of slips, and with the pencil fully in the spine and his finger up to the second knuckle, a folded sheet of yellow paper came out of the top. After a quick glance around to make sure no one was watching, Charisma carefully took hold of the yellow paper and pulled it from the spine. She quickly realised that the paper was not as old as the book. It appeared to be a foolscap sheet of legal notepaper. She took the paper and unfolded it, smoothing it out on the desk, expecting some secret to be revealed. She was disappointed. The paper was covered with a square of apparently random letters and numbers, laid out in a large grid.

After a few seconds Charisma looked up. "I like anagrams, but this is just random letters."

"It's an encryption square. The message is set out at preset intervals and the spaces filled in between. All we need is the key."

"Where do we find the key? What will it be, a number, a word?"

"Probably a number, several numbers. You count from a set location, say the top left corner to the first number, then continue to the next number and the next etcetera for as many numbers as you have, and then start again."

"So how do we find the key?"

Grantham sat back, a look of concentration on his face. "When we were in Philadelphia, looking up information about the Liberty Bell and Pass and Stow in the Liberty Bell exhibition...there's something that's been sticking in my mind. But I can't place it."

"Well I photographed most of the information, if you want to review it."

Charisma took her mobile phone out, and with a few taps on the screen, displayed the images from Philadelphia. She set the phone down on the table so they could both see the screen and started reading the information recorded on the images.

"Hold on, I think that's what's been bothering me."

Grantham took his own mobile phone out and set it on the desk and flicked through the images until he found the image he was looking for.

"Here, the info from the Liberty Bell Centre says, *'In June 1753 the bell was again raised into place, a momentous occasion for John Stow being his 55th birthday.'* But the photo of the gravestone says *'John Stow 02.05.1807Rest in Peace'*. It's not very often that dates of death are shown numerically like that is it? And if he was fifty-five in June 1753 and he died in May 1807, he'd have been almost 109 years old. I don't think that's very likely."

"I agree, but how does that help."

"Maybe the 02.05.1807 is the key rather than the

date Stow died."

Grantham smoothed out the encryption square and counted along the top row and noted the second and fifth letter on the notepad that Charisma had brought back.

"Mmm...Well I can't count out 1807 to the next letter. Let's try eighteen and then seven."

For a few minutes Grantham counted out along the square and marked the letters on the note book.

ONCEROMEMEETTOMORROWAMPHITHEATER
NOONATTHENATIONSCEMETERY

Splitting up the words Grantham got:

ONCE / ROME / MEET / TOMORROW / AMPHITHEATER / NOON / AT / THE / NATIONS / CEMETERY

"Okay, so we've got some words, but I'm not sure of the meaning," said Grantham.

"Well Rome is the Italian capital, and the best known amphitheatre is the Colosseum, but what's the Italian national cemetery?" said Charisma.

"Well the best know Italian cemetery is Anzio, about seventy miles from Rome. It dates from the Second World War. But it says Once Rome, i.e. not now Rome."

Charisma picked up Grantham's phone and tapped away at the fold out keyboard, doing an internet search. A few minutes later she frowned and looked up.

"Rome, the capital of Italy is built on seven hills with the River Tiber running through it. Washington DC, the capital of America, was originally called Rome. It's also built on seven hills and was built on a small watercourse called Tiber Creek. The Washington

Rome was originally a small community of people centred on what became Washington DC."

"Interesting," said Grantham. "If Rome means Washington then the nation's cemetery would be Arlington National Cemetery, and it also has an amphitheatre. But how could any message arrange a meeting time when it wasn't known when it would be read?"

Chapter 30

12:20hrs, 21st April
Washington DC

Grantham and Charisma walked from the Library of Congress into the bright light. Even though the impressive interior of the building was light and airy, the bright sun of the outside still made them squint slightly as they came out.

"What now?" asked Charisma.

"We could go to Arlington Cemetery and see what's there before tomorrow."

"So we are going to the meeting tomorrow?"

By now they had walked over to the balcony at the front of the raised plaza. Grantham leant against the railing and looked out over 1st Street and Independence Avenue across the Congress Gardens towards the US House of Representatives in the distance.

"It's always worth scouting out the ground before a meeting," replied Grantham after a few seconds.

"But as you said, how could a meeting be arranged for us when two days ago we didn't know we would be here?"

"Not sure," Grantham said absently, still looking off along the street.

"Sorry, am I boring you?"

Grantham pushed away from the balcony and smiled at Charisma as he unconsciously massaged the back of his neck. "No, I think I can put up with you a little longer. Come on, let's get some lunch and we can decide what to do."

They walked across the street to the gardens and wandered across the large green lawn to the far side.

Several carts were set up with people buying food and drink.

"I'll get us something to eat and drink. What do you fancy?" asked Grantham.

"Surprise me."

Five minutes later Grantham returned with a large cappuccino for Charisma, a large ice-cold fresh orange juice, or OJ as the vender referred to it, a large bowl of fresh salad and fruit and a plate of waffle cones and ice cream.

"Not exactly a traditional combination, but it looks good. What did you get yourself?" said Charisma as Grantham sat down on the grass beside her.

Twenty minutes of eating, drinking and people watching later they sat back and soaked up the sun.

"I'd suggest we head over to the Arlington Cemetery and scope out the battlefield," suggested Grantham.

"You think there'll be a battle?"

"Just an expression, but it pays to be careful, remember why you asked me to join you in the first place."

"I think Lancelot has frightened the dragons away," smiled Charisma.

They walked back to Independence Avenue, crossed the wide street and waited at the tour bus stop. From here they could catch an open top double-decker bus that would take in all of the best known tourist attractions.

Ten minutes later they saw the red bus with the star spangled banner decorating the paintwork come around the corner and pull up at the stop.

Sitting at the upper front as they travelled along, they listened to the running commentary telling them about the history and culture of the nation's capital. When they arrived at the Lincoln Memorial, Charisma suggested they get off and walk the mile or so to the Arlington Cemetery, crossing the Potomac River by one of several bridges.

The sun was still warm and bright, dappled shade was cast by the trees that were just starting to shed their blossom which was forming a mottled white and pink carpet.

After spending some time at the Lincoln Memorial, they headed out across the four-lane bridge before stopping to look at the river. Several boats were moving up and down, with many more tied up along the banks and at public and private berths. Grantham unconsciously put his hand to the back of his neck and massaged the slight ache, and then realised what he was doing. He looked around, there was a constant flow of traffic going both ways, dozens of people walking across the bridge. A silver car pulled up fifty feet away, drawing Grantham's attention. He recognised it as a newer Mercedes CLS, although he was not sure of the exact model. There was a driver, blond and athletic looking, but no passenger. As he watched, the driver's door opened and the man stepped out, he was tall and fit and looked around before casually walking in their direction, a map held out in his hand.

Charisma screamed and Grantham spun around. Another man, one of the pedestrians, was approaching quickly with a gun held close at his side.

"In nomine Patris." The forty something man, black hair, Vandyke beard with a dark Mediterranean complexion, was within fifteen feet and started to raise the gun.

Grantham quickly glanced around, there was no cover and no help at hand. He pushed Charisma to one side and stepped in front of her. "Get down," he said over his shoulder.

As the man pulled the trigger a shot rang out from

behind Grantham and the man twisted as a bullet slammed into his shoulder, throwing off his aim, his shot going high.

Grantham put his head down and charged the man in a fast jinking run. The man fired another shot which caught Grantham a stinging blow on the left shoulder. Grantham slammed into the man, but had not caught him with as much surprise as he had hoped for. The man twisted to one side, his arms high so that Grantham could not pin them to his side and doubled over to absorb the impact rather than trying to resist.

A staggering blow came down on Grantham's head, glancing off the side and scraping down his temple as the man slammed the butt of the pistol down. Grantham pushed the man away slightly and delivered two vicious uppercuts to the man's body, the second causing the man to grunt and expel his breath. Grantham jerked his head up and smashed under the man's jaw and heard a satisfying crunch as the man's teeth slammed together.

Grantham felt the sting of the crease in his temple and the slight dizziness from the blow, but ignored the sensation. The man seemed to have not noticed the blood running freely from his broken teeth and lips. He regained his balance quickly and brought the gun around towards Grantham. Without conscious thought, Grantham stepped in and brought his foot up in a vicious kick to the other's wrist. The man was fast and pulled his hand away, but not fast enough. The kick caused the man's fingers to jerk open and the gun to clatter to the floor. Grantham followed the kick by stepping in and delivering two hard blows to the head, but the man was fast and pulled his head back, riding both blows, before feinting a kick to Grantham's legs causing him to step to one side while the man hit out at Grantham's throat. But Grantham was also fast and twisted his whole body, taking the savage jab to the uninjured shoulder. Continuing the turn, Grantham brought his left elbow up, aiming for the man's head but connecting with the jaw and nose which caused a fresh burst of blood. Grantham's right fist came around in a massive haymaker. It surprised Grantham that the blow was blocked, and blocked with strength.

The man jumped back, opening a few feet between them. With a flash of steel a vicious looking short bladed knife appeared in his hand.

It flashed through Grantham's mind that the man was displaying no fear, he had clearly had at least basic unarmed combat training and even injured he was a dangerous opponent. But his attacks seemed to lack imagination. He was fast, strong and fearless, but each blow was either a defence or a killing blow. There seemed to be no strategy. Grantham could exploit that.

Grantham backed up slightly and adopted a loose boxer's stance. He threw two quick jabs and a right hook, all three connected but the man was still riding the blows and the knife flashed forward and across Grantham's arm, cutting the cloth but only just nicking the skin. Grantham again threw a jab and telegraphed a right hook. The man rode the jab but saw the hook coming and pulled back, pushing Grantham's arm to the right and forcing him off balance.

Grantham allowed himself to stagger slightly and bend over to regain his balance, exposing the back of his neck. The man saw the opening and kicked up at Grantham's stomach and slashed down with the knife.

This was what Grantham had expected. In one movement he staggered to the side, seemingly off balance, jumped and curled himself over the man's kicking leg, taking the man's shin across the solid muscle of his stomach. The knife sliced through empty air and Grantham tucked and rolled out of the way, taking hold of the leg and pulling it with him.

Most people would have tried to resist the pull on their leg, but with Grantham's full weight twisting the leg this would have ended in a dislocated hip.

As he rolled over, Grantham felt resistance from the man, but before the pressure could build up, the man relaxed and allowed himself to roll over, following Grantham rather than trying to resist. But Grantham had planned the move and had spent years honing his hand to hand skills, the man was simply reacting.

Grantham hit the ground and rolled up onto his feet in a crouch before the man had finished hitting the ground. Before the man could regain his feet, Grantham's foot shot out, connecting firmly with the other's jaw. The man staggered, half on his feet, clearly stunned and off balance, but still holding the knife. His shirt had been pulled open and Grantham saw a tattoo of a shield in front of a cross, with crossed swords in front of the shield, yellow streaks radiating outwards, the same tattoo as the attacker on the aircraft.

Grantham saw the man's bewilderment and slight hesitation and delivered a perfect roundhouse kick, the man's head whipping around as he went down, unconscious.

Before he could check the man, Grantham heard a scream and looked around to see the tall blond man that had got out of the car dragging Charisma away, almost at the car.

Charisma kicked out at the man and managed to scrape her insole down his shin. His grip loosened and she punched him hard across the face raking the nails of her other hand down his cheek. Seeming to have not noticed, the man jabbed out at Charisma's jaw and she went limp. He picked her up with ease and threw her into the open rear door of the large Mercedes.

Grantham started to run towards the car as the man

jumped into the driver's seat and pulled away. Grantham stepped into the road, jumping to one side when it became clear that the car was not going to stop. As the car swept past, there was the gentle growl from what sounded like a V8 engine.

Grantham looked around, the gun was still lying on the ground a few feet away. He took three quick steps and dove for the gun, rolling as he hit the floor and coming up into a kneeling shooting position. His right knee on the floor, left foot flat and to the side, right arm out straight holding the grip, his left hand under the gun's butt and his right hand.

The gun was a Taurus Model 85 .38 SPL in stainless steel with a black rubber grip. It had a five round chamber with two shots fired. The weapon had a short 2" barrel, not designed for accuracy over more than thirty feet. Grantham sighted along the barrel at the fleeing car, already a hundred feet away, and squeezed the smooth trigger. There was a gentle kickback and Grantham re-centred the sight on the man's head and squeezed again and again. The rear window of the car shattered and the car fishtailed before straightening up and continuing to accelerate.

Grantham stood up, powerless to stop the car. He looked around at the man still lying on the ground, was he acting with the driver of the car? It seemed too much of a coincidence that two attacks could take place at the same time, but it seemed that the blond man had shot the one on the floor in front of him. Could it be a falling out amongst thieves?

As he looked back up, the car's brake lights flashed red and the car slowed quickly, before turning a sharp right and heading down the slip road from the high bridge.

Without thought, Grantham pocketed the small gun and set off at a sprint to the handrail overlooking the road which ran parallel to the wide river. The car was circling back on itself as it drove at speed down the slip road. Grantham ran another fifty feet and vaulted over the handrail. He landed heavily twenty feet down on the sloping embankment that led down to the road. He rolled and came up on his feet, running to the edge of the embankment which was still ten feet above the road.

Looking up, he saw the Mercedes approaching, slowing as it prepared to merge with traffic on the smaller road.

Grantham timed the jump perfectly and landed on the bonnet of the slowed car as it passed along the side of the embankment. He landed on his feet but allowed himself to drop down onto all fours and then lay flat. He scrambled for a hold on the wipers, but they were tucked away under the bonnet. However, the edge of the bonnet gave a reasonable handhold and he quickly shuffled across to the driver's side, grabbing the large wing mirror. He was in luck, the driver's window was down and he leant over the side of the car to reach in and grab the driver. But by now the driver had recovered from the shock of Grantham dropping onto the car and had started to swerve the car from side to side, braking and accelerating.

Grantham managed to get a hold of the man's shirt, lost his grip and lunged further in, grabbing the bottom of the steering wheel as his feet slipped from the bonnet and started to scrape along the road. More by luck than judgement, he yanked the steering wheel to one side, causing the car to veer to the right into the embankment which was now only five feet high. The car scraped along the embankment for a few feet, the sound of grinding metal filling the air with intermittent sparks flying up from the wing and passenger door. The car shuddered to a halt as Grantham regained his feet. He slammed his fist into the side of the blond driver's head, who leant away from the blow, lessening the impact but still taking a hard hit.

Cars were passing close by, but swerving to avoid the stopped car and Grantham standing on the carriageway. Grantham looked into the back of the car. Charisma was lying on the floor just in front of the rear seats. He tried the rear door handle only to find the door locked. Unable to open the rear door, Grantham turned to the driver's door. The blond man stayed down away from the open window as Grantham tried to open the door, but turned and lifted an automatic pistol up to point a Grantham. Grantham was mesmerised by the man's eyes. Until now they had simply been a mid-blue to match his blond hair, but Grantham now saw that a contact lens had been displaced revealing a reptilian looking bright yellow left eye.

"Eight, eight," said the blond haired man with a smile.

Grantham snapped back to his senses and dove to one side as the gun barked a loud retort. From the fleeting glimpse he had of the weapon, Grantham recognised it as a Desert Eagle, probably a .357 magnum, a very powerful weapon that could take his head off at this range.

The man sat up to get a better view of Grantham and bring the gun out of the window to get better aim. But Grantham was faster. His right hand came down on top of the weapon, his right thumb slipping behind the trigger to stop it firing, gripping the top of the slide. The man reached up with his left hand to try and grapple the gun free. In the brief struggle, he pressed down on the magazine release and the matt black bullet holder dropped to the ground, clattering and bouncing away from the car. Grantham's left hand pushed up under the front of the barrel, levering it from the man's grip.

Grantham took a step back, bringing the weapon up. Before he could pull the trigger a large semi-truck sounded its ear splitting twin air horns, the large wing mirror passing no more than two inches over his head. Grantham jumped forward away from the truck and slammed into the silver Mercedes.

The man mashed down on the accelerator and yanked the wheel to the left. The car shot forward, metal scraping against the wall for five feet until it pulled itself clear. The violent motion threw Grantham away from the car and into the speeding traffic. He jumped back out of the stream of traffic as horns blared and tyres screeched, one car hitting the side of another, but neither slowing for some distance, maybe they had seen the large gun in Grantham's hand.

The Mercedes was already seventy feet away and accelerating quickly. Grantham raised the gun and took careful aim. Unlike the small revolver, this was a powerful weapon, accurate at well over 150 feet and deadly at three times that. Grantham squeezed the trigger, the slide on the gun slamming back and locking open as the windscreen of the Mercedes shattered and disappeared. But the car kept going.

Grantham looked around, he needed to follow the car, but there was no way the speeding traffic was going to stop. He looked down, the gun's magazine was a few feet away, but before he could get to it another large semi-truck ran over it with three wheels. He needed a car.

Looking around he saw that under the bridge the area opened out to a wide grassy area leading to the waterfront. A service road ran parallel to the waterfront and the main carriageway. The road access was from the slip road and then back onto the main road several hundred yards down.

Grantham ran under the bridge, staying close to the wall and then jumped over the low safety barrier and across the grass area towards the road. He looked both ways. There was a small hatchback almost at the road end, a pickup stopped near the slip road. As he watched, a 2011 model dark red Dodge Charger with dark tinted windows pulled onto the service road and drove steadily towards the waterfront.

Grantham jogged over to the road just as the powerful muscle car passed him and turned into a parking bay. He did not want to alarm or hurt the driver, but he needed the car. He crossed behind the car, coming down the driver's side. As he approached, Grantham released the slide on the Desert Eagle, there were no bullets, but he could use it to intimidate. As he got to the driver's door he leaned forward and took hold of the handle. Before he could open the door, it slammed open, hitting Grantham's arm and spinning him through a quarter turn. It was the black haired man from the bridge.

The man jumped from the car and kicked out at Grantham, connecting with a glancing blow on the thigh. He then stepped in closer and slashed out with the knife. It had taken Grantham by surprise, but he recovered quickly, blocking the blow and stepping and twisting out of immediate range.

He was now on the footway next to the river, the drop to the water was around ten feet. The man was still coming and Grantham met the attack with two quick blocks. The second block put Grantham's left hand near the man's right wrist. With practised ease, Grantham turned his left hand over the man's wrist, pushing it down to stop the blade being of use, his right arm going under the man's upper arm and lifting sharply up, bending the arm the wrong way against the elbow.

The man dropped the knife and tried to twist free, but Grantham was a match for his strength and he was on balance and knew how to use his opponent's strength and movement against him. Grantham pushed the man's wrist away from him and up behind his back while bringing his own right hand to the rear of the man's arm, feeling hard triceps and pulled the upper arm towards him and down. The man automatically bent forward to prevent his arm being broken. He then quickly stepped to one side and kicked up into the man's face, which was still a bloody mess from their previous encounter.

As Grantham's foot came back down, preparing to deliver another kick, this one to the now exposed throat, the man dropped down, grabbed Grantham's leg and pushed back. The two men fell in a twisting, tangled heap into the water. Although it was a warm day, the water was still cold, barely seven degrees centigrade. What most people did not realise was that falling into very cold water made the body go into thermal shock. Their breath would be expelled from the lungs and they would try to breathe with short sharp intakes of breath, often breathing in water and drowning. The sudden cold water also cools the blood at the extremities which can then cause a heart attack as the cold blood reached the heart. Muscles quickly lose oxygen and go into lactic acid overload and shut down, the cold making them shiver and become uncoordinated. If the body can survive these conditions for the first minute, it is only then that hypothermia will start to set in over five to thirty minutes depending on the person and the conditions.

But the human body can be trained to cope with these conditions. An ice bath twice a year for fifteen minutes trains the body to deal with freezing water conditions. While in the SAS, Grantham had been

341

forced to endure cold emersion every six months and Arctic training once a year. He also swam regularly in open water, staying in condition for the triathlons he entered.

As they hit the water with a splash, the men submerged and started to sink slowly into the gloomy murk of the river. Grantham looked up, they were perhaps ten feet down. He could feel the needle like sting of the cold pricking his whole body, but this was not a new sensation and Grantham put it to the back of his mind.

The man started to struggle to free himself from Grantham's grip, kicking out to regain the precious air at the surface. But Grantham did something unexpected, instead of heading up, he kept hold of the man and kicked strongly down.

The man struggled harder, kicking out at Grantham, his movements starting to have the edge of desperation, but the water cushioned the blows, making them ineffectual.

Grantham could feel the heat start to build in his lungs, the craving for air, but he was at home in the water, he knew his limits and knew that once he felt this, even when swimming hard, he could stay submerged for at least another sixty seconds, a little longer with effort.

They were now at least twenty feet down, the man's struggles were weakening fast and Grantham stopped, allowing himself to drift with the man still held fast. Suddenly the man convulsed, several air bubbles erupting from his mouth as spasms ripped through his body, quickly subsiding to a shudder and finally limp stillness.

Grantham allowed himself to drift for a count of twenty and them pushed the man away and down and kicked upwards for the surface.

As his head broke into the air, Grantham took a huge breath and looked around. There were flashing blue and red lights on the bridge, but the area along the waterfront was thankfully still quiet. No one seemed to have noticed the two men fall into the river. The current this close to the bank was slack and he had drifted no more than fifty feet from the Dodge. A ladder was fixed to the wall a few feet away and Grantham turned and swam to it, easily climbing back to the footpath.

It was still quiet along the service road, but Grantham knew it would not stay that way for long. He quickly considered his options. Wait for the police and tell them what had happened and ask for help in finding Charisma, or get away and rely on his own resources. He was already known to the police due to the incident on the aircraft and another incident, especially a shooting and the death of a man at his hands would not go down well. By nature and training he was self reliant. There was no real decision to make. He jogged over to the dark red Dodge Charger and slipped into the leather driver's seat. The man had left the keys in the ignition and the car started instantly at the turn of the key, the 5.7L V8 engine giving out a guttural roar as Grantham reversed from the parking bay and accelerated hard away from the waterfront, leaving twenty feet of black tyre marks on the smooth concrete carriageway.

Chapter 31

16:00hrs, 21st April
Washington DC

After leaving the waterfront, Grantham drove for ten miles out of the city before pulling off the road and heading into the woods along an unmarked track. It was likely that by now the police would be looking for him, at least the man who was involved in the attack and shooting. He needed to regroup and think.

There were some witnesses to the attack on the bridge, but as soon as the first gunshot was fired, the witnesses left quickly, although photos on mobile phones could not be ruled out. The fight on the highway was witnessed by dozens of motorists, but they would be of little help to the police as they had mostly had to concentrate on their driving. The attack at the waterfront was not witnessed as far as he knew. As for physical evidence, the shot to his shoulder had produced enough blood to soak his shirt, but it was unlikely that there was any on the floor. Had he touched the handrail of the bridge? He did not think so and if he had, so had thousands of other people so that would not hold up as evidence. He would have left prints and probably DNA on the Mercedes when he jumped onto it, but the driver has kidnapped Charisma so would probably dispose of the car for his own reasons. As for the dead man in the river, he had probably left DNA on him, but with luck the river would take care of that, if he was very lucky so would the wildlife in the river. The small revolver was still in his pocket. The larger Desert Eagle was at the bottom of the Potomac River.

Was there any CCTV in the area of the bridge? The attack and kidnap seemed, at least to some extent, to be professional. Maybe they had planned it in an area without CCTV coverage. He had not noticed CCTV on the waterfront or the main road, but he had to assume it was there. He also had to assume that they would be looking for this car, which was not exactly inconspicuous.

With time and effort the police may be able to track him, but it would not be easy. If he could ditch the car he probably had some time.

He checked his mobile phone, there was no sign of life. Although it was waterproof, it had been damaged in the recent encounter allowing water into the screen.

Three quarters of a mile along the track he came across a small log cabin just off the road. He pulled up and went to the door and knocked. After several more knocks and checking the two front windows he decided that no one was home. He went to the rear and, using the butt of the small revolver, he broke a window and climbed in.

The cabin was single storey with three rooms and a toilet/bathroom and had the feel of somewhere that had not been occupied for some time. The kettle and cooker were completely cold. There was a thin layer of dust on every surface including the floor. The bedroom held a small wardrobe which contained a selection of woodland and hunting clothes.

Grantham selected a plaid shirt, a hunting jacket, and a pair of trousers, all two sizes too large. But with a belt on the trousers and the shirt tucked in they would pass as baggy. He also took a long-peaked baseball cap with some sort of hunting logo on the front.

He cleaned himself up in the bathroom and dressed the wound to his shoulder, making sure he cleaned everything up after himself. He left a $100 note on the table with the kettle from the stove stood on top. Maybe it would dissuade the owner from reporting the break-in to the police.

He drove the car along the track for several hundred yards before veering off to one side and stopping fifty feet from the bank of a large pond. He then wiped down every surface he had touched and every surface he could reach from the driver's seat. The best way to destroy evidence would be to set fire to the car, but smoke rising through the woods would attract too much attention. He looked around and found a stick of about the right length. He then started the car and jammed the accelerator partly down with the stick before pulling the automatic gearshift into drive and diving backwards as the car drove forward at a steady twenty miles per hour and plunged into the pond.

The car floated and drifted further out into the water before slowly tilting to the left and sinking.

Grantham jogged back toward the cabin, quickly checked around to make sure he had not left anything and set off back towards a picnic area he had passed on the way in. Part of the way there, he dumped his wet clothes under several different bushes.

Once at the picnic area he headed over to an old Toyota and, with a glance around, he smashed the rear window with the butt of the small revolver. He reached in and opened the driver's door, ripped off the cover of the steering column and pulled the wires from the ignition switch. With a few twists of the wires he started the engine and, using sharp twisting movements, he smashed the inbuilt steering lock.

Grantham needed new clothes, but did not want to use a mall with CCTV. After thirty minutes he was back on the edge of town and found a camping and outdoors store.

Half an hour later he stepped from the men's toilets

with a new change of clothes and a wide brimmed floppy hat favoured by fishermen. His stolen clothes were in one of the store bags. He also needed a new mobile phone, but only the most basic models were available and he needed internet access.

After leaving the shop he drove to a multi-screen cinema, parked the stolen car away from the CCTV and walked half a mile before flagging down a cab. Twenty minutes later he climbed from the taxi at the Washington Monument, a giant version of Cleopatra's Needle. Although the sky was darkening by now, with floodlights illuminating the large obelisk, there were still plenty of people around. He mingled with the tourists and took twenty minutes to make sure no one was following him. He then walked the mile and a half to their hotel. Before entering, he observed the outside for half an hour from a small cafe across the street. There did not seem to be any undue activity so he entered the lobby and took the stairs to their room. Here, he quickly changed, packed and checked the interactive channel on the TV. This showed that there were no extras to pay, just the basic room rate which he paid with his secure credit card. Back in the lobby, he placed the swipe card room key in the reception desk slot and took the lift to the underground garage.

The BMW started at the first touch and he drove from the garage into the early evening twilight.

09:20hrs, 22nd April
MoD London

Professor Billie Lee walked away from the large screen and sat down.

"This is the latest data?"

"Yes Professor. The data was uploaded," Danny Barrett checked his watch, "just over fifteen minutes

347

ago."

"And all of these sites have been transmitting and receiving constantly for the last two days?"

Barrett nodded. "Since the increase in data transfer two days ago, the rate has been fairly constant. The land based site emits a microburst roughly every thirty minutes. The subterranean sites transmit every two hours or so. We assume that is because the land based sites have fixed transmitters whereas the water based sites have to raise and lower the transmitter and receiver."

"And we now have signals from South America?"

"Apart from the ground station in Costa Rica, there are now several along the north east and west coast, Brazil and Argentina. But the central area is still clear."

"I think that still points to the base being in South America somewhere," said Professor Lee.

"Have you made any progress with tracking the origin of the ground based signal?" asked Air Marshal Colridge-Stewart.

"Yes sir. We piggybacked a virus on one of the larger data signals. It was risky as the signal would be checked for continuity and any virus found and filtered out. Worse still, if it was found it would tip them off that we were onto them. So we disrupted the signal as if it had been corrupted by atmospherics. It was a risk, but it seemed to have worked. A few minutes later the transmitter repeated the signal so the receiver had recognised the signal as corrupt and asked for a repeat. There has been no change of style or frequency, so we seem to have gotten away with it."

"We've done well. What has this virus told us?" Air Marshal Colridge-Stewart sounded a little smug.

"We know that the signal to the ground station has been sent by ground based relay stations. We've tracked three relay stations so far to Panama, Columbia and Brazil. But we can only get the next relay when one of the systems accesses the internet on an automatic connection. So we're not in control of when the information comes in."

"Is there anything you can do to speed up the search?"

"No sir, all we can do is wait."

"Well, keep at it. You need to get the location of the base as soon as possible," said the Air Marshal with a dismissive air.

"All this data that is flying back and forth, do we know what it means?" asked General Clive Simmonds.

"We've translated a lot of the signal, but without a frame of reference we don't know what it means," replied Danny Barrett. At the quizzical look from the General, Barrett went on. "The signal is complicated and we have only deciphered about thirty percent. But even the part we can understand doesn't actually mean anything to us. If we deciphered a piece of data as 'three', we don't know three what. We don't know if three is better or worse, good or bad, higher or lower than two. Whilst we know the word, we don't have a point of reference."

General Simmonds nodded and sat back. "Thank you," he said and pursed his lips, a clear sign that he was thinking and about to speak again. "We're assuming that this increase in data is the build up to an attack, eruption...whatever you want to call it. Can we tell when it will occur?"

"Sorry General, same problem as before, we have no point of reference."

"Are any of these places," General Simmonds gave a broad hand gesture in the direction of the large screen. "Are they showing any signs of disruption?"

Professor Lee cleared her throat. "In my normal life I'm a fellow of the British Geological

Survey, the BGS. I've asked for an update from all of these locations and a general update on background noise. Background noise is the general rumblings that the Earth does all the time. There has been a slight increase in background noise, but it is within normal variations. These sites specifically, at least the ones that we are monitoring, which is about two thirds of them, have also shown some signs of increased activity. Again, they are within normal variance, but we have never seen an increase across the board before. I think I can say that there is most definitely some external force acting on these locations and it seems to be getting worse."

Professor Lee thought for a few seconds. "As to timescales, it's very speculative, we don't have enough data points to make anything approaching an accurate prediction. If we take the readings from six months ago as a baseline and then look at the readings from last week and last night, we would get a prediction from now to an incident of between two weeks and two months. But we can't predict if the increase will be a straight line, speed up or slow down, or even plateau. If this was a natural phenomenon at one location, we would not be looking at an incident in the next few days, probably not even in the next few weeks."

Michel Fortnum looked across the table at one of the other members of the ERG, Gideon Pearce the still slightly disgruntled C, head of MI-6. "Does Six have assets in South America?" In this case 'assets' referred to agents of MI-6 and it was less of a question than a statement of fact.

"South America is a big place, we do have assets in residence in some of the larger centres." Pearce looked over the top of his gold rimmed half moon glasses at Fortnum. His hair was more salt than pepper but was still thick and naturally glossy. It was difficult to believe from the look of his slight paunch and soft jowls that he had been one of the country's top agents during the Cold War.

"Can you task them to make enquiries as to possible sources of the origin of the signals?"

"Enquiries are already underway."

Michel Fortnum nodded, but did not rise to the bait.

"For now we are still in the data collection and monitoring stage. But I have a feeling that may change very quickly."

09:05hrs
Grüssmire Gewerbe HQ

Hans Eigel sat in his usual place at the head of the table. The glass wall looking over the grounds showed the rain coming down in an almost solid curtain. By midday it would have stopped and the heat would be building to form steam clouds hugging the ground.

The door to the meeting room opened and Joseph Adler came in, walked around the table and took his seat without any word of greeting or apology for being five minutes late. The Master, Eigel, repressed his smile. He would not accept such behaviour from anyone other than Adler. In truth he had little choice. Adler could not be intimidated, and he held almost as much power as Eigel. However, Eigel was loyal to the cause, if not necessarily to the man, and if he was late he would have a very good reason.

"Thank you for joining us, Herr Adler," said Eigel.

Adler bowed his head slightly, "No thanks are required." Eigel was not sure if sarcasm was lost on the man or if he viewed it as beneath him.

"Do you have something special to report?" asked Eigel.

"I can wait for the appropriate agenda item."

"Karl, update us on Project Genesis."

All eyes turned to Karl von Papen, the small rosy cheeked scientist with the immaculate hands, the hands of a surgeon that could assemble the most delicate of electronic equipment capable of killing billions of people, but who balked at the sight of blood. Eigel, when carrying out the ceremony as the Master often saw von Papen's eyes closed during the bloodletting.

"The response to the calibration is going well. There is slight variation in the sites, but results so far are promising."

"Can we bring all of the disruptors to full power and set off all of the events together."

Von Papen looked slightly uncomfortable, a common expression for him. "It depends on the definition of together. The predictions show that the events would occur within three days of each other." His voice rose at the end, and he was clearly expecting criticism or rebuke.

"Excellent, three days in these terms is the blink of an eye. Three days will allow the world long enough to savour the effects, but without sufficient time to respond. It will also allow us time to take credit for the destruction without the possibility of retribution."

The relief washed over von Papen, his face lit up with pride in the knowledge that he had pleased the Master.

"Herr Spielmann, what of the Messiah Project?"

The younger man unconsciously rubbed the scar on his right palm, it was the first time he had been without the bandage since the ceremony five days ago.

"We have moved the embryos to the bunker, all are responding well without any adverse effects. As so many are stable, well beyond our predictions or hopes," Spielmann looked sideways at von Papen and stroked his Vandyke beard, "we have used one to test a new procedure. We are accelerating the growth process. If it goes well the embryos would come to term in three months and grow to physical maturity in six years. We could stop the acceleration at any time with the injection of hormones to reverse the process. It may also be possible to halt the aging process altogether."

"This is a new branch of research that we have only discussed in theory. I do not want to risk damaging the embryos unnecessarily." Eigel's blue eyes seemed to grow darker as his eyebrows came down and together. Spielmann recognised the far from veiled threat.

"We have far more embryos that we expected. They are remarkably stable, far more stable than even our best predictions. We have tried the new process on only one embryo and it is working well. There do not appear to be any adverse effects." Spielmann looked around the table, his eyes stopping on the imposing and deadly threatening Joseph Adler. "As Herr Adler said previously, the DNA seems to be superhuman."

Eigel looked at the men around the table and then nodded slowly. "Very well, proceed. But use only the one embryo. The new race is the most important project we have ever undertaken." He looked around the table again.

"Any other business?"

Spielmann lifted his hand from the table to keep the Master's attention. "We have just confirmed that we have both male and female embryos."

Eigel stared at Spielmann, his dark blue eyes penetrating to the man's soul. Not for the first time, he realised that the cutting edge DNA research was beyond his own knowledge.

"I thought that you had removed all DNA from the egg and replaced it with the DNA we have recovered from various sources. Surely one DNA should produce one clone, the same clone each time."

"So it should. But there seems to be some sort of natural mutation, we have eighteen male and eleven female."

"You are sure?"

"Yes. I checked twice myself and then had someone else carry out the tests to be sure. There's no mistake."

Eigel could not understand what he was hearing, so he simply accepted the information as fact.

He continued to look around the table, deliberately looking from man to man, leaving Adler until last, the thought of making the man wait amused him, although nothing showed on his face.

"I have an update on the daughter of the Templar Knight. Adam has captured her and will be leaving America tonight. He had to unfortunately intervene when one of the Church's henchmen was trying to kill the girl. The man also offered some resistance, but Adam achieved his goal and has the girl. He should be here by this time tomorrow. We will then see what she can tell us." There was the glimmer of a spark in the black eyes.

"We will have as long as we need. Once Genesis is complete we will have over a year before we can venture out into the new world. And with the Messiah Project going so well, finding the relics of the Templars is less important. Although we will want them to be returned to the new race who will be their rightful owners. And any additional information that can reveal the truth from those past millennia will of course be of interest. Anything else?" No one spoke up.

"Very well, carry on with Project Messiah, but only experiment on the one embryo. Bring Genesis to the next stage, aim for full effect in one week."

Chapter 32

10:30hrs, 23rd April
Arlington Cemetery

After leaving the hotel the night before, Grantham had driven out of the city, stopping at a rural motel with wooden cabins. As was customary in most hotels and motels around the world, the check-in clerk, actually the owner of the motel, asked for a credit card imprint. It surprised Grantham every time that credit card users in America still used imprints rather than chip and pin. Grantham had used one of his fake credit card accounts. The payment would be honoured, but would not trace back to him. He parked the car around the back of the cabins so that it would not be seen from the road.

The cabin was remarkably clean and under different circumstances he would have enjoyed the motel and the countryside. But he had two things running around his mind. Charisma was missing, kidnapped and he had not been able to stop it, and the fact that he had killed a man. It was not the first time he had killed, not by a long way, but no one and nothing died easily.

But it was Charisma that was worrying him. Clearly the blond man had the opportunity to kill Charisma but had chosen to kidnap her instead. That meant that he wanted her alive, at least for now. But what of the dark haired man? Had they been working together? The blond man had shot the dark haired attacker, could it have been a bad shot? Grantham did not think so. The blond seemed cool and knew how to handle a weapon. It was the dark haired attacker that appeared to be the fanatic.

But now what? He needed access to the internet to activate the tracker on Charisma's phone. His old mobile was destroyed by the immersion in the river. It was sealed but had been damaged in the struggle allowing water into the screen, and there was no internet access at the motel. The inaction was killing him.

By 2:00am he had gone over everything in his mind at least a dozen times and forced himself to lie on the bed and relax. He had slept fitfully for four hours, rising at 6:00am and setting out on a two hour run through the Virginia countryside. After covering fourteen miles of hilly wilderness, he had returned to the motel to find the smell of cooking bacon wafting around the cabins. The owners had prepared breakfast for their guests and Grantham realised just how hungry he was. After a long hot shower followed by a two minute freezing cold rinse, he had walked over to the breakfast lodge and eaten a large breakfast. As he did so, he realised that his training was taking over and, at least in his mind, he was now on operational duty. He was taking on energy when he had the chance, not knowing what the rest of the day would hold.

The run had helped clear his mind. He had no other leads, so he would go to Arlington Cemetery and see if anyone turned up.

After breakfast he had checked out and driven back to Washington. He stopped on the outskirts of the city at a small mall. He quickly found what he needed and purchased an internet ready, pay-as-you-go phone. He then sat in the mall's cafeteria and set up the device, quickly accessing the internet and initiating the tracking software on Charisma's phone. After waiting for ten minutes it was obvious that no signal was coming back. As he expected, Charisma's phone must be turned off, maybe destroyed and ditched.

He checked news from the local area and found a report of the attack and shooting on the bridge with a report of both men. The descriptions were non-specific which meant that the body was unlikely to have been found yet.

He also found a second, separate report of the attack on the Interstate under the bridge. The report made reference to the close proximity of the first incident but did not directly link the two. There was also a description of a man the police wanted to interview, again generic but different enough from the other to not be too obviously the same person. There was also a description of the Mercedes, but no registration number. Unless the police were holding something back, it seemed he was safe for now.

He had arrived at Arlington Cemetery by 10:30am and walked around, taking in the sights and atmosphere. There were a few visitors around, all seemed normal and seemed to pay him no attention.

By 11:30am he had walked around the Amphitheatre twice.

The Amphitheatre was a sea of glistening white marble. The outer edge was divided into dozens of arches with Doric columns either side. Each arch displayed an American national or state flag. Rows of concentric marble benches capable of seating 5,000 people faced the large stage and ceremonial area.

Grantham stood at the rear under cover of the outer ring of arches, casually watching the people coming and going. There were perhaps thirty people in total in the large arena, mostly couples or family groups, several individuals of varying ages. An old man was walking slowly around the outer covered area, stopping occasionally to read the inscriptions. Grantham watched the man for a few seconds. He was easily in his eighties, possibly nineties, an old soldier remembering his comrades, his friends, his family. Keeping his back to the wall, Grantham looked around. There were two security guards at the front of the Amphitheatre, but they seemed to be casually doing their rounds. Three separate service men in uniform were taking in the sights and Grantham estimated another three who were not in uniform.

"Mr Grantham, I assume," the man made it a statement, not a question.

Grantham turned to look at the old man he had seen a few seconds ago.

"Have we met?" Grantham weighed the man up in a glance. Confident, intelligent, probably at least in his late eighties, maybe ten years older than that, he had definitely been fit but looked as if age had caught up with him and started to nudge him towards frailty. He probably did not pose a physical threat, although Grantham was not about to turn his back on the man, again.

"No, we haven't met, but I know a lot about you and Miss Valentine. We have been keeping an eye on the young lady for some time, and you since you came into her life in Oxford. You are an interesting man, with an even more interesting background." The man gave a slight smile.

"Really? You think you know my background? And who are 'we'?"

The man indicated to a seat and headed over, Grantham hesitating for a heartbeat before following.

"You joined the British Parachute Regiment before transferring to the SAS, where you served with more than distinction. As with most SAS officers, much of what you did has gone officially unrecognised. But you have seen action behind enemy lines in most of the trouble spots of the world, including a three month mission in Russia and you played a key role in preventing a major biological attack on the west. Since you left the service, rather than taking promotion, you have officially been working privately, but much of your work comes through JTAC, the Joint Terrorism Assessment Centre, where you have assisted in preventing an attack on a political delegation in Sierra Leone, helped get St.John Dalziel out of an ambush and most notably rescued the American President and his daughter."

Grantham re-evaluated the man, he may not be physically dangerous, but someone with the pull to get that sort of information was most definitely dangerous. Grantham was not going to admit to anything, but the man clearly had access to information that was supposed to be top secret.

"If we are going to talk, what should I call you? And what interests you so much about Charisma?"

"Miss Valentine is the daughter of a colleague and friend. We may not ride around on white chargers these days, but we still take our vows seriously. And the protection of family and friends is one of those vows. And you may call me Richard."

"So you're a member of the Knights Templars." It was Grantham's turn to make a statement. "How did you know I would be here?" asked Grantham.

"I didn't for certain. But where else would you go? We had an appointment, I thought you would keep it."

"But how did you predict this time and place? The message in the book could not have been planted as we got to the Library." Grantham looked levelly at the old man who had a half smile on his old, wrinkled face. And then realisation dawned on him.

"Of course, the message was planted some time ago. But you tracked the book. And you knew when we asked for it and simply turned up here the next day."

The old man nodded. "What better way to track

information than to have Knights on staff at the Nation's library? Over half of the curators have been Knights Templars. I was notified you had asked for the book even before it was given to you."

"So what was the idea behind the treasure hunt?"

"The Templars are split up into small groups to help with security and maintain secrecy. If anything goes wrong and normal communication channels are not available they need a back up. So each Knight has a way of tracking the leadership down. They have a clue that leads them to the next and so on. That way they can find the leaders if they need to, but don't actually know who or where they are. And each Knight has a different clue, leading to a different book. Any time any of the books are accessed we are informed."

"Do you have Charisma?" Grantham asked out of the blue and watched the old man's reaction closely.

The old man looked serious, the slight smile disappearing from his face as he shook his head. "No, we do not have Charisma. We would not kidnap a lady. But I think I know who does. Of course a man of your background knows of the Ahnenerbe. They are not a group that has died out. They may have changed their approach and they no longer go around in black uniforms in public, but they are still more than a force to be reckoned with. Have you heard of Grüssmire Gewerbe?"

Grantham thought for a few seconds, "The name rings the faintest of bells, but I can't place it."

"They are the leading research group in multiple cutting edge technologies, notably genetics, IT and Earth sciences. They succeeded in human cloning before the rest of science cloned the first mammal. And they have continued to search for holy relics, particularly anything that has a physical link to Jesus Christ."

360

Grantham looked at the man, questions flooding through his mind, but he was not sure where to start. "We were looking for the Knights, is that why they've kidnapped Charisma, to get to you?"

"It is difficult to fathom their motives. They have schemes within schemes. But yes, I'm sure that your search for the Knights played a role. And no, that was not an accusation."

"Why do they want to find you?"

"For the same reason that they spent years looking for holy relics."

Grantham was trying to order his thoughts, put the pieces together, not sure he could get the questions in a coherent order.

"But what changed their plans? They killed the three Knights, then tried to kill Charisma by bringing down the aircraft over the Atlantic. Now they kidnap her. Why change from killing to kidnap?"

"There are more people interested in the Knights Templars and what we possess and know than the Ahnenerbe."

"Like who? And why?"

"The church for one, at least factions within the church."

"The Catholic church?" asked Grantham.

"Well, originally the Catholic church was the main opposition to the Knights. They feared what we could do. But now it's less clear. There is still opposition from the church, but I think it is a hardcore faction rather than the whole church, although no one in the church would lose sleep if the Knights ceased to exist or if the church could gain possession of all of our secrets."

"Do the members have a symbol by any chance? A cross with light beams coming from the points and a shield?"

"They do indeed. Sometimes a pendant or more often a tattoo, usually over the heart."

"The man who tried to kill us on the bridge had the tattoo and the man on the aircraft."

Richard nodded thoughtfully.

"But what threat do you pose to the church these days? I understand that when the Knights were powerful they could have been a threat, but the Knights are now a secret society. So secret that most people don't even know you still exist."

"The threat has never been directly about power, but what we know, what we could let the people know." Richard shook his head at the thought of the situation and what it all meant. He took a deep breath.

"Much of the Christian belief is based on what the church has taught over the years. We, the Knights, could disprove a lot of their teachings that are accepted as fact. Who Jesus was, what he did, where he learnt many of his beliefs and teachings."

"Can you tell me any details?"

Richard shook his head. "I can't tell you details. But I could pose you some questions, the type of questions that the church has asked." Richard paused for a few seconds, lost in thought.

"The core belief of the Christian church is that Jesus was crucified and died on the cross. He was later resurrected before ascending to Heaven. What if Jesus did not die on the cross, but was instead rescued and cared for secretly for a few days until he had recovered enough to travel and it was then he was seen and thought to have been resurrected? What if his teachings were based on beliefs that were already old when he was born? What if he brought His teachings to the world, not just Israel and Europe, but to most of the world that was known at that time? And that those teachings developed into most of the established religions around today, that they are all just different versions of the same belief system?"

Grantham considered the questions. "I see how that would undermine the established Christian church. Maybe turning people away, and taking their money with them. And numbers of followers and money is what gives any church its power."

Richard slowly nodded as Grantham spoke.

"So the Church, or a group within the church, wants the Knights and Charisma dead to prevent any of the secrets coming out. But the Ahnenerbe want holy relics, so they want to find the Knights. And that must be because they believe you have holy relics. So are the stories of the Knights true, do you have relics that have some sort of power, relics that they're after? Information that leads back to Jesus? Secrets that...that...could change history?"

"We are the keepers of many items, several of which the Ahnenerbe would quite literally kill to get their hands on and the church would kill to either gain possession of or destroy."

"Richard, you clearly know some of my background, I may not be a man of faith in the religious sense of the word, but when I ask if the items have power, I'm sure you know what I'm referring to."

Richard pursed his lips, clearly thinking of a way forward, how much he should say.

"I assume you have heard of the Spear of Christ?"

"The spear that pierced the side of Jesus while he was on the cross. It's had several different names and many men have sought it throughout history for the power it could bring them. There's some sort of legend that says an army that has the Spear cannot be defeated."

"You are pretty well informed. Although I think you may be mixing the Spear up with the Ark of the

Covenant."

"And do you have the Ark as well."

"You want to know if items have power?"

Grantham noticed that Richard had not answered his last question, but let it go.

"The Spear first came into the possession of the Knights in the 12th Century. Over the years it has been taken from the Knights, usually by force, and eventually taken back, again usually by force. In the mid-thirties the German Nazi party was scouring the world for any and all religious relics they could lay their hands on. One of the ones they found was the Spear of Christ. They took it back to Wewelsburg Castle, the home of the Ahnenerbe. For the next ten years the German nation, especially the Nazi party, went from strength to strength, dominating the best part of Europe." Richard paused, weighing up Grantham to judge his reaction. Grantham was clearly waiting for more of the story.

"Let me ask you something, why did the Germans lose World War Two?"

Grantham was clearly not expecting the question and took a few seconds to consider his answer.

"The accepted wisdom is that they spread themselves too thin, especially on the Russian front. Their supply chain could not cope and eventually they were overrun and driven back, especially during the Russian winter which they were not equipped to cope with."

"And you think that is accurate?"

"Well, it is what happened. But I've read quite a lot about the era, I'm surprised that an army that was so well organised previously could fall apart in such a short time. Some people have speculated that there was more to it than simply a lack of organisation." Grantham paused again, marshalling his thoughts.

"The German nuclear research programme was more advanced than the American or British. They already had working missiles, the V1 and V2 and were planning the 'New York' rocket. But the early hydrogen bombs were far too big to mount on missiles so they would have had to find another method of delivery. They had two options, fly them in, like the Americans did in Hiroshima and Nagasaki or," Grantham paused, this time he was weighing up Richard. "Or they could plant the bombs, bury them in an occupied town or city and then withdraw. Let the enemy occupy the area and then detonate the bombs remotely."

Richard nodded, the story did not seem to have surprised him. "So why didn't they do just that?"

Grantham shrugged, "The German nuclear research was split between two teams. Together they had all the answers, but they didn't share the results. Eventually the war was going badly and they cancelled the research. Some say that the scientists didn't agree with the intended use and deliberately slowed the research, deliberately not sharing their results."

"Mmm...interesting. Let me continue my story. The Nazis got the Spear and became even more powerful. The Knights tried to regain the Spear but it was not easy. Eventually we became aware of the nuclear threat and tried one last ditch attempt to get the Spear back. Thankfully we succeeded, although not without loss. A team of Knights took back the Spear but made it look as if the Germans had thwarted the plan and had kept the Spear."

"You actually left them a fake," said Grantham, nodding his approval.

"More or less. But we had the real one back. That was in January 1945."

"That's when most researchers agree that the

German military started to fall apart."

"The war was still on and leaving the country was not easy, we could not risk the real Spear falling back into the hands of the Nazi party. So the Knights hid it in plain sight. Are you familiar with the Brandenburg Gate and the statue on the top?"

"I've seen it several times. The statue's a chariot drawn by four horses. I think it's Victoria, the Roman Goddess of victory?"

"That's correct. Victoria holds a standard and down the side of the chariot are several spears."

Grantham looked almost shocked. "They hid the Spear on the chariot?"

"In plain sight, where millions of people must have seen it over the years. After the war we intended to collect it. Unfortunately Berlin was split up and eventually the wall went up. Recovering the Spear was not easy. Over the years Germany as a country prospered. I've heard more than one person say that it was as if Germany won the war. But eventually when the wall came down we had to get the Spear back. After all, once the wall came down contractors, even the public, could gain access to the statue. So in November 1989 two Knights went to Berlin and collected the Spear.

"Charisma's father and Francois Bertrand."

Richard looked down and nodded his head, the smile completely gone.

"Yes, I was friends with John and Francois. It was a great loss. They retrieved the Spear but they were attacked by an Ahnenerbe, a creation known as Adam. He killed John and severely injured Francois. But Francois got the Spear to safety and we collected it a few days later while he was recovering in hospital."

After a short pause Grantham spoke up. "Wait a minute, you're saying the Nazis became so powerful because they had the Spear and when you took it back they started to fall from power. And that Germany after the war prospered because it had the Spear still in its capital?"

"As I said before, I have no proof to give you. I'm simply reporting the timeline. It may be simple coincidence. Maybe the Nazis believed they had a relic with powers and they acted differently, boldly and with less fear. Maybe the Spear truly has power. But whatever, we can't afford to let these relics fall into their hands. It may let them finally fulfil their ultimate goal."

"You mean world domination," said Grantham.

"More than just domination. They want to wipe out mankind and replace us with an earlier race."

"The Aryan race. But they were just mythical."

"I agree. But the Ahnenerbe may now have the ability to genetically create the master race. We think that they have been after any relic that has the blood of Christ, so that they can get the DNA. They believe that Jesus was the last of the Aryans."

"Okay, but how would they wipe out humanity? No nation would accept the death camps again."

"Oh, they have far more advanced methods than that. They have tried biological methods, Aids and HIV. And although thousands have died, thankfully it's coming under control."

"They created Aids?" the incredulity was evident in Grantham's voice.

"Many conspiracy theorists have speculated that some nation's intelligence agency did it, the CIA has often been favourite. But the Ahnenerbe created it and released it in Africa to wipe out the black population and then let it spread into the world."

Grantham shook his head, not sure what to make of the story. "You called this Adam a creation, did you have any reason for that?"

"The Ahnenerbe have researched in many fields since the war. One of their main areas has been in genetics. It is said that Adam was their first genetically modified human clone. He may not be superhuman, but he is special, fast and strong with no conscience or fear."

Grantham considered this for a few moments before asking Richard, "Do you know what 'in nomny petris' means?"

Richard looked sideways at Grantham. "In nomine Patris et Filii et Spiritus Sancti, is Latin for 'In the name of the Father, the Son and the Holy Spirit.' Why do you ask?"

"The dark haired man said it just before he tried to shoot Charisma and me. The blond man, this Adam, he said 'eight, eight,' before he also tried to blow my head off with a Desert Eagle."

"You are lucky to have survived, do you know what the eight, eight means?" asked Richard.

Grantham nodded, "It refers to the eighth letter of the alphabet. The letter H. It stands for Heil Hitler. Does any of this help me find Charisma?"

Richard nodded. "I think so. After the war, many German immigrants, amongst them war criminals and scientists, escaped to South America. The scientists carried on their research forming Grüssmire Gewerbe. They have several research facilities around the world, but their headquarters are in Paraguay. I believe that is where they will have taken Charisma."

Grantham nodded, if the Ahnenerbe still existed and were involved in Charisma's kidnap, it made sense.

"But you will need help. You cannot take on the Ahnenerbe alone."

"Will the Knights help?" asked Grantham.

"Sadly we are not the fighting force we once were.

There are few of us today. But I think you will find that help is closer than you think. I do, however, have something I hope will help. Please..." Richard stood up and started to walk towards the exit from the Amphitheatre, Grantham looked around before standing and following the old man.

The two men walked in silence, Richard seeming to soak up the spring light, Grantham constantly looking around and taking in his surroundings.

As they reached the car park, Richard walked to a large dark blue estate car and opened the rear hatch. The rear of the large car was empty, but Richard reached in and lifted the floor panel. Underneath was an old looking wooden box. Twelve inches wide and deep and as Richard pulled it from its concealed area, he revealed it to be about six feet long. The box was clearly old, maybe ancient, but it looked as if it had been kept cool and dry and well cared for. Two leather straps with thick padding kept the box closed. Along one side were three metal catches. The bottom two had clearly been broken many years ago, although the third looked as if it was still intact.

With surprisingly supple fingers Richard unbuckled the leather straps and flicked open the one working catch. The lid opened on concealed hinges revealing a vivid green and gold silk cloth. Richard folded this back to reveal a wooden shaft and metal head of a clearly old spear.

For a few seconds Richard stared at the Spear, looking as if he was lost in thought or memory. A look of peace, almost love, maybe reverence on his face. Slowly Richard turned to Grantham.

"Please Mr Grantham, examine the Spear."

Grantham looked from the old man to the Spear and back to Richard. "Is this *the* Spear?"

"It is the Spear that many people for two thousand

years have fought over. The same one that the Nazis stole in the thirties and the Knights recovered in 1945 and Charisma's father gave his life for in 1989."

Grantham slowly reached out, not sure what he was feeling, not sure what he *should* be feeling. The shaft was smooth and cool. It looked like old wood, smoothed over the years by countless hands, but it seemed to sap the heat from his skin, more like metal than wood. He lifted the Spear from the case and felt the weight. Just below the centre was a short metal balancing point. The shaft and head were well weighted, it had the potential to be a very effective weapon in the right hands. As he moved upwards along the shaft, he felt a small tingling in his fingers as they brushed the metal head. It reminded him of the sensation of putting his tongue on to a three volt battery but the sensation passed so quickly he was not sure he really had felt anything.

"I don't know what to say, what do you expect me to do with it?"

"Anything you want, Mr Grantham. The Spear is yours. On behalf of the Knights Templars, I give you this spear to do with as you want. Keep it, sell it, throw it away. It is up to you."

Not much surprised Grantham, but he was momentarily struck dumb.

"But...why?" asked Grantham.

"Maybe it will help you, maybe it will do nothing at all. But there are no stories that say that the Spear is bad luck."

"Well, thank you. But I can't very well carry it with me."

"You don't need to. Owning it is what counts. You can simply store it somewhere. The Knights would be happy to look after it on your behalf. We can keep it safe and you can recover it any time you want. Until you decide what you want to do with it long term."

"I presume you would like it back?"

"The Knights have been in possession and kept the Spear safe for most of the last nine hundred years and would be happy for its return. But we give you this with no conditions and no expectations. The Spear is yours."

Grantham still held the Spear, his finger brushing the metal head. After a few seconds of thought, he almost subconsciously made his mind up to accept the Spear, but to ask Richard to keep it safe. The tingle again spread into his fingers. Although it passed as quickly as before, this time there was no mistaking the sensation as it quickly spread up his arm.

With care, Grantham placed the Spear back in the box, rewrapped the cloth and closed the lid.

"Thank you. I accept the Spear, although I'm still not sure what it all means. But I would like you to look after it for me."

Richard bowed his head in acceptance.

"Good luck and God speed Mr Grantham. Remember, your friends are closer than you think. I know you will be victorious. We will meet again."

Richard fastened the case, placed it back into the rear compartment and walked to the front of the car, got into the driver's seat and drove away.

Chapter 33

11:00hrs, 24th April
Ruins of Pompeii, Italy

Antonio Nertari stood up and stretched his back. He had been interested in archaeology since he was at school. But bending over all day scraping at the ground with a miniature trowel was not so interesting for his back.

"Only another hour, Antonio, and we can go down to that small cafe you have been telling me about and sample some of the local wine," said Wendy Redmond.

Nertari smiled and stretched again, working his knuckles into the small of his back. "It is not just a local wine, it is Greco di Tufo, which is the wine and the grape. This region has been growing grapes and making wine for 4,000 years. The Greeks called this area the Land of Wine."

Pompeii was buried under four to six metres of ash following the eruption of Mount Vesuvius in AD79. So sudden was the eruption and so fast the ash and pumice flow that the people were killed and frozen for all time going about their everyday business. Since it was rediscovered in 1599, the city has been providing scientists with a detailed view of everyday life in Pax Romana. Today Pompeii is a UNESCO World Heritage site and welcomes two and a half million visitors a year.

For years Antonio Nertari had visited the site, marvelling at the figures frozen in time. He was one of the 900,000 people that lived in the nearby city of Naples, and this year he had taken two weeks off from work to take part in the latest dig.

"I warn you, the niceties of wine are lost on me. If it comes in a glass and isn't too dry, I'm happy." Like Nertari, Wendy Redmond was an amateur archaeologist and had also taken two weeks off work to participate in the dig. Unlike Nertari who travelled less than ten miles to be here, Wendy had travelled over 1,100 miles from the UK.

"That just means that you have not had the opportunity to experience the...what is the word? The...fineness of the good wine."

Wendy smiled at the richness of Nertari's accent.

"I think you mean the finer points of a good wine."

Nertari nodded at the correction, his English was good, certainly better that Wendy's Italian, but he did not have many chances to practise. And Wendy was a nice person to practise on.

At forty-six, Nertari was a widower of ten years, eight years older that Wendy, but they shared a love of archaeology, the outdoors and most importantly, a sense of humour.

Wendy had only completed a messy divorce six months ago and had used some of the settlement to fulfil one of her dreams to come to Pompeii.

Wendy stood up and also stretched, stepping to the side of the trench and taking Nertari's offered hand as she stepped up.

Looking back into the trench, they considered what they had achieved in the last six days, uncovering almost eight feet of wall.

"Not the most exciting of finds, is it?" said Wendy.

"Uncovering the treasures, the people and inside the dwellings, is not for the amateur. That is the work for the professional."

Wendy looked up and around the area. She could not imagine anything more beautiful. The sky was a rich blue with several dark green trees just coming into full leaf. The walls of the ancient city were red and orange brick with ribbons of grey mortar. The old roads were a brown/grey and the best of all, the slightly misty blue conical shape of Mount Vesuvius rising as the perfect backdrop.

"Is that smoke coming from the volcano?" asked Wendy as she shielded her eyes against the glare from the sun.

"Ah, the old lady she is also stretching."

"Is it safe?"

Nertari smiled and shook his head. "There is nothing to worry about. It is not unusual for Vesuvius to smoke sometimes. The old lady, she is just clearing her throat, there is nothing to worry about."

15:00hrs,
Washington DC

Grantham sat in the motel cabin and checked his watch then looked at the glowing red numbers of the bedside clock, both showed the same time.

Since meeting with Richard yesterday he had been trying to make travel plans to get to Paraguay. Based on the information that Richard had given him, it sounded as if the headquarters of Grüssmire Gewerbe in Paraguay was the best lead he had for finding Charisma. He had tried to research the firm, but even on the Internet, which these days seemed to be the font of all knowledge, there was surprisingly little information. The facility seemed to have been founded in the early fifties but nothing was listed on who the founders were or where the funding came from. The firm itself had no web page and did not appear on Facebook or Twitter. As far as Grantham could tell, there was no way to contact the firm electronically. He had rung the international operator from the room but even though he could provide the name and country location of Grüssmire Gewerbe, no telephone number was listed. He asked to be put through to the Paraguay International operator, but after almost ten minutes of trying to make himself understood he gave up.

When he had asked Richard for the location the old man had simply shrugged. It was based in Paraguay, but the exact location was a secret even to the Knights. Richard had told him that any meetings with people external to the company were conducted off site. The Knights had tried to infiltrate the firm, but never managed to get beyond meetings outside of Paraguay, and had suffered several losses in the attempts.

Grantham's only real lead was the German settlement of Hohenau, Paraguay. He knew that the settlement had been established around the turn of the 12th Century and it seemed logical that the Nazis, after the Second World War, would have felt at home in the area. With this in mind, he tried to arrange flights to Paraguay. But this had proven far harder than he thought.

There were no direct flights from Dulles International, Washington. The closest he could get a direct flight to was either Sao Paulo, Brazil or La Paz, Bolivia. But travelling on from these was not easy and there were no flights for four and five days respectively. The fastest he could arrange was a flight to San Salvador in El Salvador then on to the new International airport at Quito, Ecuador. From here he had an overnight stay before he could get to Santa Cruz, Bolivia and then on to Asuncion, Paraguay. From here he would be travelling overland, but to where? The Hohenau settlement was 288 miles north of the airport, but he was not even sure if this was the right location. It would have been far easier if he could have chartered a flight, but he did not have that sort of money to call on when he was working privately.

It was time he called in some favours.

He reached for his new mobile phone and hesitated. His old phone, although it looked perfectly normal had inbuilt encryption and several other special facilities. The new one did not. He revised his plans and called a different number. The number rang five times and switched to answer phone. Grantham left a brief message and hung up, staring at the phone. After three minutes it rang.

"Thanks for calling back, we aren't encrypted." Grantham deliberately did not use his name or the name of the man who was calling back. He had hoped that the key phrase he left on the answerphone would be picked up and passed on to the other's mobile phone as a flash message. The other was Danny Barrett, one of his contacts from GCHQ.

"Okay, what can I do? But make it quick, I'm in a meeting."

"I've had to buy a new mobile and haven't had it updated. I need to make some private calls, anything you can do from your end?"

There was a pause of a few seconds. *"You're lucky. I've just completed a secure web site where you can download the basic software. Only went live yesterday. Hang up and I'll send you a text with a web address. Log on and follow the instructions, It'll give you the basics."*

"Thanks," said Grantham, and hung up.

Five minutes later the phone beeped and Grantham read the text and followed the link to a web site. From here he selected the search facility and searched for what seemed like a random set of letters and numbers. A new window opened and Grantham entered his ID and sixteen digit password. Grantham read through the instructions before selecting several pieces of software to download. It was almost ten minutes later that the screen finally showed that the download was complete and the phone automatically shut down. After a quick reboot, Grantham was pleased to find several hidden icons on the phone, including basic encryption software.

Grantham dialled the number he was originally going to call. The call was answered on the second ring, but no one spoke. A series of beeps and screeches erupted from the speaker. After five seconds there were three beeps followed by silence.*"Hello?"*

"It's Grantham, I'm on a new phone."

"With only level one encryption. What can we do for you?" The voice on the other end was soft with no discernible accent, but Grantham recognised it as William Windsor, one of his two contacts at JTAC.

"The daughter of the man you looked up last week, I've lost her. I need the location of a firm to visit where she may be." Grantham did not want to be too specific with only a reduced level of encryption available.

Windsor could tell from the granite tone of Grantham's voice this was not the time to make jokes and he could read between the lines, if Grantham had 'lost' the girl, it had been by force.

"What's the name of the company?"

"Grüssmire Gewerbe in Paraguay."

"Can't say I've heard of it. I'll do some checking and get back to you. Anything else?"

"I don't suppose you have any assets in the area I could call on?" By 'asset' Grantham was referring to field operatives or troops, probably SAS, known to JTAC as Sierra Units.

There was a quiet chuckle down the phone line. *"You aren't on the clock, so no."*

"If I was working officially?"

"The answer would still be no."

"Okay, get me what you can. Thanks."

Grantham put the phone down and considered his options. There was a flight tonight from Dulles to San Salvador. He could get to Paraguay in three days. He couldn't see any other options. He rang the airport and booked his ticket, booking the connections as well. He then sat back and considered the situation. He had a few hours before the flight, was there anything else he could do? He mentally replayed his meeting with Richard. One thing stuck out. Richard had said that help would be provided from his friends, but that was not the Knights. Grantham thought for a few seconds and then picked up the phone.

"Hello?"

"Mac, it's..." The voice on the other end cut Grantham off.

"Boss, bloody good to hear from you. How you doing?" Mac's friendly Geordie accent was clear.

"I could be better. You busy?"

Like Windsor, Sergeant Major 'Mac' Maguire could read between the lines.

"The team's been training in America for the last few days. We've just finished up. What do you need?" Mac's voice had changed from jovial to crisp and businesslike.

"I could do with some backup."

"Off the range?"

"Completely off the range and very unofficial. Mac, I've no right to ask, if you or any of the lads can't do this, there's no hard feelings. This could be a life changer."

Until he retired two years ago, Grantham had been the unit commander of several SAS squads, including Mac's. They had served in some of the world's hell holes, lost men, took lives and saved many more.

There was a chuckle from the phone. *"Boss, you*

378

know everyone of us owe you more than our lives. If you need something we're there. Where do you want us and when?"

"Do you have transport?"

"Only ground based. We've used the Yanks' helos for assault training. I think they'd notice if we borrowed one without asking."

"Okay, can you get to Paraguay under your own steam? I'll cover the cost."

"Bollocks boss, we can stand a couple of flights. We're owed some leave. We'll get travel details from Washington and make the arrangements."

"Washington? That's where I am." Richard had been right about friends being close by. "Get a pen and I'll give you the details."

Five minutes later Grantham hung up and took a deep breath. He was asking men he respected and trusted to risk their lives for him. The only redeeming thought was that if the situation were reversed he would do the same for each and every one of them.

He had one more thing to do before he left for the airport. He needed to check in with Boston Detective Yeman, let him know he was leaving the country rather than risk being detained at the airport. He dialled the number and was put through to the detective's desk.

"Grantham, nice to hear from you. Decided to tell me something useful?"

"I just wanted to let you know I'm leaving the country, if that's okay?"

"You've been cleared of any wrongdoing on the aircraft. We won't even need you for the trial. The attacker lawyered up. We aren't sure how, he didn't speak to anyone or make any calls, the lawyer just turned up. After a brief meeting he informed us that his client would not be speaking to us. We had him arraigned and he was remanded pending trial.

379

Yesterday he killed himself. Never spoke to anyone except his lawyer. No warning of anything, he was just found dead in his cell yesterday."

"How did he do it?" asked Grantham.

"It was a hell of a thing, he climbed on top of his bed and dove head first at the floor, broke his neck."

"Did he tie his hands behind his back?"

"No, he just jumped off headfirst onto the floor."

"Hell of a way to do it, and it would take tremendous willpower not to break the fall with your hands."

"You said it. So, where you heading, home?"

Grantham considered simply saying yes, but if Yeman was still suspicious he could check and stop him last minute.

"No, I'm heading into South America, doing a bit of a tour."

"Okay, enjoy and keep clean."

"Thanks detective."

Grantham hung up and checked the clock. Time to head for the airport.

22:00hrs
MoD London

The conference room was starting to feel like home to the Emergency Response Group. For some time the group seemed to be going round in circles. Snippets of information would come in and it was not even clear if they had any bearing on the situation. But little by little the pieces were starting to fit together. GCHQ had tracked down the signals, started to track the transmissions back to their source. Seismic readings were now clearly rising, albeit slowly.

The door opened and Howard Thomas, the UK Secretary of Defence came in. He had the usual half smile on his face, but his eyes showed the sunken shadows of someone who had not had enough sleep over the last few days.

"Thank you all for the time and effort you have put in. You've made great progress starting from almost nothing." He smiled, but the smile did not make it to the eyes. "Things are getting a little tense in the upper reaches of government. It seems that the attack is underway, but we have no response and no defence. Do we evacuate the areas under immediate threat along the coast? Will it make any difference in the long run? Will it make any difference even in the short term?"

Professor Lee looked around the table. No one seemed willing or able to provide an answer. "If we can't stop the disasters before they occur, there will be nothing we or anyone can do that will make a difference. Apart from the privileged few, mankind will be wiped out."

Across the table Danny Barrett's phone gave three quick beeps. Although he had diverted all incoming calls and texts, certain numbers still had priority and if a key phrase was used when leaving a message the phone would let him know with the three beeps.

Barrett picked up the phone and saw the message. It was a priority message from someone who knew how to get access to him. Barrett considered taking the call, but thought better of it and put the phone down.

"Are we any closer to narrowing down the controllers of the devices that are causing the problems?" asked Thomas.

"Yes sir," said Barrett. "As you know, the satellite signals originate at Costa Rica. We've now tracked that via ground relay stations to one site in Panama, two sites in Columbia and one in Peru. But we're still only at relay stations, not the origin."

"Is there any way to speed up the search?"

Barrett shook his head. "I'm afraid not, we're in the hands of the computer search that we downloaded."

Barrett's phone gave another three beeps.

"Mr Barrett, if you need to take a call it is quite alright. I know you have other duties as well as this team."

Barrett was not sure if there was sarcasm in Thomas's voice, so decided to take the comment at face value, excused himself and went out into the corridor. He quickly accessed the answerphone and listened to the message. The key phrase was from a field operative and Barrett recognised the voice as Hugh Grantham, a man he had never met, but one he had dealt with on several occasions. Barrett did an auto call back, the phone only rang once before it was answered.

"Thanks for calling back, we aren't encrypted."

Barrett noticed that Grantham did not use his name.

"Okay, what can I do? But make it quick, I'm in a meeting." He did not want to keep the group waiting any longer than he needed to.

"I've had to buy a new mobile and haven't had it updated. I need to make some private calls, anything you can do from your end?"

Barrett considered the request. Ideally he would have the phone in front of him so that he could install the customised software, but he did have alternatives.

"You're lucky. I've just completed a secure web site where you can download the basic software. Only went live yesterday. Hang up and I'll send you a text with a web address. Log on and follow the instructions, It'll give you the basics."

"Thanks." The phone went dead.

Barrett quickly entered the new secure website and selected several programmes. He changed the security settings and logged off. The new settings would only stay active for sixty minutes. He then composed a brief message to Grantham with the web address and the time limit and hit send.

"Ah. Mr Barrett, welcome back. Professor Lee was just updating us." Thomas nodded at Professor Lee as Barrett sat down.

"Almost all the sites we're able to check are showing increased activity. At the moment the levels are still within normal parameters, but that will not stay the same for much longer. Within a few days it will become obvious to any observers, shortly after even the public will know something is wrong."

"What type of signs will people start to notice?" asked Thomas.

"Volcanoes will start to smoke more, maybe the occasional tremor, the smell of sulphur, heat increase at the surface. Maybe fissures will open. For earthquakes there will be tremors which will increase in intensity and frequency, starting with mini tremors and getting bigger. Tsunamis will not exhibit much outwardly. Maybe some small tremors as the plates slip, but as they're out at sea there will be little sign until BANG," Professor Lee slammed her hand on the table, making everyone jump.

"And we are sure of the outcome?"

"We've run over a dozen simulations in the last few days, the details may change, but the final outcome is always the same, ninety-five percent of life on the surface of the Earth is lost."

"So we need to stop it before then," said Thomas.

"Actually, we think we need to stop it well before that point. The Geology Society is monitoring the situation. All of this is new you understand, but we are speculating that at some point we pass the point of no return. Stop the devices after that time and it won't stop the incidents. The pressure will have been built up so much that it cannot simply dissipate naturally, it will carry on building until the breaking point is reached and there is an explosive release."

"Let me guess, we don't know when we will get to the point of no return?" said Thomas.

"Not only don't we know when we'll get to it, we may not even be able to recognise it when we do get to it."

"So what can we do?"

Gideon Pearce, head of MI-6 leant forward and removed his half moon glasses. "We are making enquiries in South America, but it's a big area and we don't actually know what we are looking for."

Thomas sat back and heaved a large sigh. "Okay, keep going and let's pray that we can find the bad guys soon. Or we'll all be out of a job very shortly."

22:30hrs Zulu
Pacific Ocean, 500 miles East of Manila

The control room of the Royal Navy Fleet submarine HMS Ambush would not have looked out of place on the set of a Hollywood sci-fi blockbuster. However, unlike a Hollywood film, the commander and crew of the submarine went about their duty calmly and quietly. There was no fuss, no rushing and little noise. Indeed, everything about the submarine was designed to reduce noise.

Commander Markus J Reems looked up as the 'newbie' walked onto the command deck. This was the man's first trip to sea in a submarine and as yet he had not gained his coveted dolphins, the insignia awarded to submarine crew after they have successfully completed their training and qualification in ship's systems on board their first posting. As a newbie, one of his unofficial jobs was to keep the commander of the deck supplied with coffee.

"Sonar, bridge, any surface or subsurface contact?" asked Reems over the comms.

"Bridge, sonar, surface contacts as previous, four tankers, three merchantmen, one Russian frigate at extreme range. Nothing subsurface."

"Very well. Commence survey, but keep your ears out for contacts heading this way."

As far as the crew were concerned the ship had been moved from its planned patrol to carry out some seismic surveys. Only Commander Reems and his first officer knew the full truth concerning the potential attack and destruction of large parts of the world and its population. Whilst Reems' orders had made it clear how important the mission was, they had also told him that the results of the survey were unknown, they may pick up nothing.

Reems looked up as Lieutenant Commander Jenkins, his first officer, entered the bridge.

"Afternoon Captain, I hear we've started the survey." Although Reems held the naval rank of Commander, when in charge of any naval vessel all officers were referred to as Captain regardless of their actual rank.

"That's right, about two minutes ago. No results yet."

As was common at sea, the officers and crew did not wear service caps so there was no need to continually salute each time an officer walked into a room.

Jenkins looked around the bridge, all of the men present were concentrating on their own tasks. He stepped closer to Reems' command chair and lowered his voice.

"I know we've been told that the possible eruptions and earthquakes are not imminent, but I've been doing some research. The amount of energy released in one tsunami incident is greater than all the energy of all the nuclear weapons in the world. What would happen to the Ambush if we were in the area when these plates slipped?"

Reems looked around and replied equally quietly. "I wondered the same thing and also did some research. There are no reported incidents of a submarine being close to the source of an actual tsunami. But the best advice is that it would not be too bad. You're right about the energy release, but that energy is spread over a huge area. The force should do little more than produce a gentle shove against the hull, even though it may be travelling at several hundred miles an hour."

"Just how good is this advice?" asked Jenkins with a crooked smile.

"Let's just say I'd rather not put it to the test."

"Bridge, sonar." The voice of the sonar operator came over the bridge intercom.

Reems picked up the microphone. "Sonar, bridge, go ahead."

"Sir, we have multiple seismic signals over an extensive range. It sounds like someone is squeezing the sea bed in a giant vice."

"Can you localise the signal?"

"Sir, it seems to be coming from as far as we can trace, hundreds of miles at least, all along the subduction zone."

Chapter 34

06:00hrs, 25th April
Paraguay

The aircraft rolled to a halt at the end of the runway. An ambulance that had been waiting drove from the terminal building and stopped at the bottom of the short staircase. A member of the ground crew climbed the stairs and opened the door which swung in and out before lying along the fuselage of the large executive jet.

Three ENAER T-35 Pillán trainer aircraft were stationed across the far side of the airfield with a larger Embraer EMB 312 Tucano ground attack aircraft sitting a few yards away. The aircraft represented almost a quarter of the total force of the Paraguayan air force. All were single engine prop aircraft and at least ten years old. The open doors of the hangar showed the outline of an old style Bell UH-1 Iroquois helicopter.

Although a military airfield, Grüssmire Gewerbe maintained several aircraft in private hangars with their own private security. Any three of the Grüssmire Gewerbe aircraft cost more that the entire Paraguay air force combined.

Adam stood at the top of the stairs, looking out and surveying the airfield. All was quiet as he had expected at this time, the sun was just rising in the east and casting long shadows across the airfield. Satisfied that everything looked in order, Adam stepped back into the jet and allowed the two medics carrying a stretcher to enter. After ten minutes, the medics appeared again carrying the stretcher but this time with the prone body of a dark haired woman securely strapped on. With care they carried the stretcher down the stairs to the waiting Bell helicopter. As Adam following the stretcher, the ground crew removed the stairs and a tug hitched up to the front wheel and pulled the executive jet into the waiting hangar.

Adam sat in the back of the UH-1 'Huey' helicopter watching Charisma. Since capturing her in Washington, he had kept her sedated, it was far easier to explain an 'injured woman as a result of an accident', especially if he had the correct paperwork, than hiding her away. He believed in the old adage of 'hiding in plain sight'.

They would be back at Grüssmire Gewerbe in just over an hour. The last he had heard, Project Genesis was progressing and they would shortly be taking to the bunkers for the next year. They had all the time in the world to find out everything the girl knew of the Knights Templars.

As the helicopter passed over the dense ring of trees that surrounded the headquarters, the sun finally broke through the cloud cover making the buildings shimmer in the bright light.

Ten minutes later Adam was in one of the underground laboratories. The bare white walls, clear worktops and empty shelves allowed the laboratory to be used for whatever purpose was required. In this case, the revival of Charisma from her drug induced coma.

Adam lifted a small bag onto the worktop and unzipped the top. He removed several items he had been travelling with until he reached a sealed bag. When he had captured Charisma she had a mobile phone which he had opened and taken out the battery and SIM card so that it could not be traced. But here in the shielded laboratory it was now safe to reassemble the telephone and see what information he could gain from it.

After a few seconds, the phone came to life and Adam searched through the contacts, files, images, texts, internet search history, which was so minimal that it had clearly been wiped recently. When nothing specifically stood out, he wirelessly connected the device to the computer and downloaded the whole contents to the network so that he could search it more thoroughly later.

The door opened and Adam looked around, it was Joseph Adler, his hook nose and soulless dead eyes marking him as the compassionless predator that he was.

"Adam, nice to see you again. You have done well." Adler came as close as he ever did to a smile.

"I did not complete the full task. The man escaped. He was very persistent. I believe he was a professional and well trained."

Adler nodded, "He is an independent security consultant. He was trained by the British Parachute Regiment. So you are right, he has been well trained. But you did not fail, you have brought the girl back, and she will tell us everything." Adler's smile held equal parts anticipation and malevolence. "Make sure she is secure before leaving her to come around in her own time."

12:50hrs
Quito, Ecuador

Quito, the capital of Ecuador and formerly called San Francisco de Quito, sits at an elevation of 9,350 feet making it the highest capital city in the world and houses the administrative, legislative and judicial functions of the nation. It is located on the eastern slopes of Pichincha, an active volcano in the Southern Andes mountain range. With a population of two and a half million, Quito is the second most populous city in Ecuador. The historic centre of Quito is one of the largest, least altered and best preserved historic areas in the Americas. Quito straddles the equator at zero latitude with Ecuador being the Spanish word for equator.

Grantham sat in the shade of several large palm trees. The park was a short taxi ride from Quito airport. In the past sixteen hours he had seen the inside of three airports, spent nine hours in the air and seven hours inside airport terminals. He needed some fresh air, to see the sky and stretch his legs.

He had arrived at Dulles International airport, Washington at 19.20hrs the previous night and registered for his flight, thankful that there had been no questions from security or customs. He had taken a seat in the departures lounge waiting for the flight to be called, ostensibly reading a magazine whilst maintaining awareness of everything around him. As he entered the lounge he had seen, but in no way acknowledged, Snake and Jez Stinger. Ten minutes later Mac had arrived with Nick Perkins, who had joined the Regiment only three months before Grantham had retired. Danny Fathom arrived a few minutes later. It was almost thirty minutes later that John 'Bird' Sparrow had walked in and taken a seat. All of the men ignored the colleagues they had not arrived with. Grantham had smiled inwardly, he could not ask for a better team and they were all following SOP, standard operating procedure by not making it obvious they were travelling together.

Fifteen minutes before the flight was due to be called, Grantham had gone to the men's room. A couple of minutes later Mac had come in and, once he saw that he and Grantham were the only occupants, had finally acknowledged Grantham.

"Nice to see you Boss. What's up?" Mac's Geordie accent brought a smile to Grantham's face for the first time in what seemed like forever.

"I've been travelling with a woman, Charisma Valentine..."

"Nice name."

"Very nice lady. Anyway it's a long story, but she thought she was in trouble, being followed, maybe her life was in danger, so I tagged along. It turns out she was right. She was kidnapped from under my nose. She was taken by a firm called Grüssmire Gewerbe."

Mac shook his head. "Never heard of them."

"But you have heard of the Ahnenerbe."

"Bloody hell Boss. That is the big time. They still exist?"

"After a fashion. Again, it's a long story, but in short form, after the Second World War they went to Paraguay, set up a research facility that became Grüssmire Gewerbe. They specialise in genetics and want to get their hands on anything that contains the DNA of Jesus to build the master race. Charisma's father was ex-Regiment and a Knight Templar. So they think she could lead them to the Templars' treasure, including holy relics."

Mac just looked at Grantham, lost for words for a few seconds.

"You're serious."

Grantham just nodded, his face without any hint of humour.

"If you were anyone else I'd call you insane. But we've been through too much for me to doubt you now." Mac shook his head again, his eyes wide.

"Okay Boss. It sounds like a plot by Dan Brown, but I'll go along with it."

"Do you have any equipment?"

"Oh yes, full mobile equipment, CQB and assault

with black kit and camouflage. We've also got spares that you can use. And it's all travelling in a secure crate under diplomatic cover. I've booked it in and arranged for secure transfer at each connection."

"How'd you manage that?" asked Grantham.

"As I told you, we're here on an FBI training course. Cross fertilisation the brass call it, bullshit I call it. Although to be fair, they are pretty good and the training facilities are brilliant. I wish we had the budgets they have."

"I hope you didn't let the side down?"

"Course not. And we took a big bite out of their training budget when we stormed one of their buildings. Lots of damage…unfortunately." Mac had a grin on his face. "I can't believe we were lucky enough to all get on the same connecting flights. The last two only managed because of cancellations." Just then there was an announcement over the public address system and their flight was called.

"Time to go. I'll see you in Paraguay," said Grantham.

And now fourteen hours later, Grantham sat taking in the sun and watching the mix of white and grey clouds drift by. The park was directly under one of the flight paths and aircraft were flying by at about two thousand feet. He checked his watch, three hours to the next flight to Santa Cruz, Bolivia. It was about two miles back to the airport and Grantham decided to walk and stretch his legs.

As he stood, his mobile phone beeped. He took the phone out and read the message and then re-read it. It was an automated message from Charisma's phone. The software he had loaded onto it was programmed to identify its location whenever it was switched on and to update the location every thirty seconds. It would also monitor any messages sent to the phone and act on instructions. Obviously wherever it was it did not have a signal, maybe it was somewhere remote or in a shielded location. But another thing it did automatically was to seek out any internet networks within range and piggy back onto them to ascertain its location and send out a message that would be relayed to Grantham. So now Grantham knew where Charisma's phone was. He just hoped that she was in Paraguay with the phone.

07:30hrs, 26th April
JTAC

William Windsor walked into the JTAC office carrying a large mug of coffee with the emblem of HMS Battleaxe on one side. He sat down at his desk and started to go through the overnight reports, the smell of polish and air freshener still hanging in the air from the overnight cleaning crew.

He was often in at this time, but for the last few days most officers had been in early with the raised alert status. Although they were on high alert, no one seemed to have any idea why. They were preparing files for transmission and archiving, preparing to direct security and police services for civil unrest, arranging to move hundreds of VIPs to underground shelters. In the last two days several old World War Two bunkers had been reopened and were being stocked ready for use. But even amongst all this action, no one knew why any of it was happening.

Tensions were clearly running high. But all foreign threats were at the same level as for the last year or so. North Korea was still posturing and threatening to stir up trouble. There were the usual threats from terrorist groups. Occasional probes electronically as hackers attempted to gain access to supposedly secure

393

networks. Although troops were gradually returning home, there were still enough trouble spots with British troops to keep the threat levels raised. But it seemed they were preparing for a major invasion or nuclear attack. And no one was giving them information.

Windsor looked up as the door opened. Phil Everett came in also carrying a steaming cup of coffee.

"Have we heard why we're doing all this?" asked Everett.

"Nothing yet." Windsor indicated the two computer screens. "I'm just going through the overnights. America and Europe are also gearing up the same as we are. And," Windsor scrolled further through the reports. "Also Australia and New Zealand. What the hell is going on? Someone is going to have to tell us. At this rate the press is going to start to get wind of something. And once that happens..." Windsor left the thought hanging.

By now Everett was sat at his own desk and flicking through the reports. One report caught his eye and he opened it to get more details. After a few seconds he started to laugh quietly.

"It looks like our Mr Grantham got his way."

Windsor looked up and across the office.

"We've got a report from America. Flight details of Sierra One. They've finished the training at the FBI and have flown out of Dulles International heading south to Paraguay via El Salvador, Ecuador and Bolivia."

What was not widely known was that JTAC kept covert track of various people as they travelled the world. Predominantly the targets were suspects or people thought to be dangerous to the state. But they also included many of the staff, such as Sierra units and private individuals like Hugh Grantham.

"Paraguay is the home of the company that Grantham was asking about. Has he flown out as

394

well?"

"Same flight and connections. They should be arriving in Paraguay around eight pm tonight. One other thing, Sierra One has taken their full kit with them as diplomatic cargo," said Everett.

"Oh dear, that's a bit of a no, no. We should call them back straight away," said Windsor with a smile.

"But we aren't going to?"

Windsor sat back and stapled his fingers behind his head. "Well we are very busy, and this is just a standard report that could easily get lost in all the background noise and day to day reports. We have been told to concentrate on...whatever the problem is." Windsor shrugged with slight irritation at not knowing the background to the current situation.

"So lose the report, then."

"Temporarily shelve it. Until we're less busy."

"And if Sierra One has gone rogue and goes on a killing spree?"

Windsor laughed with real mirth. "Well one, the only people they are likely to encounter in South America are drug lords and white slavers. A few less of those would be doing the world a favour. And two, if they have gone rogue, do you want to get in the way of a highly trained and heavily armed SAS unit?"

Everett laughed as well. "Well, put like that...what report?" Everett tapped a few keys on the computer. "Did you get the info that Grantham was asking for?"

Windsor nodded as he took a mouthful of coffee. "There wasn't much info about. Most of it was unsubstantiated rumours. Hints about their research, the occasional disappearance of scientists. Even some suggestions that major robberies and attacks were down to them. But very few hard facts. It was hard enough to even pin down the location. Members of the public would stand no chance. But Grantham did get lucky in one respect. You know that new private GemSat?"

"The one that we were offered free use of for a month to see how it performed?"

"That's the one, well during the free month's trial the filming covered wide areas of South America, and it picked up the compound and surrounding area of this Grüssmire Gewerbe. And to be honest, the extracted data is bloody good. It even converts the visual image to a scale plan complete with measurements and suggestions as to the security measures based on the EM signature from the devices on the ground. I'll compile the info and get it sent off to Grantham this morning.

07:00hrs, 26th April
Santa Cruz, Bolivia

Grantham turned over in the double bed and looked at the glowing red digits of the bedside clock. Sleep had taken until the early hours to come, but when it did he had fallen into a dreamless sleep for five hours. He knew he could go days with little or no sleep. He had trained to be able to perform to his full potential even when severely sleep deprived. But having a few hours of solid sleep under his belt was always good and he had managed to fully recharge his batteries. Grantham sat up and stretched before getting up and heading for the shower.

The hotel was surprisingly clean, spacious and well equipped. Built only five years ago, it served the airport and specialised in the international business trade. It offered several conference rooms of various sizes, four international standard restaurants, a huge very well equipped gym and swimming pool and Wi-Fi access throughout. One of the most interesting and attractive features was the foyer. At five storeys high, it featured a four storey waterfall dropping into a pool surrounded by tropical rainforest. Seating and walkways were spread throughout the area with open grass areas to allow for quiet relaxation. A more dramatic view was available from the fifth floor balcony that went over the waterfall and the third floor balcony which went behind the waterfall.

Grantham came out of the shower still wearing the towel around his waist and opened his suitcase for a clean set of clothes. As he lifted the clothes out, he realised that he was on the last clean set. Grantham stood up and thought for a few seconds. He could do some laundry, but would he really need clean clothes? Although he had not formulated a full plan, actually he had barely formulated a basic plan, he saw combat gear and assault weapons in the near future, rather than casual evening wear. But he still had a day's travel by aircraft and some ground transport once they got to Paraguay. And not knowing what would happen in Paraguay made his mind up. He sighed and picked up his case. He had several hours to spare anyway so why not spend it getting some clean clothes?

As he dressed his phone buzzed and Grantham saw it was a text from Windsor. He opened the message and found a brief note directing him to a secure website. He quickly accessed the site and scanned through the documents.

He headed off to the laundry room and loaded the clothes into one of the large American style washers and selected quick wash. He had ninety minutes to kill so he went back to the web file and looked at the documents in more detail. Most were articles reporting scientific breakthroughs with notes from Windsor suggesting that although not credited, they were down to Grüssmire Gewerbe. The second file contained circumstantial reports suggesting various nefarious acts attributed to the firm over the last fifty years. But it was the third file that was the most interesting. This contained aerial photographs showing the whole compound and surrounding areas. Overlaid on the photographs were infrared images showing heat signatures with analysis notes. Best of all, there were even scale plans showing the layout of the compound and the CCTV, motion, infrared and laser detection grid. Grantham shook his head, he did not know how Windsor had found so much detail in such a short time, but he thanked his lucky stars they had.

10:00hrs
Bombay Beach, California

At 224 feet below sea level, Bombay Beach is one of the lowest areas of mainland America. Sitting on the south-east shores of the inland Salton Sea only 100 miles from the Pacific Ocean, the small town is today mostly abandoned. Those people that do still dwell there do so mainly in mobile homes and self made trailer parks. Most of the shacks are derelict with only a small shop, Baptist Church and three bars in a good state of repair. The only modern building is the Academy Research Centre set up by the American Geosciences Institute, or AGI as it was more often known. As well as being the lowest point of America, Bombay Beach also lies directly on the San Andreas Fault, the geological fault line that runs up the west coast of America.

Dale St. Joseph, Randy Goodwin and Sally Foulds pulled the beach buggy up at the shore of the Salton Sea and stepped out onto the sand. They had been here for two weeks and had another four to go before returning to university to continue their studies.

"I know that field trips are part of the course and not

designed to be exciting, but could the university have picked anywhere more boring than Bombay Beach?" said Sally Foulds with a pout of her slightly too large lips.

"We're on a beach in California rather than a stuffy classroom, doing practical work for the AGI and we have a beach buggy at our disposal, what's not to enjoy?" replied Dale St. Joseph with a crooked smile and glint in his soft grey eyes. He enjoyed winding up Sally. She was used to getting her own way with almost any man that looked at her, and was not happy that she had been teamed up with the only two guys on the course that had not fallen for her artificial ample charms, cheerleader's legs and enhanced lips. Dale knew that she was completely out of his league and had given up trying to impress her after the first week of the four year course. Randy Goodwin was even more annoying to her. An athletic, basketball playing academic, with wavy black hair and Hollywood good looks, he had a steady girlfriend he had known since kindergarten and had no intention of being unfaithful. He was friendly with most of the students, male or female, but whilst being polite was cool with Sally, who even now felt that he should find her irresistible.

"That was a rhetorical question, Dweeb," said Sally with the usual scorn she reserved for Dale. "But this isn't exactly a Californian beach, is it? I mean, that isn't the Pacific, it's some stagnant inland lake. And that," she waved vaguely back towards the mostly abandoned town, "is not my idea of a Californian town. That is not even good enough to be called a rundown trailer park. And this so called fieldwork, it's just day after day of collecting numbers."

Randy Goodwin shook his head as he bent down and rinsed the container out in the water before filling it and taking the first of the day's samples. "Sally, why did you ever take the Geoscience course? And what did you think the fieldwork was going to be? Fighting rushing lava like Tommy Lee Jones in the film Volcano, or Pierce Brosnan in Dante's Peak?"

Sally stared at Randy as if trying to think of a witty or stinging reply before giving up and simply pulling a face, stamping her foot and storming off along the beach.

Randy walked out of the water and divided the water between several flasks they would take back to the lab for sampling later. While he was doing this, Dale walked out along the small landing stage and took a reading on the depth gauge fastened to the end, 12' 8".

"Any idea why Sally did choose the Geosciences course?" asked Dale.

"I think she thought it would be 'cool'. She told me the first week, while we were still on good terms."

"You mean while she was still trying to get you into bed," grinned Dale.

Randy nodded, "I don't think she was bothered whether it was bed or the back seat of the car. But she told me that some celebrity had spoken out about protecting the environment while she was looking for a course and Geoscience seemed to fit the bill."

"Typical. Talk about shallow, she's all show and no substance. Do you think she'll actually pass next year?"

"To be fair, I've done some course work with her as part of other groups and she's far from unintelligent."

Dale looked up at Randy and shook his head, "Don't start to fall for the act, she'll split you and Toni up if she can."

"No chance," smiled Randy. "I prefer women natural and less self-centred."

As they looked out across the water, they felt a slight vibration in the ground as if a train were passing close by. Looking around they saw the row of telegraph

400

poles start to lean and sway in an almost perfect S wave along the row of columns. Looking back out across the water, they saw ripples extending out from a spot about 200 yards offshore. The ripples were growing in size to almost a foot in height.

Dale staggered and fell to his knees as the sandy beach buckled under him. Without warning, the ground opened and Dale started to slip into the gaping hole that had appeared, his legs dangling in open space as he scrambled to get a grip on sand that was offering no handholds.

As the rumbling continued Dale finally lost the battle to grip the sand and slipped into space. Just as a scream was forming in his throat, Randy grabbed hold of his wrist, jerking his shoulder and causing him to gasp in pain.

"Hold on," said Randy.

"Bloody pointless comment," gasped Dale.

"It looks like it's only about fifteen feet deep," said Randy, trying to pull Dale up and stop himself falling in. The hole was made up of sand cascading over jagged rocks, the bottom appeared to be wet sand, but as Randy looked down a head sized rock broke away from the side and hit the sandy bottom, almost immediately disappearing into the apparently liquid sand.

The rumbling started to ease and the hole that Dale was hanging in started to close. Randy heaved up and started to work Dale from the hole.

"Climb up me, quick, climb!" shouted Randy.

Dale reached up with his free hand and grabbed Randy's sleeve, pulling himself up as he felt the rocks scraping against his shins.

Climbing and pulling frantically, Dale managed to get onto Randy's back and pull himself onto the beach with Randy getting hold of his feet and providing a foothold.

Dale rolled onto his back and scrambled away from the hole, Randy springing to his feet and taking several quick steps before pulling Dale to his feet and both of them running higher up the beach.

By now the rumbling had stopped and the two young men looked back at the beach. The only sign of anything unusual was the depression in the sand where the hole had completely closed up.

Dale dropped to his knees and then sat down.

"Thanks man. I'd have been under the beach now if it wasn't for you."

"Well that certainly livened things up."

Dale climbed to his feet and looked around. After a few seconds, he hesitantly walked out onto the beach. Everything seemed okay and he headed for the landing stage, returning a few seconds later.

"I thought that the water looked lower, it's now just over 12' 5", that's a drop of three inches."

Both men looked around as they heard Sally approaching.

"What the hell was that?"

"That was a minor earthquake. We are on the San Andreas Fault, remember?"

"Oh no. I can't believe it. It's a disaster."

"Well it nearly was for Dale, but it was actually a minor tremor. They get them like that every couple of years."

"Sod the tremor, look at that." She pointed down the beach. The others looked around to where she was pointing. One of the telegraph poles had fallen over, crushing the beach buggy.

"We'll have to walk the three miles back now," she said with a pout.

Chapter 35

16:45hrs, 26th April
Paraguay

Grantham sat in the passenger seat of the Toyota Land Cruiser while Mac drove. A second identical car was following a couple of hundred yards behind.

Grantham and the team had arrived at Asuncion thirty minutes ahead of schedule due to favourable weather and hired the two Land Cruisers to carry them and their equipment north. Short of finding two Range Rovers in Paraguay, the Toyota was an excellent second best. Both vehicles were 4.5L turbo diesel V8s with plenty of room for the men and their equipment. The hire company had been very proud of the new vehicles, only two months old, and had expressed how good they were and asked that the men treat them with care. Grantham had nodded and agreed to look after the vehicles before taking out fully comprehensive insurance with no excess and no waivers. After all, he could not be sure of returning the vehicles in one piece, maybe not even in several pieces. But they had been lucky. When they arrived, Grantham pictured them having to use several small hatchbacks rather than the two large, rugged off roaders.

"So what's the plan, Boss?" asked Mac.

"I've not made final plans yet, I want to see the site first. But I'm thinking a two man covert assault to secure key sites followed by an aerial assault. That's where you come in, Mark. That would give us a bottom up and top down approach."

Mark Smedley, their assault pilot was in the back with Snake.

"Do you have enough info to allow a covert assault?" asked Mac without taking his eyes off the road.

"Not as much as I'd like, but a hell of a lot more than I could have hoped for. The info from JTAC was very detailed. The new satellite coverage is brilliant."

"I think I can add to that, Boss," Smedley said with a lopsided grin.

Grantham looked at him enquiringly. "You know we've just been training with the FBI? Well I got talking to some of the HRT guys. One of them, a senior sergeant, was telling me about a new bit of kit they've got. It's a mini UAV with some of the best sensors you've ever seen."

UAVs, Unmanned Aerial Vehicles, had been used for surveillance for several years, but had started to get incredibly advanced.

"Anyway, it turned out that his younger brother was on detachment in Afghanistan with one of the British Infantry Regiments until he got injured a couple of weeks back. It was when that tosser of an MP got ambushed?"

"A tosser MP doesn't narrow it down much," said Snake, as the others laughed and agreed.

"The right honourable St.John Dalziel, MP. Or I should say not so honourable and now ex-MP," smiled Grantham.

"Aye, that's the bloke, had to resign when he got back." Smedley's broad Yorkshire accent came out even more when he was telling a good story.

"Anyway, it was his bodyguard that saved the HRT guy's young brother. He didn't know who he was, but from calling in some favours he found out that the bodyguard was ex-regiment. He couldn't sing our praises enough. So, well let's say the HRT had an accident with the UAV and let me have the pieces as scrap. Turns out the damage weren't that bad."

"So what can this super UAV do?" asked Grantham.

"Pretty much every sensor you can think of. Broad band radio reception, infrared, ultraviolet, laser ranging and dedication. UHD video and still camera with one hundred times optical zoom, it can jam most frequencies. It's silent at twenty feet with battery life of six to eight hours. It can be flown remotely or programmed onto a preset course. Signal range of five miles. It can transmit in burst or continuous feed to the base station or lock in to any internet, mobile phone, radio or TV signal and piggyback the signal to any other source. It's got heat sensors that can penetrate twelve inches of brick. And a tag and track system. You fire a small tracker at the target and it sticks and broadcasts the position to a satellite that you can access via the web."

"It sounds like your new toy will be very useful. When we get there we'll do a full sweep."

"And it's got a bloody railgun. Equivalent of a .177 cal bullet, muzzle velocity of six times the speed of sound, effective range five hundred metres, ten round mag. It's bloody marvellous boss, but it's not going to lift the troop in for an assault. Where do we get the wings from for the main attack?"

"I'm working on it."

19:30hrs
Grüssmire Gewerbe

Charisma's head was aching worse than she had ever felt and her stomach was doing flips. Her worst hangover was nothing compared to this. If she could force herself to move she would throw up. She was not sure how long she had been awake. As a best guess it was less than an hour, more than a few minutes. Her memory was just starting to return in short flashes. She had been in Oxford when she had met Hugh something? He had been in a fight and had been taken away by the police. They had made love in a shower and, and... She was not sure. She did not know where she was, but felt she was alone.

There was a screeching sound that seemed to cut through her head. She realised that it was the sound of a door opening and opened her eyes only to shut them again. The light was just too intense.

"Miss Valentine, welcome back. I have been waiting to speak with you." The voice sounded accented but Charisma was in no state to analyse where it was from. At the moment it was all she could do to stay conscious without throwing up.

"I know you must feel terrible at the moment, your senses are ultra alert. It is a side effect of the anaesthetic."

The man came closer and she felt a sharp sting in her arm. Charisma opened her eyes and saw an IV tube trailing from her arm to a hanging bag.

"You are also dehydrated. These intravenous fluids will help." The man gave a small guttural laugh. "And also make you sleep until tomorrow night when we have something special planned for you."

Charisma heard the footsteps and the screech of the door as the man left the room. It was only then that she realised the man had been speaking in barely a whisper.

She tried opening her eyes again and to bring her hand up to shield them, but realised she was strapped to the bed, unable to raise her arms or legs. The room was very dim, yet the light still struck like needles. With watering eyes she looked around. The room was not big. She was on a hospital bed three feet from one wall, maybe five feet from the other. The walls were dazzling white. She closed her eyes.

She had been snatched, kidnapped. Someone had jumped from a car and put something over her nose and mouth. Grantham, that was his name, had been fighting with another man, the man had a gun. She shook her head and immediately regretted it. Had Grantham been killed? Where was she? What was going on? Her mind started to wander as she drifted into unconsciousness again.

15:25hrs, 27th April
MoD, London

There was an air of despondency in the conference room. All of the Emergency Response Team was there. Danny Barrett had started the day off with good news, but that had just been cancelled out with new information.

The double doors opened and Howard Thomas entered, his dark blue suit, crisp white starched shirt and purple tie had become almost a uniform.

"Good morning all. I hear we have good news?" While Thomas was not exactly smiling, he did seem a little more upbeat than he had been for the last few days.

Those in the room looked from one to the other, their faces etched with despondency.

"I'm guessing the good news has not lasted?" said Thomas.

Danny Barrett looked up and shook his head. "We've narrowed the location of the signal to a few square miles."

"I thought that would be good news?" asked Thomas.

"It is, or it would have been if we'd done it quicker."

Thomas looked around the table, clearly seeking

answers without opening his mouth.

It was Professor Lee who spoke up. "The research group of the Geological Society have been running constant scenarios and compiling data. There are incidents happening all over the world. A lot are now starting to make the news and many press agencies are starting to ask questions."

"But it's more than just the press asking questions?" Thomas was starting to look stern.

"All of the simulations show that we are past the point of no return."

Thomas looked around the group and walked to the head of the table. But instead of sitting down he pulled the chair out and leant on the back.

"What would happen if we could narrow the signal to a specific building and then levelled the place?" He again looked around the table from one to the other, waiting for an answer.

General Clive Simmonds broke the silence. "The nearest navy asset is over two thousand miles away, it would take forty-eight hours to move them into cruise missile range. We could ask the Americans, but..." his voice trailed off.

"We would have to persuade them that we were right before they would commit assets. And that would take even longer. How about an air strike?"

"With what, sir?" Everyone around the table detected the sarcasm in General Simmonds' voice.

"Well the Tornado and Typhoon are our strike aircraft I believe?" The sarcasm in Thomas's voice was just as evident and thankfully he even had a slight smile.

"Well both aircraft have a ferry range of two thousand miles, fifteen hundred with armaments. From the UK to Paraguay and back is a round trip of over seventeen thousand miles, even if we staged the return leg in America that is still twelve thousand miles. That would mean," the General paused to consider the maths.

"We would need between eight and twelve mid-air refuels. And the tankers would need refuelling, and those tankers would need refuelling, etcetera etcetera. As a junior officer I was involved in the planning and coordination of the Falklands' bombing in eighty-two. That raid used Vulcans which have twice the range of the Tornados and Typhoons and the operation originated from RAF Ascension Island covering a range of just less than seven thousand miles. That operation took eleven tankers for two aircraft and took two weeks of planning to set up. It was also the longest ever bomb raid up to that time. And to cap it all, we don't have the refuelling aircraft available now. We could bring some out of retirement and convert some others, but it would take weeks."

"Mmm, ground forces?" asked Thomas.

"Flight time to Paraguay, with stops and refuelling is twenty-four hours. Add in briefing and set up, at least another twenty-four. And the team would be going in blind. No intel, nothing on the location, defences, force numbers. I'm sorry Mr Thomas, but we just don't have the assets these days to mount this sort of attack."

Thomas opened his mouth to speak, but before he could Professor Lee cut him off.

"Just in case you are going to suggest a nuclear strike, I'm afraid levelling the location would do no good. As I said, we are past the point of no return."

"Well if the inevitable is going to happen, making sure the instigators don't profit may be the best we can do."

"There may be another way." Professor Lee looked around, she had everyone's attention.

"We don't know how it would work, but it's been

suggested that if the eruptions are manmade, caused by these vibrations, then maybe using the same technology could cancel the vibrations out, release the energy slowly. Nullify them so to speak."

Everyone at the table looked at each other, not sure what to say.

"Could that be done?" Thomas seemed to ask the room as a whole although he looked from Professor Lee to Danny Barrett.

"Well we have made progress with the code. But we aren't there yet."

"If you could work it out, would you be able to intercept the signal and amend the instructions, reverse the effect."

Barrett slowly shook his head. "We may be able to get the code worked out, maybe. But we can't intercept the signal. It's got a built-in address and verification sequence. Any interception or change of the signal would be picked up. What would happen then would depend on the security protocols. But I'd guess that the new signal would be ignored and the receivers would go into lockdown, carry out the last valid instruction and not accept any new input."

"So even if you do crack the code, it wouldn't do us any good. Overall we're screwed." Thomas slumped into the seat.

"The only way it would work is if we could access the actual server where it originates and transmit from there." Barrett also slumped back into his chair.

"General, absolutely no chance of a ground assault?"

General Simmonds simply shook his head.

"Just out of interest where is the base? Is it as Professor Lee said, central South America, away from all the activity?" asked Michel Fortnum.

Barrett sighed and sat forward. "Actually I haven't

viewed the data. I just got the message that the location had been narrowed down to a few square miles in Paraguay." He shrugged and started tapping away at the computer keyboard. As the others watched the wall sized screen at the end of the room switched to a view of the Earth as seen from space. The globe spun around until South America filled the screen. As the viewers watched, the image zoomed in. As the view got closer, figures across the top of the screen showed coordinates, viewing area and apparent altitude.

Finally the view stopped at an apparent altitude of 12,000 feet. The image showed an indicated area of six by eight miles. A red outline circled about three quarters of the area. As they watched, the computer labelled several points. To the eastern edge of the screen a thin ribbon of dwellings lining a straight road was labelled as Hohenau with population, height and coordinates listed. To the north a second settlement was listed as Villa Choferes del Chaco, again with associated data. To the south west was a third label. A large clearing was shown in the surrounding forest, a central building and several outbuildings could be seen with the label 'Grüssmire Gewerbe, Research Centre'.

"So the signal originates from somewhere in there," said Michel Fortnum.

"Em, yes..." Barrett's brows knitted together as he frowned.

"I can't say the area looks anything remarkable," commented Air Marshal Colridge-Stewart. "I say we nuke the area anyway."

Thomas gave a half smile. "Something wrong Mr Barrett?" he asked.

"Em, no... It's just a coincidence, I'm sure... Just a bit odd."

"Illuminate us."

"It's just the second time in a couple of days that

411

I've come across the name Grüssmire Gewerbe."

"It sounds vaguely familiar, what was the last time," asked Michel Fortnum.

"Well, it was a request for satellite info of the area."

"Who was the request from?"

"Er, well you. At least JTAC."

It was Fortnum's turn to frown. "Who from exactly?"

"I'm not sure. I could find out?"

"Please do."

Barrett picked up his phone and speed dialled a number.

"Greg? It's Danny Barrett. I passed a sat and intel search to you a couple of days ago for Paraguay, a research firm called," Danny glanced back at the large screen to make sure he got the name correct, "Grüssmire Gewerbe."

There was a pause as Danny looked around. "Yes, that's the one. Who originated the request and what's the status?"

Barrett made some notes before saying thanks and hanging up.

"The request came through from William Windsor. He wanted everything we could give him at short notice on Grüssmire Gewerbe. We had very little background data but as luck would have it we have been evaluating a new satellite system and South America has been one of the test sites. Apparently we got some very good data which was passed through to Mr Windsor."

Michel Fortnum already had her phone out. "Windsor, it's Fortnum. Why did you want data on Grüssmire Gewerbe in Paraguay?" There was a short pause. "And why did he want the info?" This was followed by a lengthy pause interspersed with a few nods of Fortnum's head and several cursed exclamations. "I'll be in my office in an hour, I want you there five minutes later." She hung up and looked around the room.

"We have an operative, Hugh Grantham, in Paraguay. Technically he's private, no direct link to JTAC, but he's one of the best, ex-major in the SAS. He's been in every trouble spot in the world in the last few years both covert and overt. Anyway, his partner has been kidnapped in South America and it looks like he's going after her. For whatever reason he thinks that she's being held at Grüssmire Gewerbe in Paraguay."

Several of those around the table looked a little blank, others incredulous, but Gideon Pearce, head of MI-6, and Air Marshal Colridge-Stewart exchanged a slight nod.

"I've come across Mr Grantham. As you say, he's one of the best. But even he can't hope to go up against a terrorist stronghold singlehanded," said Pearce.

Michel nodded. "I agree. But he's called some friends in to help him. We had a Sierra unit, that's a dedicated SAS assault team," she looked around the table to explain to those who may not be familiar with the term. "They were training in the US and have travelled south to assist."

"So you have an operative and an assault team on site?" asked Howard Thomas, UK Secretary of Defence.

"It would appear so, sir. I'll know more once I get back to the office for a full brief."

"Well get them on side, we need them. If Grüssmire Gewerbe gets their way, they will release Hell on Earth."

"No offence Mr Secretary, but if Grüssmire Gewerbe have Grantham and a rogue SAS assault team on their tail, they've already unleashed Hell."

18:00hrs
Swiss Alps

Jean-Claude loved this time of year, the snow was still deep and white on the high slopes, reflecting the bright sunlight across the more rocky sections. But there was fresh green grass on the lower slopes, even some Alpine flowers forming colourful cushions of colour.

The signal ahead changed to 'all clear' and Jean-Claude eased the throttle to position three, the electric motor rising in pitch slightly as the additional power was transferred to the multiple driving wheels of the train.

The third of the tunnels was approaching, Jean-Claude glanced down at the control panel and saw the driving and carriage lights automatically switch on. He looked back up at the mountain face above the tunnel. There was a covering of snow across the rock, but most of it was clear showing that the majority had recently fallen from the face.

The tunnel entrance loomed larger and as the train entered Jean-Claude had the usual feeling of the train and himself being swallowed whole by the mountain. In his imagination, the tunnel entrance would close behind them and the train and all the passengers would disappear forever. Jean-Claude smiled to himself, his wife always said he should be a writer.

The train's headlights picked out the silver strands of the rail tracks heading away to infinity, the natural rock walls hidden behind a layer of concrete, the light grey walls reflecting much of the illumination from the powerful halogen lights.

Jean-Claude's heart leaped as he saw that the rails ahead were buckled. His hand leaped for the brake lever and then paused. How could the rails be buckled, they were solid steel? Surely it was a trick of the light?

414

But Jean-Claude had travelled this route for almost twenty years and had never seen this trick of the light before. All this flashed through his mind as he saw the bent rails a second before the gaping cracks in the solid stone and concrete walls that looked as if they had been sliced by a knife and moved sideways by three feet. Jean-Claude pushed the brake lever hard forward, fully to the stop and continued to push as if he could lend his own feeble strength to the massive power of the locomotive's braking system.

The train lurched forward, shuddering as the steel wheels locked and tried to grip the rails. Sparks flew off along both sides of the train and cast irregular flickering shadows along the tunnel walls. The shrill scream from the distressed metal drowning the base roar from the tortured motors.

Jean-Claude was thrown forward with the momentum as the train decelerated at almost 1g. The train was not just slowing, it felt as if it were convulsing, ripping itself apart.

Jean-Claude could now see not only the warped rails, but table sized rocks laying scattered across the tracks, the tracks themselves looking as if a giant hand had bent the rails through forty-five degrees to the right and then back to the left.

The front of the train hit the first of the rocks and threw it forward, colliding with another of similar size causing it to cannon off as if on a giant's billiard table. The wheels connected with the first section of twisted rail, skipping up and off to the left, the engine leaning to the right, balancing for a second until the carriages hit the twisted section of rail and pushed it beyond the balancing point.

The engine and then the carriages tipped to the right, the tops hitting the concrete wall and gouging a deep furrow as the engine and carriages were crushed in, the windows shattering and explosively spraying small pieces of safety glass around the carriages.

Jean-Claude lost his grip on the controls and was thrown from his seat, the back of his head colliding with the flat wall causing him to see stars. For what seemed like hours, but could only have been a few seconds, the tortured scream of metal against rock echoed through the tunnel before the train came to a shuddering halt.

Jean-Claude pushed himself up from the floor and groggily walked over to the control panel. Although the train had derailed and was leaning at an angle against the wall, amazingly it was still more or less upright. With luck and a little blessed intervention there would not be any serious injuries. Jean-Claude muttered a quiet prayer, please God, no fatalities.

Dust from the devastation in the tunnel was pouring into the carriages making it difficult to breath. Jean-Claude picked up the radio phone, with surprise he got an immediate response. He made a quick report and was promised that help was on the way. Jean-Claude looked around, he needed to check on the passengers and train staff but he could not access them directly, he would have to climb out into the tunnel and walk back to the carriages.

The lower side door on the right was jammed tight against the wall. The left side appeared undamaged but was raised high on an angle. Jean-Claude was still unsteady on his feet, but with effort he managed to climb to the door and to pry it open. He got his arms and shoulders through the gap and levered himself up, sitting on the edge of the frame.

Jean-Claude looked down at the tunnel around ten feet below and his heart leaped into his mouth. The tunnel floor had disappeared. The front forty-five feet of the engine was hanging over open space. Only the rear ten feet was still on solid ground and being held in position by the coupling to the first carriage.

Jean-Claude eased himself back into the driving compartment as the engine shuddered and settled a few inches. He prayed that help would not be too late.

Chapter 36

12:30hrs, 27th April
Paraguay

Grantham put down the binoculars and looked sideways at Mac. "No guards on patrol. It looks like they rely on electronics."

Mac nodded with the binoculars still to his eyes. "I suspect the real security will be inside the building. Even so, it doesn't look exactly cutting edge."

The two men looked very different to the casually dressed tourists that had flown into the country fifteen hours ago. They were both dressed in forest camouflage, a mix of brown, black, green and grey. Although not dressed in Ghillie suits, they were wearing Ghillie head gear, a mixture of netting and camouflage pieces to disrupt their shape. The binoculars they were both using had non-reflective lenses and were also covered in camouflage netting. If they remained still they were undetectable to the human eye at fifty feet. At the quarter mile distance from the buildings they were undetectable even with powerful binoculars. To each side and buried slightly below ground level, were two small battery powered fans that blew air across the front of the men disrupting any detection of their heat signature by infrared imaging.

Distantly they heard the sound of rotor blades cutting through the natural sounds of the forest. As the sounds grew louder both men naturally sunk a little deeper into the undergrowth. A black Bell UH-1 'Huey' helicopter appeared over the far tree line and proceeded to circle the area before settling across the far side of the compound on a helipad about five hundred metres from the main building.

Grantham watched as the passengers disembarked and boarded a minibus for the short trip to the building. As they exited the bus Grantham saw that none of the passengers had any sort of military bearing and they were all carrying suitcases or rucksacks, all but two of them were blond. The bus driver followed the passengers into the building.

"Looks like they're bringing the Aryan race in by bus," said Mac with a smirk.

After ten minutes the blades of the Huey started to slowly turn, gradually building up speed.

"Sierra Nine, do you still have the toy working?"

"Roger Mamba, we're about three quarters done with the mapping." Smedley's voice was clear over Grantham's headset, his voice displaying only a hint of his Yorkshire accent.

"Do you see the helo spooling up? Can you tag and track it?"

"Roger Mamba, wait one."

As Grantham watched through the binoculars the helicopter lifted from the ground, hovered for a few seconds and turned north, slowly climbing and heading away. As he watched, a small movement behind the helicopter caught his eye. It was only because he was watching closely that he saw anything and even then it was indistinct and too fast to get any detail.

"Mamba, Sierra Nine. Tagged and tracking. Going back to continue the survey."

"Roger that Nine, nicely done."

The weather so far had been hot and clammy. Both men knew that this was nothing compared to the height of summer. However, in the last few minutes the bright sun had given way to the dark grey clouds that were rolling in. The temperature had also dropped and a refreshing stiff breeze had blown up.

A few minutes later the comms earpieces clicked and Danny Fathom's voice came over the link.

"Err, boss. I've got a red flash alpha message just come in for you."

Grantham looked sideways at Mac. No one was supposed to know they were here. Grantham's priority was to rescue Charisma, but even with that in mind he could not ignore a Red Flash Alpha communication, the highest level urgent message within the British Security Services.

Grantham edged back a couple of feet so that he was in deeper cover.

"Who's the message from?"

"Message from Jupiter Control."

Jupiter Control was JTAC Headquarters, London.

"Patch them through, Six."

"Roger Mamba." The connection went silent for a second.

"This is Mamba, who am I speaking to?" asked Grantham.

"Mamba, this is Claymore at Jupiter Base." The voice had the characteristic metallic ring and slight stutter of an encrypted communication, broadcast as a tight beam burst transmission. A method of communication via satellite that was almost impossible to intercept. Even with the slight distortion, Grantham recognised the voice of William Windsor.

"Claymore, I'm not exactly in the market for new orders. I'm a bit busy at the moment."

"You and one of our Sierra units."

It crossed Grantham's mind to wonder how Windsor, and presumably JTAC, knew that the troops had followed Grantham to Paraguay. They were probably tracking their passports, but that was not a concern now.

"You know why I'm here, Claymore."

"And your plans coincide with ours. This is too complicated to go into details. But Grüssmire Gewerbe, Tango HQ, is causing world-wide disruption with earthquakes and volcanoes. We're talking ELEs, extinction level events."

Grantham's brow furrowed, he had not been expecting this. "So you want us to stop them. We'll do what we can."

"It's more than that. We need you to get access to the main computers and connect through to GCHQ so that they can send some alternate commands to the devices they have in the field."

"Is that all? What resources are at our disposal?"

There was the slightest of pauses before Windsor answered. "The reason we need you is that you are the only unit within range. This operation is time critical."

Grantham slumped down, his head resting on his hands. He needed to get Charisma out, but he could not simply ignore an ELE.

"Once we get Charisma out, can you flatten the complex?"

"Negative, Mamba. It's critical that we connect to the communications to reverse the commands to the devices causing the eruptions."

"Okay, let me have the details."

12:50hrs
Grüssmire Gewerbe

The large interior of the reception area was still, quiet and airy. Yet only minutes ago it had been crowded with new arrivals and reception staff. Each new arrival had to pass multiple levels of proof of identity including fingerprint, retina identification and speech recognition. The final stage of identification was an analysis of the subjects' DNA against a stored sample.

However, whilst the facility could carry out DNA sequencing faster than any facility in the world, it would still take an hour to sequence each sample. The process was not quick, but it was extremely thorough. Each new arrival would be allocated a room in the bunker, but until they passed the DNA check they would be kept together in one room.

In the boardroom the directors were assembled, Hans Eigel, the large framed, balding Master sat in his usual seat at the head of the large oval table with Joseph Adler to his right. The rest of the 'Elite', as they thought of themselves, were looking at the Master.

"How is everything going with the new arrivals?" asked Eigel.

Adler's head turned to face the Master. "The security checks are proving effective and efficient. The next batch of DNA should be ready in a few minutes. I do not expect any negative results."

The Master looked around the table, a half smile on his face, his gaze settling on the youngest of the order, Michael Spielmann. "How are the embryos doing?"

The young man looked back levelly at the Master until he caught the eye of Joseph Adler and looked away. He took his rimless glasses off and started to clean them, giving himself a physical thinking space.

"Everything is going well. Their progression is at the top end of normal. The female embryos are actually maturing slightly quicker than the males. The one embryo that we have been boosting the growth rate of is responding excellently." There was the slightest hint of rebuke in Spielmann's voice as he glanced at Adler and quickly looked away.

"We expect it will be viable in two months, mature in a little under three."

The Master nodded his approval. "How long before we can clone from the embryos?"

Spielmann shrugged his thin shoulders. "In theory we could do that now. But I would recommend, with your permission, that we bring them to term and carry out extensive testing before we progress to the next generation. There are signs that the genes are, well there isn't really a technical term for it, but dominant."

The Master looked a little lost at the news. "I thought dominant was a term that was used in genetics?"

"Yes sir, it is. But this is a different context. In normal reproduction, the male and female genes are mixed, some come out on top by random variation, some because the genes from one source are dominant. But in this case, the whole set of genes from the embryos are dominant."

"So any offspring would be clones even if the other DNA was not cleared out?" The Master knew he was fumbling for the right terminology, but was comfortable that no one would rebuke him.

"No sir, well not quite. This is still early days and we need to carry out a lot more testing. But it would appear that there would be perfectly natural variation, as with normal progenation, but that where there was a choice the new genes would dominate."

"And is this good or bad news?" asked Eigel.

"Definitely good news, sir. If we had to do this by pure cloning we could do it, but we would end up with lots of the same subjects. And there would be the possibility of building in genetic abnormalities. But by mixing the DNA, and with the subject being dominant, the gene pool would be diverse and much healthier."

"And what about the mutation that is creating female embryos?"

Spielmann looked a little guilty as he answered. "We still do not know. I've checked the original DNA from each artefact and they are definitely the same and perfectly normal apart from the small fraction that we can't classify."

"Could that small part cause the mutation?"

"By all accepted knowledge there is no form of human DNA that could mutate in this way. But, by definition we may not strictly speaking be dealing with *human* DNA."

"Mmm, well keep an eye on them. The embryos are the key to the Messiah Project. They are the first generation of the new race."

Eigel turned to von Papen, until recently the small almost invisible man would shy away from direct questions. But since the Genesis Project came into its own his confidence had grown in leaps and bounds.

"Are the disruptors all working as planned?"

"They are working excellently. We have passed the point of no return. Even if we switched them off, the effects have gone too far, the eruptions and outbreaks would still happen, maybe less coordinated, but they would still occur." The little man suddenly smiled, the expression was not natural on him and it made his face look cadaverous. "And almost all life on earth will die." His voice sounded as if he were about to break into a laugh. Several of the elite group around the table looked almost shocked at the small man's outburst.

The Master pulled himself together and turned to the man at his side. "Joseph, what of our visitor?"

Adler's lifeless black eyes seemed to almost sparkle. "She's well. I'm keeping her sedated until the ceremony. I've debriefed Adam and it appears he acted just in time. The church was preparing to kill the girl and her minder. But Adam snatched the girl before any harm could befall her."

"Who was the church's attacker? Michael?"

"Yes. But this Grantham took care of him. They both went into the Potomac River. At least one body

424

was later recovered."

17:30hrs
Outside Grüssmire Gewerbe

"Okay, so much for phase one. Phase two. We know the guards' routes and schedule. Not that they are that regular, unfortunately. There are cameras monitoring the approach, front elevation and garage doors. But there are noticeable gaps, here, here and here." Grantham indicated the makeshift map that he had made on the floor of the forest clearing where they had all gathered. "What is the range on the new UAV?"

"Around two miles Boss."

"Good enough. After phase one I want the assault team staged here." Grantham indicated a large clearing to the south of the compound on the map they had downloaded from the data that JTAC had provided. "Can you get in and out of there okay?"

Smedley looked at the map for a few seconds, weighing up sizes and angles. "Tight, but no problem."

"Good. Me and Mac will go in following this route," he scraped away at the ground providing a visual accompaniment to the briefing. "I want you monitoring the infiltration with the UAV and providing an overview of the area. Once we access the building, we're playing by ear. When we call you'll need to move fast."

Smedley nodded. "From call to first foot on the roof, ninety seconds."

"You all up to speed on fast rope?"

"Up to speed and well practised. We did several assaults last week with the FBI," said Mac.

Grantham looked each man in the eye, holding their gaze for a couple of seconds each. "This is not going to be easy. We're lucky to have more info than we had

425

any right to expect. The compound is a secure research facility and it's not been set up externally to repel a professional assault. But what's inside and what the opposition is we can only guess at. There are no guarantees."

"Never is, Boss. Besides, life would be boring if we knew everything," said Snake with a grin.

"Get some food and rest. We move out in three hours. Mac, set a watch on the compound, one hour on, two off. I need to make some calls to London."

18:00hrs
Yellowstone Park

The blue cloudless sky stretched from horizon to horizon. The mostly flat countryside of the region seemed to emphasise the vastness of the open space. The scattering of trees and rocky outcrops, although huge in themselves, seemed dwarfed in the massive outdoors. Not a breath of wind disturbed the spring stillness.

Ranger Clive Two Rivers pulled the 4x4 off to the side of the track and stepped out, took a deep breath and looked around, "Ah, the Great Spirit is at home today," he said with a smile. As a National Park Ranger he was responsible for keeping the park and the people in it safe. But the park meant far more to him than most. He was a native Shoshone, the Native American tribe that had roamed these lands for countless generations before the white man arrived and he only felt truly at home when in the open.

The Ranger station had received a report that a couple had failed to report in. Anyone planning to camp in the park overnight had to register their planned route and schedule. They had probably just lost track of the time, he could not really blame them. Still, he had to check it out and gently remind them that they should check in.

He checked their registered details and set off for the low rise half a mile away. He was used to the outdoors and his tall, lean frame covered the distance quickly and effortlessly. A few minutes later he topped the low outcropping of rocks and looked down into the shallow depression. There was their tent, a dayglow orange, impossible to miss in the natural environment. He took his binoculars from the pouch on his belt and scanned the area. There was no sign of the couple, but the tent was in one piece and zipped up so they were unlikely to be far away. He took a deep breath, the climb had winded him more than he thought. He laughed quietly to himself, at fifty-six he was not as young as he used to be. Ten years ago he could have walked all day up the steepest of slopes with a full backpack anywhere in the park and never have broken a sweat. Partly that was down to his ancestry, but mostly due to his love of, and regular visits to, the wilderness.

He set off down the slope and approached the tent, calling out the couple's names. He looked around, still no sign of them. He put his hand up to shield his eyes, he could feel the start of a headache. Clive walked up to the tent and shook the front pole, calling their names again. Three years ago he had come out to find a couple in similar circumstances only to open the tent and find them making love.

He bent down and unzipped the flap, again calling their names. As he looked in he saw the couple still in their sleeping bags and not cavorting naked on top of them. He called their names and reached in to shake the foot of the man. There was something wrong, the man's feet and legs were too stiff. He dropped to all fours and crawled into the tent. Quickly checking for a pulse, he noticed that neither was breathing and that their lips had a distinct blue tint.

Clive backed from the tent, his head now splitting and his breath coming in short gasps. Finding two dead bodies was not pleasant, but these were not the first dead bodies he had seen, it should not be affecting him this badly. He backed away from the tent and felt his head start to spin and he staggered, dropping to one knee, he was finding it hard to get air into his lungs.

His thoughts were foggy, but something was trying to surface. He reached unsteadily into his pocket and took out his lighter, although he did not smoke, starting a camp fire was far easier with a lighter than rubbing two sticks together. He flicked the lighter several times before it lit, only for it to fizzle out quickly. The couple's blue lips, his headache and trouble breathing, the camp was in a hollow and the whole area was still a slowly active massive volcano, a caldera. If gases had escaped then carbon dioxide, which was heavier than air, could form in hollows. He needed to get to higher ground, out of the hollow.

He tried to stand but after two faltering steps fell back to his knees, gasping for breath. He tried to breathe deeply, his lungs and throat starting to constrict as he crawled away from the tent. His mind was wandering, he imagined that an eagle, his spirit guide and protector, was calling to him, beckoning him to the great hunting ground.

His breathing had almost stopped, his mind was wandering, there was nothing but the slope, the hard packed mud and sand under his hands and knees. The heat was fading, he was starting to feel cold. Suddenly he took a huge gasp of air, the oxygen rushing through his system as his head came above the CO2 layer. It was sweet and warm and probably the best sensation he had ever experienced. With the one gasp of air he had gained enough strength to push himself up and climb a little further.

His strength was returning quickly, as was the pounding in his head, but at least it proved he was alive. As he reached the lip of the depression he turned onto his back and looked up into the sky, the warm sun caressing his face. He needed to call the station, get help out here and warn others of the potential problem from the volcanic gas seeping out of the ground. He saw a movement out of the corner of his eye and turned his head. The clear blue of the sky was still unbroken. An eagle was riding the thermals, climbing higher and higher. As he watched, the eagle gave one long call and left the thermal having reached the height it needed and set off across country.

Clive Two Rivers smiled, his spirit guide had been looking out for him today.

Chapter 37

00:40hrs, 28th April
Paraguay

"Sierra Two to Mamba, on site, all set," reported Jez Stinger.

"Roger Two. How's it look?"

"Target is on site, security strictly second rate."

"Roger Sierra Two. Stand by," replied Grantham who, along with Mac, was still at the Grüssmire Gewerbe complex.

It had taken the Sierra unit four hours to get to the airfield but they were now in position and checking the defences.

The airfield had dim patches of irregular lighting. The meagre security force guarding the airfield would be night blind, their night vision would not be developed as they passed in and out of the lit areas. This would hinder their response to any attack. Whereas the Sierra unit would have night vision goggles in place with automatic filters to dim the enhancement when they were in or near a light source.

Sergeant Jez Stinger, Sierra Two, raised the binoculars to his eyes again. There was little wonder that the airfield was so poorly guarded. For one thing, this area of the country was very sparsely populated and what people were around were poor locals that simply wanted to keep their heads down and not attract attention. Secondly, the airfield seemed to contain very little of interest. Two ENAER T-35 Pillán aircraft were across the far side of the airfield with a third in one of the smaller hangars being worked on by mechanics. A larger Embraer EMB 312 Tucano was half in and half out of one of the larger hangars. But the target of the Sierra unit was one of the closed, well maintained hangars containing the UH-1 Huey which had been tagged as it left the research compound. The hangars appeared to be all of the same age. But some were far better maintained. In fact, the ones that were maintained were almost pristine. No flaking paint, no broken panes of glass, the roofs were all in one piece and all of the doors were closed. The less well maintained generally appeared shabby and run down, most had either main doors or personnel doors standing open.

The only visible activity seemed to be military personnel, sloppy and poorly coordinated but military none the less. They were working in and around the badly maintained hangars so maybe the hangars in good condition belonged to someone else? And that raised the question, would the security in the helicopter hangar be better?

Stinger's earpiece crackled and Grantham's voice came over the radio.

"Mamba to Sierra Unit, all set?"

"Sierra Two, all set Mamba."

"Phase one is go."

Stinger slowly stood and moved forward, scanning the area around and to the sides with his combination night vision and infrared goggles. It took eight minutes for him to cover the two hundred yards to the edge of the compound. Once there he crouched down behind and adjacent to some small bushes intending to cut through the compound fence. But as he crouched down he raised his goggles and saw that several large holes were already in the fence from simple age and ill repair.

"Sierra Two in position, ready for entry."

Within two minutes the rest of the team had reported in.

"Sierra Two to all units. Commence entry."

Stinger crawled through one of the openings and stood to a crouch advancing towards his attack point, ensuring that he stayed in the darkest of the shadows and that he was in front of the dark background of the forest to avoid any silhouettes.

As he reached the closest building, he flattened himself to the wall, his MP5 assault rifle held at the ready. Nothing had changed, the noises were all constant. There was a radio playing some distance off where the maintenance crew were working. Voices were coming from the same area, casual with occasional laughs.

Stinger shouldered his rifle and stowed his goggles. He took out a radio and microwave detector and started to sweep the area.

"Sierra Two, in position, no readings." Stinger was now whispering even more quietly, but his throat mic still easily picked up the sound.

The rest of the unit checked in, also confirming that they had no new electronic readings, all was ready.

"Sierra Nine, put the blanket down."

Stinger counted to five before he heard the radio in the distance turn from music to static, the electronic jamming was in place.

"Sierra Team, go, go, go."

Stinger ran towards the corner of the building and raised his MP5, scanning the area before rounding the corner and heading for the maintenance hangar. The personnel seemed to be concentrating on the work they were doing on the aircraft or the now unresponsive radio. He reached the side of the building and flattened himself against the wall, careful to not collide with the metal surface. Pausing for five seconds to make sure he had not been spotted, he clicked his radio once, getting a double click in return. He then gave three clicks on the radio, paused and three more clicks. Count to three.

Stinger swung around the corner, he raised the gun in a classic shooting stance. His feet were shoulder width apart, the left forward and straight, the right under the body with the foot at forty-five degrees to the side. The front knee was slightly bent and soft, the rear straight and pushing forward. His body was bent slightly forward at the hips to put weight behind the gun. From this position Stinger was perfectly balanced to shoot or change position.

Stinger sighted on his first target and pulled the trigger. The gun gave two short barks.

Turning at the hips without moving his feet, Stinger levelled on the second man and squeezed off another two shots. Turning back the other way he sighted on two other targets, the red dot from the laser centred on the first and the MP5 jumped again. Stinger turned slightly and brought the gun to bear on the last man but saw that the man had drawn a hand gun and was levelling it at Stinger.

As the man's finger tightened on the trigger two sharp cracks rang out from across the hangar. Sierra Three, the fabled 'Snake' was covering the area from the opposite side. It was his weapon that had fired the two shots, two shots that had put down the mechanic just before he could pull his own trigger.

Across the hangar Stinger could see Nick Perkins, Sierra Five, in the same stance and covering four targets that were now on the floor.

Waiting for all movement to stop, Stinger and Sierra Five moved in to check the targets: four were unconscious, four were dead.

A sound from the back of the hangar caught the men's attention. Two of the mechanics had been at the rear of the building. As Stinger looked up he saw them disappear through a personnel door.

"Sierra Four, we have two runners," said Stinger into the radio.

"Roger Two," came the reply.

Three seconds later a sharp crack rang out across the small airfield, followed by another.

"Runners down."

Stinger looked around, apart from their team nothing was moving in the hangar. "Snake, Nick, go get the runners, be careful, they're down but we don't know their condition."

Snake and Nick Perkins nodded and ran across the hangar and out of the door. Stinger could hear Sierra Four directing them to his targets and offering cover.

"Sierra Six, any movement?" asked Stinger quietly.

John 'Bird' Sparrow and Danny Fathom were stationed away from the hangars covering the west and south. But the cover was not perfect, ideally Stinger would have liked at least two more men, four would be better. Still, you worked with what you had.

"No movement, Sierra Two. But there may have been a brief flash of light from the secure hangar just after Four took out the runners."

"Sierra Two, one runner is permanently down, the other not far behind," reported Snake.

"Roger Sierra Three, bring them back. Sierra Six, keep an eye on the hangar."

Rushed footsteps from behind made Stinger turn, his MP5 coming up. Three men in utility uniforms were running towards the hangar, all three were brandishing guns of different types. Stinger shouldered his machine gun and fired off a double tap, changed targets and fired twice more. Two of the men went down. Before he could bring his gun to bear of the third, the man simply stopped, dropped his shotgun and crumpled to the floor.

"Man I love this thing," came Sierra Nine's voice

over the radio. *"One shot from the rail gun and the guy just dropped."*

Two minutes later Snake and Perkins returned with the two runners.

For five minutes they checked the hangar but found no one else and nothing of interest. Five minutes later the unconscious mechanics had been patched up, tied up and unceremoniously dumped into a small supply room which they also sealed securely. They would need someone to let them out or starve to death, but at least they were alive for now.

"The second runner, make that ex-runner, joined his mate," said Stinger when he checked the two bodies. Although Snake had given the man first aid, sealing his wound and stopping the blood flow, the wound had been too severe. Bird was too good a shot.

Stinger checked his watch, fifteen minutes since the start of the assault.

"Sierra Team, form up."

Two minutes later they were outside the secure hangar, where they expected to find the helicopter.

"Snake, you got your door pick?"

"Never leave home without it," Snake grinned as he took the twelve gauge shotgun from his back and pumped a round into the chamber.

The others stood back as Snake fired a solid twelve gauge slug into the door frame at the site of the lock, the frame and door developing a hole large enough to get a man's head through. Stinger was first through the door and went low and left, followed by Perkins who mirrored him to the right. Danny Fathom followed Stinger to the left but stayed high, passing behind Stinger and covering up and wide, his field of fire overlapping Stinger's. Last through the door was Snake, having stowed the shotgun he was back to the MP5 and covered high and right.

435

The hangar was of a similar size to the first, but with only the one helicopter it seemed twice as large and echoed with every sound. The men scanned the building checking for movement or heat. The combination goggles casting the area into shades of grey and green overlaid with multi-coloured infrared heat images. Most of the area showed a consistent heat range of four degrees. But there was a slight rise in temperature high up the side wall and several small pads heading across the ground as if someone had walked across the floor recently leaving ghostly footprints.

Using hand signals, Stinger directed the men across the hangar, spreading out and covering each other's sides and backs.

Unlike the first hangar, this one was neat and tidy, a few fifty gallon drums, a long workbench, an enclosed area that was probably stores and office. An open mesh staircase led up to an open mezzanine area. A low, squat vehicle with a fixed tow bar sat to one side, obviously used for towing the helicopter in and out of the building.

As they advanced across the large open floor area, a small rustling sound and movement from the upper area caught Stinger's attention. He swung his rifle up towards the movement, as the distinctive sound of a Kalashnikov on full automatic filled the building, the sound echoing and reverberating from the metal walls and roof. The image in the goggles flared into bright focus as the flash from the automatic rifle illuminated the area and the infrared goggles screened white heat from the gun's flashes.

The SAS men dove to the floor, each rolling to stop the shooter getting a clean shot at them. Snake and Danny Fathom rolled up to one knee and levelled their weapons at the upper area and released several controlled bursts. This stopped the shooter and allowed Stinger and Perkins to quickly advance. While Snake and Fathom continued to fire short bursts, Perkins flattened himself against the wall under the open walkway and pulled a flash-bang grenade from his webbing.

"Fire in the hole!" he shouted loud enough to carry to the team. He stepped forward and tossed the grenade high and back so that it arced up and over the upper area.

The grenade exploded five feet over the upper walkway. The flash was a searing white light that would burn after-images into the eyes of anyone looking even in the general direction and the concussive bang was so loud it temporarily overwhelmed the hearing, leaving the ears ringing and numb and the body swaying from temporary inner ear damage.

Knowing what to expect, the SAS men had looked away and clicked up their night vision goggles, shielding their eyes. Their earpieces were designed to act as radio microphones and to filter out the worst of the sound.

Before the echoes had died away, Stinger was already charging up the stairs, stopping as soon as his head and shoulders drew level with the walkway. He could see the figure half in and half out of a doorway, leaning against the frame, one hand raised to it head, the other still holding the Kalashnikov. Stinger raised his MP5, it was useless shouting a warning as the man would be deaf for some minutes yet. Besides, the man had already sealed his fate when he opened fire on the unit.

Stinger fired a short burst of three shots, two striking the man mid-mass, the third impacting on the door frame as he fell back.

Stinger advanced slowly, keeping wide on the stairs so that he could see the legs and body of the man where he had fallen and watch for movement.

He heard movement behind him at the same time as he heard Perkin's voice over the radio. *"Sierra Five right behind you Sierra Two."*

Stinger saw that there was slight movement from the man, the shots had not been fatal. As Stinger reached the open doorway, the man must have sensed movement and raised the Kalashnikov. Before the man could squeeze the trigger, Stinger unleashed two more shots, these hit the man in the upper chest and throat and he slumped to the ground, not moving. Cautiously Stinger approached the man and kicked the rifle away while quickly scanning the area for movement and heat. Nothing.

"Tango down," he reported.

As Sierra Five arrived a few feet behind him, Stinger bent and quickly checked the man who was wearing body armour, no wonder the first two wounds were not fatal.

The upper area consisted of just three rooms. A twin bedded bunk room, a combination toilet and shower room and a combination kitchen, dining and sitting room with microwave, fridge, a large screen TV and DVD player and two large sofas. In less than a minute Sierra Two and Five had searched the area for possible hiding places and announced it clear.

"Lower area clear. Just the chopper to check," said Sierra Six over the radio.

A few seconds later all four men were surrounding the Bell UH-1 helicopter. Both side doors were closed and these offered the only entry. The UH-1 Huey was armour-plated around vital components, and could also be armoured along the cabin and flight crew areas. But without opening the doors the SAS team could not tell if the walls were solid or simple thin skin aluminium. It was also common practice for Hueys to be armed with mini guns so anyone on the inside could potentially be armed with a very deadly weapon.

Using hand signals, Stinger stationed the men around the helicopter such that if they had to return fire they would not hit each other rather than their target.

Stinger carefully walked up to the left side door and reached out for the handle. With a deep breath he pulled hard allowing the door to slide easily back as he dove for the ground under the chopper. Apart from the sound of the door sliding back and thumping against the rubber stops, all was quiet.

Stinger raised himself up, covered by the side door and stepped cautiously forward. Without warning a single deep boom erupted from inside the helicopter. Stinger felt an agonizing blow to his chest and slumped to the floor. Two shots rang out from Sierra Three and Six, both aiming for the flash from the large calibre handgun inside the Huey and the warm fuzzy image shown by their goggles. There was a strangled cry from inside the UH-1 and three more shots echoed around the hangar quickly followed by another five from Sierra Three and Six.

There was a deathly pause and silence as the echoes died away.

Snake moved cautiously forward around the back of the helicopter, keeping the machine between him and the approximate position of the shooter while Danny Fathom covered him. Taking a quick look around the door, Snake saw that the figure of a man was lying in a crumpled heap on the floor of the helicopter.

While Snake kept the man covered, Fathom quickly ran over and climbed into the cabin, kicked away the hand gun and checked him. Dead.

Snake bent down and checked Stinger who was

cursing with every oath he could think of. The .45 cal bullet had struck him mid-chest but had not penetrated his body armour. But the blow was enough to drive the air from his lungs and cause severe pain and a bruise that would be various shades of purple, yellow and red for several weeks.

"Chopper clear, target down," announced Sierra Six.

Stinger accepted a hand from Snake and stood up, rubbing his chest and still cursing.

"Sierra Four, any movement?" asked Stinger.

"Negative Sierra Two, all quiet." John Sparrow was still watching the whole compound from his sniper position in the tree line.

"Sierra Nine, objective secure, get in here."

"On the way, Sierra Two," replied Mark Smedley, the team's pilot.

"You three, go check the rest of the compound and buildings. By the count from earlier we've accounted for everyone, but make sure. I'll cover Sierra Nine while he checks the chopper. If you come across any opposition call out and we'll go in mob handed. Destroy any comms equipment and set a radio suppressor."

"Sierra Two to Mamba," said Stinger ten minutes later.

There was a short pause. *"Mamba to Sierra Two, report."*

"Objective secure. Several targets down, more immobile. No casualties," Stinger rubbed his chest. "We'll be wheels up in five."

02:45hrs
Grüssmire Gewerbe

Grantham and Mac had been in cover since the rest of

the unit had left for the airfield. On opposite sides of the facility, they had maintained watch to ascertain the guards' routine. If he were being generous, Grantham would say they patrolled at random, if he were being a little harder he would say haphazardly.

"Sierra Team to Mamba." Grantham heard the slightly metallic voice through his earpiece.

"Mamba, go ahead."

"Sierra Team will be at LZ in five."

"Roger that. Report when you're in position," replied Grantham. "Sierra One, you ready?"

There was a small laugh over the radio before Mac replied. "I was born ready, Mamba."

Grantham crawled back from his OP, observation point, into deeper cover. He then quickly checked his equipment before crawling forward again.

"Mamba, Sierra Team all set. New toy is up and heading your way, on site in two."

Grantham scanned the compound with combination binoculars, infrared and night vision glasses.

"Sierra One, move to forward position, we go after the next patrol."

With practised ease, Grantham quickly stored his equipment, crawled back and stood up in thick cover. He mentally repeated the mantra his old training instructor had drilled into him. Shine, shadow, shape and silhouette. As he moved, Grantham was continually aware of his background and how he would appear against it.

He was nearing the compound perimeter fence, a sturdy double mesh steel construction. But it was not electrified or alarmed, as far as they knew. Grantham took out a small hand held electronic detector and passed it along the fence, careful not to touch it. No reading. He advanced the detector until it touched the steel mesh.

"Mamba, Sierra One in forward location. No reading from perimeter."

"Roger Sierra One, same here. Cutting."

Grantham took a pair of cutters from his pouch. They were the same size as a pair of large scissors, but they were ratcheted and made of some exotic material that Grantham could not pronounce. What he did know was that they would cut through carbon steel like traditional cutters through copper sheet.

The blade closed on the mesh, locked and stopped. Grantham opened the handles and squeezed again. The blades edged closer together. On the third squeeze the blades met and the mesh parted with a slight twang. With the tension gone the next few cuts went quicker and easier. In less than four minutes Grantham had a hole large enough to crawl through. Two more cuts would do it.

"Mamba, Sierra One entering."

Damn, Mac was good. Maybe I'm getting old, thought Grantham.

"Mamba, Sierra Nine, new toy in position. Have you and Sierra One in sight. Three Tangos on patrol."

Grantham scanned the night sky, no sign of the small UAV. He cocked his head to one side, no sound either.

He headed for the small stand of tall weeds, they were not great cover but unless someone was looking directly at them and within twenty feet or so he should be fine.

"Sierra One in position."

"Mamba also in position. Hold."

From his vantage point Grantham could see one of the guards sauntering around the large compound. He seemed to be enjoying the night air more than taking any real interest in checking the area for intruders.

A small rustle to Grantham's right caught his

attention, movement shifted the grass and Grantham saw a body the thickness of his forearm slither from the long grass and head towards him. Carefully he drew his combat knife, a variation of the American Ka-Bar knife. It had a razor sharp seven inch matt black blade, needle point with an inner curved cut out above leading to a serrated back. The handle was a mottled black nonslip rubber.

The snake stopped, head raised and its forked tongue flicking in and out sampling the air. It was only three feet away and there was no mistaking the broad swell to the rear of the head, distinctive in pit vipers, and even in the moonlight the diamond pattern along the back stood out. A diamond backed rattlesnake.

Grantham realised he had tensed up, ready to slash with the wickedly sharp blade if need be. He forced himself to relax. The snake could probably detect fear, or at least the pheromones given off by possible prey. Grantham took a deep breath and visibly relaxed his body, keeping the knife ready but under no illusion that he could beat the snake in outright striking speed. The one good thing was that the snake was still pretty straight, not coiled in a striking pose.

The rattler raised its head higher, still sampling the air. Grantham could see at least five feet of thick body just starting to taper at the far end, it must be almost six feet long.

The snake tensed slightly and drew its head back and its body forward forming a tight 'S' shape, poised for a strike.

Grantham forced himself to slightly loosen his grip on the knife, relaxing his arm. Without warning the snake snapped straight, mouth wide and fangs pointing forward. The strike was too fast for Grantham to react until the snake was at full length, and by then it was too late to stop it. But the strike had not been at Grantham.

He looked down to see the snake withdraw its head from the largest rat he had ever seen. Its body had to be at least fourteen inches plus the tail. The rat froze for a few second and then ran off away from the snake. Grantham looked back at the snake which again had its head raised and its tongue flicking in and out looking after the departing rat. The snake looked directly at Grantham and then started to slither after its meal.

Grantham took a deep breath and replaced the knife.

"Sierra One to Mamba, last tango just returned to base. Ready to move?"

"Oh yes Sierra One, I'm ready to move."

Ten minutes later Grantham flattened himself against a concrete wall. The building was three storeys high, the front was a mixture of mirrored glass and concrete. But the side that Grantham was on was almost completely concrete with a large roller shutter door. Three single doors were evenly spaced along the length, and only four windows looked out. There was no light coming from any of the windows.

Grantham checked his watch, it was twelve minutes since the last guard had returned to the building. It was now a question of waiting. The plan was to jump the guards as they started on their next rounds.

A noise from the front of the compound caught Grantham's attention, a vehicle was approaching. Quickly but carefully he ran to the front corner. Across the clearing the bus they had seen earlier came through the barrier and made its way slowly to the front of the building, stopping at what appeared to be the main entrance. The doors opened with a pneumatic hiss and the driver stepped down and walked into the building. After a few seconds there was the unmistakeable sound of the metal roller shutter doors opening.

"Sierra Nine, what does the new toy show at the front of the building?"

There was a pause then, "*Mamba, front looks quiet. Some windows show residual heat but no tangos. I can see one definite heat source, one possible in the entrance area.*" The definite heat source would be the driver the possible was a guard or receptionist.

"Sierra One, change of plan, we're taking the bus."

"Roger Mamba, I'm at the corner, be there in ten."

Grantham stepped from the cover of the building, stepping away from the wall but staying in the shadows. Luckily the driver had turned off the vehicle's lights.

As Grantham approached the bus he had his MP5 trained on the front of the building, he also glanced up at the mirrored windows. If there was someone up there without lights this assault was going to end quickly and noisily.

"Sierra One behind the target." Mac's voice whispered in Grantham's ear.

"Roger Sierra One, get aboard."

Grantham saw a shadow move along the side of the bus and enter the open doors. He quickly edged his way sideways, keeping the building covered with the MP5.

As he got to the bus he lowered the gun and turned to check behind. Mac was crouched in the bus's doorway, covering the area until Mamba arrived. Without a word, Mac crouched his way into the bus and headed to the rear. Grantham stepped up and walked three rows back before crouching behind the third row of seats on the driver's side.

Two minutes later the driver walked from the building and back onto the bus, closed the doors and started the engine. The bus drove forward and around to the side of the building before turning sharp left and heading through the open roller shutter door and down a steep ramp.

As the bus levelled out and came to a halt the driver

445

stopped the engine. The lights in the large garage had come on automatically and cast sharp shadows into the bus.

Grantham stood and in two strides was behind the driver. Before the driver realised what was happening, Grantham had pressed the muzzle of his 9mm Sig P228 pistol against the driver's temple, his left hand clamped on the driver's left shoulder.

"Do you speak English?" asked Grantham.

"Ja, err yes, I speak English," stammered the driver in a thick German accent. He was in his late fifties, a little overweight and with thinning light blond hair that made him look bald from a few feet away.

"Good, answer some questions and you'll be okay, if you don't I'll put a bullet in your brain and look for the answers elsewhere. Understand?"

The man tried to nod but found it difficult with the gun pressed to his temple.

"Are there any other vehicles due in or out tonight?"

"Nein, das ist… err, no, I am in late because of a, err a engine problem. I should have been back many hours ago."

"How many security men are there?"

"I do not know," the driver shrugged his broad shoulders. "Four, five that patrol outside, one or two that patrol the err, I do not know the word. There are management and scientists and others that work with hands like me and caretakers who are not as clever as the scientists. There are one or two guards that patrol our living areas. But most of the non-clever staff have gone so less patrols now."

"How many guards on site altogether?"

"I do not know." The man was obviously mentally counting. "Maybe twenty?"

"Who are the people coming in?" asked Grantham.

"New scientists. Some come from long way,

different parts of world."

"Do you have a map of the complex, the building?"

"No sir. I do not go other places, we are not allowed."

"No maps?" pressed Grantham.

"I do not have map. I think maybe one in caretaker office."

"How many floors are there in the building?"

"Three above, some underground. I think more than one. I do not know how many."

"Where is the security and communications centre?"

"Some security near non-clever staff area but some other place. Communications I do not know. We are not allowed telephones or radios in grounds or building."

"Where is your living area?"

The man gave a brief description of the manual staff areas. They all appeared to be on this lower level with no direct access to the outside. There were two exits, one to the garage and one to the reception area. One lift served the three upper floors, but the driver did not know the areas it accessed and said it needed a key card to call the lift. With a few more questions Grantham managed to find out the location of the scientists' rest areas, canteen and gymnasium, all of which were on the ground floor. The management areas, which were on the upper floors, seemed to be the ones with the mirrored glass.

"Okay, I'm going to tie your hands together and tie you to this pole," Grantham tapped the metal pole behind the driver's seat. "And I'm going to gag you. Understand?"

"Ja."

The driver stood up and turned away from Grantham. With practised ease Grantham patted the man down, checking for weapons and backed him towards the pole where he told him to wait. He then stepped to the door and checked the garage. Several expensive cars, BMWs, Mercedes, a Porsche were parked in numbered parking lots. Half a dozen utility vehicles were spread around as well and a tractor and three sit on lawn mowers. A bus the same as this one was off to one side, and parked near the exit door was a large blue motorcycle.

Grantham felt more than heard movement behind him and started to look around.

A shot from a handgun rang out, echoing around the bus. Grantham dropped to the floor of the bus and spun with his own handgun raised.

The driver was slumping to the floor, half of his face a bloody mess, a small revolver in his hand. Grantham looked towards the rear of the bus, Mac was pointing his own Sig 9mm towards the front.

"He pulled the gun from the side of the seat," said Mac.

Grantham nodded to Mac and looked down at the seat, a small flap hung down revealing a padded pocket obviously designed to hold the small revolver. Slumped next to the seat, the driver was obviously not going to move again.

"Okay, let's move out."

Mac came forward and the two stepped to the still closed door.

"Think they heard?" asked Mac.

"Don't know. Guess we'll find out pretty soon if they did."

"I see one camera."

Grantham nodded. "Sierra Nine, can the new toy come down here?"

"Don't see why not Mamba."

Grantham explained what he wanted for a few seconds.

448

Twenty seconds later they saw a small movement near the top of the wall coming down the entrance ramp. The briefcase sized UAV was matt black and difficult to see in the shadows.

"I can see the camera Mamba, can't block the signal, it's hard wired."

"Okay Sierra Nine, take it out."

Without warning or sound the camera simply disintegrated. The hypersonic railgun projectile carried so much momentum the camera case shattered and the inner electronics spilled to the floor.

"Nice shooting Nine. Okay Mac, let's go."

The door leading from the underground garage was of a heavy metal construction but not locked. The corridor outside was well lit and straight in both directions for at least seventy feet.

"Do we trust what the driver said regarding directions and locations?" asked Mac in barely more than a whisper.

Grantham shrugged, "We have nothing better to go on."

They stepped into the corridor, one to each side and quickly moved along. One would move forward while the other watched the corridor to the rear, they would then swap and the second would move while the first watched the rear. In a few seconds they were at the door the driver had described as the security office on this level.

Grantham covered the corridor while Mac placed a small box the size of a matchbox against the solid metal door. After a few seconds he shook his head at Grantham. The box was a highly sensitive microphone that was capable of hearing through solid doors when in contact with them.

Changing positions, Mac covered the corridor while Grantham slowly tried the door, it was unlocked and moved easily. At the first sign of a sliver of light he stopped and nodded to Mac who turned to face the door. With a hard steady push, Grantham swung the door open while Mac covered the interior with his Heckler & Koch MP5.

The room was about forty feet on a side. A wooden table with eight chairs was at the far end, a small open plan kitchen next to it. Several cheap looking and well used easy chairs and sofas were spread around the room. The only tidy area was to the left. There were three desks with several large log books, three office style chairs and a keyboard with a monitor in front of each.

As the door swung open a guard looked up from an easy chair, realised that the two men at the door did not belong and jumped up, reaching for a gun on the side table. Before the man was fully on his feet, Mac had placed two 9mm bullets in his chest. Movement across the far side caught Mac's eye as another guard stood up from behind a large backed chair facing away from the door. He was already swinging a large revolver towards the door. Before Mac had his gun half way towards the man, two shots rang out, echoing around the room. Both bullets entered the man's head, destroying both brain and face.

Quickly sweeping the room, Grantham and Mac made sure there was no one else in residence.

"Two tangos down," reported Grantham over the radio.

Once they were sure the room was empty, they did a quick search. The logs were written in German but from what Grantham could tell they appeared to be entry and exit records of personnel and vehicles. Two of the computers seemed to be basic models, both had connections to the internet. The screen of the third was showing static. After a few clicks of the mouse it appeared that the computer was dedicated to monitoring the CCTV. So the men had probably not seen anything that happened in the parking area. With a few clicks Grantham determined that the computer had two other CCTV links, one to the outside covering the front of the building, including the garage entrance, the other was the reception area. The outside was all quiet, the reception area had one guard sitting behind the desk, his feet on the desk, his head resting against the seat back.

"What now Boss?" asked Mac.

"First I'm going to connect to JTAC with one of these," Grantham indicated the computers, "See if they can hack the system."

Grantham changed channels on his radio and within twenty seconds was talking to Danny Barrett six and a half thousand miles away. After a few seconds Grantham stood back and watched the curser on the screen take on a life of its own as Barrett started to probe its memory and the network.

"I want to see the caretakers' room, see if they have a map, like the driver said."

A minute later they were in a large store room about half the size of the guards' room. Shelves and cupboards lined three walls and contained everything a building needed for cleaning and maintenance. A desk against one wall held several ledgers, again all in German. Four large maps of the complex were fastened to the wall, one for each of the upper levels, one for the garage. Mac scanned the maps with a small camera and transmitted the image to the rest of the team. At least they now had a layout of the complex.

Grantham's earpiece came to life. "*Mamba, this is Jupiter. No go on the computer link. We need access to the main computer network. The comms centre or a computer with high level access.*"

"Roger Jupiter. Are you ready at your end?"

There was a pause before Barrett answered. "*Almost Mamba.*" Grantham looked across at Mac who was rolling his eyes.

Grantham was examining the floor plans of the building, tracing different sections and following conduits and ducting.

"Mac, have you got any smoke grenades?"

"Two, what you got in mind."

Grantham quickly scanned the shelves and found a five litre container of bleach and put it to one side. Moving along the rows of shelving it took him a minute of checking labels before he found what he wanted.

"Mac, grab a couple of metal buckets from that cupboard."

Mac got the buckets and came back to look at the two five litre containers: bleach and toilet cleaner. He hefted the toilet cleaner and scanned the label on the back.

"Bleach and acid, are we making chlorine gas?"

"The air conditioning room is on this level. Mix those two with half a bucket of water and we'll get a cloud of chlorine gas. Add some smoke from a grenade and pull the fire alarm. Should be enough to flush everyone out."

"The gas will be too dispersed to cause any harm."

"I'm not looking to hurt anyone. Remember Charisma's in here somewhere, hopefully. I just want to add an irritant to the smoke, give a bit of urgency to the evacuation." Grantham pressed his mic button. "Sierra Team, ready to move in five. We're about to have a fire here and I expect a lot of people to be leaving in a hurry."

Chapter 38

03:45hrs, 28th April
Grüssmire Gewerbe

Grantham poured the toilet cleaner and bleach into the water and watched as a thin green mist rose from the buckets. Mac stepped over to the control panel and turned the fan control up to maximum. The fumes were clearly being sucked into the vent.

"Grenade," said Grantham, his voice muffled behind the gas mask.

Mac pulled the pin and tossed the small cylinder into the vent. Three seconds later there was a muffled pop and smoke billowed into the room before quickly being sucked back into the vent.

Grantham and Mac left the room and at a quick jog headed for the stairs at the end of the hall.

The stairs had one landing at half way and a larger second one at the top. The door was clearly metal with a stout lock and a card reader to one side. Grantham swiped a card he had taken from the security guards and was rewarded with a snap as the lock disengaged.

The guard behind the desk had his feet propped on the table and opened his eyes at the sound of the door swinging back. The slack, sleepy look disappeared instantly when he saw the two troops dressed in camouflage and gas masks. He sat forward trying to get his feet off the desk and reach for his side arm. Mac's MP5 fired twice and the man slumped back and to the side, falling from the chair, one foot still on the desk which twitched twice before falling to the floor.

"Tango three down."

Grantham took off his gas mask and sniffed the air.

There was a definite tang that made his nostrils twitch and a small wisp of smoke coming from the air conditioning grille high up on the wall.

The desk top contained nothing but a computer screen, mouse and keyboard. But the side of the desk nearest the guard had a panel with a series of buttons and lights. Clearly alarms and call buttons of several kinds. Grantham looked down the list, 'feuer', German for fire.

"Sierra Team, we are about to go noisy, start the approach."

Grantham reached into his jacket pocket and took out a pack of baby wipes. It was a standing joke amongst the troops that baby wipes were the best thing to remove camo-paint, and it gave them beautifully smooth skin. Grantham took two out and handed the pack to Mac. Both men quickly scrubbed away at their hands and face.

"Set the smoke at the top of the stairs." Grantham nodded to the door leading to the garage.

Grantham checked the panel again and pushed the button marked 'feuer'. Instantly the dim lighting flared into harsh white light and a wailing siren rang out. With a hollow pop the second smoke grenade exploded at the top of the garage steps. Mac had closed but not latched the door so smoke was seeping out around the edges, spreading across the floor of the reception area.

Raised voices and movement came from the corridors leading to the reception area. The upper floors formed a mezzanine that started to fill with people looking around, heading down the stairs, looking for the exits. Grantham walked purposefully over to the stairs and started to wave the people down, many of them holding cloths or their hands to their noses and mouths.

"Schnell, schnell," said Grantham waving the

people down and pointing them towards the main entrance.

The people were a mixture of ages, mostly men with a few women. They were mostly blond and blue eyed, the brunettes standing out from the crowd. And the majority looked soft and pale, as if they spent their time in darkened rooms and rarely saw sunlight. Scientists, thought Grantham.

He put his hand to his ear and pressed transmit while still waving the people out.

"Mamba to Sierra Team, expect collaterals to be leaving the building. Direct them away from the buildings in German via the PA. Collaterals are free to go unless they offer resistance. Tangos are guards, probably dressed in black and probably armed. Weapons free on Tangos."

"Roger Mamba, just crossing boundary." Grantham could hear the rotor noise from the helicopter in the background of the transmission just before he heard the same from the outside.

Sergeant Mark Smedley, Sierra Nine, slowed the helicopter and came to a hover over the flat roof of the large building. The side doors were already open and 35mm diameter ropes had been tied off and coiled on the floor. Just before he arrested the forward motion, the rest of Sierra Team kicked the coiled ropes out of the open rear doors.

"Go, go, go," called Smedley over the comms system.

Jez Stinger, Sierra Two, and Snake Dunhelm, Sierra Three, were the first out, one to each side. Before they hit the roof they were followed by Nick Perkins, Sierra Five and Danny Fathom, Sierra Six. As the team sniper Bird Sparrow, Sierra Four, had already set up beyond the boundary.

Smedley released the ropes before pulling up on the collective and twisted the throttle grip, increasing power and lift. At the same time he pushed the cyclic gently forward taking the Huey up and over the edge of the roof. He pressed the anti-torque pedals and turned the helicopter sideways, allowing the machine to side-slip away from the building so that he could look down at the stream of people.

He flicked the PA system to broadcast. "Von dem Gebäude entfernen." It was some time since he had spoken German, he hoped he was actually saying, "Move away from the building."

All of the people leaving the building were looking up at the helicopter, some still drifting away from the doors, but most simply standing and staring. He flicked a switch and the powerful night-sun searchlight illuminated causing those below to shield their eyes or look away.

"Von dem Gebäude entfernen. Schnell!" He put some steel in his voice and was pleased to see that he got the required response. "Schnell! Schnell!" Many of the collateral targets were now moving briskly away, heading for the boundary. As a quick head count he came to thirty with more still coming out.

Grantham stood at the bottom of the stairs waving and encouraging people out of the building, he estimated forty had left so far.

"Who are you, what is going on?" A guard in one piece black overalls was coming down the stairs, pushing past the scientists.

Grantham glanced at him and then deliberately continued to evacuate the now thinning crowd.

"You, I said what..." The guard got within arm's length of Grantham and was reaching out to take hold of his collar. With a smooth, easy movement Grantham took hold of the man's wrist in one hand and bent it back while twisting and pulling the man forward. The guard was still two stairs up and fell forward, a grunt escaping his lips as he hit the ground and his wrist snapped. Grantham bent quickly and in an open hand strike broke the guard's nose, stunning him. Still holding the guard's wrist, Grantham grabbed a handful of blond hair and slammed the man's head into the floor. He went limp.

"Tango four down."

Grantham stood up and continued to direct the last few people out. Several started at the fallen guard, but they all carried on to the outside.

Mac was standing at the back of the reception area, his MP5 held at the ready but keeping a low profile, not wanting to panic the scientists as they headed out.

As the last of the crowd were exiting the building, shots rang out from the side. Grantham instinctively ducked behind the stairs as Mac returned fire, two short bursts on full auto. Grantham rolled from cover and came to a one kneed crouch, the MP5 pulled into his shoulder. One guard was down and as he pulled the trigger both his and Mac's short burst drilled eight 9mm bullets into the man.

"Tango six down," announced Grantham over the comms.

Mac ran over to the two fallen guards, did a quick search and removed their security cards. Grantham did the same with the guard who had come down the stairs.

"Which way Boss?" asked Mac.

"Sierra Team will be coming from the roof down. Let's find the entry to the lower levels."

The troops on the roof cleared the landing zone while the sound of the nearby helicopter washed over them, seeming to make the whole building vibrate.

Stinger stood back from the door. "Sierra Team ready for entry." He crouched down and turned away from the door as the detcord cutting charge exploded with a sharp crack that was lost in the din from the hovering helicopter.

"Sierra Team entering."

"Sierra Team ready for entry." Grantham heard Stinger's voice a second before a different alarm sounded, overlaid on the wailing of the fire alarm.

"Sierra Team entering."

Grantham and Mac ran over to the lift. There was no call button, just a card reader. After three attempts, they found one of the security cards activated the lift. After a few seconds the doors slid open, Grantham and Mac poised to fill the compartment with automatic fire, but the lift was empty.

Grantham stepped in and quickly looked around. A CCTV camera was in one corner, monitoring anyone who entered. With one shot Grantham destroyed the device. The control panel had buttons for three upper levels, and three sub-levels.

"Next stop ladies' lingerie, all aboard," said Grantham.

As the door blew back, Sierra Team saw the steep stairway leading down from the roof, white light coming from below. They entered at speed, removing their night vision goggles and leapfrogging each other down the stairs to the top floor. Jez Stinger hit the lower landing, his back against the wall as the door was thrown open and two guards started to enter with assault rifles raised. Stinger pulled the trigger, his MP5 on full auto, releasing the full thirty round mag. in just over two seconds. The guards dropped to the floor, one rifle firing wildly into the ceiling.

"OUT," shouted Stinger as he raised the MP5 and ejected the empty magazine before slamming a new one in place. "Tango eight down," reported Stinger.

Fathom and Snake leaped over the fallen guards and covered both ways along the corridor. Perkins came through and turned right, Stinger followed him turning left. The corridor was about one hundred feet in both directions. It was well lit with doors spaced along both sides. The walls appeared to be a light brown veined marble with a white marble floor and matt black ceiling. Noise and movement to the right drew the team's attention. A door about fifty feet down had opened, more guards were running through. Fathom and Snake dropped to a one kneed crouch at each side of the fifteen foot wide corridor, Stinger was against the wall behind Snake, all three covering the approaching guards. Perkins covering the opposite direction to make sure they were not outflanked.

The three troops of Sierra Team opened fire, releasing three round bursts with deadly accuracy. The front two guards dropped almost immediately, the next two returning half a dozen shots before bullets slammed into their heads and upper torsos. The final guard turned to leave through the same door he had entered by. Snake fired one shot at the retreating figure and saw him stumble as he made it through the door.

Fathom was already on his feet and sprinting down the corridor, pulling a hand grenade from his webbing and throwing it through the closing door. He slammed himself flat against the wall as an ear splitting explosion rocked the almost closed door, supersonic shrapnel from the fragmentation grenade shredding the door and peppering the opposite wall.

"Tango twelve down," reported Stinger from back along the corridor.

Fathom kicked the door open and sprang back as

Perkins took up a firing position, more than half covered by the wall and door frame, sweeping the room with his MP5. The room was large, forty feet by twenty with several doors leading from it. Two guards were on the floor, both ripped apart by the fragmentation grenade.

"Tango fourteen down," said Perkins.

Two guards stood outside of the lift doors on sub level one, watching the level indicator of the approaching elevator. They braced themselves as the doors parted and opened fire, one with a pump action assault shotgun, the other with a fully automatic machine gun. The sound filled the corridor and echoed around the lift. The walls of the elevator shredded with each shot, nothing inside could have survived the massive onslaught.

As the shots died away the doors started to slide shut, stuttering in the damaged slots and grinding as metal rubbed against metal. Just before the doors met, a small black ball, slightly smaller than a tennis ball, hit the floor and bounced between the guards who turned to watch it as the high explosive hand grenade exploded.

The overpressure turned the guards' organs and bones to mush and they slumped to the floor, little more than bloody sacks of skin.

The lift doors squealed and ground slowly open. Grantham moved to the side with the left hand door as he checked the corridor for more guards. Mac dropped to the floor behind him and let the ceiling hatch slam shut.

"Tango sixteen down," said Grantham.

Sierra Team were moving room to room, clearing each in pairs. One would open the door, the other would sweep the room with his MP5 ready to fire at any threat, while the first prepared to toss a flash-bang grenade.

The first room had clearly been a guards' quarters. There were bunks and seating for ten guards. After a quick search, Stinger had found a computer control point and killed the incessant alarms. The rest of the rooms seemed to be quality self-contained living quarters, all empty.

"Top floor clear, mostly high class accommodation for ten people. Odd sense of decor, lots of Nazi memorabilia and what I'd guess at devil worship stuff? Plus swords and knights' stuff, that knight with a K."

"The Ahnenerbe were into all forms of occult, including knights of the round table and chivalry."

"Not Dungeons and Dragons, then?" said Stinger as they opened the door to the stairs. "Going to two."

Grantham looked along the corridor. The right walls were spotlessly white, the floor and ceiling a smooth light blue. The ceiling had strips of glowing white along the centre, no bulbs, it seemed as if the paint itself were glowing. At the junction of the walls and ceiling were electric blue LEDs. The left wall was solid glass, the first twenty feet shattered by the grenade. Grantham could see several large laboratories spread out behind the glass walls. Quickly heading away from the lift, Grantham and Mac started checking the half dozen doors along the right hand wall.

The first two were large storage areas, seeming to contain all things 'scientific' as Mac described the products on the racks and shelves. The third door revealed a large open plan living area. It appeared to be empty, but had several doors leading from the main area. These opened to a series of self-contained flats with a large communal kitchen/dining room, several toilets and bathrooms and sleeping space for around twenty people.

"Sierra Nine, how many people left the complex?" asked Grantham.

"About seventy Mamba. Most are heading away along the road."

Three more rooms showed the same set up, most of the beds appeared to be used. Another four rooms seemed unused, as if waiting for their occupants.

As they came out of the last room, a door further down opened and a middle aged man in a white lab coat came out. He paused and looked at Grantham and Mac, his face at first displaying curiosity and then panic. He reached under the lab coat, obviously grasping for something.

"FREEZE, DON'T MOVE," shouted Grantham.

The man ignored him and started to back up, still scrabbling under his coat.

"HALT, SIE BEWEGEN SICH NICHT."

The man hesitated at the sound of the German, and then pulled his hands from under the coat. In his left hand was a German Luger pistol.

Grantham did not hesitate, the double tap of shots took the man in the neck and head. He slumped to the floor, the shot to the throat having severed the spine preventing any last signals getting to his hand and causing a stray shot.

"Tango seventeen down."

The last three rooms were of a similar size, but were clearly set up as office workspace. Each had twenty workstations with printers and copiers. Six large 100" ultra flat TV screens covered one wall. Another wall contained floor to ceiling bookshelves with obviously old titles, some appeared to be bordering on ancient.

Grantham stepped to one of the computers that was displaying a screen saver and moved the mouse. The background screen came up asking for fingerprint access.

"Mac, drag that scientist in here."

A few seconds later Mac came back easily dragging the dead body across the smooth polished floor, leaving a vivid irregular swath of bright red blood in a wide trail. Grantham pulled the man to the computer and swiped his right index finger across the pad. The computer gave a chime and an incorrect message. Of course, the man had held the Luger in his left hand. Trying again with the man's left forefinger the message on the screen cleared and multiple icons appeared.

Grantham changed channels on the comms and again called GCHQ. It took less than thirty seconds to log onto the GCHQ web and for Danny Barrett to start probing the system.

"It looks like we can access the full system. There are multiple firewalls and security levels," Barrett's voice sounded dreamy as if he were concentrating on something other than talking.

"Do you have the programme ready to download?"

"Err, almost," replied Barrett.

After a quick check of the rest of the labs and living quarters, Grantham and Mac carefully took one of the two staircases down to the next level. Suspecting an ambush at any moment, the men descended one flight at a time, covering each other and up and down the stair well. But it was not an ambush that took them by surprise as they opened the door to the lower level.

Upper level two appeared to be a work area. The rooms were mostly offices. At least two of the rooms were large meeting rooms, but one, in the centre of the corridor, was an impressive looking boardroom. It could sit twenty around the highly polished mahogany table. Chairs around the outside could sit at least another forty. Large plasma screens were suspended at the centre of each end and side wall. Small control units were set into the table in front of each seat. The outer wall was one solid piece of glass looking out over the grounds. There were chrome and LED lighting bars along all walls and the centre, which were dimmed down to give a low even light to the room.

Stinger looked out across the grounds, he could see the high intensity searchlight of the helicopter sweeping the grounds, making its way around the perimeter. As he watched, the helicopter jinked in mid-air and rose steeply. The bright searchlight winked out and the helicopter side-slipped before starting to drop.

Several bursts of automatic gunfire from the corridor made Stinger turn and head out of the impressive boardroom. The gunfire had the distinctive twang of a Kalashnikov machine gun, a weapon that none of Sierra Team were using. As he reached the door a concussive blast and searing light came from an open doorway several doors down. Stinger broke into a run as more shots rang out, these were a mixture of the Kalashnikov and the quieter and faster stutter of an MP5.

"Sierra Nine, taking fire."

"Tango eighteen down. One casualty, Sierra Three, cat three." The voice on the radio was Fathom, Sierra Six. A category three wound was non life-threatening and not debilitating.

"What happened?" asked Stinger as he entered the room.

Snake was holding his left arm up as Sierra Six strapped a field dressing to the open wound.

"We kicked the door in, swept the room visually and didn't see anything. We were just entering when this guy," Snake nodded to the guard on the floor who had been stitched by at least eight shots to the abdomen, "he

464

came out from behind the door and opened fire. I rolled away and Nick threw a flash-bang. Short fire fight and I got winged."

"Okay to go on?" asked Stinger.

"I've had worse shaving," grinned Snake. "But have you seen the heap of crap he shot me with?"

Stinger bent down and picked up the Kalashnikov 74, the newer version of the much vaunted 47 that was used the world over by every terrorist, rebel and revolutionary. The Kalashnikov 74 was a well built, sturdy weapon that had been issued to Russian troops since the early '90s. Firing a 5.45mm calibre bullet, the standard version held a 30 round magazine. But this was most definitely not standard. An eighteen inch needle point bayonet was sticking out of the front. A grenade launcher was underslung on the barrel with a powerful spotlight to the right. The magazine was double size, 60 rounds. On the top of the weapon was a combination wide-angle zoom sniper scope and laser red dot sight. The solid plastic butt stock had an SS death's head on both sides. The attachments had almost doubled the weight of the already heavy weapon to around 7kg. The AK-74 was designed as an assault weapon rather than one for CQB, close quarter battle, and the additional weight and length from the ridiculous bayonet and attachments made it almost unusable.

Stinger placed the weapon on a table and headed out of the room. "Come on, enough rest, let's keep moving."

Mark Smedley turned the Huey through 180 degrees and started back along the perimeter of the large compound. A metallic crack focused Smedley's attention. It was a sound he had heard on more than one occasion, the sound of a bullet passing through the outer skin of the helicopter.

Smedley banked the helicopter left and up, pushed the nose down to gain forward momentum and dove down and right. He switched the searchlight off, no point in making the target easier.

"Sierra Nine taking fire." Another twang rang out as another round shot through the rear passenger compartment.

"On it Nine," said Bird.

Corporal John 'Bird' Sparrow scanned the area in front of the large building. There was no one immediately in sight. He flicked the telescopic sight from starlight to infrared and scanned again. There, a small red image crouched in the shadows. Bird already had the distance and elevation to the building dialled in. With a smooth motion he pressed the safety trigger forward and moved his index finger to the firing trigger behind. He took a breath and let it out slowly, paying attention to his heartbeat, a steady regular 62bpm. As he watched, the image in his scope flared bright white and flashed back to red. The target had fired another shot.

Bird applied even steady pressure to the trigger of the CheyTac M-200 until between heartbeats the long rifle kicked back hard against his shoulder as the .357 bullet exited the barrel at 1500 feet per second. The distance to the target was just over 500 yards meaning the bullet covered the distance in a little over one second. Bird watched as the target displayed a burst of warm red splatter as the main heat source slumped into an unrecognisable heap. Something warm had just erupted from the target. Bird worked the bolt action of the sniper rifle and chambered another round. Sighting by infrared he could not be sure what part of the target he had hit. The second shot displayed the same splatter of heat, but with no further movement from the target.

The bullets decelerated as they left the barrel, but after 500 yards they would still be travelling at almost the speed of sound. The amount of momentum they would deliver to a human target would be devastating.

"Tango nineteen down. All clear Sierra Nine."

Grantham and Mac exited the modern stairwell and entered what appeared to be a medieval passageway. The walls were large stone blocks, the floor slate, with age worn grooves. The lighting was from regularly placed flaming torches, although Grantham noted the actual flame was coming from a small central gas filament made to look like an old fashioned torch.

Grantham and Mac looked at each other, they were both clearly taken aback.

"I knew the SS were into some medieval crap, but I didn't realise they would go this far," said Mac.

"They used several real castles during the Second World War. I suppose we shouldn't be surprised. Let's hope that they're using medieval weapons as well."

They advanced along the corridor, checking front and rear as they went. The first two doors they came to were wooden with barred openings, cell doors. Looking in they could see the cell was dark and damp, the far wall had chains and manacles. Thankfully they were empty. The next two from the outside looked the same, but the interiors were very different. Rather than the dank traditional cells they looked more like operating theatres. A large operating table was in the centre with straps along the sides. One wall was filled with glass cabinets containing chrome instruments, many of them with what looked like wickedly sharp edges. The opposite wall held racks and cabinets of multi-coloured chemicals. The rear wall had racks of vessels of varying sizes, all empty. What the hell were they doing here, thought Grantham.

467

A snap behind them made Grantham and Mac start to turn as a mini-gun opened fire. As he dove to one side Grantham felt the heavy impact of several slugs slamming into his back and side. He hit the floor and rolled onto one knee, bringing the MP5 to his shoulder and aiming back for the target, expecting to see at least one guard. There was no one there. Instead a small grille had opened up and no more than four inches of mini-gun muzzle was pointing through, and this was twisting right and down, targeting Mac for a second burst.

"Mac, move!"

Grantham opened fire on full auto, emptying the thirty round magazine at the small target. Every shot landed within three inches of the opening, at least a third hit the muzzle itself. The mini-gun opened fire, but the impacts had caused the operator to pull partly back and the sustained burst raked the far wall and ceiling, kicking up plaster and dust.

The muzzle pulled back and the flap ground shut.

Grantham shuffled over to Mac who was pulling himself to a sitting position against the wall, a thick smear of blood on the slate floor.

"How bad?" asked Grantham as he ejected the magazine from the MP5 and slammed in a new one.

"Thigh and hip. Not fatal, but it's going to slow me down a bit." Mac grimaced in pain. "Deal with them, Boss. I'll get some dressings on."

Grantham checked the corridor and moved across to the now obvious hatch. He removed his combat pack and took out a breaching charge. About the size of two TV remote controls, the device was packed with C4 explosive in a shaped charge that would direct the explosive power in one direction.

Grantham removed a paper strip to reveal a putty like base. He slammed the charge against the wall directly under the hatch and pulled the pin. He quickly went back to Mac and pulled his gas mask into place and shielded Mac from the blast.

Although directional, the blast still washed over them like a hammer blow.

Grantham sprang up and stepped over to the gaping two feet hole. It was unlikely that anyone inside could have come through the blast unscathed, but Grantham lobbed a fragmentation grenade in and stood to one side until it exploded two seconds later. He then swung around and sprayed the interior with thirty 9mm rounds. As the dust dispersed he saw three bodies dressed in guards' black overalls.

"Tango twenty-two down. One casualty, Sierra One, cat two."

"I'm not the only casualty," said Mac, nodding at Grantham's neck.

Grantham put his hand to his neck, it came away red.

Mac was already injecting his wounds and pressing field dressings in place. Grantham wiped away his own blood and Mac confirmed it was, "little more than a graze".

Grantham helped Mac to his feet, both men grunting with the effort, Grantham pressing his hand to his side.

"I think I've got broken ribs as well," said Grantham.

"I've had some of them, don't worry, they only hurt when you breathe. What now?"

"I find Charisma and rescue the damsel in distress. You make your way out."

"I'm okay, you can't go on alone boss, let's get one of Sierra Team down here."

"Sorry Mac, you'll slow me down and it'll take too long to get someone else down. You exfil and we'll meet at the extraction point. I'll make it an order if I have to."

Mac grinned, "You aren't in the Regiment anymore, you're retired remember? Or is your memory starting to go?"

"I'm serious, Mac. I want you out."

Mac opened his mouth to speak and then closed it and nodded resignedly. "Good luck, boss. Don't be late." Mac turned and hobbled back the way they had come, leaving bloody footprints on the floor and hand prints on the wall as he steadied himself, the painkilling injections already taking effect.

Grantham opened his jacket and pulled the straps on his body armour tight to support his ribs.

The next few rooms were deserted, Grantham checked half a dozen that appeared to be cells, actually more like torture chambers, some old fashioned, some modern, all frightening.

The end of the corridor turned through ninety degrees. No sound, and no sign of movement but he had a bad feeling about this. Grantham readied his last flash-bang, released the handle and let it brew for two seconds before tossing it around the corner. Gunshots rang out until the grenade exploded and Grantham sprang around the corner spraying the area with automatic fire.

"Tango 24 down," announced Grantham.

The corridor went on for about fifty feet before ending in a large oak door with burning torches to each side. Grantham checked his MP5, only five shots left. He strapped the machine gun to his back and drew his close combat Sig 228. Not as powerful as a Browning High Power, the Sig was the SAS's preferred weapon for close quarter combat. A little lighter and shorter, the Sig could be moved, aimed and fired quicker.

Behind the door was a steeply descending stone staircase leading down about thirty feet. At the bottom was a similar oaken door.

Grantham slowly made his way down the stairs. The door was heavy but opened easily.

The room was a large locker room. The lockers modern but decorated to look like ye olde timber. A shower room with ten communal showers was off to one side and an even more imposing door stood opposite. Ornate carvings and inlaid gold runes covered the solid looking door.

The room was dimly lit with flickering torches, shadows danced around the room, reflections bouncing off polished surfaces. Several black robed and hooded figures were standing in a semi-circle facing a white robed figure that was at the head of some sort of bench. The men turned to stare at Grantham seemingly taken aback that someone had burst into the room and disturbed their ceremony.

But it was the figure on the bench that caught Grantham's attention. Charisma, dressed in a simple, pure white, long dress was lying supine, seemingly unconscious.

Grantham was a split second too late to react to the figure that had appeared at his side. The blow to the temple could have been fatal if Grantham had not pulled his head to one side at the last moment. The blow rocked him and made him see stars. His Sig 228 was twisted from his grip and the MP5 snatched from his back as he rolled to the floor and away from his attacker.

"Welcome Mr Grantham. I've been looking forward to meeting you again since we bumped into each other in Washington."

Grantham looked at the man standing at ease in front of him, his vivid yellow eyes giving him an almost alien appearance. The man he knew as Adam was dismantling the Sig 228 and dropped the pieces to the floor. Grantham reached for his K-bar knife, but as he drew it from the scabbard Adam's foot slammed into his wrist and it slipped from his fingers, skidding across the floor.

Just then a mechanical voice echoed around the dark chamber. "Zehn Minuten, um sich selbst Vernichtungsdatum." Suddenly the tension in the room escalated tenfold. The men looked around and at each other before staring at the standing figure in white. There was a second's pause before the voice sounded again. "Ten minutes to self-destruct."

Chapter 39

09:02hrs, 28th April
GCHQ Cheltenham

"What the hell do you mean 'self-destruct'?" General Clive Simmonds almost yelled from behind Danny Barrett.

Barrett was sat in his own office, a large twenty feet by twenty feet room dominated by a semi-circular desk with three computer consoles. The centre keyboard sat in front of two 32-inch screens, the two keyboards to either side sat in front of two 20-inch screens. Barrett was furiously tapping away at the centre keyboard, occasionally switching to one of the others to enter a command and then back to the centre.

"It activated when I accessed the mainframe security index. It's a dead man's switch. No sign of it, no way to bypass it. It's to stop anyone accessing the system and disabling the security protocols. If you know what you're doing you can still disable the protocols, but before you have chance to get in and do anything..."

"The whole place goes up in smoke. Can you disable it?" Simmonds was still shouting.

"I'm checking, but I don't think so."

"So why did you go that deep into the system? Just idle curiosity?"

"No. I needed to access the security protocols to link in the new instructions to the remote machines."

"And have you got them? How long will it take to get the instructions uploaded?"

"A lot less time if I didn't have to keep answering bloody stupid questions."

It was definitely insubordination, but Simmonds

473

knew better than to pull Barrett on it, at the moment.

As Simmonds watched the screen a countdown clock appeared in the upper right corner. 09:15 to detonation.

04:02hrs
Grüssmire Gewerbe

Grantham lunged for Adam before the shock of the mechanical announcement wore off. But Adam did not seem to have even noticed the voice forecasting their destruction and easily sidestepped Grantham and punched him in the ribs as he drew level, causing Grantham to gasp in pain.

The tall white clad man started to cross the room, heading for the door followed by his black clad disciples.

Adam stepped up to Grantham and threw a one, two, three combination of punches. Grantham blocked them, but he could feel the easy power in the blows.

The hooded men were exiting the room and there was nothing Grantham could do to stop them.

"You made a mistake coming down here, Mr Grantham. You are now trapped in here with me."

Grantham forced a half smile. "Actually I think you'll find it's you that's trapped in here with me." As he said the last word, Grantham delivered a snap kick to Adam's knee and was rewarded with the sound of a heavy thud, but no snap. Adam returned Grantham's smile but he displayed a slight limp as he adjusted his stance.

Grantham stepped in closer and threw his own combination of blows. Adam blocked them with solid counters and landed a hard blow to Grantham's cheek before taking hold of his arm and executing a perfect hip throw, launching Grantham easily ten feet across the room.

Grantham rolled to his feet, just to the side of Charisma. He glanced down at her, she was still unconscious but her breathing seemed strong and her head turned slightly.

Adam was stalking towards the altar while Grantham backed up to the raised dais, preferring room to fight.

The mechanical voice sounded again, first in German and then in English. *"Nine minutes to detonation."*

Adam seemed completely unfazed by the announcement or Grantham. He approached Grantham and threw a dummy punch before stepping into the blow and reversing the attack with a sharp elbow to the face. Grantham was just fast enough to pull his head back, taking a glancing blow. Under the conditions the attack had not been conventional, it was too showy. It had come close to landing simply because Adam was so fast. Grantham got the impression Adam was starting to put on a display.

Grantham dropped to the floor, sweeping Adam's legs from under him. As he dropped, Grantham twisted and aimed a crushing blow for Adam's throat. But Adam saw it coming and took hold of Grantham's arm, pulling it along the same direction, and threw Grantham across the floor. Grantham rolled, but still hit his back hard against the ornate pedestal with a horned skull that seemed to serve as the focus of the room. A large swastika was hung on the wall behind and two imposing suits of armour stood proud at either side.

Grantham climbed to his feet, the pain from his ribs getting considerably worse. Adam casually approached, seemingly confident. Grantham leant against the dais, struggling to get his breath back, but as Adam closed in, he pushed back and delivered a roundhouse kick that connected with Adam's mid-section and drove him back with an explosion of breath. For an instant Adam's face displayed shock before he again advanced and blocked Grantham's blow and bent his arm in a vicious lock, slamming him towards the dais. Grantham allowed himself to fall away from Adam, straightening his arm and giving himself room to reach under Adam's groin and heave him off his feet and slam him down against the dais and floor.

The two men crashed to the floor, knocking several items from the shelves under the dais. The items clattered to the floor, including a golden bowl, mortar and pestle and two ornate daggers. Both men grabbed for the evil looking curved blades and stepped back, brandishing the blades between them.

Adam advanced slowly, his guard down and Grantham feinted with his left and delivered a fast backhand slash to Adam's throat. Grantham stepped back at the sight of a thick red line of blood that appeared from under the other man's right ear, all the way across the throat to just under the left of the jaw.

Adam gasped and put his hand to his throat. But after a couple of seconds he took his hand away and smiled as he wiped the blood off, leaving nothing but a faint pink mark.

"You should choose your weapons more carefully," said Adam with a grin. "These two blades are almost identical, but that one delivers a pumped flow of blood from the hollow, blunt blade. The Master uses it in ceremonies to impress his acolytes. But this one," he held up the other dagger, letting the flickering light glint off the curved blade before drawing it across his own palm. "This one is very sharp, and the one he uses on the actual victims." The blood dripped to the floor and Adam closed his fist, cracking several knuckles.

"Eight minutes to detonation," announced the

mechanical female voice.

Grantham quickly thought back across the last two minutes. Adam was fast and powerful, he was also confident to the point of arrogance. He suspected that Adam was supremely confident as he had never had to face defeat, unlike Grantham and every member of the SAS who did not complete their basic training until they had been utterly broken. If Grantham could hurt the other man he could maybe dent that confidence.

Grantham allowed Adam to close in. He backed up slowly, breathing heavily. He was betting that Adam still wanted to play with him, demonstrate just how good he was.

Adam slashed out several times at Grantham, who kept his head and arms just out of reach before throwing a hard but slow punch at Adam's head. Adam caught Grantham's left arm and grinned. But before he could do anything with the arm, Grantham stepped in and under his own left arm, slammed his right arm into Adam's ribs with every ounce of strength he could muster. He then brought his right foot down on Adam's right knee, causing him to release Grantham's arm and fall to one knee. Grantham spun around and delivered what could easily have been a killing blow to Adam's neck. But Adam fell forward and rolled away, before coming to his feet and turning to face Grantham. However the smile had gone to be replaced by a grimace and what could be a glimpse of fear.

Adam advanced in a crouch, holding the dagger out in a fighting stance and displaying perfect balance. He was now taking this seriously. Grantham had got to him, he hoped it had been the right approach.

Adam slashed out, once, twice, the third time striking Grantham across the chest, cutting easily through the camo jacket but only grazing the body armour. Grantham saw his opening and stepped inside the man's reach, delivering two punches that destroyed Adam's nose and shattered his eye socket. Grantham dropped to one knee as Adam started to close his arms around him and punched up hard into Adam's groin before rolling away and coming to his feet.

Grantham was now really breathing hard, his ribs digging into his lungs, threatening to push through and puncture them. But Adam was also suffering, physically he was damaged, but still seemed strong. But the look on his face was now clearly a mixture of anger and desperation, maybe even fear.

Adam slashed out with the blade, hard and fast, three potentially killing blows, but Grantham kept out of reach, backing up until his back was against the wall. He had nowhere else to go. He glanced around as Adam closed the distance, to one side was the old red, black and white SS emblem draped on the wall, to the other an ancient looking suit of armour, both were out of reach. Adam paused, just out of arm or leg reach, a grin returning to his face at the anticipation of the kill. As he drew his arm back there was a piercing shriek from behind.

Charisma had regained consciousness and had screamed at the top of her voice. Adam hesitated and glanced over his shoulder, Grantham did not. Throwing everything into the blow, Grantham hit Adam with every ounce of strength fully in the solar plexus. Adam gasped and started to double over, his breath ragged, spittle on his lips. Grantham took the brief opportunity and sidestepped to the suit of armour. With one fluid motion he drew the sword from the grasp of the armoured gauntlets, spun through 180 degrees with the blade at neck height.

Adam was just straightening and pulled his head and neck away from the sharp blade. Grantham's momentum was too great to simply stop and he continued on, the large blade hitting the wall and dropping to the floor along with Grantham.

Adam took one step forward and smiled. The smile froze on his lips as blood bubbled between his teeth and a large gash opened across his throat. A strangled gurgle came from his lips and he dropped to his knees before slumping face down, his head and face slamming into the stone flags.

"Seven minutes to detonation."

GCHQ Cheltenham

"Well?" barked General Simmonds.

Danny Barrett continued to tap away at the keyboard for a few seconds. "I've got the protocols I needed. I'm attaching them to the new commands." He tapped away for a few more seconds before hitting several keys with a flourish. "That's it, the new commands are uploading."

"How long will it take?"

Barrett pursed his lips, considering his response. "Several data packages, all quite big. They need to go through half a dozen relays, two minutes. Integration at the far end before transmission, another two or three minutes. Upload and transmission two minutes. Give or take thirty seconds either way. Total of seven minutes?"

The countdown in the corner of the screen clicked over to 06:59 to detonation.

Grüssmire Gewerbe

Grantham helped Charisma off the altar. She was still wobbly but now fully aware of her surroundings.

"Where are we? What's been happening?"

Grantham was holding his arm to his ribs and

grimaced as he spoke. "No time to explain, we need to get out of here. Come on." He put his arm around her to stop her falling and glanced back at Adam before shuffling across the room, collecting his Sig 228 and quickly reassembling it before heading out of the door.

"Mamba, Sierra One." It was nice to hear Mac's voice. *"I'm on the ground floor with the rest of the team."*

"Roger One. I've got Charisma, heading up. Sierra Nine, get everyone to five miles."

"Coming in, I'll be waiting for you Mamba."

"Negative. I've got other plans for our escape. Get going."

"Boss, we've got time to wait. We'll head down to cover you."

"Negative, Mac. I want you all out. That's an order. I've got a different exit strategy."

There was a pause. *"You'd better be right Boss or you'll answer to the whole team."* Despite the situation Grantham smiled, that was not a prospect he relished.

"Got you Mac. And if anyone sees some weirdos dressed in black or white monks' outfits with hoods, they are fair game. In fact I'd take it as a personal favour if they were dead before this place blows." The climb up the long stairs had taken its toll on Grantham who was still breathing heavily. But it seemed to have had the opposite effect of Charisma. The exertion seemed to have helped drive the drugs from her system and she was steadier and more clear headed.

"Where are we?" she asked.

"A research facility in Paraguay, run by your friends the Ahnenerbe. Come on, we've got two more floors to go."

The second floor seemed oddly deserted, Mac's blood leading the way to safety. Grantham was starting to recover, his ribs were screaming in pain, but his breathing was easing and he was getting back in the rhythm of checking the front and rear.

As Charisma opened the door to the stairs Grantham swung the Sig up and around, seeking a target. There was no one in sight, but Grantham was sure he saw a door two floors above just closing.

"Six minutes to detonation."

Stinger led the way out of the large glass front doors. The Huey was hovering at fifty feet about one hundred yards off. Stinger reported their exit and Smedley quickly lowered the chopper until the skids were just touching the ground. Sierra Team advanced quickly, Fathom helped to support Mac as the rest of the team covered their exit. In twenty seconds the first two were at the Huey and took up positions to cover the rest of the team's approach.

Mac hobbled up to the low floor and sat down before pulling himself in and shuffling out of the way.

Movement near the building caught Snake's eye and he swung his MP5 around, sighting through the telescopic laser sight. The target was a thickset man dressed in a long black robe with a hood shielding his face. At least two other men similarly dressed were standing just inside the open main doors. Snake placed the red dot on the centre body mass and squeezed the trigger twice. The black clad figure seemed to pause before crumpling to the floor.

"Weirdo one down," reported Snake.

Footsteps to the right caught his attention and he swung around to see Bird running in. With one easy jump he landed in the Huey followed by Stinger. Snake stood and stepped up into the helicopter as the tempo of the rotors increased and the machine lifted off.

"Five minutes to detonation."

Charisma opened the ground floor door, Grantham covering the area beyond. They were at the far end of a wide corridor, the area well lit from the emergency lighting. Grantham stepped through the doorway and started along the corridor. The area felt deserted, their footfalls echoing off the marble floor and walls, but Grantham had a prickling on the back of his neck, danger was close.

They passed several doors, Grantham knew they should be checking and clearing each, but they had no time and he had no back-up.

A gasp from behind made Grantham spin around, the Sig held in a two handed grip.

A medium height man dressed in a hooded black robe was holding a Luger to Charisma's head. The hood was down revealing light blond hair fading to grey. The hook nose gave him the appearance of a predatory hawk, but it was the soulless black eyes that caught Grantham's attention. Two other men similarly dressed were standing just inside a room with the door half open looking out into the corridor.

"Drop the weapon or I'll take delight in blowing this young lady's brains all over the wall."

"Kill her and you follow a second later." Grantham's weapon never wavered. He was under no delusion of self-modesty. Grantham knew he could hit the small target the man was presenting as he crouched and hid behind Charisma, if he would only stay still. But the man obviously knew what he was doing. He constantly moved both his head and Charisma from side to side, never presenting a target for more than a second.

"No one else has to die here. Call the helicopter back and we can all leave."

"That helicopter is carrying an SAS assault team, just how far do you think you'd get?"

"Once they leave the helicopter without their weapons we will board and fly off. This young lady can either stay with you or she can come with us. The choice is yours."

Grantham hesitated, there was no way he was calling the team back. This was turning into a Mexican standoff.

The man kept his constant movement up, but to Grantham's surprise Charisma smiled and opened her mouth to speak.

"Hugh, remember me to Snake, tell him I know how he felt."

Grantham's mind flashed back to the story he had told Charisma as she coughed and drooped down slightly before the man's arm tightened around her throat.

With a snap, Grantham adjusted his aim and pulled the trigger. A bright red hole appeared in the shoulder of Charisma's pure white dress as the 9mm bullet passed through her upper shoulder and slammed into the man's chest.

The man gasped with shock and Grantham put a bullet in the outer right side of his brain.

Adler went limp and Charisma drooped to the floor. Grantham fired two more shots, one to the mouth severing his spine, the other just to the left centre of the chest, destroying the heart.

"Four minutes to detonation."

Grantham rushed over to Charisma where she was lying on the floor. She was conscious and in obvious pain. Grantham pulled out his first aid kit and withdrew a preloaded syringe.

"This is a coagulant, antibiotic and strong pain killer. It'll help to stop the bleeding, prevent infection and make you more comfortable." Grantham pushed the needle quickly into the wound and heard Charisma gasp. As he did so the nearby door opened and two men in similar black robes stood there, both holding Kalashnikovs as if they were not sure which end should point forward. Grantham snatched for the Sig 228 from the floor where he had placed it.

"Halt. Don't move." The man holding the machine gun was clearly nervous, and that made him unpredictable.

"Call the helicopter. Get them to come back or I'll shoot." The man was clearly on the edge, there would be no reasoning with him.

"Three minutes to detonation." The mechanical voice announced in German.

The man holding the Kalashnikov looked up at the voice coming from the ceiling speakers. Grantham rolled and grabbed the Sig. Before he could bring the gun to bear, at least eight shots rang out from two machineguns. As he brought the gun around he saw the two men stagger against the wall and slide down, leaving bloody smears against the white marble.

Grantham rolled over as he heard footsteps running along the corridor behind him. A wave of relief washed over him as he saw Stinger, Snake and Perkins running towards them, their MP5s held at port, the camouflage clothing and face paint enough to instil fear into anyone seeing them. Stinger bent down to Grantham and Charisma while Snake and Perkins covered the corridor.

"What the hell are you doing here?"

"We took a vote and decided to come back."

"Since when was the SAS a democracy?" asked Grantham and started to cough, dark red blood smearing his lips.

Stinger ignored the question. "Come on Boss, we need to get out." Stinger helped Grantham to his feet as coughs racked him again. "Nick, grab the girl, we're leaving now. Boss, you shot?"

Grantham shook his head. "No, but I think a rib has punctured my lung."

"That all? We'll sort you out on the chopper."

Perkins slung his MP5 on his back and picked up Charisma as if she were little more than a child. Stinger put one arm under Grantham's arms and half carried him, half dragged him along the corridor. The pain in Grantham's chest was excruciating, but he made no protestation.

"Two minutes to detonation."

The corridor seemed endless as the troops dragged and carried Grantham and Charisma along. Snake seeming to move effortlessly at the side, constantly swinging back and forth, covering the front and rear.

They reached the large open foyer, Bird was covering them from the open doors, and as they approached he stepped outside and swept the area with his CheyTac sniper rifle. As the others passed, he followed them, continually sweeping the area.

"Fail safe engaged. Detonation cannot be cancelled. Sixty seconds to detonation. Sechzig, sixty, Neunundfünfzig, fifty-nine..." The doors closed behind them.

The Huey was only thirty yards away from the entrance, the rotors a blur, the skids barely touching the floor as Mark Smedley kept the power on, ready for an immediate lift off.

As they approached, Grantham could see Mac sitting at the edge of the open doorway covering their approach.

Perkins placed Charisma onto the floor of the helicopter and jumped in before helping to pull Grantham up. This time a muffled growl of pain escaped Grantham's lips. Stinger jumped and dove out of the way.

"PUNCH IT," yelled Mac as Bird leaped for the chopper from six feet away. Smedley fed full power in and dipped the nose of the Huey to gain forward momentum. The aircraft was rising fast but only just cleared the trees at the outer edge of the clearing.

GCHQ Cheltenham

Danny Barrett sat back, nervously twirling a pen in his fingers.

"Has it worked?" demanded General Simmonds.

"I don't know. The upload has worked and the security protocols were accepted. It's compiling the new commands to broadcast on." The counter in the corner showed 0:22 and the flashing words, 'Fail safe engaged. Detonation cannot be cancelled'.

"How will we know if it's worked?"

Barrett sat forward and pointed to a flashing egg timer. "If that turns to a green smiley face, the compilation has finished and the broadcast has been completed."

They watched the countdown seconds tick down, seeming to accelerate as they approached zero.

The egg timer stopped flashing, it paused and flicked out. The screen went blank. The countdown timer read 00:00:00

Grüssmire Gewerbe

The black helicopter skimmed the treetops, the whole airframe shaking with the full power feeding through the whirling rotors. Smedley banked the helicopter in a sharp right turn, aiming for the lower ground to the north.

Grantham was lying on the floor, an oxygen mask covering his nose and mouth. His breathing was ragged and a few spots of blood were spattered on the inside of the mask. Bird was checking his vitals and had already pumped him full of painkillers and tranquilizers, but did not want him comatose.

Perkins was checking on Charisma, the shot to her shoulder was not fatal, she would need a few stitches but that could wait until they were more stable. He had taken a thin silver Mylar blanket from his pack and draped it around her upper body.

"How long?" asked Smedley.

Mac checked his watch, "Fifteen seconds."

"Everyone hold tight, this is going to be hairy. Give me a countdown at five," called Smedley.

Mac took hold of the grab handle and braced his legs against the forward bulkhead. Bird pushed Grantham against the same bulkhead and braced them both. Perkins already had Charisma strapped in so braced one arm onto a hand hold and the other across Charisma.

"FIVE SECONDS," called Mac.

Smedley cut the power and pulled the nose of the speeding helicopter up at an incredibly steep angle. Flat out the Huey had been travelling at 135mph at 200 feet, the manoeuvre bled 100mph in three seconds. Everyone on board was thrust down and forward with the rapid deceleration. Levelling the aircraft out, Smedley rapidly descended and continued to bleed speed.

A flash of white light from behind signalled the detonation of the complex. They had covered almost one mile in the last forty-five seconds, but no one knew the blast radius of the explosion.

The skids hit the ground hard, but the Huey was solidly built and the last of the forward speed rapidly disappeared as the helicopter skidded ten feet along the overgrown grassy clearing.

A second before the blast hit, there was a violent vibration through the ground. With no time to react, the shock wave slammed over the helicopter, lifting the tail several feet into the air before slamming it back into the ground. With a creaking snap dozens of large trees tilted and snapped, toppling into the clearing, landing with a shattering roar as thousands of tons of timber settled to the floor.

21:00hrs, 29th April
Sorsogon Bay, Philippines

The early evening was refreshingly cool compared to the sultry heat of the day. The sky was black with stars that could never be seen from any populated area. The fifty foot luxury yacht was several miles off the coast riding the gentle one foot swell with ease.

Amanda's nose crinkled at the bad egg smell and she turned to complain to Alan before realising that he was still underwater with the rest of the group. Amanda had met Alan almost two years ago and this was the second diving holiday they had been on. Alan and the other divers had been friends for years having met at the local scuba club and had been holidaying around the world at top dive spots twice a year since they were just out of their teens. Although not a diver, Amanda still enjoyed the holidays, after all, the best diving spots were also some of the best holiday destinations.

At the sound of movement on the stairs coming up from the galley below, Amanda turned to see Pam carrying two mugs of coffee.

"Whew, that's a bit of a stink," said Pam.

"I know. I turned to complain to Alan and then realised they were still down," replied Amanda.

"They'll be down for another fifteen minutes."

Amanda shook her head and smiled. "How do you

do that, you know the dive times and never wear a watch."

Pam shrugged, "Just a lot of practice, I seem to have a built-in clock. Mind you, I'd never rely on that when diving, assuming I ever get back in the water."

Pam had burst an eardrum in a car accident a few months ago and had to avoid diving until her doctor gave her the all clear. At least she was company for Amanda while the others were diving.

"Where is that smell coming from?" asked Amanda.

Pam walked to the back of the yacht and looked around. Apart from the dim lights of the fishing town of Castilla three miles away, the only lights were the millions of twinkling stars and galaxies in the night sky.

"I suppose it's just volcanic gas seeping up from the seabed. This whole region was formed by volcanoes, the islands, the bays, everything. They're inactive now, although there are minor eruptions from time to time."

"Is it safe to dive?" Amanda asked.

"It's fine. Tourism is about the only industry the islands have and diving is a big part of that. Besides, with the right conditions, like we have now, the water is so clear that diving is like swimming through air, it's amazing. Mmm, that's strange. I wish I was back diving..." Pam's voice quietly trailed off.

Amanda walked across the gently swaying deck to the rear of the yacht to see what Pam was looking at. As she looked down she saw a faint glow in the water, it looked like the divers were coming back up, their lights sending out a dim glow.

"If that's the dive lights, they're coming up early aren't they?" asked Amanda.

"Yes, they've got another ten minutes yet. But I'm not sure that's just the dive lights, it's too widespread."

A noise off the starboard bow caught their attention

and they both looked to the side. At first they thought that a large shoal of fish was broaching the surface, but as they watched, they realised that the disturbance was bubbles rising from the depths and bursting at the surface.

"That smell's getting worse, and is it me or is it getting warmer." Amanda pulled the top of her blouse open and blew down her front.

Pam wandered around the edge of the deck, looking out at the water, the glow was spreading. As she watched, several fish floated to the surface, all white and bloated.

"Amanda...get the engine started."

"Why? The others aren't up yet." As she spoke there was a small splash from the rear of the boat and she looked out at the water. One of the divers, she couldn't tell which, had surfaced but was floating face down.

Amanda leant over the low gunwale, reaching out for the scuba tank.

"AMANDA DON'T!" Pam ran over to the rear of the yacht, making a grab for Amanda.

Amanda turned at the call and her hand dipped into the water, causing her to give an involuntary scream and jerk her hand from the near boiling liquid. As she grasped her hand to herself, she saw it was already turning red and blistering.

"We need to get out of here," said Pam with force.

Amanda was clearly in pain and maybe starting to go into shock.

"But, the divers..." she looked over the rear at the diver that had surfaced. As she watched one and then another diver surfaced around the boat. All were lifeless. The first and second wore full wetsuits. But the third only had the scuba tank, mask and mouthpiece. Instead of a suit he wore pale blue swimming trunks. With shock, Amanda realised it was Alan. And his body... he looked as if he had been boiled alive. His flesh was bright red and covered in white and yellow blisters, the skin already starting to fall away from the bones. Amanda's mind started to block out the horrors as she started to scream.

Pam pulled Amanda back from the edge of the boat, forcing her to sit on one of the benches while she rocked back and forth, incoherent burbling coming from her mouth. Pam then bolted for the cabin, she could hear the fibreglass hull starting to crack as it turned brittle in the now clearly boiling water.

The engine caught on the first attempt and Pam eased the throttles forward gently, not wanting to overstress the boat's structure.

From the raised deck, Pam could now clearly see the hundreds of fish floating to the surface and surrounding the boat. The sea was boiling in all directions and in the darkness she could not see more than a hundred yards and the subsurface golden glow seemed to spread in all directions.

Pam eased the throttles a little further forward. She looked around the control panel, she was sure there were switches for the lights somewhere. There, she pressed the three buttons and lights all around the boat lit up the water surface and a large spotlight to the side of the bridge deck cast an intense white light forward. As the lights came on, the glow from beneath the surface seemed to retreat back into the depths.

A sharp retort like a gunshot echoed from the rear causing Pam to spin around. A large crack had appeared around the rear transom, allowing water to spill onto the deck. Pam gasped as she saw the water splashing against the engine cover. If too much water flooded the engine it would drown and stop. And then the hull would disintegrate and they would both end up boiling to death.

Pam turned back to the control panel and pushed the throttles forward, not now worrying about stressing the boat's frame. The 300hp engine growled deeply and the yacht leaped forward, the rear digging into the water. Pam looked around the panel, desperately looking for the pump controls. There were several buttons on a panel labelled 'pumps', each with different references which meant nothing to her. Pam pressed all of the buttons and heard different noises coming from below deck. Hopefully at least one would pump water from the engine compartment.

Pam looked forward, her eyes straining to see the water surface which was now covered in a thick layer of steam. The engine started to splutter, and then evened out for a few seconds before starting to miss unevenly.

"Amanda, AMANDA."

Amanda looked up at the sound of her name.

"Get the inflatable ready, we might have to abandon ship."

Amanda seemed completely at a loss as if Pam were speaking a foreign language. But slowly she stood and looked around, before walking towards the inflatable that was fastened to the side of the cabin. Pam realised how much shock she must be in when she saw her feet turning red and blistering as she waded through the ankle deep scalding water.

Pam looked out at the water, she could see the boiling surface surrounding the boat. The engine sputtered and died, before coughing and restarting to run unevenly.

Pam steered toward the nearest shore, still at least a mile away. She lifted the radio microphone and clicked the dial to 'emergency'.

"Mayday, mayday, mayday. This is pleasure yacht Calypso. Please help." Pam's voice broke as the enormity of the situation started to strike home. She looked back across the rear of the yacht. The water was not just boiling, great plumes or water and steam were starting to erupt hundreds of feet into the air.

Epilogue

Three Weeks Later

Grantham sat on the five-seater corner unit with his legs up and a cup of strong tea on the table in front of him. The TV was tuned to the national news. Charisma reached for the remote control but Grantham asked her to leave the station for the moment.

"So Professor Lee, the high level of activity has ended?" asked the reporter as she sat on the large sofa in the studio.

"Well that's impossible to say." Professor Lee was well past her first flush of youth, but clearly well versed in her subject and obviously at home in front of the camera.

"The seismic activity that we expect is simply an average of past experience. We can have long periods of steady activity or times of especially high or low activity. What we have experienced over the last few weeks has been an unusually high activity period. Some of the events were unusual although nothing was actually unprecedented. If you look at the events and their severity it looks as if there was a slow build-up over several weeks and then a slow decline over the last two weeks or so. But taken as individual incidents they were just that, individual incidents that had little, if any, connection."

The reporter nodded along with the explanation. *"But the effects are subsiding?"*

"It would appear so. The incidents have declined in number, frequency and severity. Although nothing can be guaranteed, it seems safe to say that normal service has been resumed. With the release of so much energy

recently, it may be that we will enter a period of low activity for some time."

The reporter smiled, displaying a set of teeth that were too perfect to be natural. *"Thank you, Professor Lee."* She turned to the camera before continuing. *"Now, a recent survey has shown that crime is on the increase in the southern counties faster than in the north. We'll shortly be talking to two experts who think that they have an explanation for this. But first, we are going to meet the boys of One Direction right after they perform their latest single."*

"You can switch over now, please," said Grantham.

"So the world is safe?" asked Charisma.

"I don't know if I'd go that far. But GCHQ got the new instructions sent out just in time. As the Professor said, it looks as if everything is returning to normal. The experts think they can modify the system to detect seismic activity a lot sooner than they have in the past. Maybe even to offset the effects. Some university student is apparently set to make a fortune out of the thing after patenting some sort of technology."

After escaping the explosion, Grantham and the SAS team had headed north to Brazil where Grantham and Charisma had been hospitalised for five days before being allowed out to return home with instructions to rest and relax for at least another two weeks before gradually returning to normal activity over the next month. Grantham was getting fidgety, longing to get back to being physically active.

Grantham reached for the large mug of tea, but paused to cough, wrapping his arms around his ribs as if holding them in place. He quietly admitted to himself that it would be a few days yet before his ribs were ready for anything beyond a steady walk.

There was a knock on the door and Grantham slowly stood and straightened up. A minute later he walked back into the room followed by an old man.

"Charisma, this is Richard. I think it's time you two met. He knew your Dad, and the rest of the Knights."

Grantham left the two alone for a few minutes while he made fresh drinks, even adding some biscuits to a plate before taking them in.

Charisma was listening to Richard who was talking about her father. For almost an hour Grantham sat back while the two talked. Charisma was learning things about her father, and her mother, that she had never even dreamed of. Her father had been one of the leaders of the Knights Templars.

"So, that leads nicely to one of the reasons I'm here." Richard's deep, clear voice belied his obviously old age.

"As the daughter of one of our generals," he paused and smiled at the look on Charisma's face. "General is only a term of authority not a strict rank as in the army. He could be called a commander or even a manager. It just happens that the term is general. So, as the daughter of a Knight Templar, you would be welcome to join the order."

Charisma was clearly at a loss for words. "I'm not sure. What would I have to do?"

"How much you do, how much you get involved would be up to you. But your obvious research talents could be very valuable. And our resources are better than any university or library. We have many original documents that most scholars do not even know exist. But how far you went within the order and how much access you had would be up to you. Please think about it, your talents and knowledge would be very welcome. And you Mr Grantham." Richard turned to Grantham. "We are always looking for new recruits, especially ones with your talents."

"I'm honoured. But I'm not sure I'm ready to sign

up again. Would I be right in assuming it would involve six months or so away somewhere?"

Richard smiled and had an obvious twinkle in his old eyes. Grantham noticed even with his advanced years he was not wearing glasses. "I see you have done some research."

Grantham shrugged. "Simply put two and two together. It seems that at least three former Knights dropped out of sight for several months. I assume it's some sort of selection process."

"Yes...and no. It's very much a two way thing. As much for the recruits to see if the Knights fit them as the other way around. As I said to Charisma, please think about it before you answer. But there is something else. Have you thought what you would like to do with the gift I gave you in Washington?"

Grantham thought back across the time since he had last seen Richard at Arlington Cemetery. How much good luck had he had? His old unit were on hand when he needed them, he had helped saved the life of the Hostage Rescue Unit member's brother who had given Mark Smedley the UAV that had been so useful. He'd had access to intelligence on the compound better than a lot he had got while on active duty. They had all been able to travel together to Paraguay. They had obtained the Bell UH-1 which had not only got them in, but more importantly got them out. On the other hand several of the unit, including himself and Charisma had been injured. On the other hand, they had not been killed.

"I'd like to thank you for the gift and give it back to the Knights."

Richard bowed his head. "Thank you. It will be kept safe as it has always been." Grantham thought he detected a tear in the old man's sparkling eyes.

"Could I ask a favour? Can I give it back to the

order from midnight tonight?"

Richard had the sparkle back in his eyes and a smile on his face. "Of course, but it may not work well for personal gain. Good fortune is not always what you want."

"But what you need?"

"Maybe so. But midnight it is."

Richard spent the rest of the afternoon with them until he said it was time to leave.

"Are you going back to America so soon?" asked Charisma.

"No. I'm going to spend a few days in Britain, visiting sites I've not seen for many years. See what has changed. Give me a call, both of you, if you want to talk or you reach a decision." Richard handed them a card with two numbers on before taking his leave.

A week later

The pub was just over half full. Most of the crowd were split into small groups, almost entirely male. It was the first time Grantham had been in the pub since he retired from army life. He looked around the pub and recognised over half of the men. This was the regular haunt of the SAS in Hereford.

The group were sat in one corner of the large room. Mac was still walking stiffly. Snake was back on active service from tomorrow. Charisma's shoulder was healing well and she had almost full motion back. Grantham was now out and about, walking was no problem and the doctor had given him the all clear to ease back into training from the weekend.

They had arranged to meet the previous week, to catch up and, Grantham had hinted, something else.

"So no problem with going off the reserve?" asked Grantham of Mac.

"We got a good bollocking, usual threats. But the fact that we helped stop the attack and that your name still carries a lot of weight helped."

"Good. Well you all have my thanks and gratitude. If there's anything I can ever do to return the favour you only have to ask."

"That goes for me as well," said Charisma, raising her glass along with the men.

"Well, as you're offering..." said Snake with a wicked grin.

"Snake," said Grantham with a mock serious tone.

"Sorry boss."

"Do you know what it was all about?" asked Mac.

Grantham snorted. "What's it ever about. Some bloody nutters think they can run the world better than anyone else. In this case the old SS had decided to wipe out mankind and replace us with a super race. In the last three weeks the authorities of twenty countries have tracked down eighteen bunkers with almost thirty thousand people waiting for the end of the world. Ten thousand were troops with enough firepower to finish off anyone who survived. The authorities are still finding more bunkers and clearing up the mess." The men around the table shook their heads.

"While we're talking about the job, I've been meaning to ask, what were your exit plans?" Mac looked from Grantham to Charisma and back.

"Remember that bike, the one in the garage? I was going to use that."

Mac raised his eyebrows and nodded. "Okay, I suppose that could have worked, if you'd had the time and could still stand and breathe."

Grantham smiled and nodded. "Yes, that would have helped. Okay, well there is one other thing I want to share. Last week I bought a lottery ticket and had a win. It wasn't the jackpot, but five numbers and the bonus, fifty thousand quid. Which makes a share of five and a half thousand each." Charisma took out several envelopes and passed them around, each contained a cheque.

"Boss, you know there's no need to share this," said Mac, several of the others nodded.

"That will pay you back for the air fares and expenses. It's not much but we got it as a result of the adventure, sort of."

The SAS team looked inquisitively at Grantham and Charisma, but when it was clear they were not going to elaborate Mac went on, "We'll put it to the exit fund. Thanks Boss, Charisma," the team again raised their glasses.

"What's an exit fund?" asked Charisma.

"Mac, care to explain?" said Grantham.

"Well, some of the missions the SAS undertake are black ops. That means that if we're rumbled and pursued or caught, we're denied. And denied means that the government says we are not part of any official force and we are just individuals acting alone. In some circumstances we may even be prosecuted by our own side if we make it back. So we have a fund that we can call on if we need it. An exit fund."

"Well I hope you never need to use it. Thank you for all you did for us."

"So what's next?" asked Mac.

"Well I'm going back to the private work, so maybe our paths will cross again, officially or unofficially. And Charisma is taking up a new position with a research facility that has made her an offer she couldn't refuse. Apparently their head, a guy called Richard, says they have access to artefacts and documents that no other organisation could dream of."

Charisma nodded. "And for my first job I'm going to get to examine an object I've been applying to see for years."

Mac and the others raised their glasses again. "Well it's onwards and upwards. Here's to us all."

Author's Notes

Although this is a work of fiction, much of the historical references and quoted 'research' and 'opinion', especially that by Charisma, is true. At least it is held to be true by researchers.

The case of Russian reporter, Nicolai Notovitch travelling in India and being rescued by Buddhist monks who had values and tales similar to bible stories is well documented.

The tombs of Roza Bal referred to in Chapter 16 exist and can be visited.

Native American tribes still hold that 'a pale faced healer' and 'Cheezoos, the God of the Dawn Light' came to their land hundreds of years before the first recorded Atlantic crossings.

In the bible (whichever version you read) Jesus, the son of God, disappears for around 15 to 18 years, reappearing as a fully fledged preacher.

The holy relics that are referred to, the Spear of Christ (Spear of Destiny, Lance of Longinus etc, etc), the Holy Blood in Bruges, the Crown of Thorns in the Treasury of Notre-Dame de Paris are all documented and can be seen by visitors (or are they copies, the originals held by some secret order?)

The Ark of the Covenant is widely held to be in the church of St. Mary in Axum. This used to be paraded every year but now a copy is used to protect the original which is getting fragile (?).

The Knights Templars were real and their arrest on Friday 13th October 1307 is historical fact and gave rise to unlucky Friday the 13th. Many of the Knights escaped, some went to Scotland and later set sail westwards, again this is well documented. What happened to them later isn't.

Where 'fact' merges into fiction I'll let the reader decide. But remember, 'fact is stranger than fiction' and does art mirror reality, or vice versa?

Best regards
Brian Phillipson.

www.ingramcontent.com/pod-product-compliance
Lightning Source LLC
Chambersburg PA
CBHW022235020726
47496CB00004B/919